THE
WILD
BETWEEN
US

THE WILD BETWEEN US

A NOVEL

AMY HAGSTROM

LAKE UNION
PUBLISHING

Text copyright © 2023 by Amy Hagstrom
All rights reserved.

No part of this book may be reproduced, or stored in a retrieval system, or transmitted in any form or by any means, electronic, mechanical, photocopying, recording, or otherwise, without express written permission of the publisher.

Published by Lake Union Publishing, Seattle

www.apub.com

Amazon, the Amazon logo, and Lake Union Publishing are trademarks of Amazon.com, Inc., or its affiliates.

ISBN-13: 9781662511486 (paperback)
ISBN-13: 9781662511493 (digital)

Cover design by Caroline Teagle Johnson

Cover image: © Samuel Sutherland / EyeEm, © Trevor Williams, © oxygen, © Gina Bringman / Design Pics / Getty; © Theus / Shutterstock

Design elements used throughout: Mountain
© Modern Visual Agency / Shutterstock

Printed in the United States of America

For my grandmother Joan Morrill and my mother, Julie Hagstrom, whose love of reading and writing blazed the trail before me.

PROLOGUE

November 19, 2018
5:25 p.m.
Marble Lake Wilderness, California

Spencer Matheson hops the creek skirting the edge of the meadow, then jets up the Lakes Loop trail, his Nikes churning up dust in their wake.

"Wait up!" Cameron calls, from somewhere down-trail. "Spenc-*er*! Wait for me!"

He slows, partly because he knows to be a good big brother, but also because it's steeper than he remembers, the trail strewn with rocks he has to keep dodging.

Cameron catches up, face totally red, jeans all dirty. Maybe he already fell, trying to keep up, and Spencer feels a little tug in his tummy, the kind that reminds him to be nicer. Cameron is only five, too little to do things on his own, like lead the hike. He's not already a first grader like Spencer, seven years and three-fourths.

"You're going too fast," Cameron says. Only a little bit whiny. "Plus, I don't know if this is the way, Spence."

"It's the way. We hiked this hill last week, remember? All the way up to the ridge."

"With Dad," Cameron points out.

Spencer huffs out a hot breath of air, watching it disappear like smoke. "We don't need Dad." This doesn't sound very true, not even to Spencer, but he doesn't take it back. They've already waited forever for Dad to be done working tonight. Cameron probably just wants a piggyback ride on the uphill parts.

He offers the next best thing: the last gummy bear in his pocket. Red, Cameron's favorite. When he accepts it, they carry on up the rest of the slope, stopping only once more when it doesn't seem like there's enough air for their lungs. Spencer reminds himself that when Dad was a kid, he hiked all over these mountains, knew every turn on the trail. It's enough to get him trudging uphill again.

Only once the trail finally flattens out does he let himself rest, hands braced on his knees. He doesn't even poke fun when Cameron flops down on a boulder instead, acting all worn out. Once he's caught his breath, he straightens, taking stock. Spencer can see all the way down to where they started at Marble Lake Lodge, where the metal snow roofs of the guest cabins wink at them like tiny jewels. The wind is crazy, though, rushing through the trees so fast it sounds like a river, all rumbly and loud.

"It's cold up here," Cameron says.

Spencer feels cold, too, but sweaty at the same time, which makes the wind kind of sting when it hits his face. He stretches his arms out wide, his sweatshirt billowing like a kite. Now that the hard part is over, he decides he likes it up here, where he's taller than the trees. Down in the forest, it's different. There, Spencer is just a little ant of a person weaving this way and that through towering pines, sage, and manzanita, no landmarks to go by. Not at all like in the parks back in Portland, even the big ones, where he knows every secret trail through every grove of green, leafy trees. Dad calls this place *the real deal*, but sometimes, Spencer wants to say *big deal* instead, with a little kick at the dirt besides, even though that's talking back. Even though he wants to prove that he can hack it here in the Sierra, just like Dad.

He straightens his shoulders. He made it this far tonight, didn't he? And practically on his own, because Cameron only counts a little. And now that they've made the ridge, they might as well explore. Spencer hops from rock to rock along the trail.

"The ground is hot lava!" he tells Cameron, right before his next big leap. He sticks the landing onto a big fallen log as Cameron gets up and joins in, and they jump from rock to log to rock, all the way down the other side of the ridge, through forest they haven't hiked before. Cameron trips once, landing in the lava, but Spencer pretends he didn't see. It's not Cameron's fault his legs are shorter.

By the time they reach the bottom of the hill, it's gotten all shadowy, maybe because the sun doesn't reach down into this wash. Spencer decides they should go back up, to where they can see better, but maybe they should hike it kind of sideways, like Dad showed them to do, in a zigzag pattern instead of straight up. Switchbacks, he'd called them. Spencer could do the climb no problem, but the switchback trick will make it easier for Cameron.

It feels like it takes ages, going sideways back up the hill, and by the time they reach the ridge again, it's getting hard to see anything at all, even though they're back above the trees. Even more worrisome: the trail doesn't seem to be there anymore, and even though he looks really hard, Spencer no longer sees the lodge below.

"How come we're not in the same place as before?" Cameron says.

"Shush. Yes we are." Where else could they be? They went down the wash, and then they went back up. So what if they zigzagged? Starting points don't just change. The ground doesn't just move on its own.

"I don't like that it's getting so dark."

Neither does Spencer, but what good would it do to say so?

"Let's just go back, Spence. I want to go home."

Home. That twisty feeling in Spencer's tummy returns, tightening itself into a knot. He misses Portland, even though nothing of his is there anymore . . . not their house, not his things, not even their mom. *Marble Lake Lodge will be home now,* Dad had said with a firm nod, as they'd left the city behind. Usually, that tone works—*confidence is key,* Dad always says—only nothing about this wilderness feels like home yet, no matter how hard Spencer tries. No matter how bravely he explores. And now he can't even find the lodge, which should be right down there, next to the creek and the meadow, which have also disappeared.

"This way," he tells Cameron, trying to copycat Dad's confident voice. He points them downhill in the opposite direction from which they just climbed. This has to be right. It's just too dark to see the trail, is all.

But they walk downhill for a long time, and the meadow doesn't appear. There's no creek to hop. Instead, it's just endless trees in every direction. He's an ant again, dwarfed by the woods. They're both shivering now, and Cameron is starting to cry. So is Spencer, but he pretends to himself that he isn't. They keep walking, tripping on roots and stones and maybe other things. Spencer can't see in the dark. He doesn't like to think about what all is out here, in these woods.

"Are we lost, Spence?" Cameron asks over and over, every time they turn a corner just to find more darkness. More trees.

"No," Spencer whispers. "Course not." But the knot in his gut is like lead now, reaching all the way up to his throat. It hurts to swallow, and his voice comes out all shaky, not fooling anyone. Not even fooling Cameron. Because of course they need Dad. Just like they need familiar, friendly trees and a home Spencer can find his way back to in the dark. Instead, all they have is each other.

Holding hands is babyish, but Spencer takes Cameron's, and he doesn't let go.

1

SILAS

Two weeks earlier
November 3, 2018
Feather River, California

Silas Matheson keeps his eyes trained on the ribbon of road before him, all his focus necessary to navigate the sharp mountain turns. No matter how raucous it gets in the back seat, he can't swivel around to scold the boys, warranted as it may be. "Settle down," he instructs for the fourth time, as, in the rearview mirror, he watches Cameron hurl an empty juice box at Spencer's head.

"Ow! Da-*ad*!"

"Oh, he missed, and you know it." They've been driving six hours already today, and if Silas is being honest, he'd like to throw something, too, if only to distract from the relentless doubt that's ridden shotgun for every one of the past four-hundred-some miles. What kind of father whisks his kids away from everything they've ever known?

One who's determined to keep his head above water with these two, who've never bickered so much in their short tenure on this planet until now. Is it this move that has his children grating against one another like rocks in a tumbler in the back seat? The upheaval in their family life? Both?

"Apologize," Silas tells Cameron, who mumbles something under his breath as Spencer makes a show of scooching away as far as the back seat of the Chevy will allow, pressing his body into the side panel of the door.

"I said *sorry*," Cameron says again, pouting on his own side of the bench seat.

Sorry won't cut it, though, will it? Spencer has heard *sorry* far too often lately—from his mother upon her acceptance of a dream job in another country, from Silas himself as he logged far too many work hours of his own—for this apology to soften his seven-year-old resolve.

Children are malleable, Silas was told by well-meaning acquaintances when he and Miranda split years before, not long after their youngest's birth. *Children adapt*, teachers and day-care providers assured, while Spencer and Cameron bounced between two households and two professional parents nearly the entirety of their lives. Has Silas finally pushed this theory to its breaking point, uprooting the three of them for a much-needed fresh start that, for Silas at least, might prove to be anything but? An uncomfortable feeling of uncertainty still gnaws at his determination as they cross the river they've been paralleling and the road finally straightens.

Spencer sits up taller to peer out his window. "What's this place?" he asks as they pass a city-limits sign.

"Feather River." The last place Silas had lived before being forced to grow up. It's been fifteen years since he fled this town, the sun at his back instead of hitting his eyes through the windshield. He flips down the visor and forces renewed enthusiasm into his voice. "Which means we've only got thirty more minutes to go."

"Until we get to the lodge?"

"Until we get to Marble Lake Lodge," he confirms.

The imminent end of their journey should have the tension draining from Silas's shoulders, but instead, the forested landscape rolling off the transparent arc of the windshield has the opposite effect. Because Feather River, cradled at five thousand feet within the rise of the California Sierra, hasn't changed a bit. How can this be, when Silas himself has changed so exponentially, the boy he'd been when he lived here becoming a man nearly overnight?

Over five nights, to be exact. And five excruciating days.

He grips the steering wheel tighter. There's the railroad trestle spanning the river, underneath which his friends had once fished. And the diner on the corner where he killed time over baskets of greasy fries. The highway takes them past the same laundromat, burger joint, and dilapidated tavern it always did, and the landmarks instantly conjure the faces of the people he knew here best: young, laughing, blissfully unaware of what life had in store. He shuffles through them, until he lands mercilessly on Jessica Howard at seventeen. *Perpetually* seventeen, to Silas. Her face eager and fresh and flawless.

He forces this thought back, trying to see this place with fresh eyes, but it's useless. Even the trim color of the Feather River Frostee is the same shade of red it was the day Silas had driven in the opposite direction, leaving for good, or so he thought.

When he picked up the phone last month to hear his aunt Mary's voice, rough as ever from all the Marlboros, he couldn't have imagined their conversation would lead him back here.

"So I've been thinking," she said, which, with Aunt Mary, translated to *I've decided something.*

Silas proceeded with caution. "And?"

"And I've earned myself some Arizona sunshine."

"You've been saying that for years, Aunt Mary." At least five, anyway, since Silas's uncle Les had passed of a stroke, leaving far too much responsibility on the shoulders of his aging widow. Throughout the summers of Silas's youth, culminating in the summer that overshadowed them all, he had worked side by side with his aunt and uncle at Marble Lake Lodge as they made repairs to the buildings, cut new trails, and taken care of guests; made up cabins and stacked wood; whipped up endless batches of French toast and blueberry muffins in the cavernous kitchen. Even with all the hard work, some of which, Silas was embarrassed to admit now, he'd shirked as a teen, Marble Lake had been an idyllic haven of his youth, right up until it hadn't been. "You really going to sell?"

"No, I'm going to gift."

Silas didn't follow.

"You and your boys could use a change of scenery, from how you tell it."

"Mary—"

"Silas," she said softly, her voice a gentle rasp. "I understand your reluctance, really I do, given all that happened, but this place was meant for you, and you were meant for it. We both know you were the one who loved it most."

Her words were a punch to the gut. Had he? Loved it most? Or had he just loved who he'd spent the most time with there, that last summer of high school? Finite memory, tactile and raw, rose in his mind's eye in a startled rush, like a bird flushed from its hiding place. The girl he'd loved, tanned and happy. So impossibly young. He hasn't been able to banish it since.

Sensing victory, Mary pressed her case. "With your ex out of the picture, and you and your boys on your own now—"

"Miranda hasn't disappeared from their lives, Aunt Mary." Even if Silas suspected it might feel like it to Spencer and Cameron, with her on the other side of the Atlantic. *Malleable*, he reminded himself.

"With your situation changing," Mary carried right on, "those kids need stability. You've always found that here."

He nearly laughed at the irony: a rough bark of aggression painful to swallow. He couldn't deny that Miranda's departure and his subsequent foray into full-time fatherhood had yanked the proverbial rug out from under all their feet. He'd underestimated everything: how much time the boys would spend in childcare, the difficulty of balancing family time with his career in environmental law. Cutting back his hours had only added to the emotional toll; his work protecting vulnerable wilderness had always served as a touchstone, tenuous as it was, to the outdoors he loved.

Maybe, he decided, it was time to return to the root of that love, even if it did hurtle him back to his past. "Do you mean it?" he asked Mary, while trying to imagine it: he and his boys carving out a new home in the High Sierra.

"I'll transfer the ownership on Monday," Mary said with soft satisfaction. "Look at us, coming around full circle."

Back to where it all began, Silas thinks now, with the addition of two little passengers. How will the three of them be received? In other words, how long is Feather River's memory? Not quite ready to find out, he drives right past Clark's Market, even knowing they could use a few essentials. He presses down on the accelerator instead of topping off at the Quik Save, willing back a trepidation no one should associate with a homecoming.

The boys resume their roughhousing in the back seat as the highway opens back up and they begin their ascent up the mountain pass north of town. By the time they reach the weather-faded *Marble Lake Lodge, est 1953* sign, it's full-on road-trip WrestleMania, but now Silas doesn't mind the distraction; it makes his initial reunion with the lodge a bit less weighted. It seems unfathomable that this unassuming cluster of eclectic buildings can somehow hold his most cherished memories and his most desperate nightmares, but the second Silas eases to a stop, he knows Marble Lake Lodge can still make room for both.

The boys tumble out of the Chevy like pent-up puppies, legs churning as they race each other to the entrance, and he watches them go, glad to see their little-boy energy redirected from any newfound sibling unrest. He forces himself to make his own reacquaintance with this place more slowly. Perched on a shelf of granite, the main building's bank of south-facing double-story windows stare toward eight-thousand-foot Marble Peak. Its foundation is laid with river rock, the remainder of the walls constructed of thick pine planking, and a huge stone chimney draws the eye to the entire far outer wall. In the muted light of the evening sky, its metal snow roof seems to shimmer.

The green trim on the shutters has faded, and the dried remains of last summer's geraniums still cling to the soil in the planters around the cavernous front door. Silas feels a stab of guilt for allowing self-preservation—and shame, if he's being honest—to keep him away so long. He should have been here, helping Uncle Les and Aunt Mary during their golden years.

The boys have run around the side of the building to discover the path that weaves through the property, and Silas trails behind them as they take a whirlwind tour. They pass guest cabins 1 through 6, the two-story recreation building with its own river-stone fireplace, the housekeeping-supply building and toolshed, the woodpile, and, finally, cabins 7 through 9. Just beyond these: the meadow, the creek, and the trail system that, once upon a time, took Silas all over the wilderness that was his backyard.

He corrals the troops, and they return to the Chevy to empty it of their possessions, carrying loads of boxes through the main lodge entrance and past the guest dining room, where memories assault Silas anew. He allows himself only quick flashes between instructing the boys and carting duffels and luggage up the stairs to the living quarters: himself, at age eighteen, sitting right there on that dining-room chair, sweat dripping down his back, stomach in knots. His friends sitting across from him, unable to meet his gaze. People everywhere: asking questions about Jessica.

He pinches his eyes shut and draws in a deep breath. Draws forth the good memories this lodge can offer instead. Like sitting in the windowsill on the second-story landing, feeling the sun on his face. Cleaning cabins for Les with his besties, Danny and Meg, the smell of Comet and Pledge cloying but somehow homey. Taking off after work to trek up into the wilderness, where a cannonball leap from the cliffside into ice-cold Long Lake would elicit a whoop from Danny and a shriek from Meg.

Standing here in the dining room, staring at the massive mantel over the fireplace, he spots something that sends a shock of recognition through him. Yet another memento Marble Lake Lodge has stored for him for safekeeping, though he can't decide if this particular one is pleasant or terrible. Both, somehow. Definitely both.

"Hold up, boys," he calls as Spencer drags a sleeping bag, half out of its stuff sack, behind him across the wooden floor and Cameron trails after, his arms overflowing with stuffed animals. "I want to show you something cool."

He lifts the smooth chunk of Sierra obsidian from the mantel with exaggerated show for the boys' benefit, who have engaged in a tug-of-war with a stuffed dragon while his back was turned.

"What is that?" Spencer asks, rising on tippy-toe to inspect the shiny black rock.

"This," Silas tells him, "is a type of stone I've only ever found right here, in these mountains." He must have left it here, by the fireplace, when he left in such a hurry so many years ago.

"So it's special or something?"

"Yeah," Silas confirms, after the ache this question elicits eases from his chest. "Very special."

He continues to stand by the mantel, studying the obsidian even after Spencer has lost interest, trying to decide whether the stone still belongs here. Whether any of them do.

I should call them, he thinks. It would be perfectly normal to reach out to the two people he once called his best friends, now that he's back for good, but then another thought follows right on its heels. *I don't deserve to.* He burned that bridge years ago. Now, here at the lodge, he somehow feels even further from them both than he had in Oregon.

Over the past decade and a half, he's kept up with the Feather River gossip as best he can, mostly thanks to Aunt Mary, who would offer what she heard at the beauty parlor or post office. *Meg and Danny? Yeah, they're still in town. She works for the sheriff's office now, as a secretary or some such. Yes, they're still together, last I heard. They volunteer for the county search-and-rescue unit in their spare time.*

Of course they do. Silas wouldn't expect anything less. Not from those two. Not after what happened. Suddenly he's very ready to call it a night. "Boys! Let's wrestle up some dinner."

"Pizza Hut?" Spencer asks hopefully.

Silas pretends to consider this suggestion, picking up his cell phone. "Hey, Siri, closest Pizza Hut," he intones, then waits, head tilted in concentration, for dramatic effect.

When no tinny reply comes, the boys both gather around the phone. "What's wrong with it?" Cameron asks. "Where's Siri?"

"Seems Siri forgot to catch a ride with us from Portland," Silas says. "No cell service up here, kiddos. And no Pizza Hut."

"No Pizza Hut?" Cameron echoes, his voice incredulous.

"Not within seventy miles or so." The closest is probably in Reno, or, in the other direction, Sacramento. He gauges his boys' reactions to this stark reminder of the distance they've put between themselves and the suburban existence they've always known. Will there be tears of protest? Fear or uncertainty? Cries for their mother, past co-procurer of pizza delivery? He's not a man who's used to second-guessing himself, and he doesn't enjoy the feeling now, as a fresh wave of doubt, laced with a healthy dose of guilt, washes over him. Has he just made everything harder on them all instead of easier? But his boys surprise him.

"Cool," Spencer decides after a moment of consideration. "We'll be like Bear Grylls, hunting and trapping stuff."

Silas smiles, giving himself a mental pass for all those hours of Discovery Channel he allowed when he'd still been wrapping up his cases in Portland. But then he sobers, because while Cameron nods along, following his big brother's lead, his face is clouded with a vague confusion that's become all too familiar of late. *He's only five,* Silas chastises himself. What sense could Cameron possibly make of the adult decisions that have brought him here? Miranda testing the limits of their co-parenting arrangement to pursue her dreams. Silas deciding to return to Marble Lake to face his demons. He pulls Cameron in close, bending down to breathe in the scent of him as he tucks his head into Silas's side.

"How about breakfast for dinner?" he suggests, which instantly earns him the popular vote.

"Yeah!" Spencer agrees as Cameron looks up, a spark of remembered joy in his hazel eyes. Breakfast for dinner has always been Silas's weeknight go-to.

They find left-behind pancake mix in the pantry, along with canned peaches and applesauce. They have so much fun cooking on the massive Viking stove, Silas forgives himself for allowing cowardice to prevent him from making a grocery run. After dinner, he lets the boys play in the rec building, where they unearth dusty Monopoly boards and poker sets. Cameron finds a giant puzzle, and Spencer digs ping-pong paddles out of a cupboard.

"We need to get a new table, though," he decides, eyeing the weathered and warped one propped against one wall. Silas used to play on that one, whooping Danny's ass game after game. He smiles before that damned memory trail leads him further down the same path again, to Jessica and all that had ensued, and he frowns.

It takes entirely too long to make the beds and find the toothbrushes, and by the time the boys are settled in their new room—once Silas's room—at the top of the lodge stairs, the day has fully caught up with Silas. He settles into one of the Adirondack chairs on the lodge porch and peers out into the night.

He'd forgotten how dark it gets up here, in the Sierra. At least until he looks up, and then it's like the heavens have iced over, each blazing white star blending into the next. He just stares for a while, letting all that whiteness bleach his brain.

The silence of the mountains settles in around him, packed in like cotton, and for just a few minutes he doesn't have to question his decision to uproot his boys. He can forget that he is now solely responsible for this lodge, aka his new livelihood, and that it will be up to him entirely to ensure his kids are happy, healthy, and whole.

He doesn't enjoy the peace for long. He remembers too late that this type of stillness has always left him with too much blank space inside his head, an empty slate like a rolling expanse of virgin snow, undisturbed and untouched. Tonight, he finds it leaves him vaguely restless, fretful about digging too deep and overturning too much.

2

SILAS

Fifteen years previous
August 30, 2003
Marble Lake Lodge

Search teams. Sheriff's-department officials. Sirens. And sitting. So much sitting. Silas wasn't sure what he'd expected a search-and-rescue operation to feel like, but it sure as hell hadn't included this much time stuck in this chair, waiting in the cloying heat of the lodge while a blur of humanity spun around his periphery. With the focus so squarely on him and his friends, he would have thought they'd be at the center of things, able to *do* more. Instead, here in the eye of the storm, the air felt heavy and silent and thick. Instead of adrenaline, there was only dread.

A full call-out, that was what they called it. Dozens of vehicles. Hundreds, probably, of volunteers, from who knew how many counties, all combing the forest for Jessica. Dogs. Dive teams, even, in sheriff's-department boats they launched from trailers into Marble Lake. What could those divers possibly see, Silas kept asking himself, in that murky water? Duckweed and algae, maybe. Tree roots long submerged, slowly decaying in their aquatic resting place. Surely not Jessica. It made no sense for her to have ended up there. But then, where?

It was what the guy from the sheriff's department, Lieutenant Halloway, had been asking Silas, Meg, and Danny from the moment they'd reported Jessica missing, back on Day 1. Like if he just asked enough, he'd get a different answer than *We don't know.* But nothing in this narrative had changed since that very first night of the search, when Uncle Les had first put out the folding chairs in the lodge great room, and they'd all sat there, the three of them, sweaty and spent from looking for Jessica, hungry but not wanting to eat the sandwiches Aunt Mary made, not even tired, though they should have been. Sometime around midnight, their little sharing circle had widened to include Meg's mother and Danny's father. Then, just before dawn, Jessica's mom had appeared in the doorway of the lodge, accompanied by a sheriff. *The* sheriff, Halloway told them, of the whole county.

"Greg Walters," this man had said, "at your service."

Silas's first impression: he didn't look anything like the grizzled sheriffs in the old Westerns Danny liked to watch on TNT, the only free movie channel he got. Thin and fit, with a neat mustache, this guy looked more like a city cop.

He'd recognized Teresa Howard only vaguely . . . earlier that year, hadn't she chaperoned a school trip to a production of *Hamlet*? To his surprise, however, Mrs. Howard had made her way across the room directly to Meg. For one brief, horrific second, Silas had thought she meant to hit her. He'd actually braced for it, on Meg's behalf. But instead, Mrs. Howard had enveloped her tightly.

"Honey, honey," she'd cried, "what *happened*?"

And Meg had only been able to shake her head, crying into this woman's coat sleeve.

It didn't stop anyone from imploring them to remember. To retrace their steps. Like Silas or Meg or Danny might magically remember where they'd left Jessica up in these mountains, like when Uncle Les looked all over the lodge to find his truck keys. But unlike keys, Silas wanted to shout, people didn't just stay where you misplaced them, waiting for you to discover the glint of them again, shining up at you from the dirt. People did unpredictable things. Brave things and stupid things and, sometimes, things they regretted. Silas should know.

The only place to escape Sheriff Walters's relentless questioning was upstairs, by the window ledge on the second-floor landing of the rec building. Every few hours, when Uncle Les and Aunt Mary insisted the kids took breaks from their vigil, Silas retreated there, where he knew he could catch a breeze even on the hottest of summer afternoons; all August he'd taken his shirt off to catch a tan as he'd cleared bugs and dirt from the screens, working alongside Uncle Les. Now, on Day 4, he straddled the ledge, staring out at the woods and watching a knot of mosquitoes the size of his fist buzz in a spiral just out of reach. Trying not to think.

He didn't hear Danny climb the stairs. When he looked over, he was just suddenly there, as Danny had a habit of being, and Silas had to grip the sill with his thighs to avoid tumbling out in surprise.

"It's going to get called off," Danny said, his voice hollow. "The search."

He looked . . . wrong somehow. Amped up and unnerved. Not his usual dependable self. He hated it as much as Silas did, not being able to help.

"They won't call it off yet," Silas argued. Because they just couldn't. "Not until they find her." That was how these things worked, wasn't it?

Silas looked back out the window, over the grounds of the lodge. Plenty of trucks and trailers still dotted the parking area. Plenty of people in orange shirts still milled around. But someone had begun attaching big yellow ribbons to some of the trees. For missing people, Aunt Mary had explained. In memory. Which had caused Silas to clench his fists in despair. Jessica was missing, yeah. But she wasn't . . .

she shouldn't be . . . memorialized. Why were these searchers skipping so many steps, jumping directly to the end?

"I'm just the messenger," Danny said. "I heard that guy, the sheriff? He said this was it, Silas. In a few more hours, no one's even going to be looking anymore."

Not. Looking. Anymore. The three words hung there, taunting Silas, like they dangled from individual strings, just out of reach. It made him want to bat the air with his fists. He pushed off from the windowsill ledge. Enough sitting around. "We should *do* something, then."

Danny just eyed him warily, like he did most of the time these days, before turning away, like Silas was some kind of lost cause. "When are you going to get it?" Danny said. "You can't power your way out of everything."

Silas stared him down. "I'm not trying to get *out* of anything." Typical Danny, with his bizarre need to beat him to the moral high ground. He wanted to take him by the shoulders and shake him. "*Something* happened out there," he pressed, his voice rising.

"Well, we can all agree on that," Danny snapped, his voice somehow obtaining an even higher air of superiority.

"It's not me who—"

"Stop it."

Meg. He hadn't heard her climb the stairs as they'd been arguing. He spun to look at her just as Danny, too, turned to face her, and for a moment, the familiar triangulation of their friendship caught and held, the three of them legs of the same stool, propping one another up by sheer shared experience alone. And then Danny's eyes gleamed with something like challenge and Meg shifted her gaze to the floor and the stool was kicked out from under him.

"Sheriff Walters is trying to get us to turn on one another," he told them both. "Can't you see that?"

That gleam of Danny's flashed fire. "And we would *never* do that, would we, Matheson? Turn on each other?"

18

The accusation sliced cleanly, right to the bone, but Silas stood his ground. What had Meg so often said? He was like a rock in a current. That was it. A wall to the wind. He couldn't budge now. Not with so much at stake.

"We're not to blame," Silas said firmly. "None of us."

If he willed this to be true, would it set in stone? Or would it just solidify the guilt sluicing through him into granite as ancient as the peaks of the Sierra, destined to outlive them all? He was still trying to decide as Danny pivoted and retreated down the stairs. He turned back to the window, eyes stinging, until he heard Meg's footsteps following suit.

3

MEG

November 8, 2018
Feather River

Meg Tanner stands for the customary Pledge of Allegiance that opens every meeting of the Feather River Search and Rescue team, then settles in for an afternoon of mind-numbing bureaucracy, interspersed with much more welcome training, protocol, and fifteen-minute coffee breaks. Over a decade into these weekly meetings, she knows to sneak a granola bar or two into the sheriff's department, just in case they go over the ninety-minute time allotment. Which they always do.

She nudges Danny, sitting to her right, and offers him a bar, which he accepts with a grateful nod. Her commute from her day job as department secretary to the sheriff is less than fifty yards, but he's come directly from work at the fire station, still in his navy-blue uniform pants and Feather River Fire T-shirt. Meg will cook dinner tonight, she supposes, since Danny has pulled mess-hall duty two nights running.

Lieutenant Julian Santos, second in command, is at the podium, announcing this month's budget, or lack thereof, and the K9 team is restless in their seats toward the back, mumbling about the new training harnesses promised to them.

Santos holds up one hand. "No one was *promised* anything," he reminds the group. "Not during this budget year, anyway." Something about tax dollars diminishing, that bill they so desperately needed passed last election not going through.

Meg has known Lieutenant Santos for his entire tenure as special officer in charge of Feather River County Search and Rescue operations, and he's always shown impressive patience while dealing with the same old thing: never enough money to spread around, the hospitality team begging for upgraded cookware, the ATV team hoping for a new trailer, the dive team petitioning to attend that training seminar in Sacramento. Meg waits it out. They've already debriefed on the four searches they've had this month—hunting season is always busy—and she's anticipating what's next on the meeting agenda: SAR's yearly stats. They're still a month shy of the end of 2018, but she compiled the data herself at work just today, at the request of her boss, County Sheriff Greg Walters.

Walters himself approaches the podium to deliver what Meg already knows to be good news. She's smiling before he's even finished shuffling the papers in his hands and has located his reading glasses, which were already perched on his nose. "Well, looks like we'll do it, folks," Walters says, his normally gruff intonation softening at the edges. "As of today, we have one hundred percent finds for 2018."

Applause erupts, chased by a few whoops and one earsplitting whistle from Craig Bonway, head of the K9 group. Meg winces even as she laughs.

Then she sobers. Because next to her, Danny has crossed his arms over his chest, his shoulders tense. Meg allows herself a prickle of resentment. Can he not just take the win? Instead, per usual, he seems to insist on self-flagellation. And it's not for the benefit of the old-timers in the room, who are, at this very moment, probably glancing their way. No, Danny brings this punishment on himself.

A 100-percent find rate does not mean every search victim is found alive in a given year, but it does mean they're *found*. Which means a recovery effort, complete with answers for the friends and family. Meg glances sidelong again at Danny. Is he thinking what she's thinking . . . what she's *always* thinking: What about 2003? What happened to Jessica Howard that August night?

It's why they're both here, when it comes right down to it. Meeting after meeting, search after search. It's why they've both dedicated their professional lives and their free time to this county. To comb the wilderness that swallowed up their friend all those years ago. Because it sure isn't for the bad coffee and the end-of-year barbecue at the river, where ATV-unit captain Chuck Roland can be counted on to break out his ukulele.

"There's only so much a person can do to make amends," Danny told her through a clenched jaw more than once after the Howard search ended with no resolution in sight. No answers. The bitterness in his tone had made her wince. In it, she'd heard what he'd left unspoken: *Nothing we do will ever be enough.* And yet here they still sit, shoulder to shoulder, forever trying to tip those scales.

When the meeting ends, she and Danny drive out of the department lot in silence. It's Tuesday night, and Tuesday night is usually reserved for darts and IPAs at Conifers off the highway with the rest of the SAR crew, but Danny suggests they drive directly home.

"I don't exactly feel like socializing," he says.

She doesn't really, either, but there's also River Bend Brewery, where the crowd is younger and livelier, even midweek, and the cacophony of voices and clank of pint glasses might help keep any lingering questions resurfaced in the SAR meeting at bay. But they never go to River Bend on Tuesdays, and Danny's mouth has already set in a firm line, his brow knitted against the oncoming headlights of the few cars on the road. "We have your dad's retirement thing tomorrow night anyway," she offers, by way of concession. "Not to mention Thanksgiving coming up."

And next Monday, they'll have bowling league, because they bowl every Monday at the Cosmos with Charlotte from call-out and Steve from the fire station, who are expecting their second little girl next month. Meg supposes there will be a temporary reprieve after Char's water breaks, though she can count on another SAR meeting on Tuesday, of course, as well as the Tuesday after that, and so on and so forth. She stares out the windshield of her SUV, making each familiar turn as the road parallels the river, wondering how long she can stand to be stuck in such a rut.

I could apply for the promotion, she reminds herself. Walters said the victim-advocacy position that had come across his desk had her name written all over it, but Danny worried it would be triggering. *Triggering for me or for you?* she'd just managed to bite back. But all she had to do was think of that horrible week at the end of August 2003 to know she was no more immune than Danny.

"They were all staring at us," Danny says now. "The search veterans, I mean. McCrady. Santos. Even Walters."

"They weren't," Meg counters automatically. She knows how much it pains him to feel the condemnation of his peers, real or imagined. "And Santos wasn't even here in '03." But even as she insists on this, Meg's mind is playing a familiar, and always morbid, loop in her head. Running through the forest. The scream she can never unhear. She clenches her jaw tight to keep from suddenly crying. "Trust me," she tells him. "No one thinks about this more than we do. No one."

He turns to regard her, his face awash with misery in the glow cast from the dashboard lights. "I can think of *one* person who *should*, at least," he mutters. "That is, if he even still cares."

That bite is back in Danny's tone, and Meg's sympathy dissipates. "That's not fair. We can't possibly know what he's thinking."

"He should never have come back," Danny counters. "I know that much."

Meg exhales, eyes determinedly on the road. They'd heard Silas Matheson was back in town just two days ago, from Janice Hall, the checkout clerk at Clark's Market; the moment his name dropped, Meg's whole body turned to lead. Danny, too, went rigid.

Should they feel insulted that he has evidently been here for days already, taking over Marble Lake Lodge for Mary Albright without so much as a courtesy call? At Clark's, it was all she could do to retrieve her share of their groceries from the conveyer belt before the apples and lettuce collided with the eggs. A paper bag under each arm, she and Danny escaped in record time, only to sit in the car in the parking lot, processing this news in what felt like parallel universes.

Silas had left town fifteen years ago without even saying goodbye. And now he was back, reinstating himself at the lodge like nothing had happened? Meg wasn't insulted, she decided then. She was hurt, the wound she'd deluded herself into thinking had scarred over years ago still raw.

"I hear he's got kids," Danny says.

Meg nods numbly. "Two boys." She debates saying more, then adds, "He isn't with their mother anymore, though."

Danny glances at her. "Well, it's nothing to us," he says.

He stares her down as she drives, his expression now a dare, and Meg lifts her hands from the steering wheel in a gesture of surrender. What other recourse remains to her? She's always suspected that behind the bravado, Danny is a man who doesn't want to know. Not really. Not all of it. Despite his dedication as a volunteer with SAR, despite working in public service, he never combs through the well-worn Marble Lake topographical maps and archived search notes on his days off, like she does. And every year, he shoots down her suggestion to put in a formal request with Sheriff Walters, imploring him to reopen the Howard search. His argument: "How can any of us heal if we keep picking at the scab?" True to his word, as far as Meg knows, he's never even set foot in that terrain since.

Now, bitter victory shines in his eyes at her lack of rebuttal. He looks away first, saying, "On second thought, I think I may grab a beer at Tomahawk before calling it a night."

He knows the dive bar isn't her scene, but she doesn't have the energy for a conflict right now. Certainly not about this.

She sighs, and Danny reaches over and gently squeezes her shoulder. "It's just that after tonight's meeting, I know I won't be good company."

She can't argue there. They're both just doing the best they can, but it will be a relief not to feel his angst tonight, to get out from under his gaze. But twenty minutes later, after dropping herself off and giving him the use of the car, she can't seem to shake herself of his condemnation of Silas. She still feels the heat of it, like coals glowing under her skin, searing her from within.

This is precisely why they never talk about this, apart from when statistics and unexpected news bring it all crashing back. It's easier that way. Meg can skim along the surface of their routine life—work, friends, family, SAR—without dipping too far under it. She pinches her eyes shut, blocking out the haunted look on Danny's face, the tension in the car, and the echo of Walters's announcement at the meeting. She forces her thoughts away from the Marble Lake wilderness. Refuses to visualize the path of each trail, blazed into rock and dirt. Doesn't allow herself to wonder if it's already feeling like winter up at the lodge, two thousand feet higher into the Sierra range.

Not while she's down here in town, spiraling in what feels like endless circles.

4

SILAS

To say this lodge is a mess would be an understatement, and Silas has officially almost run out of daylight. It's not just the landscaping and exteriors Aunt Mary had been forced to let slide following Les's death; all the chimneys needed cleaning, new storm windows should be installed on the cabins, and now, after almost two full weeks of nonstop repair work, Silas has discovered a decaying wasp nest in the corner of the upstairs hallway of the rec building.

"Stay put," he calls down to the boys, who are making a ruckus downstairs. The wasps once occupying the nest have probably long since taken up residence elsewhere, but the last thing he wants—or needs—is for someone to get hurt.

He gets only a vague reply from Spencer; from the sound of it, they have uncovered the pool cues and a sword fight has commenced on the staircase. By the time he's found a dusty can of Raid in the utility closet, the battle has mercifully moved to the porch.

His relief to have them out of his hair comes with the usual chaser of guilt. He brought his boys here so they could create a new life *together*, not so Silas could keep reshuffling their spot on his never-ending to-do list. It's hardly their fault he's given up a more than satisfactory salary to take a gamble on this place. It isn't their fault day-to-day custody has proven more daunting than he cares to admit after years of successful co-parenting.

"You have to take the job," Silas had urged Miranda the day she'd been offered the position in Manchester, even knowing she couldn't take the boys with her, given the demands of the new position. "I got this," he promised, his brain already buzzing with the implications for his own life. Their relationship may not have gone the distance, but they'd always supported one another's pursuits. They'd never stood in each other's way. *Kids are happiest with happy parents,* Miranda always said.

But can they be? Happy here? Aunt Mary's words echo back to him in answer. Silas *was* always the one to love this lodge most. Surely his boys will discover all there is to love, too. They're already settling in, he reminds himself, if the din downstairs is any indication. It's loud, sure, but the boys aren't bickering for a change. With all this open space and room to breathe, they'll find their stride, just as Silas once did. It's already started: in the sparks of creativity as Spencer and Cameron make up new games combining incomplete chess sets and checkerboards, the laughter as they build forts outside out of logs and sticks. They've only been at Marble Lake a few weeks, but that camaraderie between the boys Silas always loved seeing in Portland is blossoming again: Spencer is Cameron's best friend, and Cameron is Spencer's.

The thought of *best friends* has uncertainty creeping its way back in, so Silas picks up the can of Raid with renewed enthusiasm, ignoring the sting of the fumes. Each new discovery the boys make—the stairwell at the top of the lodge that leads to a jumble of old gear in the attic, the constant sound of the wind in the pines that lulls them to sleep, the way the stars appear like a solid ceiling of white—will continue to remind

Silas why he brought them here. Will reinforce his parenting instincts. No more second-guessing.

And no more distracting himself from the past by way of DIY. "Hey, guys!" he calls from the landing, coughing from the Raid cloud he's created. "How about the three amigos take a quick hike before dinner? Just give me a few more minutes."

He's rewarded with a chorus of whoops from below, and he's smiling as he rips the Raid-saturated wasp nest from its prime square foot of real estate at the dark far corner of the hall. And then his smile fades.

He's face-to-face with the most acute case of mold he's ever seen. *Goddammit.* He's no contractor, but he knows that where there's mold like this, there's a leak, and not a small one, either. He's still assessing the situation when Cameron calls, "How many minutes is a few?"

"Five," Silas decides, frowning at the wall.

Five minutes turn into twenty, maybe more. Silas loses track, his head buried in the depths of the hall closet. What if a pipe has burst? But even as he peels back wood paneling and pries away rusted nails, he can still hear Spencer's and Cameron's voices rising and falling as they work out the rules to yet another made-up game. His boys are resourceful, he reminds himself. Resilient, just like everyone always says.

Until their patience finally wanes.

"Dad?" Spencer's whiny tone. The one that used to be reserved for his mother. "Are we *ever* going?"

"Da-ad!"

"Almost ready," he calls, though this time, he already knows he's full of shit. So do the boys. One of them answers with an angry clunk on the ancient upright piano downstairs while the other whines, "But that's what you said before!"

But Silas keeps staring at the stripped closet, because he's finally uncovered a full-blown water stain blossoming across the drywall. The damage trails all the way to the floor, which means, what? A compromised foundation? What began as a simple project has morphed into a complete headache, but even as Silas tells himself that the second floor has remained standing for decades and isn't likely to collapse tonight, he doesn't table it. Ignoring Uncle Les's voice in his head, chastising him for barreling forward, per usual, he goes after the source of the issue buried under the floorboards.

He ignores Cameron on the piano, ignores the general scuffle of sneakers on the floor below. He returns to the hallway for his toolbox, then for his mask. It's not until he has half a dozen more boards pried loose on the landing that he registers the silence.

He pauses, knees smarting on the hard surface. Listening harder.

Definitely no more noise coming from downstairs. He contemplates investigating, but he's almost done here. He'll finish just this one section and then figure out where Spencer and Cameron have gone off to. Probably one of the guest cabins, where they like to play house. Or back to the main lodge to find Cameron's hydro pack for the hike. He'll join them soon and apologize to them while they cobble together dinner.

By the time he's removed the last board, he's surprised to note how dark it's gotten in the hallway. Out the upstairs window the sun has set behind Marble Peak, and he glimpses the forest beyond, the darkness not yet complete enough to reflect his own image back to him on the glass. Downstairs, the rec room is still silent. No ruckus. No whining. Not even the hint of a footfall on the floorboards.

He calls out to the kids anyway, then opens the heavy front doors to step onto the porch and yell their names in the direction of the main lodge. Maybe they got too hungry, he thinks with a fresh ping of guilt. Maybe they decided to start dinner without his supervision.

The thought of them breaking out the boxes of mac and cheese they finally picked out at Clark's and trying to operate the Viking stove has him trotting toward the lodge kitchen, heart in his throat, a reprimand already on his lips. But the kitchen is empty, the lights off, the stove cold. Pushing back a prick of alarm, he doubles back, calling toward the direction of the cabins.

No response. No one in cabins 1 through 6, no one in 7 through 9. *Shit.*

Back in the rec building, he nearly trips on the toys on the floor: the oversize puzzle Silas asked them to pick up hours ago, the pool cues, the Nerf golf set, the foam clubs discarded by the fireplace. And then he sees it, on the arm of the couch: a note printed on the back of a roofing invoice in Spencer's careful hand:

Gon to exsplor the rig wile you work. Be rite back. Have bude sistem

Cameron has added his mark, too, illustrating the final point with two carefully drawn stick figures, one just a bit taller than the other. The two brothers.

Dammit. It's supposed to be the three amigos. This time, the expletive comes out of Silas's mouth on a soft exhale, like maybe this note won't be true if he doesn't shout. Doesn't draw attention to it. He knows exactly which ridge Spencer means; Silas has hiked it with them half a dozen times already, thanks to its proximity to the lodge. But they're entirely too young and too green to navigate it solo. God, has he implied otherwise, in his gusto to get them to love this wilderness? He knows the answer, and swallows a quick swell of nausea. He whirls to look at the clock on the wall by the fireplace. 6:25. Right back? What does "right back" mean? When did they write this? When did they leave? Surely they're already overdue. Surely they didn't mean to be out past dark. Dammit, dammit, dammit. His kids don't realize yet how fast night descends up here; the mountains reach up like arms outstretched, meeting the sinking sun far sooner than in Portland.

The pink slip of paper feels impossibly thin in Silas's tight grasp, his pinched index finger able to discern his rising pulse in the pad of his thumb. He wills himself to think. How long ago did they last call his name? Thirty minutes ago? Forty? How many times did he ignore them? How many seconds—minutes—does his neglect of his children now equal?

Something inside Silas seems to weaken and then crack, crumbling in a wreckage of that god-awful uncertainty and guilt. All he's been working so hard to avoid comes crashing down around him: the move, the stress of the renovations, Miranda's departure to the UK, his obvious inadequacy in caring for these boys alone, evidenced by this note. He grabs the Maglite always on a peg by the door—too high for a child to reach, he realizes with a pang—and, on shaky legs, he exits the rec building. He sets out at a fast clip along the Marble Lake trail . . . through the meadow, over the creek, and up the lake loop. He stumbles all the way up the ridge, thinking with every step: *Be there. Be there. Be there.*

But when he crests the top of the trail, no one is here.

Silas is no stranger to fear, but the terror coursing through his veins now is a new and oppressive acquaintance, pushing its way past reason to scatter his thoughts like so many broken shards of glass. As he scrambles farther along the wooded trail, he can no longer keep the thread of the past, that thread he's been so careful not to tug, from unraveling. It trips him up as the worn tread of his boots slide on the exposed granite and tree roots with each crushing footfall, taking him one step backward for every two steps forward. It'd be poetic, given how often he's found himself in this precise position in life, if it weren't so damned tragic. His breath comes in heaving bursts, and his mind buzzes in agitation, reminding him—unnecessarily—of the insistent ticking of a clock reverberating outward from the pulse pounding behind his ears.

"*Spencer!*" he shouts as he runs. "*Cameron!*" And then again. And again.

At the crest of the hill, he pauses only the briefest of moments to take stock, hands braced on his knees, lungs screaming. Even as he gasps for breath, he curses the necessity of this moment's rest. The minutes are accumulating too quickly. Every second that passes is a second more he's separated from his children.

He should call the authorities. Right now. He should ignore the voice in his head that's reminding him what happened last time. To Jessica. To all of them. Because these are his kids it's happening to now. His *kids*.

But it's only a philosophical question anyway: the closest cell tower is miles away, on Banner Peak near town, and the nearest landline is at the lodge, now half a mile or more back in the direction he came from. He cannot fathom turning back so soon, and so he resumes his punishing pace long before his body is ready, half running, half stumbling onward. In under five minutes, he's turned the final corner of the well-traversed trail above his mountain lodge and arrived on a lower ridge. He jogs along it, still shouting his two sons' names repeatedly into the gathering night.

"Spencer!" He doesn't pause. *"Cameron!"*

Still nothing. No one returns his call, save for the screaming in his own head.

He yells until his voice is a thick croak, the back of his throat burning as he sucks in the chilled air, but still gets no response. The wind—whooshing now through the tops of the conifers high above his head like an invisible river—has picked up. He'd forgotten it's even more pronounced up here, bringing his own cries back to him.

After another five minutes he's forced to stop again, his lungs screaming in protest. He fumbles for the flashlight clipped to his belt and flips the switch. Below him, he can no longer make out the lights from his lodge; if he were still lower on the ridge, he'd see the living quarters and recreational building shining brightest, surrounded by the metallic roofs of the cabins and outbuildings, illuminated by the new moon like beads of a necklace slightly tangled. Can Spencer and Cameron see these lights, from wherever they are? Or are they in blackness, too?

Cameron's afraid of the dark, his brain conjures up against his will. Silas installed a star-shaped night-light in their bedroom just the day before, ignoring Spencer's protests. Though that night, it was Spencer who asked for it switched on as Silas tucked them in, wasn't it?

The whisper of dread he's been trying to outrace snakes back into his thoughts, ensnaring him. Is it time to turn back? Time to pick up the phone? No, he carries on, stumbling in his haste and fatigue, falling and finding his footing repeatedly as he runs on in ever-widening sweeps through the sea of trees in every direction.

This is real, his brain screams between gulps of breath. This is truly happening to him . . . to his *children.*

Silas can barely process the fact that less than an hour ago, they were safe and sound. Annoying to him, even! He summons the rec room to his mind, the well-worn sofas and the cheery fireplace, and the homey warmth of it makes the threat he feels closing in from all sides seem bizarre, as far removed from this life he's trying to carve out for his boys as a fairy tale in one of their books.

How, he asks himself, fingers raking impulsively through his hair, the heels of his hands grinding into his eye sockets, could a person go from the end of an average day—chores, responsibilities, irritation at rowdy play—to this level of terror in the span of only a few minutes?

He, of all people, knows how, and so he calls their names out into the darkness again. And again. But now that he's spent, reality is a brick wall he's having trouble scaling. Amid his calls, he begs aloud for this to be a dream, though he isn't awakened. The earth remains still and silent, save for the wind in the trees. There's no nudge to spur him out of his warm bed, no jarring signal of morning.

He closes his eyes tightly and wills all three of them back into the kids' new room where they belong. With their Star Wars comforters on the twin beds. The Nerf guns and Legos cluttering the floor.

When he opens his eyes, Silas is looking down at his own clenched fists. The thought of his boys out here alone, without light, without water—God, he hopes Cameron has the hydro pack—explodes in his brain anew, inadequacy tearing like shrapnel. His boys may have stood here, right in this very place, only minutes before, and the thought spurs him back into action. Running again, he screams on repeat for his sons.

After thirty more minutes, some corner of his mind reserved for cold, calculated logic tells him what he already knows in his gut: *I'm not going to find them like this.* He knows his way back—a fact that sends a new jolt of guilt shooting down his spine—and a few minutes later, he's returned to the lodge porch steps. His back to the rec-room door, he yells one last time, because how can he not? He shouts from somewhere desperate and guttural, his voice ringing out a full octave lower than he planned, and his throat burns strangely with the effort. He yells until he thinks his lungs may burst, but it's useless. His words are snatched from his mouth and carried away by the night.

He throws open the door with all the aggravated energy he cannot exert elsewhere. Inside, the lights are still on, cardboard puzzle pieces still scattered across the floor. One booted foot sends the puzzle box— Dinosaurs of the Jurassic Period—skidding from the entry to the worn rug by the fireplace.

Once he reaches the staircase, Silas cranes his neck up toward the second-floor landing, looking. Listening. He knows he's delaying the inevitable, but maybe, just maybe, the boys returned while he was out looking. Maybe they were playing a trick on him—the irony slays him—and maybe they're hiding from him right this minute, giggling in the upstairs closet amid the Raid. Maybe they'll all laugh about this just as soon as he's done reprimanding them within an inch of their lives.

"Cameron!" he yells one more time. *"Spencer!"*

Nothing. No one.

"Come out right this minute! This is not funny!"

Impenetrable stillness.

They are not hiding. They are not taking a page out of their old man's book, playing a joke and laughing. They're both *gone*.

The sickening sense of déjà vu Silas has been holding at bay throughout his search finally overpowers him, because he has been here before, calling out into the night, grasping at thin air. As he crosses the room, lunging blindly for the phone, dialing 911, four words are repeating on a loop.

This cannot happen again.

Surely, lightning cannot strike twice.

5

MEG

November 20, 2018
3:14 a.m.
Feather River

Meg is fast asleep when the shrill insistence of her ringtone cuts across her darkened bedroom and into her subconscious. So much for a full night's rest. Blearily, she picks up, because a call at this hour can mean only one thing.

"Morning, Meg," Charlotte mumbles into the phone.

Meg runs one hand through her tangled hair, reaching with the other to shut off her alarm, which had been set for an optimistic 7:00 a.m. "Yeah. Hey, Char. I'm here."

"We've got a full call-out. We're meeting at the station in thirty minutes. Can you make it? We'll be headed up in the Marble Lake direction."

The words *Marble Lake* have Meg instantly sitting up straighter, but the question is purely rhetorical: Meg always makes it. She says a silent goodbye to a lazy morning and then nods. Realizing belatedly that the visual affirmation won't suffice, she answers audibly. "Yeah, Char. See you soon."

She nudges Danny, who has slept right through the call, then swings her legs off the bed and stands, swiping blindly for the light. He groans, flinging an arm over his face, but a moment later, he, too, is up, no more likely to skip a call-out than Meg.

Their field uniforms are easy to spot in the closet, the obnoxiously bright orange button-down shirts and olive Carhartt pants standing out in sharp contrast amid the row of flannels, tees, and jeans. As Danny debates his footwear choices, Meg grabs her favorite thermal undershirt before layering her uniform over it, then pulls wool socks and her hiking boots on. It may still be fall, but this is the High Sierra, and they'll be lucky if the temperature clears the low twenties before sunrise.

In the kitchen, they skip coffee, knowing there will be plenty of it, although admittedly bad, later, opting instead for a handful of energy bars and packets of instant oatmeal, which they stuff into the two go bags sitting in the front entryway. They're both always search-ready, repacked after every mission.

In a routine born of long practice, they snag their water bottles from each side pocket, fill them silently at the kitchen sink. Usually, they're both too bleary for conversation on early-a.m. call-outs, and today is no exception, but Meg stops Danny by the door anyway, a hand on his forearm.

"You okay?" He'd gotten in late. She was too tired to revisit the tension in the car after the SAR meeting, and the lack of resolution hangs in the air between them.

But Danny just says, "Why wouldn't I be?"

He snags the keys from the sideboard, and Meg takes the cue with a bit-back sigh, grabbing her orange-and-black parka, *Feather River County Search and Rescue* stamped in large block letters across the back. As they head out the door, she tells herself to let it go. When Danny broods, less is more. The challenge for Meg is not hearing the echo of past trauma in the silence. It takes effort, but she decided long ago that making it work with Danny was worth it. Otherwise, what did she give everything up for?

In the car, the digital display on the dashboard reads 3:25 a.m., and as they retrace the short drive to the department station, she worries her lip, trying not to overanalyze today's search location. She's been on plenty of other searches in the Marble Lake area during her SAR career, in addition, that is, to the one that started it all. This one won't be any different. Right? The guest season is well over, so she suspects this search is for a missing hunter, the most common scenario at this time of year. She won't know for sure until their first debriefing, but there's no reason for Marble Lake Lodge—or its new owner—to be directly involved in any way.

She glances sidelong at Danny, wondering if he agrees, but even though she knows he's now seen the search location on his call-out text, his face remains unreadable. Silence it is, then, which comes as no surprise; they never talk about Marble Lake Lodge or what happened there.

She retrains her eyes on the road, letting the darkened tableau of green pines and winding river rise up to meet her, their reflections rolling off her windshield like waves lapping at the glass. A Northern California town with a population of two thousand probably calls to mind images of country charm and rolling foothills, maybe a winery or a Silicon exec or two, but not here. In this western corner of the Sierra Nevada, the mountains framing Meg's view are high enough that she's forced to lift her chin to glimpse their peaks. Studded with jagged granite, the steep elevation is marked by lodgepole, ponderosa, and patches of snow that never completely melt.

She takes it all in, still trying to shake that "in a rut" feeling from the night before. Growing up in the shadow of these mountains, she took them for granted for years. At least until her eyes were opened to the fullness of their beauty. And the danger.

At the station, the parking area is already filling. Meg pulls into her usual nine-to-five spot, and she and Danny sign in to the call, scrawling their names and radio numbers on the form to confirm their presence. Most of the people are milling around outside, and Danny gravitates there, but Meg lets herself inside to wait, leaning against the side of a desk—*her* desk, it just so happens—to await the remainder of what Charlotte likes to call her call-out victims. It always takes her aback, how different this place looks at zero dark thirty, the usual bustle and noise generated by too many people sharing a small space (*Thanks, budget cuts*) replaced by an almost eerie solitude. Her reception area is still and silent for a change, the papers she'd left neatly stacked on her desk still undisturbed from the day before. The entire building, in fact, seems cast in a soft predawn glow.

It's a temporary respite. Twenty minutes later, the rest of the half-awake searchers have arrived, and everyone huddles around the call-out desk, awaiting orders. They're all fueled by the same adrenaline that got Meg and Danny out of bed in a hurry, peppering the team leaders with questions she knows they aren't at liberty to answer. Rideshares up to the search staging area are quickly organized, and Meg and Danny's rig pulls out just before 4:00 a.m., cruising out of Feather River and then higher into the mountains up Marble Lake Road, each twist of the pavement as familiar to her as the inside of her own home.

It feels good to get moving again, but *another* twenty minutes later, the remainder of Meg's initial rush of adrenaline has failed her, the hum of the engine lulling her back against the seat. She's just leaned her head against the passenger-side door of the sheriff's-department 4x4, welcoming the wash of dry heat blowing across her face from the adjacent air vent, when her driver slows and then turns the wheel. She sits up only to blink in surprise and then dismay: of all the acreage of the Marble Lake wilderness, they had to choose *this* exact spot as the location for the day's staging area?

There it is, right before her: the Marble Lake Lodge sign, pointing toward the old stomping grounds and new home and business venture of Silas Matheson. They've rolled right into the guest parking area, beyond which she can catch glimpses of the metal rooflines and stone chimneys of the lodge proper. Though she's taken it upon herself to hike the nearby trails dozens of times in the last fifteen years despite her requests to reopen the Howard case falling on deaf ears, she's studiously avoided the lodge itself. What if she ran into Les or Mary Albright, who'd want to fill her in on their nephew's new life in Portland? Or, worse, what if they'd want to revisit the past, Mary Albright pinning her direct gaze on Meg before enfolding her in one of her signature hugs?

She looks at Danny again, whose poker face has finally failed him. He looks every bit as unsettled to be here as Meg, glancing anywhere but directly at the lodge. The relatable attempt at self-preservation sends a stab of sorrow through Meg. In her experience, out of sight is never out of mind.

That feeling of ill ease settles more firmly in her gut. Again, she tries to talk herself down. Surely, it's coincidence that the search is centered here, epicenter of both Meg's longest-running nightmares and her most recent misgivings. The lodge must simply be the most strategic base for today's operations. That's all.

All the same, as she and Danny join the rest of the searchers who have already assembled, she once again feels wide awake. Is Silas here somewhere, assisting? Has he opened the lodge up to the operations team? She's grateful that the parking area is set about a football field's length away from the smattering of buildings. As curious as she's felt about Silas's new life, she's not sure she's ready to face him in casual conversation. Too many unanswered questions still churn through her mind when she lets her defenses down: Does he blame her for what happened? Is that why he left? Or has he been punishing himself all this time by casting himself into exile?

She can't go there, certainly not today. Danny must feel similarly, because he's shut back down, his face carefully neutral now that they've joined the others, so she makes a beeline for the coffee carafe at the cook van. At this point, it's more for something to do than out of any need of caffeine.

"Hurry up and wait," someone groans, and she smiles tightly, acutely aware of the bureaucracy of search-and-rescue operations. The red tape, the spitting contests, the trampling of various agencies' toes that you'd think would be limited to the movies is all true, in spades.

"What's the holdup this time?" she asks her closest neighbor to the coffee carafe, an old-timer to the team. He rocks a signature Santa Claus beard but lacks the accompanying apple-red cheeks and twinkle in his eye. *Barry,* Meg remembers. She always struggles with his name, so un-Santa-like.

"Hell if I know," Barry tells her. He juts his chin toward the bright-yellow van, nicknamed the Lemon. "They've been holed up in there for what feels like forever."

Interpretation: the incident commander has been sequestered in the communications van, com van for short, with their boss, Sheriff Walters, and whoever is today's Feather River Forest Service representative, for over thirty minutes. Santos is probably in attendance as well. Meg studies the van, the bright paint peeling around the rims and along the undercarriage, where the snow and mud thrown up by the mountain roads alternately freezes and thaws all season long. Inside, the powers that be must still be strategizing.

Even out of earshot, stomping her feet to ward off the cold, Meg can guess at the gist of their conversation. They'll have topographical maps spread out on the com-van table by now, with highlighted segments squared off. And if they aren't still arguing about *where* to look, it's about *who* will look. Every big search starts with a squabble about who's better equipped, which agency is superiorly trained for the mission, even where the county boundaries fall and the jurisdiction shifts. Everyone wants the glory, even if it means their own county will be temporarily understaffed. When Meg first joined up, years ago, it seemed unforgivably petty. How, she asked her senior team members, could management be so shallow and crude as to bicker about the credit and the glory at the moment of some family's anguish? At perhaps the very moment of a victim's somewhere-out-there suffering? As someone who had once been on the other side, sitting and waiting, wrapped up in guilt and terror, it felt unacceptable to her.

It still does. Despite the early drive up and the predictable wait, her heart is beating quickly. She stirs her terrible coffee, watching the steam rise to cut through the cold air, and tells herself again that it's not the unsettling location that's keeping her heart rate up. No, this is the way it always is with her. From the moment the search-and-rescue text lights up the screen of her phone, something ignites inside Meg.

Admit it, Charlotte has told her on more than one early morning, *you live for this shit.*

Char's right, but what choice does Meg have? The alternative is to forget, and she couldn't do that if she tried. She gulps a mouthful of bitter coffee too fast, trying to swallow the irony of this, which she's never been able to outrun. Luckily, distraction is in sight, in the form of her friend Phillip McCrady, approaching from the parking lot at an awkward hop-step gait while grappling with the slip-on traction cleats on his boots. Meg waves him over to offer a steady shoulder; his breath clouds the air as he bends forward, his gloved hand still attempting to tighten the rubber tread over the sole of his boot.

McCrady smiles gratefully. "Thanks, kiddo."

Like Barry, McCrady is at least thirty years Meg's senior, and the first time they were thrown together as a hasty rig team five years ago, she'd bristled at the nickname. Today it doesn't even register in her brain. So what if she's thirty-three years old, surrounded by retirees and career law-enforcement professionals? These are her people. From the moment she applied for her first admin job with the county right out of high school, directionless and hurting, SAR has been her family.

McCrady slides her an affectionate grin, as though he's read her mind. He gives the tip of her hair a playful tug. "At least I stopped calling you Red," he adds with a chuckle.

Meg frowns. "It's not *red*, exactly."

"Sure, okay. Auburn, then." McCrady pulls his gloves off and thrusts them at her. "Hold these, will you?"

She tucks them under one arm and takes a long drink of her coffee, wondering if she should dig her traction cleats out of her bag as well. The ice is only the thinnest sheet of frozen condensation here in the parking lot, but it's unpredictable, crunching unevenly under their feet. There's no snow yet, but Meg guesses the first big storm of the season is only days away at best.

When she lifts her head, Danny has materialized back at her side, letting his pack slide down his arm and fall with a thud to the icy pavement as he fishes out his own cleats. He still looks somber, which is apropos given the circumstances, of course, but she's just wondering if he's going to finally broach the subject of their search location when McCrady, never one to pass up the opportunity to use a nickname, acknowledges him with a jovial "Hey there, Boy Scout."

This particular moniker has been chasing Danny most of his life, and Meg thinks he's going to bristle, but instead, he manages to call up the same boyish charm that has drawn her to him since they were kids, brushing his light-brown hair out of his eyes as he straightens.

"Hey there, Phillip. Kathy keeping you busy in your retirement?"

"Probably busier than they're keeping you out at the station." McCrady chuckles.

"No rest for the weary public servant," Danny answers wryly, only adding credence to his do-gooder status. He carries it well, though, probably because he comes by it honestly, and McCrady rewards him with an affectionate pat on the shoulder.

The dawn is fully upon them now, but the sky remains ominously opaque, closing in like a low ceiling just out of reach. Meg surveys the incoming clouds, trying to shake off an irrational sense of claustrophobia.

Danny follows her gaze. "Storm coming in, most likely. We know anything yet?"

"We will in a minute." She nods in the direction of the Lemon. The com van's door has crashed open, and today's incident commander steps down with a sheaf of papers under one arm.

Danny lets out a low groan, and a few feet away, McCrady swears under his breath. "Shit, Susan Darcy." Meg leans over and kicks the steel toe of his boot to silence him.

As with any job, some IC appointees are better than others. Personally, Meg has never had a problem with Darcy's style—a combination of smart-ass gumption and raw impulse—but not everyone agrees with her assessment.

"All right, people," Darcy calls, climbing up onto the running board of the Lemon. It's a necessary maneuver, to ensure her five-foot-zero frame is viewed by all. "Gather around. We have two subjects. The first is a seven-year-old boy. The second is his brother, age five."

Instantly, sounds of dismay pick up volume through the crowd at this unwelcome news. Next to Meg, McCrady says, "Well, shit."

Barry kicks at the ice at his feet. "Not a kid search. Goddamn."

Meg's heart, too, sinks. Maybe that awful intuition *was* right, in a way. There's nothing worse than searching for children. But then her brain makes an immediate, lurching leap and her stomach does a horrible flip: Children. Marble Lake Lodge. Silas. But it can't be, can it?

She tells herself no, she knows nothing yet, but her stomach is still turning over on itself as Sheriff Walters steps in front, shushing them all with two beefy hands in the air. "I know it's rough. All the more reason to get teams out there, get a move on. The boys have been missing since just past sundown last night. First responders have been out since twenty-one hundred hours, with no luck."

Another collective moan arises from the crowd at the news that these kids have already endured a full night out in this cold. Meg's heart constricts further in her chest as Darcy lets a blaring whistle fly so she can begin reading out names, calling each searcher by radio number to issue GPS units and search vests.

As she works and the crowd starts to move into their groups, Meg listens for her own name, eyes on Darcy. First, however, she hears two others.

"The names of our search subjects," Sheriff Walters calls from the com van, "are Spencer and Cameron. Last name: Matheson."

Meg freezes, this sentence delivering a second punch to her gut in as many minutes. Danny, too, stills beside her. She must lose whatever color had graced her cheeks, because on her left, McCrady doesn't miss a beat. "Hold on. You know these kids?"

She can only shake her head tightly, her eyes now trained on Danny, who finds his voice first. He flings Meg a look that conveys both disbelief and despair, and most likely masks much more. It usually does. "No, not the kids."

"We know their father," Meg supplies, barely able to speak through the rising dismay threatening to drown her.

"Knew him," Danny corrects swiftly, while Meg's throat constricts still further.

Now she's the one unable to meet *his* gaze, but when he reaches for her hand, she squeezes, wondering when exactly this morning of protocol shifted out of their control with such devastating thoroughness.

6

MEG

Eleven months prior to Howard search
September 2002
Feather River

One day, it had just been Meg and Danny embarking on their senior year as Feather River High School's longest-standing couple, and the next, in a torrent of energy and whirlwind charisma that left her dizzy, it was three.

Meg had clocked the new guy on campus twice already—once in the school office, picking up a schedule, and once in calculus, where he'd been seated next to her—and had dismissed his interference in her life in any way. His looks and novelty alone placed his social trajectory eons above her own ordinary orbit. And then she'd exited third period to witness the impossible: serious, studious Danny—*her* Danny—shouting with unrestrained glee over the din of locker doors crashing shut.

"Silas *Matheson*? No freaking way!"

She watched as he pushed his way through the rush-hour hallway traffic to lock in to an exuberant embrace with the grinning, entirely overconfident, probably completely self-absorbed new guy. This Silas.

And Silas hugged him back. Actually lifted Danny up off the ground in his enthusiasm, the two of them tumbling into people trying to get to class like exuberant puppies. "What's up, Boy Scout?" Silas laughed.

Boy Scout? Was that a dig at Danny? Because he was already almost an Eagle Scout. But Danny just said, "It's been *ages*. How come I didn't know you'd be coming to school here?"

Ages?

"'Cause I didn't know myself, not until last week anyway," Silas supplied. By this time, Meg had somehow migrated toward them without realizing it, and he stuck his hand out. "Hey. I'm Silas."

"Megan Tanner," Meg said cautiously, taking the proffered hand, while Danny said simultaneously, "Meg is my girlfriend."

Silas gripped her hand with enthusiasm. "Your boy and I go way back."

Danny jumped in as more people started to gather around, interested to know how Meg and Danny, of all people, knew the cool new kid. Hoping, probably, to be introduced next. "Silas used to spend his summers here," he said to the hallway at large, "living up on Marble Lake Road with his aunt and uncle. You staying with them again now?"

"Yep." Silas grinned. "Talked my folks into letting me finish out high school here, instead of dragging me along on yet another mission to save the planet." For the benefit of everyone else, he explained, "My parents are environmental activists, which is cool and all, until you don't want to spend your senior year homeschooling on the sidelines of a damming-project protest."

"Totally," someone sympathized, and Meg turned to see what amounted to the entire cheer squad behind her, Stephanie Adams and Jessica Howard leading the pack, assuming, just as Meg had, that their social status as most popular in the class gave them priority access.

"How do you know Danny?" Jessica asked.

"Well, he saved my life," Silas deadpanned, only breaking into a grin when the tension had drawn taut enough for Danny to flush in protest.

"Hardly." All eyes turned to him, Meg's most certainly included, so he continued. "I was up at Marble Lake Lodge—"

"For a Boy Scout thing," Silas said.

"Cub Scouts," Danny corrected. "It was forever ago. We were, like, ten or something. And Mr. Albright—"

"My uncle Les—"

"Was leading us on a wilderness-badge project, teaching us how to read animal tracks by Marble Lake. Silas tagged along. Mr. Albright was explaining how you can identify different animals, and even know if they were feeding, or nesting, or . . ." He trailed off, sensing that he was losing his audience.

"It was totally boring," Silas interjected, earning a laugh from the cheerleaders, "but then I had an idea." All eyes turned back to him, except for Meg's. She was still looking at her boyfriend, whom she'd known since kindergarten. And whom she'd never known to grand-stand, or even remain in proximity with anyone who did.

Silas went on to set the scene: It was almost time for the troop to leave the lake, and Silas decided it would be funny—"hilarious," to be precise—to leave his own tracks in the mud by the lakeshore and then hop into one of the rowboats waiting there for guests and row out onto the lake. See if his uncle Les could follow *those* tracks.

"But he didn't even notice I was gone!" he declared, to more laugh-ter. "And there I was, floating farther and farther out onto the lake, totally losing the battle against the wind, the oars slapping the water every which way, like a complete idiot." He paused then, for dramatic effect, Meg supposed, then flung an arm around Danny's shoulders. "Only my man Dan here saw me, and he tried to call out to my uncle—"

"But he was too far in front of me—"

"And we all know Danny," Silas added, "and he just had to be a hero, didn't he?" More laughter, though with Danny, or *at* him? Meg wasn't sure. And Danny didn't even seem to care. Silas just leaned in to his captive audience. "There I was, adrift and alone. Night falling."

"No, it wasn't." Danny's face flushed again.

Silas waved this away. "And then, suddenly, there's another rowboat, and this kid, who seems to know how to actually use oars, is coming to my rescue."

"It wasn't quite like that."

"I waved my arms at him—dropping my own oars into the water, since I hadn't rigged the oarlocks"—more laughter—"and then there he was, figuring out how to hop from his boat to my boat, *with* his oars, no less, so we could combine our spindly ten-year-old strength"—here Silas flexed what were no longer spindly biceps—"and get ourselves back to shore."

The gathered crowd cheered—actually *cheered*—and Silas ended with a flourish. "The only casualty that day? One rowboat, retrieved later, two oars, never to be seen again, and my backside, after Uncle Les heard the tale."

Everyone laughed so hard now, the closest teacher popped her head out of her classroom and made a shooing motion, urging them to move along to where they needed to be.

"And we've been friends ever since," Danny added shyly as the crowd reluctantly dispersed, "hanging out the next few summers Silas came back after that."

Before Meg and Danny had become a thing. She braced for more laughter. But it didn't come. Quite the opposite, actually. The cheer squad looked at Danny like they'd never really seen him before. Which had always been just as well, in Meg's opinion.

"My uncle decided he was a good influence on me, I think." Silas winked in the cheerleaders' direction. "I just wish I hadn't been gone so long," he added. "Marble Lake Lodge with Dan was way more fun than traipsing all over the country."

Silas hadn't been kidding. He really did like hanging out with Danny Boy Scout Cairns. And right from the get-go, Meg was dragged along for the ride. He invited them to have lunch with him at the top-social-tier cafeteria table that first day, already playing host at their own school, and even as Meg declined—she had nothing to prove to these people—Danny was already accepting. And so she sat, waiting for Silas to realize his mistake. To bolt for the cool crowd, following Jessica Howard, maybe, who had—impossibly—been shunted over to the next table. Surely, he had a thing for blonds? But no, he remained planted between Meg and Danny, polishing off his sandwich.

Not that it mattered. Not that Meg needed to win some sort of popularity contest. Meg had Danny, who would graduate high school, get his fire-science AA degree, and then join the Feather River Fire Station 11 crew. It had been his goal to serve the public since filling out the required "*When I Grow Up, I Want to Be ____*" project in preschool, and Meg liked that Danny knew himself. It was a nice change of pace from her mother, who changed career dreams as often as hairstyles, which was often, seeing as "hairstylist" had been one of said careers. Meg liked that, unlike this new whirlwind in their lives, Danny had an actual, applicable *plan*, one she could slip right into the wake of. Because Meg didn't really have a label of her own. She wasn't Boy Scout. She wasn't Miss Popular. She wasn't prom-court material, wasn't a jock, wasn't on the cheerleading squad. Basically, she hovered just off-center of the mainstream, unnamed and uncategorized. Unseen, too. And honestly, that was just fine.

"You never told me about Silas," she said to Danny late that afternoon as they tossed their backpacks onto the Cairnses' worn couch.

"I guess after he stopped spending summers at the lodge, I kind of forgot."

Nothing about Silas Matheson seemed forgettable to Meg, but she let this pass.

"What do you think of him?" Danny asked. "And be real."

Meg be real? What had Danny been all day? Because he certainly hadn't seemed himself. "He's . . . a lot," she answered, after weighing the question with care, but Danny just smiled, like suddenly he'd decided "a lot" might be a lot of fun.

Within days, it was as if Silas had started school in Feather River at five years old, just like all the rest of them. He hit the ground running, joining every club, taking interest in every corner of the social stratosphere, and bringing his new duo right along with him. Methodical, steady Danny seemed charged somehow by Silas's energy. A switch Meg hadn't known existed in him had been flipped, and keeping up with the two of them became her breathless new normal, whether in the corridors or in the classroom or, as was the case one sunny October afternoon, on a biology field trip along the banks of the Feather River.

Following the river upstream, water-testing kit in hand, Silas had been—by far the most enthusiastic among their classmates, a habit that didn't seem to dock him popularity points. Meg had to trot to keep up with him and Danny in her clunky school-issued rubber boots, never mind that blisters were no doubt forming. Silas did that to people: he spurred them to action, set them to clamoring, even when all that awaited them was silty sand and ice-cold water. Wading through the pebbly river, fingers freezing as she sucked up samples with her plastic tester, Meg listened as Danny seemed to hang on Silas's every word, acting like it was an honor somehow, to hold all the test tubes. So what if Silas was team leader for their project? He couldn't collect his own samples? Though he did, actually, scooping up and filtering the murky stream water right along with everyone else, all the while waxing poetic about the forest around his aunt and uncle's place, about the lakes he loved to swim in, even about the crawdads they uncovered with their boots.

"You really like this stuff, don't you?" Danny asked, and Silas grinned in answer, lifting mud-caked hands up to his face to brush away a buzzing dragonfly.

"I like discovering things," he answered, which sounded ridiculous. Or should have, at least. *Would* have, without a doubt, coming out of anyone else's mouth.

Apparently, one of the things Silas had determined to discover was Meg. He constantly peppered her with questions, making her feel like she was in some sort of bizarre interview as Danny's girlfriend. He managed to coax opinions out of her she hadn't even known she'd harbored on everything from books to nature to movies, absorbing it all before rebounding it in a manner that left her vaguely dizzy. His passion at the river hadn't been an anomaly; Silas was agnostic in the purest sense of the word. He took nothing at surface value; in class, his hand remained nearly permanently raised; in his term papers, he wrote argumentatively, uncovering and overturning ideas, dismissing the mess he made out of hand.

He was such a contrast to everything Meg appreciated about Danny: his reliability, the way she could predict his moods, his easy companionship—a comfort to her since they'd been deposited together in the same after-school childcare program, both raised by single parents. So why did this contrast seem to work? The two boys balanced each other like the two sides of the same coin, Meg precariously poised on the edge between them.

The term "third wheel" never seemed to occur to Danny or Silas, leaving Meg to conclude *she* was the odd person out. As the weeks went on, she gave up trying to figure out why and simply allowed herself to be carried along in Silas and Danny's current, a loose, random bit of debris that bounced and bobbed along.

It wasn't until 4:00 p.m. each school day that she was set adrift, when Danny headed to the Feather River station to rack up volunteer hours as a junior firefighter and Silas commuted up the highway to Marble Lake Lodge. She'd go home, where a note from her mom would inform her whether or not she'd be home for dinner. She'd make herself some food before starting homework and wonder when, exactly, having her free time had stopped feeling so welcome.

7

MEG

Matheson search
November 20, 2018
6:20 a.m.
Marble Lake Lodge

Susan Darcy's briefing still burns in the forefront of Meg's mind, the name *Matheson* still echoing in her ears, when she finally sees Silas again in the flesh. He steps out of the Lemon upon the announcement of the identity of the missing kids, and, prepared as she should have been, his presence hits her with the brute force of a wind rising up over the Sierra snowpack midwinter, unyielding in every regard. She's instantly reminded that nothing about this man has ever been temperate.

He looks smaller, somehow, standing next to the sheriff, but there's a stubborn set to his jaw that's instantly familiar. It's easy to look past the day-old stubble and disheveled clothing to recognize the boy she'd known, bursting as he had from the periphery of Meg's and Danny's lives to the center in the blink of an eye.

Back then, everyone was drawn to Silas like a moth to flame, the golden boy with the bright light he was generous to share, if you could stand the heat. She reminds herself that it's been a full decade and a half since he snuffed that light out of her life.

He's shuffled to the sidelines as more leadership emerges from the com van, and Meg makes her way through the crowd toward him cautiously, Danny close on her heels, and when she finally reaches Silas she falters, her nerves at seeing him again back in full force. It's been so long. So much has changed. Will he even welcome their presence here? She can't tell. Silas's face is a study of shell-shocked misery that Meg knows has nothing to do with her or Danny. His kids are missing. Missing *here,* at Marble Lake, just like . . . *No,* she tells herself. *Don't go there. This is about his boys. Nothing else.*

Mercifully, her training kicks in. "Silas," she says, swallowing hard. She hears what's almost a plea in that simple greeting, but she manages to maneuver around it to deliver the line she's been taught to say to family members of victims in their time of need. "I promise we're doing everything in our power to locate them."

"We're allocating all our resources," Danny adds, in even more rote search-speak.

The words are so clinical, and so insufficient, Meg flinches. Silas studies this reaction, looking at her just as he always used to, as though she's left him somewhere, stranded, and not the other way around.

And then his face gives a little twitch of uncertainty, and Meg's professional demeanor cracks. Ambiguity is so uncharacteristic for the boy she knew that grief burns a path across her chest, the chronic pain she's learned to live with for over a decade suddenly acute.

She turns away, catching Susan Darcy's gaze. She's watching them all like a hawk, and not just because Meg and Danny lost focus mid-briefing. The clearly defined (and strictly enforced) boundaries between searchers and the families of their subjects is being breached. But then Walters says something in Darcy's ear, and recognition flashes across her face. She still looks conflicted but lets the reunion carry on without interference. It can't be a good thing that the sheriff has instantly remembered the connection between them all, but this, too, Meg pushes to the back of her mind. All that matters right now is finding Silas's boys.

The media has yet to make its way up the icy road for a quick clip and a sound bite, and though this image—of two searchers and a victim locked in what is clearly a moment of awkward, unspoken intimacy—would surely be their idea of front-cover nirvana, Meg knows they'll be too late. By the time the local news Jeep arrives, or the helicopter from NewsWatch 5 out of Reno, crowding the airspace, she and Danny will be gone, combing the wilderness for the boys, leaving Silas to be photographed here alone, broken in the shadow of the yellow com van.

As if he, too, realizes their time is limited, Silas looks between Meg and Danny and speaks to them for the first time in fifteen years. "I don't know how this could have happened," he says, palms open in supplication. Or penance.

Either way, the truth of such a simple statement reaches about a dozen layers under Meg's skin. She knows, of course, that he's referring to this search, to his boys lost somewhere in the mountains, and not to the three of *them*, or whatever lingers of them in this chafing air and blowing wind. Even so, she has to swallow multiple responses long buried, the sight of him eliciting a rawness in her like an exposed nerve.

He stares back at her, caught in his own pain, his blue eyes as vibrant as ever. But new lines spiderweb toward his temples, like he's spent time squinting into sunlight, and a thin, almost translucent scar curls in a half shell below his lip. It reminds Meg that there are stories she and Danny don't know. There have been adventures they have missed. She glances toward Danny. Is he thinking the same? There was a time when he made a cameo in every one of Silas's anecdotes.

But then Silas straightens. "I need to get out there!" he tells them, looking between Meg and Danny as if deciding whether to beseech them or dare them to object. "My kids have been missing since *last night*, have they told you that?"

Meg and Danny nod wordlessly, but Silas isn't finished. "They've had me stuck inside. My boys, my *little boys*, have been in this cold too long already"—he gestures wildly toward the forest—"and I can't be standing around! I need to be *looking*!"

This is the Silas Meg knows. The man of action. The leader. The memory of the long hours they spent together after Jessica's disappearance takes her firmly back in its grip: The days as hot as today is cold. Sitting on a cheap folding chair in the lodge dining room, the metal plane of the seat sticking to the backs of her thighs as she sweated in the stuffy heat. Silas had been sitting right there, too, of course. Right between her and Danny.

"You can't come with us," she tells him now. She knows her face is a mirror of Silas's misery, but she can't help, not with this. Thankfully, Danny steps forward, as Danny can be depended upon to do.

"They won't allow it," he says softly. "They'll have more questions for you—"

"I don't want to answer any more questions!" Silas yells, attracting the attention of half the ground pounders assembled and waiting. "I don't want to sit, or wait, or *think*! Those are my kids! *My* kids! *Out there!*"

From the corner of her eye, Meg can see that Darcy has decided enough is enough, making her way over to break up the party. She needn't have bothered. Silas is already making a beeline back to the Lemon. His fists are clenched, shoulders angled forward in singular purpose. Meg trails quickly in his wake.

"*Silas!*" she says as he pushes his way through the searchers, the last vestiges of their awkward reunion burning off in the heat of the moment.

He ignores her. Reaching Darcy, he takes one look at her clipboard of search teams and schedules and starts ticking off a list of the many threats faced by his kids. "Hypothermia. Frostbite. Disorientation. Dehydration. While we stand around!"

Darcy doesn't flinch, not even when Silas thrusts his hand out, demanding a radio. Despite the woman's tiny frame, Meg knows she can hold her own. Darcy meets Silas's eyes as he stares her down, his mouth set in a hard, fast line, her neck craned and her shoulders squared, matching him in both posture and expression.

Her words, however, when she speaks, are surprisingly gentle. "Give us twelve hours." She indicates the gathered searchers. "We're a team. We work well together. We train together. Give us a day, Mr. Matheson, to put our best foot forward, before you attempt to actively join us."

He's already shaking his head before she can finish her sentence. "I'm going to be a part of this!" he demands. "I can hike! I can search!"

"But today, that is *our* job," Darcy answers firmly, and even while unyielding, her tone is still kind.

Silas considers this offer for less than a second. "Not without me."

He moves as though he plans to push past Darcy to the Lemon but makes it only a few steps before stopping abruptly. Meg can see what's given him pause: Sheriff Walters himself blocks the way, his girth, more ample than when they last faced off, far more formidable than Darcy's.

Silas curses under his breath, then surrenders. Meg guesses he meant to turn and retreat, to fall to pieces somewhere away from the crowd, but instead, when he pivots, the two of them find themselves again face-to-face. In the circle of searchers she and Silas are toe to toe, locked in a miserable dual stare.

This, too, feels painfully familiar, but before Meg can say or do anything, Walters is between them. With one large palm on Silas's shoulder, he steers him away. The last Meg sees of him is the stiff, tense jut of his shoulder disappearing back to the sidelines.

"Show's over," Darcy bellows, and Meg glances back around to realize all eyes are on her. Danny, especially, is glaring at her, as if to say, *See? I told you no one's forgotten.* She can read between the lines, too: *Least of all you.*

Meg looks away, tensing at the blast of Darcy's search whistle as she picks up right where she left off, now dividing the most agile ground pounders into teams to navigate the more challenging terrain. "Danny Cairns, team leader, Team Five," she shouts, to no one's surprise. She yells off the team members from her notes on her clipboard. "Meg, you join him. Also, Phillip McCrady and . . . let's have Max Reece. You're with Cairns."

Max is a newbie, and with a sense of relief Meg hands him his copy of the USGS topographical map they'll all be referencing. At least one person in their small party won't be making comparisons to the 2003 search for Jessica. God, she sounds like Danny. She forces herself to focus, scanning her own copy of the familiar terrain. The first thing she notes: the highlighted line running in an oblong arc around the outside of the Loop trail, circling out several miles past the highway to the west and into Forest Service lands to the south and east. The search radius.

Danny explains it to Max. "Darcy used the established foot sizes of the boys, combined with any information Si—the father—might have provided about the mindset of the children. You know, whether their personalities were more likely to prompt them to hide or to run, for instance."

"From that info," McCrady chimes in, "she created a formula to determine how far they're likely to have traveled in the approximate ten hours they've been missing."

"Couldn't be too far, though, in this cold. Right?"

McCrady shoots Max a stern look while Danny says more gently, "It's important not to think like that."

Max nods, while Meg swallows the hard lump that's risen in her throat. She repeats Danny's advice in her head. *Don't think like that.*

Besides, they've only scratched the surface of the science behind search-radius determination. They can expect this perimeter to be altered two or three times over the next hours: drawn inward if, for instance, evidence of an injury to one of the boys is found—or, yes,

God forbid, the temps drop even further. Inversely, it will be expanded as time lags on. New information trickles constantly into the com van during the course of a search—a scrap of clothing is found, a new footprint is spotted—sending the incident commander back to the drawing board.

"So don't get too comfortable with this," Danny says to Max, tapping the map with one gloved hand. "No doubt Darcy will be pinpointing the location of new evidence and recalculating this whole thing soon."

"If we do our jobs right," McCrady adds, and Danny nods in agreement.

The radius is a fairly ambitious one today; it must include at least thirty square miles. Clearly Darcy has no intention of underestimating the Matheson boys, which encourages Meg somewhat. If they're anything like their father, they'll be kids of action.

When the ground pounders finally move out, Team Five hikes down the dirt drive in the direction of the lodge to await their exact assignment. The road is wide enough to walk four abreast for now, but they walk silently, and Meg concentrates on the welcome sensation of feeling returning to her icy toes.

Which brings her mind right back around to the wintery conditions. Movement helps ward off frostbite, but schoolkids in Feather River are taught to stay put if lost in the woods . . . had Spencer and Cameron Matheson gotten this lesson in Portland? Or from their father? And would that information save them or cripple them?

Her mind swings back to the haunted look on Silas's face back by the com van. If *she's* thinking these thoughts, so is he. If *she's* worrying about the boys, he must be fighting back pure panic. The Silas Meg once knew was impulsive and daring and untethered. Les joked that ice water ran through his veins. Has he instilled these traits in his kids, or has time and maturity and fatherhood brought restraint? Knowing the answer could help determine search strategy, which, as of now, remains by the book.

"We're starting with a hasty search," Danny reminds Max, explaining that searchers will be sent out on trails to key locations—the area directly around the lakes, the trail junctions, and the campgrounds. "There's still too much ground to cover for a tight, inch-by-inch grid pattern," he adds, anticipating Max's next question.

Meg knows other teams have simultaneously been sent out in trucks—when she first heard them referred to as "hasty rigs" she imagined a type of tie-down device—to travel the nearby roads that weave in and out of the campgrounds, lights and sirens running.

"Is all that really necessary, all at once?" Max asks, his breath vaporizing in the cold.

"Hell, yeah," McCrady offers. "Kids are unpredictable—scratch that, *anyone* is unpredictable in situations like this. The boys might have decided to seek out familiar landmarks, or maybe they just headed downhill, traversing the inclines in the dark. Maybe they're in full-blown panic, and then who knows where they'll head? Course, we hope they're just hunkered down nearby. Remember that autistic kid a few years back, guys?"

Meg nods. They found him right on the roadside, hiding from the search teams looking for him, disoriented but otherwise unharmed.

After a few minutes, they reach the periphery of the lodge property and stop to do a radio check. While Danny focuses all his attention on his radio dial, Meg finally lets her gaze sweep fully over the familiar buildings with their cedar siding and steeply sloped rooflines, refusing to let static from Danny's receiver crowd out room for memory. A deep ache like a long-buried bruise tightens her chest as she takes it all in, and she wonders if it has been a mistake, avoiding these buildings and grounds since the Howard search. Maybe with practice she would be better able to cauterize the flow of memory this place induces. Or has

Danny had the right idea, bypassing even the once familiar trails of the Marble Lake wilderness?

"It's morbid," he said, the fragility of his tone urging Meg to drop it, the one time she suggested they return to hike the Lakes Loop trail together, on the first anniversary of Jessica's disappearance.

She supposed it was too raw. Too fresh. And had Silas been there to chime in, he would have agreed. *We have our own reasons to steer clear,* he would have reminded her. *We have our own tracks to cover.*

In the years since, however, Danny's position on the matter has remained as unchanging as the granite peaks overshadowing them now. Still, she knows him well enough to know he'll follow orders. As he awaits Darcy's command, she can imagine exactly what he's thinking: they've been assigned to start here, at the base of the ridge, so start here they will, whether seeing Marble Lake Lodge sends them both into a tailspin of melancholy and grief or not.

"Team Five, come in."

Darcy's voice sounds gravelly on Danny's walkie, which he brings to his lips to answer. "Go ahead, Base."

"We have your team taking the Lakes Loop trail to Long Lake, then descending to the shoreline."

Dropping them directly into the epicenter of the worst day of their lives. Meg just hopes she's the only one to detect the tightness in Danny's jaw as he lifts his walkie and compresses the talk button to confirm receipt. A prickle of resentment makes itself known. Did he think he could avoid that acreage forever?

At his terse nod, they stride forward right through the lodge grounds, on a direct course for the far outbuildings. From there, they'll fan out at a bearing of 120 degrees from north until they hit the T that connects the lodge trail with the Lakes Loop trail. This particular swath of wilderness covers the entire slope below the ridge and much more besides, just for good measure. Silas has outlined the area as one of the few he's introduced to Spencer and Cameron since their arrival. According to Darcy, it quickly became a favorite.

Like father, like sons.

She pushes back against this line of thought, too, but succumbs to a glance up at the rec building as they pass it. How many hours did they log in there, helping Les and Mary with chores and maintenance? Goofing off when they were supposed to be working? The green-shuttered windows and weathered porch look the same as ever. Is the same pool table still inside, the one with the ripped felt and the missing eight ball? Are there still dusty paperbacks in the bookcase, puzzles stacked on the end table by the fireplace?

They pass through the end of the lodge grounds next, where the last of the outbuildings gives way to a meadow that come summer, Meg knows, will be carpeted with wildflowers. These buildings, too, still look achingly familiar. She bites back a painful swell of homesickness. How is it possible that it simultaneously feels like a million years ago and just yesterday that she was last here? With the exception of some new rain gutters on the cabins and storm windows on the utility room, Silas's mark upon the lodge in his few weeks of ownership gives her no insight into his future plans for the place.

She focuses back on her boots on the frozen ground, forcing a deep, cold breath of air into her lungs. Seeing him this morning felt like being yanked above water after years of submersion. For so long now, it has seemed easier to sink below the surface, allowing the lodge, the river, and lakes they loved to disappear from view.

She'd set her focus on Danny, the flip side of Silas's coin. Now, she studies the tread of his boots in the half-frozen dirt at her feet, matching his stride as she hikes. Much of the time she can almost believe they're meant to be together. But in her most honest moments, she knows it's more that she thinks they deserve one another, their shared life a sort of penance.

But it *is* a life, she reminds herself again. It's something. She relies on Danny to be steady, to not rock the boat. She enjoys the drama-free existence they share. It's a characteristic of his she's always appreciated, that she's always chosen, hasn't she? But the way she greeted Silas— all awkward tension and fear and adrenaline—and the way he greeted *her*—despair personified . . .

There was nothing drama-free about that.

Even though Silas, at least today, is not quite the commanding presence Meg remembers. Back when she and Danny knew him best, Silas took up all the space in a room.

When Danny comes to a halt at the base of the incline on the far side of the lodge to pin their location on his handheld GPS unit, she stops, too, holding up one hand to Max. Danny depresses the call button on his radio. "Team Five to Base, come in."

Darcy's voice crackles out of the speaker; muffled by the fog, it sounds grainy and otherworldly. "Go ahead, Team Five."

"We're in position and beginning our hasty search now." He looks back down at his GPS display and reads out his coordinates.

Back at the Lemon, Meg knows, Darcy is recording the numbers and checking the position they were assigned on her master map.

"Position confirmed," she says, and they spread out again in a loose line, Meg once again flanking Danny's left. Slowly, they make their way up the steep slope, Danny holding their bearing at their assigned 120 degrees. They're widening their sweep as they go, but Meg can still see the occasional flash of his orange jacket sleeve through the thick trees and knows he's keeping an eye on her as well. On the other side of her, Max is matching *her* angle, and on his left, McCrady is matching his.

They've officially started their search, and they yell out as they hike, their repeated calls for the Matheson boys reverberating back to each other against the trunks of the trees and the sharp pitch of the rocky terrain. Meg glances back at Danny through the trees, and once again, it's easy to know exactly what he's thinking: that there's nowhere on earth he'd less like to be.

8

Meg

Ten months prior to Howard search
October 2002
Feather River

Despite being born and raised in Feather River, Meg had never seen Marble Lake Lodge.

"Come up and visit," Silas said before they all went their separate ways after school one sunny October afternoon. "I get lonely, doing all my chores by myself." He wagged his eyebrows at both her and Danny.

"Well, when you put it that way," Danny laughed, while Meg intoned, "That line actually work on the girls?"

"Seems so." Silas grinned, and Meg rolled her eyes. Of *course* he'd already be playing the field; Silas probably had his pick of Feather River's most eligible singles. Maybe when he finally settled on one, Meg would stop feeling like the odd woman out in this trio.

"Dan has plenty of chores at the fire station," Meg said now. She looked to him, trying to reach the Danny she knew under whatever this new persona was that Silas brought out in him. The Danny who relished going to the fire station to sweep out engine bays and hose down trucks.

"And you have that paper for English, right?" She'd finished hers, but she could keep him company while he knocked it out.

"The station can do without its Boy Scout for one day." Silas laughed. "And last I checked, you're not Cairns's mother." He threw one arm around each of their shoulders. "C'mon." He grinned, shifting the charm into high gear. "It's paradise up at the lodge. Tell her, Dan. Besides," he whispered mock-conspiratorially into Meg's ear, "he has to read the book before he can start the paper."

Danny hadn't even *read the book*? She shot him another look, this one of complete disbelief.

She was still feeling surly and unsettled—for one, Danny didn't even *have* a mother around, so maybe Silas could cool it with the offhand jokes—as they took the highway out of town, and as they climbed in elevation after taking the right onto Marble Lake Road, she planned to be indifferent to this "paradise" of his. But as the dense pine woods fell away to be replaced by sharp, craggy rock and spindly alpine ponderosa, Meg leaned forward in her seat despite herself, taking it all in. Each turn revealed a landscape that rose and fell in jagged cliffs, stealing her breath away.

By the time they turned off at the Marble Lake sign, it was as if Meg had rolled into another world. Les and Mary Albright's lodge was a veritable fort of outbuildings, living and dining halls with river-stone chimneys, and log cabins flanked by mountains of evergreen and granite that looked like they belonged in a watercolor painting.

She was entranced. And irritated, too, because Silas had been right. Of course.

Danny misinterpreted her expression. "It's kind of basic, but it's super fun up here. You'll see."

"'Charmingly rustic,' not basic," Silas corrected with mock refinement. "That's what Aunt Mary puts on the brochures."

She greeted them on the wide front porch, one long gray braid swaying back and forth as she enthusiastically waved them inside.

"Danny boy! So good to see you again." She hugged him to her, then pulled Meg in, too, with a "Welcome to Marble Lake, my girl."

Meg startled in her embrace, unaccustomed to such a greeting at her own home, let alone from a stranger. She smelled woodsmoke and cigarettes and lemon Pledge before she was released with a hearty pat on the back. "Don't mind the mess," Mary said, wiping her hands on her flannel shirt. "*Someone* neglected his dusting duties this week." She eyed Silas with what was clearly meant to be stern disapproval, but didn't fool anyone.

"Uncle Les kept me late splitting wood," he called over his shoulder.

"Well, get on out of here before I give you *all* work."

Silas's bedroom sat at the very top of the lodge's main building. He led them through the downstairs dining area and industrial kitchen with its hanging pots and pans, through a hallway lined with old-timey black-and-white photographs depicting miners with grimy faces, women in Victorian dress posing by picnic baskets, and railroad crews working a line, and up a set of wooden stairs.

Past a wide landing storing a jumble of boxes and fly-fishing gear, a narrower, more rudimentary stairway led to a single attic dormer room. The walls had been left unfinished maple, and Silas had covered them in topographical maps and astronomy posters, his dueling passions of terra and cosmos facing off in silent challenge. An oversize bookcase stretched the length of one wall, and outdoor gear, from backpacks to trekking poles to boots, sat piled in the corner. The slanted wooden ceiling was so low that when Meg entered the room, she promptly hit her head.

"Watch it," Silas said, grinning, way too late.

Danny laughed, giving him a shove that sent him tumbling toward his desk.

Meg watched the two of them, still not sure what to make of this side of Danny that Silas seemed to coax out, this side that relaxed and didn't take things so seriously and didn't have the weight of the whole world on its shoulders all the time. Which didn't sound so terrible, really, until she remembered that it had been ages since she and Danny had been alone together. And then there was the issue of his homework. Silas seemed to get As effortlessly, but the rest of them had to actually crack open a book or two. She really did sound like Danny's mother, and she didn't appreciate it.

They spent the late afternoon ducking the threat of Aunt Mary's chores as Silas showed them around for Meg's benefit, the boys slamming ping-pong balls at one another in the rec hall, Meg climbing to the loft in the maintenance shed to get a glimpse of the owl Silas said roosted there, all three of them gathering around the lodge kitchen table when Mary proffered snacks. It was a ruse—they had to fold and stack the dining-room linens after that—but Meg didn't mind. She already felt at home here, with Mary's gravelly laugh punctuating the boys' loud bantering, with the great-room fireplace lit once Silas's uncle Les crashed through the door with an armful of firewood, tracking wood chips all over the floor.

And so when night fell, and Danny promised Silas they would return, Meg heard herself agreeing. Pretty soon, the three of them fell into a routine, retreating to Marble Lake every weekend, so Danny wouldn't miss too many weekday trainings.

Most days, the three of them hiked over the mountains, or else they all hid out in Silas's attic bedroom, because now it was the season for Les to put them to work scraping paint off cabin paneling or winterizing doors and windows. When hiding out proved successful, they lounged on Silas's bed to study or watch TV or just stare up at the stars on his ceiling until they blurred and shifted under their half-closed eyelids. When it didn't, they climbed ladders to clear out gutters, insulated pipes in anticipation of freezing weather, and swept out cabins.

On a Saturday afternoon in mid-November, rain drummed on the roof—so close it felt to Meg as though she'd feel the drops on her head at any moment—making Silas's room the perfect place to curl up and hibernate. Silas, however, had other plans. A Bureau of Land Management map lay unfurled on the bed before them.

"I want to hike the Lakes Loop trail," he declared, pointing to the thin dashed line that snaked up the ridge just past the lodge meadow.

"We've done that loads of times," Danny interjected.

Silas leveled him with a look. "I wasn't finished. There's supposed to be a few old mine shafts still intact on the slope above Long Lake. From my calculations, they're only about a mile off trail, around the three-mile mark on the loop."

"What's so special about them?" Danny asked, but Meg already guessed the answer.

"Only that Silas hasn't conquered them yet," she supplied, which earned her a grin.

"That's right. We'll plant our flag once we explore them."

Danny set down an old Etch A Sketch he'd been toying around with. "You know they're not going to name them after you, right?"

Silas didn't look totally convinced of this. Outside, the rain pummeled the window with continued vengeance, but his eyes shone with their usual unrestrained enthusiasm.

"Anyway, it's too wet to go today," Danny decided, and he was right of course, so why did this send an unexpected jolt of disappointment through Meg? This was the Danny she knew. Cautious. Reasonable. Responsible. Wasn't it good to have him back?

"Silas didn't mean today," she heard herself say.

"Maybe I did mean today," he countered, "until Dan here decided to be such a pussy." He tugged the Etch A Sketch away from Danny and held it up in the air, out of reach.

"Silas," Meg said. "Stop it." He was goofing off, but it hurt Danny's feelings. She could tell.

But Danny just jumped up and snatched the toy back. "Whatever, man. Sorry I don't want to get soaked to the bone." He resumed his tinkering while Silas went back to his map with a shrug, leaving Meg to wonder at the way guys could have a spat, shake it off, and resume where they left off, all in a matter of seconds.

It made her wish again that Silas would just find a girlfriend of his own already, so she'd at least have someone sane to talk to up here. But that forced her to actually picture some other girl right here, in Silas's room, hiking the trails with them and doing lodge chores with them, and who would that girl be? Undoubtedly someone perfect and popular and pretty—and suddenly Meg couldn't picture someone like that being here at all. At *her* lodge. Receiving Aunt Mary's hugs and eating her cranberry-oatmeal cookies. So maybe she *could* picture it. And she didn't like it.

"Who are you going to take to homecoming?" she asked Silas impulsively.

He glanced up from his map with a distracted frown. "I dunno. Why?"

"Because it's, like, in just a few weeks."

Danny looked up from the Etch A Sketch screen. "You should totally ask Jessica."

Now Meg frowned. See? This was precisely what she'd been afraid of. She shouldn't have brought it up. "If you want to be a total cliché," she said before she could bite the words back.

"What's that supposed to mean?" Silas said. Danny looked like he'd like to know, too. His hands had paused on the little white knobs of the toy.

Meg stared over Silas's shoulder at the constellation map on the wall. "I just mean . . ." Shit. What *had* she meant? "It's just pretty predictable, right? The hot new guy dating the picture-perfect cheerleader?"

She realized her stupid slip the second it came out of her mouth and flicked her eyes instantly to Danny, who looked like he was trying to work out if he'd heard that right. Maybe he hadn't. "Never mind," she said, "I'm not explaining it right."

But no way was she going to get off that easy. A ridiculously annoying smile had grown across Silas's face. "Wait. You think I'm *hot*?" He nudged Danny. "You hear that, dude? I'm hot."

"Oh, shut up," Danny said, kind of nudging him. "You know what she meant—and it *would* be a cliché."

"You don't even know her." The chastisement was for both of them, but Silas looked resentfully at Meg while he said it. "Neither of you do, and you've gone to school with her for, like, forever."

Meg felt a little lurch in her stomach, because he was right, of course, even if it *was* kind of nice to hear Danny take her side for once. She sank down on the edge of the bed, feeling shitty.

"You're right, man," Danny conceded, and Meg continued to feel Silas's eyes on her. Knew he was waiting for her to apologize, too. But she just kept on feeling awful. Day after day, she and Danny drove up here to live vicariously in Silas's world. And every time, she wished she didn't feel like a tagalong. And now maybe she wouldn't have to be, and she'd tried to throw a wrench in it. Why? Didn't she get tired of dividing her and Danny's time as they constantly hung out with *his* friend?

No, she realized, the moment she'd posed the question in her mind. She *didn't* get tired of it. She didn't miss her empty house and her and Danny's predictable routine. She hadn't dragged her heels about coming up here since that very first day, and somewhere along the line she'd stopped living vicariously through Silas at Marble Lake and had laid some sort of claim of her own. A claim she didn't want to relinquish to some mystery fourth party. They were a trio, it dawned on her with some dismay; she didn't want it to change.

After a comment, Silas grabbed the TV remote with a sigh and started surfing, and Danny hefted himself off the bed to go scrounge up a snack in the lodge kitchen. Meg settled into his spot, eyes trained on the TV, her brain still working overtime as she propped her stocking feet up on a tattered stuffed bear Silas didn't seem chagrined to have on display.

She and Silas hadn't really been alone together much, just the two of them, and she wondered if he, too, felt the shift in dynamic. Maybe it was just her, because she was lying on his bed, inches from his pillow. Which felt intimate, combined with the drumming of the rain on the roof. She was hardly ever alone with Danny in *his* room. It was just better that way, she'd decided, until she was sure she wanted to take things to the next level. Going all the way meant commitment, Meg's mom had told her, shuddering a little at the word, which made it all the more significant to Meg. She had a good thing with Danny. She couldn't risk messing it up.

After a minute, Silas diverted his attention from the movie he'd settled on, reaching across Meg to palm a Nerf football sitting on the bed. She kind of startled, given where her mind had just been, but he just lay back on the bed to toss the ball high up into the air, catching it with an easy confidence on each return. Meg watched the blur of the green-and-blue-paneled ball, spinning as it traveled up and down, glad for the distraction.

Upon his next catch, Silas said, "Am I bugging you?"

Meg turned her head on the pillow and tried for a lighthearted tone. "What, right now, or overall?"

Silas didn't answer at first. "Let's start with overall."

Meg studied the tiny muscles in Silas's fingers flexing and relaxing with every catch of the ball. "No, you're not."

His gaze flicked over—just for an instant—which was long enough to cause him to miss the ball on its next descent. It bounced off his forehead gracelessly, and he and Meg both laughed. As far as a tension-breaker went, it would suffice.

Silas didn't bother to retrieve the football. "So," he said, still smiling. "Megan."

"Meg."

"Yeah. About that. Why don't you like Megan?"

She frowned in thought, wanting to really answer, not just brush this off. It was a feeling she had a lot in Silas's presence, now that she thought about it. This new need to define herself before anyone else did it for her. "I've just never really felt it was me."

"Megan is too tame for you," Silas agreed, his voice carrying a lilt of scholarly observation. "No one named Megan does anything but fade into the background." Meg rolled her eyes, but Silas looked at her without blinking. "You don't fade. You know that, right?"

Meg did *not* know that. And she liked hearing it, rolling it over in her mind as a possibility. Still, just like before, she found herself underplaying it. "Not while I'm only seventeen, at least, I hope," she quipped.

Silas looked up at the poster of the constellations on the wall. "You're kind of like Cassiopeia." He smiled, pointing out the zigzagging path of stars in the northern plane of the chart. "Half of her stars are the most luminous in the hemisphere, but the other half aren't even visible to the naked eye."

Meg only waited, unsure how to answer. What did he mean by that . . . half visible and half unseen? Though it kind of reflected how she felt right now: half-confused, and half-intrigued.

Silas leaned back over his mattress, reaching under his bed to retrieve a well-thumbed paperback. *Constellations of the Northern Hemisphere.* "But did you know," he said, turning the pages quickly, his customary enthusiasm building, "that if you could view Cassiopeia from Alpha Centauri—that's the brightest point of the constellation Centaurus—then the sun, *our* sun, would appear as a star within her?" He pointed back at the W pattern of Cassiopeia on his wall. "There," he said, "at the far-left end, would be the sun." He turned, smiling triumphantly at Meg. "Quite a coup, huh? Unassuming Cassiopeia is actually a superstar—no pun intended—if viewed from the right angle."

Meg looked from the chart to Silas's face, glowing with its steady confidence. Her mouth quirked into a mischievous smile. She knew next to nothing about astronomy, but after years of reading every genre of fiction she could get her hands on, mythology was another matter entirely. She could dispel Silas's theory in an instant, an opportunity that gave her a bit of a rush.

"Cassiopeia was a diva long before anyone viewing her knew she included the sun," she informed him. Silas looked at her in surprise as she gestured back up at the diagram, tracing the simplistic outline of the queen's shape with one finger. "She's upside down. Do you know why?"

Silas's face sobered in an expression of anticipation that sent another small thrill of victory shooting down Meg's spine. "She was so boastful of her beauty, Poseidon hung her that way in the sky, as a warning against vanity." She scoffed then, unceremoniously lifting a loose lock of her hair and letting it fall back to the pillow in a tumble of auburn strands. "*I'm* not vain. So, you see? Your theory is disproven."

She shot Silas a triumphant grin and then felt it falter as she caught something that almost hinted at confusion in his eyes. "You're right," he conceded softly. "You're not vain."

For a moment Meg lay in place, absorbing this hollow victory, trying to make sense of an inexplicable tangle of emotions playing for dominance in her heart. And then Danny walked back through the door with a monstrous bowl of popcorn under the crook of his arm, and Silas high-fived him, and the three of them settled in to watch TV. By the time Danny and Meg gathered up their coats in the entrance of the lodge, Danny mislaying his car keys two times, it was full dark.

"Night, Cairns," Silas called from the cavernous lodge kitchen, just like normal, but suddenly he was by Meg's side, pulling her cap down over her head with a playful tug.

"Good night, Cassiopeia," he added with a smirk, and even though he said this loudly enough to bring Danny into the loop, declaring that he was not the only one with a nickname now, the shared reference between them—just them—flowed over Meg like honey, seeping with a subtle warmth into every empty space under her skin.

"Good night," she managed, and then stepped quickly out into cold air, welcoming the driving rain on her cheeks. She was not beautiful, and she was not luminous, that was ridiculous, and she had set the record straight, so why, Meg wondered the entire ride home, did she still feel the glow of being seen as such?

9

SILAS

Matheson search
November 20, 2018
7:25 a.m.
Marble Lake Staging Area

Silas looks directly into the sheriff's eyes and wills himself to behave. He can't lose his cool again, and he sure as hell can't regress to the scared, cocky boy he was when the two of them last squared off, just like this, at this exact place. He'd been fifteen years younger, and Walters was serving his first elected term. That time, Silas blinked first.

But I'm not that kid anymore. And Meg and Danny, somewhere out on the trails right this minute, can't possibly be the same scared kids they were in 2003, either, despite the instant pull toward them he felt the second he saw them again. They both may have been haunting him for years, but Silas tells himself it's Walters's presence here, at Marble Lake, that's making it seem like no time has passed at all.

"What we need from you now, Mr. Matheson," Walters says, "is as much information about the boys' clothing, appearance, and habits as possible. Let's start with Spencer's shoes."

"His shoes?" Silas says dully.

"Color, size?" This question comes from the man named Santos, who sits to Walters's left, taking notes rapidly on a waterproof binder.

Silas wills the image of Spencer's shoes to swim into focus. They won't materialize. Instead, he still sees his onetime friends where they'd been standing among the searchers, readying to mobilize to find his boys. Maybe because he knows thinking about Spencer and Cameron right now will upend him. Send him careening even further out of control.

"Knowing the shoe size helps the trackers," Sheriff Walters adds. His eyes are beady in his face. Alert and intense, but watery, too. Walters has aged. "You remember."

Silas glances up sharply at this first acknowledgment of their shared history. *That's right, old man,* he would like to say, had he any leverage today at all. *Lay your cards on the table.* Because of course it's not lost on Walters that the two of them have circled this exact same question of sole treads and imprints before. Did Silas really harbor any hope that this would have been forgiven and forgotten? He hasn't even forgiven himself.

"As you know," Santos interjects in a much gentler tone, "time isn't on our side. Anything you can recall will help."

Shoes. Spencer. Silas squeezes his eyes shut tightly, reopening them with new focus. The air inside this canvas tent they've erected in the center of the staging area is stuffy beyond reason, making a mockery of the danger his boys face, right this very minute, out in the cold. Sweating through two layers of flannel, he forces himself to think. Was Spencer wearing his Nikes yesterday? Or had he insisted on those cheap Minecraft rain boots again, the ones that were too small? The kid's feet were growing so fast. Who could keep up?

He blinks again, trying to clear his head, but a cottony feeling stubbornly clings to the inside of his skull. He wonders if this is what shock feels like. He knows it isn't panic. Panic was what shot through his body for hours earlier, sending urgent arrows of alarm from the very center of his being to his furthest recesses, from the tips of his fingers to the soles of his feet. Panic was what got him through the night, first as he scoured the woods, then after dialing 911 and calling Miranda in Manchester only to have it go to voice mail. Instead of leaving a message that would undo her, he drove the rutted roads surrounding the lodge into the early morning, headlights flashing, horn honking, first with the response team and then with the sheriff patrol. *Panic,* unlike shock, is unmistakable.

"He must have been wearing his Nikes." Yes, that has to be right, because Spencer just complained about the boots, didn't he? Something about blisters. "Black-and-white low-tops."

"Good. That's a start." Sheriff Walters tugs at his brown uniform vest, which is straining around his ample stomach. "And the size?"

Silas shakes his head. Miranda bought the Nikes. He remembers because it was just days before her flight out of PDX. Spencer acted out, throwing a fit when she wouldn't buy him Heelys instead. She called Silas in tears, and he assured her he'd talk to Spencer. Make sure he understood that his mother wasn't leaving forever. That he and his brother would be with her for Christmas, then again for summer break. And that in the meantime, they were in good hands with their ol' dad. He remembers because that talk was the genesis of the three amigos.

"You and me against the world?" Spencer questioned, kind of incredulous, after Silas rambled on about superheroes or bravery or some such thing. Had he really said that? Against the world? He tried again.

"Well, you and me and Cam. Which makes us more like the three amigos."

The moniker had brought him immediately full circle, to the trio formed so many years before, but Spencer quipped, "The three a-*mathesons,*" a slow smile spreading across his face. And then he was grinning in earnest, the pink gummy space where he'd just lost one of his bottom front teeth on full display, and Silas grinned back.

He runs one hand down his own face now. "I don't know the size. He's seven." For a moment, he stares down at his lap, a feeling of inadequacy he's beginning to feel accustomed to slicing through him in place of the wind outside the tent. "He's seven," he repeats, "so size"—he glances down stupidly at his own feet—"two? Three?"

Santos beckons a nearby deputy and issues instruction Silas cannot hear, leaving Walters free to continue his careful study of Silas's face. "The team over at the lodge will look through the boys' closet. See what other sneakers they can find to shed some light onto the size situation."

"There's a team in the lodge?"

Walters nods passively. "Checking for anything we might have missed. Standard protocol."

Silas feels his cheeks heat as frustration rises. "I've already checked the boys' room." Cameron's new puffy coat was there, cast on his bed. Ditto for Spencer's, though that had been discarded in the lodge kitchen sometime the day before. The find gutted Silas, sent him in frantic search of the boys' other various hoodies and sweatshirts. Had Cameron left one in the rec room, after playing a heated game of puzzle piece air hockey? Had Spencer discarded his favorite on the deck before dinner the night before? It was impossible to keep track.

He's already given a team of deputies an inventory of what he thinks the boys were wearing when they set out from the lodge. Which basically amounted to what they hadn't been. Deputies, questions . . . lodge searches . . . Is Silas under investigation? He can't be sure and is suddenly afraid to ask. What if they decide he shouldn't be here? What if they exile him even farther away from his boys? The mere possibility has his empty stomach clenching in revolt, even as his humiliation doubles: What kind of idiot doesn't even know if they're under suspicion?

Walters plucks these questions from his brain effortlessly. "The faster we can eliminate any possibility of foul play," he says carefully, "the faster we can allocate all our resources to the trail."

The words *foul play* have Silas ready to vomit, but it's the possibility that the department has not, yet, put every able human being on the search for his kids that has him seething. He stares the sheriff down, eyes locked, shoulders rigid.

Santos fills the tense silence that follows. "Even though there aren't a lot of shoe prints on the trail this time of year, having the specifics makes the process of elimination much easier. Easier means quicker."

"Yeah, about that." Silas swivels in his chair, craning his neck to get a glimpse of the staging area from where he's been sequestered. It looks mostly abandoned, which means the teams Walters has assigned to the search have finally all deployed. Still, it's not enough. Not by a long shot. "There was nothing all that *quick* about getting boots on the ground this morning."

"There's a process," Santos tries to interject, but Silas cuts him off.

"Your *process* could cost my kids their lives."

Walters doesn't bullshit him, which Silas supposes is one benefit of their history being an open book between them. "It's true that the first twenty-four hours are crucial," he says, as Silas's mind flashes on the stuffy heat of the lodge in the early hours of the Howard search. On Meg and Danny, rooted on folding chairs beside him. "We're all concerned about the cold," Walters continues, "especially at night, when the temps go below freezing."

Somehow, hearing it out loud is even worse than the vague terrors on a loop in Silas's mind. He moans involuntarily, letting his face fall into his hands.

Walters leans in. "Listen now, son. You've got to be strong for them." He looks directly at him. "I know you're tired, I know you've spent the whole night in a panic, but I also know you can be tough as nails, when you want to be. So, let's go over the sequence of events again."

Silas forces himself to straighten in his chair, even as the last vestige of his strength seems to melt from his body. They've been at this, on and off, for hours already. Just like last time. And like last time, he feels every bit as culpable. He has no choice but to take a deep breath and begin recounting the timeline anew.

Just as he explained to a deputy late last night, and that Darcy woman earlier this morning, he starts on the upstairs landing, with the wasp nest he had to break down, the repairs that seemed to multiply before his eyes. "I definitely underestimated the job." He turns to Santos. A fresh, hopefully unbiased audience of one. "By the time I came downstairs, I was greeted by silence. An empty room."

He has long associated that kind of deep silence with these mountains, but not ever with his little boys. He squeezes his palms to his head, as if he can coax the headache from his temples. To think he used to crave that kind of solitude! Seek it out in these very woods as a teen, when his life felt so big and loud, spinning faster and faster.

Now? In this interrogation? He doesn't know whether it's the altitude, the thinness of the air unable to act as a buffer to the raw serration of the granite slopes, or simply the fear that serves as his new, constant companion, but he's fighting lightheadedness along with the fear and the shock. Instead of allowing him to think more clearly, like they did when he was a teen, these mountains have somehow emptied him, with his kids snatched from him like this. He's hollow inside as he continues.

"That's when I went looking for them," he tells Santos. "Right after I came back downstairs." He pinches his eyes shut, but it doesn't block out the memory of running, calling, tripping over roots and sage. "And then when I returned—without them—I called you."

This time, Silas's voice *does* crack, splintering at the edges until he caves completely, bowing his head as he feels the despair sluice up within him like acid. "They were both gone . . . just . . . gone."

When he looks up, even Walters looks sympathetic. Santos lays a palm on his shoulder. "Have you had a chance to make any phone calls?" he asks. "To relatives? The boys' mother?"

He dials Miranda again right then and there, but when she picks up this time, sounding a bit breathless, like maybe she's had to quickly exit a meeting room or restaurant to accept the call, he finds he can't speak. His throat completely closes up around the words, wrapping them tightly into a parcel of misery he cannot dispel, let alone deliver. He can't do this to her, can't be the one to tell her he's failed in this simplest and most sacred of tasks.

Santos gently peels the phone from his ear and takes the call himself. He steps away from Silas and speaks softly into the receiver; Silas sees his back tense as Miranda's wail cuts through him. They all hear it, Walters bowing his head as though taking a moment of silence for the grieving mother. The sight only adds to Silas's misery. Of *course* he hates knowing Miranda is suffering now, too. Of course he'll call her back just as soon as he can offer anything but his own terror reflected back at her. But *he's* the parent right in front of Walters now. *He's* the parent gripping discarded jackets—jackets that should be on his boys' bodies right now—in his helpless hands. He's the parent staring down at his children's empty beds, scrolling through photos of them on his phone for some SAR volunteer to photocopy, trying to remember when they last ate a meal. Where is *his* moment of silence?

Walters has more questions, and Silas comes further and further undone with each effort to recall exact times and places. He can't shake the ever-present knowledge that yesterday, just yesterday, his kids were right here, within his reach, and now they are not. He simply cannot set that thought down long enough to pick up another.

Children are malleable, sure. Until they slip through your fingers as quick as lake trout, disappearing in a silver-bellied flash.

When he next cradles his head in his hands, Santos calls mercy on his behalf.

"I think we have enough for now."

Maybe the lieutenant realizes what Silas has known for weeks: that his life has been careening increasingly off-kilter long before yesterday. Solo parenting. Returning to the Sierra. Facing past demons . . . He's finally been flung off his carefully constructed axis, and his kids are now paying the price. It's all so fucking familiar, he wants to cry.

His shoulders shake as he fights it, and he feels Santos shift uncomfortably, as though this situation has risen above his pay grade. "I'm sure your boys' mother—Miranda—will be here just as soon as she can."

Walters has been quiet, scanning Santos's notes. "You really haven't been back here since high school?" he shoots at Silas.

The question feels like a swift yank on an emergency brake, jerking Silas right back to '03. "Sorry, what?"

Walters juts his chin toward Marble Lake Lodge. "You said you hadn't laid eyes on the place since you were a kid."

"That's right."

"Not even for a family visit? A quick trip? Or a reunion, maybe?"

"None of the above," Silas says. He's tense again in his seat, defenses rising as quickly as the wind flapping the walls of this canvas tent. Yeah, he should have done more to help Les and Mary out in recent years, but Walters's words imply much more, and they both know it.

Walters studies him for a moment. "Huh."

Silas takes the bait, as Walters probably knew he would. He's never been one to back down. *You don't have to meet every battle head-on,* Meg used to say. But that was back when the battles were between him and Danny, after everything had gone south. "Why?" he challenges Walters now. "What does that have to do with anything?"

"I just find it noteworthy, is all. Given that you have friends here. Friends who certainly seem to have your back."

"*Had* friends here," Silas is forced to correct. As for that second part, he has his doubts. Has he been forgiven for what had happened?

The irony is, Walters probably knows the answer to that better than Silas himself.

Another long moment passes, and then Santos offers coffee, which Silas dismisses. He does not want coffee. He wants the hell out of this glorified tent they call a command center, out onto the trail so he can continue *looking*. Outside, he hears the K9 dogs barking, their harnesses jangling as their handlers release them into the wild, and he wants to join them with every fiber of his being. Just thinking about this has his muscles jumping with tension under his skin, nerves shooting up and down his spine. The idea of coffee seems downright absurd, in fact, and he has to fight the sudden urge to laugh.

He pushes the canvas tent door open with gusto and storms across the operations area and parking lot toward the lodge grounds. They may be able to stop him from actively searching the wilderness, but they can't keep him from the only real home he's ever known.

10

SILAS

Nine months prior to Howard search
November 2002
Feather River

When the weather proved unpredictable in the High Sierra, which was most of the time now as winter neared, Silas started spending some weeknights at the Cairnses' house in town. While Danny volunteered at the fire station, Silas usually killed time on the bleachers in the gym, scribbling trig equations amid the cacophony of basketballs bouncing and the cheer squad practicing routines. Which was how he found himself peering up at Jessica Howard standing over him one random Thursday afternoon. He figured she was going to start up a conversation about the game the next day, or, better yet, invite him to join the squad at the Frostee for post-practice fries, but she just bounced down next to him instead.

"Need help?" she said, studying his work over his shoulder.

He didn't think he did, but as it turned out, Jessica was a whiz at trig, and didn't mind sharing her biology lab notes, either.

"She's also got a killer bootleg MP3 of Linkin Park live at the Fillmore," he told Danny and Meg, while eating the Cairnses' snacks later that afternoon.

"Did you ask her to homecoming, then?" Danny asked.

Silas blinked at him. "I didn't even think of it." He'd been too busy listening to "In the End" over and over again on Jessica's brand-new iPod.

Danny muttered something about some people being hopeless, and Meg said nothing at all, leaving it up to Silas to provide the trio's next distraction, as usual.

"Let's go fishing," he said, eyeing the gear stashed, as always, by Danny's front door. Feather River's namesake river divided the downtown blocks right down the middle, separating the two halves like an axe blade splitting a chunk of firewood, and Meg and Danny had traversed just about every inch of it. It was their turn to play tour guide.

Danny looked dubious. "It's the wrong time of day. Besides, I have to study." He made a show of digging through his backpack, throwing back over his shoulder, "I failed that English paper, by the way." Like it was Silas's fault. It wasn't as if *he'd* read the whole book, either.

"I told you: all you have to do is remember the important parts, and then you can bullshit the rest."

"Yeah, that didn't work," Danny said, eyeing him warily. "At least, not for me." He sighed, reminding Silas of Uncle Les when he was exasperated. "We can go fishing Sunday, if we get up early."

"But we're climbing to the fire lookout on Sunday," Meg chimed in, to Silas's surprise. They'd talked about making the trek to the top of Marble Peak, where an old tower overlooked the Marble Lake wilderness, before the snow flew, but he hadn't realized Meg was so into it.

He rolled with it, though, because Meg's vote made it two to one. "That's right. And I have to work for Uncle Les tomorrow. So if we're going to go fishing, it has to be now."

Danny looked between the two of them, then sighed again like the old man he'd probably been since birth. For a minute there, Silas had hoped he'd cured him of it. "Oh, *fine*," he said, abandoning his backpack in favor of his tackle box. "But don't expect anything too exciting," he added as he began sorting the fluorescent rubbery lures and plastic bobbers.

Silas grinned. "I always expect something exciting." He plucked three little lead weights out of a tray and juggled them until they scattered on Danny's entry floor.

"Dude! Pick those up."

"I am. Chill." No one was ever home in the afternoons at Danny's house anyway, his father, Frank, working four days on, three off as a safety engineer for Union Pacific—probably where Cairns got his crazy work ethic from.

They piled into Danny's dad's piece-of-shit truck, which was actually pretty awesome, in a retro sort of way, to his favorite fishing hole at the end of a rutted Forest Service road paralleling the river by the train tracks. They parked in the looming shadow of a trestle spanning overhead, beneath which the water eddied in deep, swirling pools.

"Sweet," Silas declared, out of the car before Danny had come to a full stop. Meg trailed behind, a book in one hand, a blanket to sit on in the other. "Not a fisherwoman?" he asked.

She smirked. "You don't know how long Danny can fish."

She was right. After equipping Silas and pointing him in the direction of a good spot, Danny planted himself at the edge of one of the deepest pools, and just . . . cast. Over and over. As the sun slanted across the sky, and the geese flew overhead, and the train whistle blew every fifteen minutes. Silas tried to emulate this semi-meditative state, but it was no use: fishing was as boring as watching a metronome wag back and forth.

Danny could keep his rainbow trout; it was the huge granite boulders framing the eddy, perfect for climbing, that had Silas's attention. Abandoning his rod and reel, he scaled the rocks until he had a view of the river all the way to the next bend, Danny and Meg just two stationary ants below him. Scrambling back down, he leaped off the rock right above Meg to pounce upon her blanket.

"Shit!" She nearly dropped her book, bringing one hand to her chest. "Stop bouncing around like a pinball and come sit down."

He obeyed, squinting into the sun, watching the light shining off the trestle, until, out of the corner of his eye, he spied Meg reaching the end of her chapter.

"Climb the trestle with me," he said, taking her book from her hands and setting it down on the nearest rock. "We can reach the underside of the train track."

"What? No way."

"It'll be easy," he said.

"But what for?"

"What do you mean, 'what for'?" He was baffled by the question. "Just because, of course."

"It's dangerous. The trains come regularly."

Silas frowned. He hadn't heard a whistle in a while. And no way was he just going to sit here waiting for Danny to tire of fishing. He said as much.

Meg sighed, a long, exasperated sound. "It was *your* idea to come," she reminded him.

Yes, but now he'd found something more challenging to do. Aunt Mary blamed his penchant for adventure on his upbringing; too much time left to his own devices in the wilds of some corner of the country or another, she'd said. But it wasn't just that. Where other people seemed to see limitations, stop signs, do-not-enters, Silas saw opportunities. And who knew where each could lead?

"We won't climb up far enough to reach the tracks," he promised.

Meg looked toward the distant form that was Danny, downriver now by a good fifty yards, and waved an arm at him, though whether to coax him to come along or just let him know their plan, Silas couldn't say. It didn't matter, because Danny didn't notice. So Silas led the way, jumping from boulder to boulder to the trestle support beam by the water, gratified when Meg followed, albeit reluctantly.

Up close, the metal trestle beam reached higher than he'd thought. The rungs were too far apart for proper climbing, and paint peeled from the rungs of the ladder, hot to the touch in the sun. Still, an adventure was an adventure. Silas was already halfway up, legs wrapped around the pillar like he was retrieving a coconut from a palm tree, by the time Meg reached the base.

"I don't know . . ." she called up to him.

Even when Silas climbed back down to her, showing her where the best footholds were, she stayed rooted on firm ground. "You go without me. I don't want to slow you down."

"No way, it's no fun by myself," he said, and held out his hand, willing her to take it. Thrilling when she did.

He guided her up a few rungs, but within a few feet, she was paralyzed again, hanging on to the pillar while Silas's feet flailed amid empty air above her.

"Grab my hand again," he said, but this time Meg shook her head mutely and clung on.

"I think you should come down," she called as a fly buzzed Silas's nose. He shook his head at it, blond hair flying about wildly, not daring to loosen his grip to swat at it.

"It's too high," Meg insisted.

"Too" anything was the wrong thing to say to Silas. Didn't Meg know that by now?

He climbed a few more feet, one outstretched arm almost, but not quite, reaching the base of the train track over their heads. "Just a sec. I just want to try to—"

He made a second lurch for it, lost his footing, and spun there, above Meg's head, for what felt like a very long count of ten, with one hand holding on to the pillar. He could feel his grip loosening, and loosening, until finally gravity prevailed, and he fell like a rock to the ground.

"Silas!"

Shock came first, as all the air was knocked from his lungs. Then pain, radiating outward from his ankle.

"Are you okay?" She hadn't witnessed the landing, her face pressed against the trestle post as she clung for dear life, but at least her death grip prevented him from taking her down with him. "I'm coming!"

And surprisingly, her limbs seemed capable of movement again, propelling her back down the trestle to the ground. "Go slow," he gasped, on a cough. Then, when she landed far more lightly than he had into the blanket of pine needles at the base, "Wow, good job."

"Guess I just needed proper motivation," she said sarcastically.

"Guess so." The thought took some of the sting out of Silas's fall.

"You okay?" she asked again, her shadow falling over his face as she bent in close. The sun cast a halo behind her auburn hair, and he was about to make a joke about an angel coming to his rescue, but then Danny's face was floating over him, too. And for some reason, it no longer seemed like a good idea.

"What happened?" Danny sounded breathless, and the bottoms of his pants looked wet. "I heard you guys shouting but couldn't get here in time."

Silas forced himself to his feet. "Wind just got knocked out of me. That's all." He looked at Danny, who, now that Silas took him in completely, had definitely splashed his way upriver to get here. "Sorry, man."

But his ankle still smarted, and he'd scraped his knee and ripped his pant leg, and Meg insisted they end their day at the river early.

"Why'd you have to push your luck?" Danny complained on the ride back into town. "It's like you have to prove yourself all the time."

Aunt's Mary's words reverberated. Uncle Les's, too, his reprimand landing lightly, but spanning all the way back to that very first time Silas had pulled Danny into his orbit of trouble, out on Marble Lake, alone and adrift.

"I was just having some fun," he mumbled. "I'm sorry I ruined yours, though." And he was. Truly. Especially since the sight of Meg bending over him, making sure he was okay, still lingered in his mind's eye, making him feel a bit uncomfortably warm inside.

As penance, he finally committed to a double date to the homecoming dance, asking Jessica with what Meg told him was unacceptably late notice. "It's a miracle she was still free," she told him, to which Danny had retorted, "I'm pretty sure she turned down at least two offers holding out for you, man." The look on his face told Silas he didn't find this entirely cool, either.

Silas didn't disagree, and he really couldn't say why he'd put off asking her. Beneath the bubbly all-American cheerleader persona, Jessica ticked all his boxes. But somehow, instead of her interests and achievements making her stand out, they blended her into a vanilla sort of popular that left him a bit . . . uninspired. What had Meg called her? A cliché. Which was harsh, though Silas kind of got why. But it wasn't Jessica's fault that she faded into the background. No more than it was Meg's fault that she sort of glowed with an aura only Silas seemed to see. He told himself he just needed to apply himself, as Danny liked to say. To focus on the things that made Jessica glow.

At the dance, she did kind of sparkle under the disco lights and streamers hung by the dance committee—headed by Jessica herself—her sequined dress sending prisms of color across the lacquered gym floor as she twirled. The gym still smelled like sweat and popcorn, kind of killing the vibe, but Silas pulled her close anyway, earning him an equally dazzling smile.

As they shuffled their way toward the three-point line, Meg and Danny brushed past them, Danny giving Silas a playful punch on the shoulder. As they spun away again, Silas heard Danny tell Meg, "You look beautiful."

She did. Silas knew he wasn't supposed to notice, but he had eyes, didn't he? She wore a dress that hugged the curves of her hips and the back of her neck, where the thin halter straps tied in a knot, and while Silas actually preferred her in jeans and a T-shirt, hiking boots at the ready, when Danny ran his hand down the bare skin along the curve of her spine, it took effort for Silas to look away, back at Jessica's open, pretty, made-up face.

Shit. He swallowed hard, and spun Jessica around playfully. Gave her his full attention.

"Having fun?"

In answer, she executed another graceful pirouette, her hair flashing bronze and then gold in the pulsing light, like tinsel on a Christmas tree.

Silas laughed, which drew Meg's eye. He had trouble reading her expression in the dark, but something flashed there—disapproval? Annoyance?—before Danny spun her away from him again and the next song drowned everything else out.

When midnight rolled around, the chaperones began to usher students out the doors, hovering in the lobby as parents were called and rides procured. Silas had planned to crash at Danny's—his dad was on his southwestern route through Reno, gone until Monday—but Meg might hang there, too, and for the first time, it felt like three might be a crowd.

When Jessica suggested late-night snacks at the only diner in town, he agreed readily, leaning into the Formica table across from her until two in the morning, sharing greasy tots and trading stories of Feather River and the wider world beyond. He learned that Jessica loved owls and classic movies in addition to Linkin Park, and that unlike Silas and Danny, she'd devoured *Sense and Sensibility* in English 12, and had secretly borrowed *Pride and Prejudice* from the library right after. When he kissed her for the first time under the neon sign of the diner, she'd tasted like salt, her lips cold from the ice in her Coke. He'd told her he hoped they could hang out again, and he'd been pleasantly surprised to realize he meant it.

11

MEG

Matheson search
November 20, 2018
8:30 a.m.
Marble Lake Wilderness

Meg's feet slip and slide as she climbs the steep terrain behind the lodge, the exposed roots and granite slick with rapidly dissipating frost. The moisture remains heavy in the air, clinging stubbornly to the low-lying shrubbery that covers the hillside. Her pants get wetter with every pass through the abundance of branches and leaves, and she cannot help but wonder what kind of seven-year-old kid could navigate this punishing slope, not once, but several times, according to the information Darcy had gleaned. And for *fun*, to boot.

Silas Matheson's kid, she reminds herself. *That's who.*

As she climbs, Meg purposely deviates from her straight upward path so that her movements produce a loose zigzag pattern. She needs to cover as much ground as possible, and at every fallen log and boulder she stops and forces herself to look beneath. It's standard search procedure, but bracing for the worst has never gotten easier. Each time she stoops, pushing aside the limbs of trees to peer into their wells or around their trunks, calling for Spencer and Cameron, she feels a quick tightening of her gut that's not quite panic, and not despair, but something in between, a hollow disassociation that toes the line between self-perseverance and optimism. Knowing the search victims' father personally adds another element to the equation: dread.

Because what if she has to look him in the eye, this sleep-deprived, despairing shadow of the man, the concept of whom she has tucked away into a time capsule in her mind all these years, and tell him the worst? She can't. She won't. And so she keeps calling out. Keeps that optimism front and center.

It's not until they've reached the perpendicular trail at the ridge that she has a moment to stop and catch her breath. The temperature has risen—mercifully—since the sun crested Marble Peak to the east, but will this reprieve be enough for the boys?

"You can develop frostbite on exposed skin within thirty minutes once the air is below freezing," Matt Bower, their chief medical consult from Washoe Medical Center in Reno, told them just last month at their annual winter-weather-training session. How long were the boys exposed last night? Hours.

"Factor in the windchill that's a constant in the High Sierra, and things get interesting even faster."

Where is Matt now? Did Darcy call him in? If—no, Meg corrects herself—*when* they find Spencer and Cameron, God willing, they'll need as swift attention as they can get. Meg's wilderness first-aid certification is just not going to cut it.

She stops short next to Danny; Max and McCrady are still a quarter mile back, making their way toward them to regroup.

"Can you believe this?" she says softly, watching his face for his reaction as he reaches around to the side of his pack, yanking his water bottle free. "It's surreal, looking for Silas's kids."

"No, I can't," he says only, eyes trained on the forest in front of him as he gulps his water. She supposes he doesn't owe her any comfort, but they *are* in this together, the two of them. They made that decision years ago, after Silas left, Danny sticking stubbornly to his firefighting career path, Meg directionless in the face of so much turmoil. At a loss, she stumbled upon a job listing for the county, only a high school diploma required. She hadn't known it reported directly to the Feather River County Sheriff's Department until she arrived, in a borrowed skirt of her mom's, for an interview, just to be faced with the presence of Sheriff Walters himself, and worse: Jessica Howard's mother sitting across the desk from him, a wet Kleenex gripped in one fisted hand.

"Meg," Teresa Howard cried, smiling through her tears, even though the last time she'd seen her, only months ago, had been at the lodge. During that awful, interminable wait for news of her daughter. "Aren't you a welcome sight. I just knew you'd never give up on my girl."

Meg took an abrupt step backward as though stung, swiveling toward Walters in confusion. What was this? An ambush?

As it turned out, just unfortunate timing. In the weeks since the search for her daughter had been called off, Teresa Howard had become a fixture at the department, putting in petition after petition to reopen the efforts. This day, she'd just happened to interrupt Walters's interview schedule.

What could Meg have done in that moment but agree with Mrs. Howard? So she told her that of course she would never forget Jessica. That if she got this job—here, she glanced briefly at Walters—she would dedicate her working hours to cases like hers. And then she went to Danny, her employee onboarding paperwork in hand, and told him she would be joining Feather River Search and Rescue. On the payroll and as a volunteer. It was the right thing to do. It was also the *only* thing resembling a path she could follow.

Danny had been there for her, signing up for SAR training the same week as Meg. Attending every training session at her side. The only thing they *hadn't* done together was discuss the Howard case or Silas Matheson. Not ever. Not if they could help it.

"Walters seemed to have a lot of questions for him," she presses now. Silas had still been sequestered in the command tent when they departed.

Danny only stares stoically forward, then takes a swig of water.

"Odd that Santos is here, too," she adds. She can count on one hand the number of times both first and second in command have shown up for the same search at the same time.

"Makes sense, kid search and all."

"Dan, c'mon! You know it's not just because of the kids." She lowers her voice. "Walters is drawing unfair comparisons to . . ." She bites off the rest, because after last night's discussion, he knows perfectly well what she's getting at, and as it turns out, she's gotten pretty accustomed to avoiding this subject, too. "Silas doesn't deserve this," she finishes softly.

This finally gets Danny's full attention. "And why exactly not?" He replaces his water bottle into his side pocket with the same poorly controlled anger with which he bagged their groceries at Clark's the day they learned of Silas's return. "It's like I told you," he says. "Everyone knows the three of us were involved back then. And everyone knows Walters failed to find Jessica. It will be on his record *forever*, Meg, as sheriff of this county. Do you think he wants a repeat? No, this time he won't botch it."

Meg takes a startled step backward. Because what's that supposed to mean? "The two searches can't be compared," she hisses. "Jessica went missing in the summer. She was an eighteen-year-old female, scared, yes, but not without any sense of her bearings that night. Surely two young boys, without adequate clothing, food, or shelter, lost at the start of winter is an entirely different scenario."

Danny just stares at her, incredulous. "Same search area, same subject questioned? Of *course* they can be compared. And unlike last time, there's only one common denominator, isn't there?"

Meg bites her tongue until she feels a sharp stab of pain. *Silas has nothing to do with this. He couldn't possibly.* She fights back a feeling of nausea, because no matter how comfortable she's gotten with Walters, working for him for years, she'll never forget the feeling of being on the wrong side of his interrogations, his piercing blue eyes relentless as he asked her the same two questions in a dozen different ways. *When was the last moment you saw her? Who else was there?* She wouldn't wish that on anybody, especially not Silas. Not again. "What exactly are you saying right now, Danny?"

"Only that '03 is the only other year we've had a blemish on the one-hundred-percent find record," Danny shoots back.

"A *blemish*? Danny!"

"All the years since, we've proven—you and me—*our* record is clean."

"Which leaves Silas to blame?"

Danny hesitates, long enough for Meg to hear her heart pounding with indignation in her chest. "You said it, not me," he mutters.

Meg stares at him. He can't *merit* his way out of this, no matter how many volunteer hours he banks. No matter how many honor badges he earns. Neither of them can. She's about to say as much, but he's not done.

"Jessica Howard's case has remained unsolved for *fifteen years*, Meg, and Silas Matheson has never once looked back."

Because he can't, she wants to yell. But she swallows hard instead. That's the problem with harboring secrets. They don't make for very compelling arguments.

At a loss, Meg stares at the tree line, watching the reflective striping on Max's jacket bob between the branches toward them, watching McCrady crest the far slope. Is it her imagination, or is he looking back at her through the lingering fog with more wariness than warmth? What if Danny is right? What if, in light of this new search, what the old-timers have always seen as the catalyst for Meg's and Danny's tireless dedication now looks like guilt? As wrong as it is, Danny's determination to separate himself from everything Howard-search-related makes tragic sense.

"Meanwhile," Danny continues, "you and I have to live with what happened, every damned day. At every meeting, when a case involving a teen girl is reviewed, or worse, when the Howard search itself comes up . . ." His voice lowers. "It makes me feel fucking helpless. Tell me it's not the same for you."

It's not the same for me. Silas may have fled, but Meg's life with Danny is her own form of self-preservation. Year after year, search after search, she's buried herself deeper into this life she chose, or that perhaps chose her, that day she interviewed at the department. She's given up too much to cut bait now.

"We can only do what we can," she manages. "Each of us."

Even Teresa Howard said as much at the ten-year anniversary of her daughter's disappearance. "The sheriff's department has gone above and beyond for my family," she conceded. Then she looked toward Meg and Danny, in the front row of the gathering. "Her friends have never wavered in their dedication."

Neither one of them was able to hold her gaze. The all-too-familiar guilt snaked through Meg, a thread of misery that wound through Danny, too, cinching them both tight. And he's right: Silas wasn't there that day to hear it. To have that blessing laid at his feet. But despite all that's happened, Danny's life is still on course. He's doing exactly what he set out in high school to do: Serve. Protect. Be the hero.

"Dan," Meg prompts now. "No one is blaming you."

He doesn't answer, and she leans back against the nearest ponderosa trunk, pack and all, just for the solidity of a boundary she can trust. The sun is trying to emerge from the fog; every few seconds the stripe on Max's jacket sleeve bursts before her eyes like a flashbulb as the sun reflects off it through the trees. *Gotcha. Gotcha. Gotcha.* She closes her eyes to it.

Maybe it's for the best that they never speak of that summer, she decides. Because with every step forward in SAR, every certificate earned, every recognition of dedication received, Danny's put distance between himself and that awful August night. He's polished his track record to a spit shine. Meanwhile, every time Meg studies the topo maps of the Marble Lake wilderness, every time she hikes these trails, her love of these mountains and her memories pull her back, spinning her in yet more circles as she tries to make sense of what she has never been able to solve. What will it take to break free? More than a new position in victim advocacy, she suspects, though that might be a place to start.

"Jessica's disappearance was the worst week of my life," she finally adds, because this, at the very least, is completely true. This is one thing they can agree upon. The chaos, the barking of the dogs, the whir of the helicopter blades batting the air . . . it all flashes through her mind in a terrible highlight reel.

As an olive branch, it suffices. The memories are mirrored in Danny's eyes as he reaches out to encircle Meg's wrist with one thinly gloved hand. "I know," he says, and it's all the atonement they have time for before Max stops at their side.

All business, Danny calls their new coordinates in to the com van, and they listen, circled around his radio, as Susan Darcy delivers their next search assignment. Danny inputs these new coordinates for their next waypoint, a high ridge overlooking the aptly named Long Lake, into his GPS, and they spread out once again, preparing for their next sweep.

The terrain becomes milder on the next set of coordinates. It's still a far cry from flat, but the placement of each footfall no longer requires Meg's full attention. If she still feels unsteady on her feet, she knows she has the sight of Silas, emerging from the Lemon this morning, to blame. Seeing him again, here, where he's always seemed to inexplicably just *belong*, has left her feeling as exposed as the blanket of pine needles beneath her boots. Because whatever she ultimately decides to do with her life, she belongs here, too. With every search, every mission, she has made it so.

They continue to call for the Matheson boys as they hike, pausing at intervals to stop and listen, but all Meg hears are her search team members' voices ringing out against the pines and the low whistle of the wind in the branches. She keeps a careful eye on her position between Danny and Max, the flash of their jackets popping out against the green of the forest here, then there, and she tries not to think. For now, she tries not to be anything more than Meg Tanner, search volunteer and sheriff's department administrator, giving up her free days to do what she feels called to do.

And who, exactly, is Silas now? Who did he become after leaving Marble Lake? Everyone changes. Even Danny, she decides, darting a glance his way as he begins his ascent up the final slope toward Long Lake. He's still ever the do-gooder, of course, but the bitterness she heard in his words earlier as he condemned Silas continues to nag at her. Is it really just Silas's abandonment of them that has Danny still so angry? And has she failed to notice this thanks to her participation in his long-standing silence on the matter?

Silas's return has the effect of hydraulic pressure wearing down rock . . . his presence, or maybe just Meg's presence back at the lodge, is stirring up the many layers of silt she and Danny have carefully built up in order to stay in Feather River together, to share a life together. A moratorium on discussing Jessica Howard. An unspoken agreement to forget that their duo was once a trio. One glimpse of Silas, and suddenly everything is murky. Suppressing 2003 and all it entailed is no longer an option, and Meg's not sure if she's relieved or terrified. Either way, she should have seen it coming: Silas has always managed to wash all but what is essential away from a person, laying bare what's underneath.

12

SILAS

Eight months prior to Howard search
December 2002
Marble Lake Lodge

Winter arrived with a vengeance, dumping over three feet of snow in the Sierra before Christmas. Silas spent most of the school break at Jessica's house, where they polished their respective college applications, watched movies, and baked cookies, laughing at the way Jessica's kid brother idolized Silas's every move.

"I think he likes me more than you do," Silas joked, at which Jessica straddled him on the couch, planting a kiss on him that said otherwise.

"I think you two could use some fresh air," Jessica's mother suggested dryly, entering the room as if on cue.

Silas convinced Jessica that the outdoors did come in at least second to a make-out session, and an hour later the two of them, plus Danny and Meg, were digging around the storage shed at Marble Lake Lodge, looking for the snowshoes he was sure he'd seen after shoveling snow last week.

"What's the plan?" Danny asked as they all struggled with their bindings a few minutes later. Because of course he had to have one. "Where are we going?"

"Surely not that trek you've been obsessing over," Meg added, digging a granola bar out of her jacket pocket and breaking it into thirds. When she realized her mistake, she offered Jessica her own portion, who declined.

"What trek?" Jessica asked as Silas accepted his share of chocolate-peanut-butter chunk and Meg retreated outdoors, ready to go.

"Your boyfriend is determined to find some abandoned mine shaft that's supposed to be somewhere near Long Lake," Danny told her. Silas felt himself stiffen a little at the label, because he and Jessica weren't really using any, keeping it casual, but she just beamed at Cairns, so he guessed she didn't mind much.

It was Meg who looked kind of weirded out, actually, chewing her bite of granola bar methodically as she observed the group from the doorway, and Silas felt a little tug of misgiving. He hoped she didn't resent Jessica being here. It was only fair that Silas didn't have to feel like the odd man out anymore.

"We'll get to the mine eventually," he said, breaking off a chunk of icicle from the eaves of the shed and lobbing it in Meg's general direction. It missed by a mile, but of course Silas hadn't been aiming to hit her. He'd just wanted to pull her back into the fray. She fished the spear out of the snow and lobbed it back at him, and he grinned.

"Today, we'll hike the old logging road to Willow Lake."

"Isn't that just a glorified pond?" Danny said.

"Is it far?" Jessica asked.

"Far enough that we should bring some packs," Danny decided. "Water, layers, you know the drill."

"That's why he's the Boy Scout, folks," Silas joked, but Jessica still looked concerned.

"What if it gets dark?"

Silas saw Meg shift a bit impatiently in her snowshoes. She glanced up at the sky, which was an endless, Northern California blue, the sunshine bouncing off the snow in a dazzling display of diamond-studded ice. Before she could say anything, though, he assured Jessica, "We'll be back way before dark."

Half a mile in, however, he was hoping this trail wouldn't make a liar out of him. The way proved steeper than Silas had anticipated, the logging road uneven and deeply rutted under the heavy Sierra powder, curving up one slope and then another in a relentless climb that left them all breathless. When they hit the first of several plateaus midway to the lake, Danny—several yards ahead of the others—finally stopped in the shelter of a large tree.

Silas came to rest beside him, panting as he pulled off his stocking cap to wipe the sweat from his brow. Steam rose off the top of his head, and Meg and Jessica laughed as he raked one hand through his hair, feeling it stand up on end. He returned their grins, feeling like the court jester and not caring.

"You guys good?"

"We're good," Danny returned, "but I'm done breaking the trail, dude."

Blazing the path through the fresh snow *was* a bitch. "Sierra cement," Uncle Les always called it, when the inches piled up against the tree wells. Silas replaced his cap on his head and turned with a purposefully casual shrug. "Ladies first, then, I guess."

He probably took too much pleasure in watching the surprise register on Jessica's face. Meg stepped right up to the challenge, however, and had already taken five long strides up the trail before he ran to catch up to her, his snowshoes churning up clouds of powder in his wake. He could hear Danny's annoyed protest, something about snow in his ear, his grumble muffled by the frosted forest.

When he caught up with Meg, Silas reached out an arm to halt her, and she turned, her face flushed with cold and exertion.

"I was kidding, Cass." He laughed.

Meg didn't. Her eyes flicked to his sharply, making him instantly aware that his hand was still on her arm, and he removed it swiftly. He hadn't meant anything by it. Danny came up behind them, Jessica trailing after, and Silas shook off the sudden self-consciousness he felt between him and Meg, because he must have imagined it. Danny invited him again to take the lead with an exaggerated sweep of one arm, and only then did Meg smile, falling back with a promise to keep Jessica company in the rear. Silas began to hike, his feet lifting and sinking through the drifts in a sure, determined march, glad, suddenly, for the burning sensation in his calves and the concentration necessary to keep his steps in line with the path only visible by the swath of trees lined before them.

After a time, the only noise around him was the rhythmic breathing of his companions and the silence of the woods themselves. This seemed to Silas like a sound in its own right, a hum as heavy as the drifts heaped around the circumferences of the tree wells. The air felt charged with an auditory humidity he could breathe into his lungs.

The next time he paused for a break, leaning against a slab of granite that immediately chilled his backside, he called out, "Hear that?"

"No." Meg's voice sounded strained as she worked to clear her snowshoes with each step. She hadn't even paused to listen, but Silas didn't allow her to deter him.

"Exactly!" he answered cheerfully, glad to put the awkward moment with Meg behind him. "Which means we're not there yet. We should hear Willow Creek when we get close."

This notion of finding something within nothing, of uncovering the hidden within the great wide-open, was what the others—at least Danny, and certainly Jessica—didn't seem to get when it came to finding the Long Lake mine, for instance. If Silas could, he would follow every trail marked on the maps in his room to its final destination, no stone left unturned.

Only Meg usually seemed to understand this about him. "Silas the Conqueror," she intoned dryly now, chucking a heavy chunk of snow in his direction as she and Jessica caught up. She stripped a layer, tying her jacket around her waist. "Lead on."

After nearly two hours of effort that should have been closer to one, they reached Willow Lake. It disappointed, as Danny had warned it might, sitting shallow and flat in a low bowl between the mountains. But Willow Creek gurgled under a layer of snow, and the center of the lake shone blue under the reflection of the frosted trees, and the peaks rose up on every side of its banks in a dramatic sweep of gray and white. It all left Silas slightly dizzy as he scanned the scene before him, and he smiled. He took a deep breath and flopped down on a rock by the reeds, his snow pants sliding on the wet surface.

"A few more weeks of this cold, and we could come back with skates," Danny noted, coming up behind him, and he was right. On this end of the lake, where the water was shallowest and the shadow of the nearest peak cast a low gloom, the lake had frozen over.

Silas immediately hopped back up, ignoring the sharp pull of protest from his quad muscles. "If you need skates, you can sit on the side and watch, Cairns."

He stooped to unclasp his snowshoes in less time than it took to finish his sentence, then pushed through the powder to the edge of the lake. Stepping out gingerly, he tested the surface with a hard rap of his heel.

"Oh, *that* looks scientific," Danny laughed, while Jessica shouted, "Be careful!"

Meg just watched, sitting on a stump, legs outstretched. The aluminum ends of her snowshoes stuck into the snow, the tips pointing up at the sky.

"Come out here," Silas called. "The water's fine!"

Danny gestured down his long torso. "I weigh more than you," he answered. "Besides, the ice is too thin this early in the season."

Silas just scoffed and then slid farther out onto the pond. "Seems okay to me!" Out of the corner of his eye, he saw Danny bend to release his own boots from his buckles. But then Meg was at his side, saying something Silas couldn't hear, and Danny's hand fell away from the clasp.

"Oh, *hell* no," Silas called as he spun away on the ice. "You are not that whipped, Cairns."

"Shut up," Danny returned, though good-naturedly enough. Silas turned to glide toward them again only to skid gracelessly to a halt as the reason for Danny's improved mood stared him right in the face. Meg sat on Danny's lap, hands snaked under his coat as he kissed her neck. She whispered something in his ear, and Danny laughed, the sound crescendoing across the lake.

And just like that, Silas felt like the third wheel again, just like old times.

Which was dumb, because Jessica was right there, standing on the lakeshore, waving to him anxiously.

Maybe it was just because Meg and Danny weren't the cutesy type, so sometimes Silas could almost forget they were a couple. That they weren't all just best buds, hanging out at the lake. He remembered the way he'd felt when Danny had used the word "boyfriend" in the same sentence as "Silas's" and "Jessica" and suddenly felt claustrophobic, even out here under this wide sky. He spun away from all three of them, keeping close to the edge of the pond, sliding and coasting through the reeds sticking up through the ice. Even by the time Danny, Meg, and Jessica were just dark blobs at the far end, he hadn't gained enough space. Didn't he want himself and Jessica to have what Meg and Danny had? Jessica was kind and smart and at least mostly keeping up.

By the time he'd turned back, the shadows had increased and the ice no longer sparkled with the light of the sun. A low bank of clouds descended rapidly, darkening the lake surface, and Silas felt suddenly melancholy.

What he needed was a diversion, something to cheer him up. With Meg and Danny still thoroughly wrapped up in one another, Jessica now walking the lakeshore solo, he left the ice and scrambled up the incline by the bank about fifteen feet, all he could manage without snowshoes. Locating the largest snow-topped hunk of granite he had any chance of dislodging on his own, he pressed his weight against it, shoulder to thigh. What would Danny do if he thought he'd been proven right about the ice? Go into full Boy Scout mode? Cry for help? The possibilities cheered Silas immensely. It took a few minutes, but pretty soon he had the large stone rocking. With one final shove it began to roll, tumbling down the slope faster and faster until finally—and so satisfactorily—it crashed through the thin ice with a splintering sound that echoed off the granite ridges.

He froze in place on the slope but didn't have to wait long. They definitely heard it. All of them. Only twenty, maybe thirty, yards away, Danny and Meg came running, navigating the debris of rocks and roots concealed under the snow along the bank of the lake. Jessica came from the opposite direction, picking her way along the shore with clumsy haste.

"Hey!" Danny yelled. "Silas?"

At first, the sight of them all scrambling toward the source of the sound, limbs flailing, felt almost as satisfying to Silas as watching the rock tumble downward in its crush of snow and exposed brush. But then they got closer. Close enough for him to register the looks on their faces the moment they saw the jagged break in the ice.

"*Silas!*" Meg screamed. "*Oh my God!*"

And just like that, the joke soured.

She continued to yell as she ran, tripping and gasping, and, hardly for the first time, Silas wondered what the hell he had been thinking. His pride held him in place for only a few seconds before he launched himself down the slope to cut them off, calling back to them. They weren't listening, so he channeled his energy into keeping on his feet instead, barreling down the hill as his legs worked triple time through the thick snow. He was ten feet upslope from them, and then five, and then the momentum proved too much and he flailed out of control, running headlong into Meg, sending them both crashing to the ground. Silas curled one arm around her stomach, drawing her flush against him as they tumbled, and when they hit the rocky debris of the pond bank with a heavy crunch, he was on the bottom, breaking her fall.

"Son of a *bitch*!" Meg shouted, and even though Silas was wet and scraped and he hurt like hell, his first reaction was relief. If she could cuss him out, she was okay.

His second reaction was to curse a bit more colorfully; a jagged rock had cut clear through his jacket to the small of his back, and the pain seared through him in steady, high-crested waves.

Meg rolled off of him.

"Are you all right?" he gasped.

"I'm okay," she answered slowly, just as Jessica caught up, panting for breath, looking between Silas and Meg and the cracked ice in utter confusion. Meg followed her gaze to the ice, and her eyes narrowed at Silas. "*You* appear to be just fine as well, not to mention perfectly *dry*—" He braced himself for more—he deserved it—but she had bent back down over him. "You're bleeding. Let me see."

She helped him to sit as Jessica pushed in close, giving a little whimper at the sight of blood. Danny just delivered a hard shove to Silas's shoulder. "What the *hell*, man?"

Silas shrugged painfully out of his coat. "I dunno," he answered. "I'm sorry."

"That's what you always say."

It was true. Silas glanced up to where he had rolled the boulder from its perch. "I just thought it would be . . ." What? Funny? "It was just a stupid prank."

"Well, you went too far this time, dumbass."

Meg peeled up his shirt carefully while instructing Jessica to breathe slowly with her head between her knees. Silas was busy adding "squeamish around blood" to the list of things he was learning about her when the cold air hit his wound.

"A dumbass who might need stitches," Meg said, with a sharp intake of breath.

Silas was still working out how else to apologize when she pulled off her own jacket and top layer. Shivering in her undershirt, she looked down at her long-sleeved tee in her hands with regret before pressing the warm cotton onto the gash in Silas's back.

He shivered, too.

The sun was fully gone now, obliterated by clouds looking heavy with snow. A low wind had begun to blow. "Time to go, I guess," Meg said, shrugging her jacket back on.

"We *always* know when it's time to go," Danny added. "It's whenever Silas does something stupid."

No one argued with this. They made their way back to their snowshoes in silence, where Silas was forced to brace against Danny, his shoulders tight with tension, while Jessica clasped his boots into the bindings. On the trail, they moved even more slowly than before, despite the fact that the way was almost entirely downhill.

After an hour it began to snow, and after two, Silas's eyes strained through the driving snowflakes on each turn in the trail for the welcome sight of the main road. The pain of his wound escalated with each step, and he hiked with an unbalanced gait, one hand pressing Meg's shirt to his back under his coat. At one point, he felt sure he saw the shape of Les's old pickup, only to realize he was looking at a mountain hemlock bent with new snow. He groaned out loud.

"We might as well have gone all the way up to Long Lake after all, at the rate we're moving," Danny said.

"Maybe we'd be warm and dry up in the mine right about now," Jessica added, note of forced brightness in her tone. She offered Silas a small smile, but she was irritated too, he could tell. Of course she was.

"You're way too nice to him," Danny declared. "He doesn't deserve you."

"I don't," Silas agreed glumly. He reached for Jessica's gloved hand with his free one and gave it a squeeze.

Only Meg stayed silent, breaking trail ahead of them all. Silas focused his attention on Danny instead. Some best friend Silas was. His screwups always came crashing down around him, and when they did, Danny was right there, caught in the cross fire. He'd lost his best lure the day Silas had fallen from the trestle. He'd practically caught hypothermia the time he'd rowed out to him on Marble Lake. And today? Silas had full-on tackled his girlfriend, while his *own* girlfriend—Silas still wasn't sure about that term—stood by, terrified. When the lodge finally came into view, its craggy features softened by a heavy draping of freshly fallen snow, it looked to Silas as isolated and defeated as he felt.

13

MEG

Matheson search
November 20, 2018
9:20 a.m.
Marble Lake Wilderness

Long Lake sits in a bowl of peaks on the far eastern rim of the Marble Lake Recreation Area. The Lakes Loop trail skirts its closest bank from above; after a long, steady uphill climb thick with ponderosa and sugar pine, the wide expanse of the lake pops into view unexpectedly, sparkling below a sheer cliff of gray granite and scraggly underbrush. It's the largest in the entire basin, and from the single overlook along the main trail it seems to sink into the very granite of the mountains, dropped to the depths of the Sierra like a puzzle piece fit perfectly into place. If the smaller lakes on the other side of the loop call to mind calm, picturesque fishing ponds, Long Lake is their polar opposite, embodying a rugged, stark beauty that for Meg has never failed to both frighten and exhilarate.

Her team stops at the overlook for a water break, and for a long moment, while McCrady fiddles with his radio and Danny helps Max adjust his pack, she just stops and stares. It doesn't matter how many times she's hiked it: this trail never fails to inspire awe. Sometime during that year of exploring these mountains with Danny and Silas, even with Jessica, this place became part of her DNA. She mainlined it, the pulse of this high-elevation air oxygenating her blood.

After regrouping, their team picks their way down a smaller side trail that provides the only marked lake access. The path is so steep here—cut into the side of the slope in jagged switchbacks—that Meg's ears pop with the change in pressure within less than a quarter of a mile. The muscles in her calves feel like rubber; in some places she half stumbles and half jogs, lacking the strength to slow herself down. They drop nearly five hundred feet before arriving at the Long Lake shore, the trail emptying out at a small, rustic boathouse. There's a narrow dock and two aluminum rowboats flipped over on the shore, their oars and fishing gear no doubt locked away for the season. The dock dips as it absorbs Meg's weight, swaying under the gentle lapping waves caused by a light but steady wind. The sun has disappeared again, replaced by a low bank of dark-gray clouds, and the surface of the water, usually cobalt blue, is a dull metallic silver.

She's shed her jacket with the exertion of the hike, stuffing it into Danny's pack at his insistence, and now the wind chills the sheen of sweat along her back and neck. It feels good, but she feels a stab of remorse. Because what does this windchill feel like to Spencer and Cameron? Are they, too, wet with sweat? She looks out over the lake again. Or wet from falling in? And if these thoughts are plaguing her like this, what must they be doing to Silas right now?

"Dan?" she calls. "My jacket?" She's just shrugged it back on when she hears the heavy scraping sound of metal on stone; she turns to watch McCrady lift one side of a rowboat and heft it up at an angle. It makes her think of the boats on Marble Lake and the story of Silas and Danny first meeting, and she glances at him, wondering if he's remembering, too. But he's just digging out his own jacket from his pack, his face unreadable.

Crouching to one side, the newbie, Max, peers underneath the rowboat before shaking his head with a look of abject relief. "Nothing," he confirms, and they both straighten, letting the sides of the boat fall back to the ground with a clang of metal against stone that echoes in the still air.

They move on to the second boat, and McCrady's shoulders stiffen as he bends again, curling his fingers underneath the rim of the bow. At the next metallic screech, Meg closes her eyes until Max's second grunt in the negative tells her they're in the clear.

The three men circle the boathouse, Danny trying the door, but the padlock is secure, and there's no sign of attempted forced entry. If the boys sought refuge here, they were denied shelter. They shout, deep and loud, for the kids, their calls bouncing off the surface of the lake and the sides of the granite, but every time they pause, there's no hint of an answer.

"I'm worried about hypothermia," Meg admits to Danny.

"It warmed up some today," he reminds her, even as he rubs his hands together. She wonders how long until they can see their breath in the air again.

"It's the windchill you gotta worry about," McCrady contributes, and Danny frowns.

"Not helpful."

"Sure it is," McCrady argues. "The more you know, the more prepared you'll be when the time comes."

"When what time comes?" Max asks.

"The time to revive someone," Danny says solemnly. "If we get that lucky." Meg thinks of her basic wilderness-medic training again, worried she may forget something if she needs it. Danny just nudges one rowboat with his boot in frustration. Or maybe exhaustion-fueled adrenaline. Sometimes, during a search, the two intertwine.

They spread out again, combing the shoreline of the lake. Meg keeps calling over and over, her eyes low as her gaze sweeps the pebbled shallows of the bank, eyeing the sandy soil for any sign of a footprint, or, worse, a flesh-toned form, blending in with the sand on the lake bottom. There's no use trying to acclimate to the possibility, so she doesn't try. Instead, she redoubles her focus on the shore and the water and the filling of her lungs as she calls their names. The access trail is the only way to the water; if Spencer or Cameron saw the boathouse from above, they must have arrived at this juncture.

And gone where? She tries to think like a kid. You're cold. You're lost and hungry . . . and the terrain is unfamiliar. Maybe you're hurt. You're definitely tired. Where do you go? *Down*, her training tells her. Lost people, panicked people, fatigued people, always go downhill. But would Silas's kids?

Anyway, there *is* no downhill. Long Lake was scooped out of the granite a millennium ago. If Spencer and Cameron dropped into this bowl, the only logical next step would have been to climb back out. The easiest way lies on the far side of the lake, where the slope is more gradual, but Meg glances that way only briefly before dismissing it. Because the possibility is unlikely, or because memories are too thick in that direction?

She tries to convince herself it's the former. At any rate, the boys did not circumvent the lake along the rocky shoreline. So far, she has only covered a distance of a few hundred feet, and already the way is nearly too difficult to navigate. What brief breaks of open sand she's been afforded at the water's edge have given way to sagebrush and exposed pine roots. She's picking her way over mossy rocks and through thick, spongy undergrowth that scrapes all the way to her knees: *her* knees . . . on a child the size of these boys, it would reach chest-high.

She looks back up at the far slope, still wishing she could access it to give it a thorough search. But before she can suggest they reroute and navigate it, Danny calls the team back to the boathouse. Meg sinks wearily onto the edge of the dock, the muscles of her thighs shaking with the effort. She wipes the sweat from her forehead and looks over to Danny, panting softly with his hands braced on his knees. The others follow her gaze, awaiting direction from their team leader.

"We need to redirect," Danny announces, and Meg starts to nod. He's noticed the possibility on the far side of the lake, too, then.

But to her surprise, he's ready to dismiss this search area entirely.

"I'm calling us off this lake," he continues.

McCrady lifts his head. "I agree there's no way they'd crash through this shoreline," he says, "but we haven't even scratched—"

"You know as well as I do," Danny interjects, "there are half a dozen *other* lakes on this loop with easier water access, lakes it would make more common sense to be searching. We can't afford to waste time where they're clearly not."

McCrady releases a breath, low and hard. "Well . . ."

"Wait, what?" Max interjects. "We're just gonna give up?"

Any other search, Meg would explain to the newbie what he'd learn eventually with experience: no search can cover every possible square mile. Hard choices have to be made, but these choices hardly make a searcher dispassionate. It takes a steady, long-burning fervor to sign on to this madness year after year, search after search, willingly woken at all hours of the night to hike in blizzards and darkness and searing heat. To stand frozen in staging areas and climb trails hungry and so tired, falling asleep standing up is not an absurd possibility.

But today? Standard practice, no matter how practical, feels completely inadequate. "I'm with Max. These are *Matheson* kids," she points out. "They're not exactly going to fit the MO."

Danny's face darkens with the usual distaste at the sound of Silas's name. But there's indignation there, too, which Danny usually uses to mask fear. She'd certainly seen that expression on his face as they were all questioned during Jessica's search. So what was it about now? Having his leadership questioned? Too bad.

"Every minute we continue along the lakeshore is a minute we're *not* looking somewhere the boys are twice as likely to be, Meg," he says, frowning at her in disapproval. "You should recuse yourself from this discussion if you can't be impartial."

This stings. Obviously she's too close to this, but then, so is he. Which means both their judgments are skewed, only in different directions. It leaves her feeling like she's been blindfolded and spun in circles. "*You're* the one refusing to acknowledge specific victim tendencies—"

McCrady sticks two fingers in his mouth and lets loose an ear-piercing whistle. Max claps his hands over his ears, and Meg and Danny both startle into silence. "Time is of the essence," he reminds them, "and the two of you bickering isn't doing these poor kids any favors." Meg feels her face heat. He's right, of course. "Danny's team leader, so let's get a move on." He shoulders his pack with surprising grace for a man his age.

"Thank you, Phillip," Danny says brusquely, already reaching for the radio strapped to his chest, but McCrady just grunts an acknowledgment.

This seems good enough for Danny, who has already twisted the volume knob on his radio all the way up. The near-constant chatter that always pollutes the search airwaves fills the silence of lakeshore and dock.

Before he can depress the talk button, someone else, on some other corner of wilderness acreage, beats him to it. "Team Seven, calling in to Base," they hear. "We've got a blue baseball cap. Looks like . . . Old Navy brand," the searcher reports.

Everyone at the boathouse goes very still, listening as the cap, discovered directly off the trail on the right-hand side of Lower Big Bear Lake, is described to Susan Darcy. She asks Team Seven to stand by, and Meg looks straight at Danny, holding his gaze like a lifeline. This could be it. This could be the clue that narrows this massive search grid. Somewhere off-communication, Darcy is describing the cap to Silas. This very second, Silas is answering.

Meg's eyes narrow in on the silent radio in Danny's hands as she waits, goose bumps once again rising along the flesh of her arms. Staring at this single connection to Silas, she feels an almost violent wrench of her gut, as though a physical part of her has been yanked back to the staging area.

Abruptly, Darcy's voice rings back out over the airwaves, and they're all put out of their misery. "That's a negative, Team Seven. Neither Matheson child owns a blue baseball cap. Bag it and plot it but assume it unrelated."

The surge of bottled-up adrenaline leaves Meg's body as quickly as it came, and she sinks down onto the splintered planks of the dock. *Unrelated.* Goddammit. She releases a pent-up breath, letting her gaze fall to a particularly round pebble stuck in the sand, polished smooth from the elements of wind and water, and then nudges it with one boot. *Dammit, dammit.*

Danny waits a moment, then calls in. "Command, this is Team Five."

"Go ahead, Team Five."

"We've reached our assigned coordinates and are holding at Long Lake."

"What's the status there, Cairns?"

Danny frowns, and Meg feels a weak smile threaten the corners of her mouth. Radio communication within the unit is casual compared to what Danny's used to in the fire department. With civilian volunteers making up the bulk of the search-and-rescue team, even search managers often discard radio-number protocol in favor of first or last names. She can distinctly remember Jan Radcliff, a member of over twenty years, conducting an impromptu lesson on the art of rolling out pie dough over the radio on a less urgent search about a year ago. The only radio conduct that's strictly adhered to is the use of a simplistic color code to categorize a victim's status: black for deceased, red for critical, blue for unharmed. Easy enough, Meg supposes, for all the amateurs like herself to remember.

Danny presses the talk button to answer Darcy's question, which will amount to more disappointing news in the Lemon. "We've got nothing."

"After the lodge-side slope, you covered the area between the Lakes Loop trail and Long Lake?" she confirms.

"In a loose grid. Yes."

"And did your grid span the lakeshore?"

"Negative." Danny deliberately shifts away from Meg's gaze. "We tried to hike the circumference, but our consensus is that the vegetation is too thick for the boys to navigate."

Darcy pauses. "Got it. Stand by, Team Five." Meg pictures her studying her topographical map, trying to determine if any sections of her search radius have slipped through the cracks, and where. "Okay," she finally answers. "Take the northern end of the Lakes Loop trail back around to the T above the lodge, then return to the staging area. No use retracing your steps, unless you think it needs another sweep."

In other words, finish the loop. "But you want us to return to staging?" Danny sounds surprised. "Because we're good to remain in the field for another few hours. Maybe heading to the north—"

Darcy's voice is firm. "No, you're not. Your team needs food and a break. Return ASAP."

Danny signs out, strapping the radio back to his chest and turning the volume down to its previous level. It's still high enough for Meg to hear the chatter, but only while she stands close to Danny.

Silently, they fall into a line, heading back up the access trail single file. If Max is reluctant to leave the lake, he knows better than to say so.

As difficult as it was to navigate her way down the slope, it's twice as strenuous going back up. By the time they've reached the fifth of the dozen-odd switchbacks, Meg's thighs are burning, and her chest aches with the effort of sucking in the cold, damp air. She pauses, bent double, at a curve in the trail, concentrating only on the sharp protest of her muscles. She welcomes the pain, because in its own twisted way, it brings relief. Just like hunger or any other human discomfort, it consumes her mind, distracting her wholly. Selfish or no, for this single moment in time, on this trail, she's not thinking about the Matheson boys. She's not thinking about being at odds with Danny. She's not even thinking of Silas, and the way his return seems to have shed light into the cracks and crevices of the life she built with Danny with such scrutiny. She's thinking only of herself, of the steady, punishing trail, and, despite the pain radiating along the backs of her calves and the headache mounting behind her eyes due to her predawn wake-up call, it's a welcome reprieve.

Once they reconnect with the Lakes Loop trail, the team resumes calling out for the boys at regular intervals but remains single file. Meg's not sure if it's simply the power of suggestion or if the miles they've covered since she crawled out of bed this morning have caught up to her, but now that they're on their way back to a meal and an hour or so of rest, it's all she can do to hike with any semblance of energy. She peers into the tangle of sage and thin lodgepole pine as she hikes, but she knows it's not adequate. Someone will have to cover this section again during the afternoon.

She dreads returning to the staging area to face Silas without any hope to offer. Will she find him still in the command center, being grilled by Walters? Or, worse, hobbled on the sidelines with absolutely nothing to do? She knows Silas; nothing would feel worse to him than inaction.

She ventures a glance at Danny as they hike. His head is down, his eyes warily on the trail in front of him, and his face reveals nothing now but the steady, hardened tug and pull of physical determination. Perhaps his own fatigue has softened the edges of his anger.

He'll get over this bump between them; he always does. This wall between him and Meg isn't anything new, and maybe he *is* more detached, the way he's worked so hard to avoid this wilderness.

They hit the T-shaped cutoff to the lodge five minutes later, and as they clear the final slope and drop down into the center of the lodge grounds, the buildings are no longer deserted, as they were on their first pass through this morning. Now deputies from the department are combing the space; the doors to the small guest cabins ringing the center common space are propped open, and she can see a growing conglomeration of brown uniforms at the entrance to the main lodge kitchen and living quarters.

Meg falters in the middle of the trail. Maybe it's not just Danny who's attempted to put up a barrier after all, because she feels wholly unprepared for this sight. And it's not just worry for the Matheson boys that threatens to disarm her. It's everything: the authorities and the lodge, the forest and the search. All of it is dredging up memories she's silently punished herself for over the last fifteen years.

It's their job, she reminds herself firmly. *Don't I know that better than anybody?* This lodge is the last known location of both Spencer and Cameron. Of *course* they're searching it. It would be nothing less than unprofessional if they neglected to turn it completely inside out, and Meg knows it.

She watches the deputies—most of whom she's known for years—shine their Maglites into the darkened cabins, hampered by both the touchy electrical wiring and the lack of light allowed through the boarded-over windows. There's no crime-scene tape, and no media, so she knows no one has found cause to charge Silas with anything, and yet Sheriff Walters himself is standing on the bottom step of the rec room porch, directing someone on his two-way radio. His presence causes Meg to remember her feet, and when she strides back into the center of the staging area, she's no longer half hoping to avoid Silas. Despite the awkwardness of their reunion, a sense of loyalty has seized her. This is *Silas*, caught in the web of this nightmare, and she suddenly doesn't care how much time has passed. There's too much history between them to not be at his side. There's too much at stake to pretend that the last time this lodge was teeming with searchers it didn't change everything. As she enters back into the fray, she scans the hastily erected tents and the com van in the parking lot, urgently seeking him.

14

SILAS

Four months prior to Howard search
March 2003
Marble Lake Lodge

Silas spent the rest of the winter with an acute case of cabin fever. The mishap at Willow Lake kept him on his best behavior, biting his tongue every time he felt the urge to suggest another cold-weather expedition. He distracted himself, and Jessica, with what she called "cozy winter time" in his dormer lodge room, tucked away from the parental eyes of Les and Mary, apart from the random "check-ins" to see if they wanted snacks or to coax them into chores. Danny and Meg still came up on weekends, too, and they all watched movies until the sun dipped below the crest of the ever-present peaks and shadows cut across the floor, or buckled down to their homework, stretching out across the worn rug that ran wall-to-wall in Silas's bedroom.

As soon as the snow melted from the higher elevations, he was back to studying his maps and plotting routes through the wilderness but managed to organize only one hike—a short ascent to Little Bear Lake on the Lakes Loop—before the next freak spring blizzard came in.

"I need wheels," he complained to Danny, spreading his map of Forest Service roads that had already been opened for the season.

Danny glanced over his shoulder and scoffed. "Those roads are all along the river. They're rutted and steep as hell, man."

"You might as well relax, Silas," Meg added. "This is just how it is in March."

"Mud season," Jessica added agreeably.

But Silas didn't really hear her. He was still eyeing Meg across the room. "Nothing is 'just how it is' unless you let it be," he argued. But then something wonderful occurred to him, and he sat up fast, chucking a pillow at Danny. "Plus, I *have* wheels. Four-by-four ones!"

Danny, Meg, and Jessica shared a *what-the-hell* look over his head, but for once, Silas didn't care. "C'mon, I'll show you."

He'd discovered the 1960 Jeep buried in the lodge utility garage last fall, rusting on three wheels under a frayed tarp. Now he kicked away the last of the frozen slush around the garage doors and yanked them wide open, pulling off the tarp for the big reveal. "She's gorgeous, right? Les said I could have her if I can get her running again."

Meg and Jessica both just stared, so Silas waited for Danny to offer up his usual caution. But he had just passed the first of his fire-science written exams for the volunteer department and was apparently feeling generous. "Dude. Cool."

The girls weren't quite as easily swayed. "But it's totally . . . it's a piece of . . . I mean, surely it can't handle those Forest Service roads?" Meg ventured.

So of course Silas had to make sure it could do just that.

At least eventually. Upon investigation, the Jeep seemed to be missing an entire side of the floor panel and doors, not to mention a hood and a coat of paint. The current color could perhaps be described as a dull dirt brown, and one wheel axle had nearly rusted out, but it screamed *challenge* and *freedom,* two things Silas couldn't say no to.

Uncle Les traded a full day's work clearing the remaining snow from the rec-building roof in exchange for mechanic services, and by the first week of April, Silas eased down Marble Lake Road with one foot pressed hard on the accelerator and the other braced on the sticky clutch, all the while straddling the gaping hole in the floorboard. The steering wheel proved stiff and difficult to turn, the windshield wipers didn't work at all, and the transmission ground with every gear shift, but rolling out onto the pavement, Silas felt alive for the first time since January.

He drove directly to Danny's, honking in celebration and laughing at the looks of bewilderment on his and Meg's faces as they emerged from the house to investigate.

"I can't freaking believe it," Danny said with a grin, clearing the three porch steps in one long leap.

"This Jeep," Silas called in triumph, "is going to get us everywhere we want to go!" He gripped the rusty roll bar above his head and swung down to the ground.

Meg approached with significantly less enthusiasm. "Will it even get you up the hill *home*?"

A valid question, though Silas wasn't about to give her the satisfaction of admitting it. "How about a joyride?"

Danny hopped in without hesitation, and even Meg was agreeable enough, as long as she got the narrow back seat that had, in her words, *a freaking floor*, and they ground their way past the high school at a whopping twenty miles per hour that felt more like fifty without the unnecessary constraints of doors or windows. They took side streets— even Silas's confidence had its limits—over to Jessica's house, where she hopped in the back with Meg. The four of them weaved their way slowly toward the rarely traveled A14 highway, where Silas pressed the accelerator again, this time all the way to where the floor *would* be, topping forty-five. When Jessica shrieked, he chuckled at his success, turning to waggle his eyebrows at her.

"Eyes on the road!" Meg begged. An edge to her voice had him complying.

A sharp wind hit them at an angle as they drove; in the back seat, the girls' hair whipped around their faces, and out of the corner of his eye Silas could see Jessica trying to wrestle hers into submission. Beside her, Meg leaned her head back and laughed, letting her auburn strands fly through the air like fire. Riding shotgun, Danny stuffed his bare hands into the pockets of his jacket. A few miles down the road, Jessica leaned forward in her seat, her face inches from Silas's ear.

"Remind me what's fun about this?" she called, nearly shouting to be heard.

"Ask her," Silas shouted back, nodding his head toward Meg. He chanced a look back at her, her cheeks bright pink with cold, her eyes sparkling.

"I love it," she called back, misunderstanding the question, and his eyes watered as they snagged hers for a fraction of an instant too long. The steering wheel jerked under his hands of its own accord—he'd have to look into that—and on Danny's shout, he faced forward again, the wind full-on in his face until tears came. When Danny finally quit griping, he could still hear Meg laughing.

Silas didn't yet dare try out the rutted Forest Service roads until Les helped him replace the axle, but on the afternoons Danny wasn't volunteering at the station and Jessica didn't have cheer practice, they continued to test out the limits of the Jeep on the highway and around town, stopping at the Frostee for shakes or a greasy cardboard basket of fries.

On the days Danny did work, Silas continued to swing around for Meg en route to pick up Jessica, to whom Meg, she assured Silas, had warmed, though she didn't have him quite convinced. There were just too many times Silas noticed her being almost too nice, like she was trying to make up for something, or maybe that was just Silas projecting, a word he'd recently learned in psych class. Because he definitely gave Danny more than his share of fries when they dropped some by the station, and he hadn't given him any shit for taking on extra hours, or called him Captain Dan, or anything like that lately, though it wasn't to make up for the fact that he was spending so many afternoons with Meg, because after all, they weren't doing anything wrong. Even Jessica agreed, laughing when Silas asked if she minded Meg tagging along.

"Meg and Danny are practically *married*," she'd declared.

"It's hardly as serious as that," Silas shot back before he could analyze why, exactly, he cared.

On the first truly sunny day in mid-April, just as Silas looked forward to not freezing in the wind for a change, Jessica canceled on him to go shopping with friends. Bummed to miss out on the prime weather but figuring he should cancel on Meg, too, he swung by her house to let her know plans had changed only to see her already on the steps, waiting for him. His swift little uptick of gladness turned to dismay when he cut the rumbling engine and stepped out. Clearly she'd been crying.

"I don't want to talk about it," she said before he could even ask, dodging him to reach for the roll bar of the Jeep and hoist herself in. She wore a T-shirt for the first time since fall, and Silas had forgotten, over the long winter, how pale her skin was, how quickly it blushed in the sun. She'd pulled her hair back in a ponytail today, and something about the foresight of this told him that she anticipated these rides as much as he did.

"Where to?" he asked, after explaining Jessica's absence, which didn't seem to deter her.

"Not the Frostee."

Okay, then. He knew exactly what today called for. He turned the engine over, and when the Jeep rumbled to life, he headed in the direction of the river, then swung onto the first unmarked road he saw.

"Deciding to test your luck, I see," Meg called over the engine. She had to lean close to be heard, and when Silas glanced at her he caught the hint of a smile on her face.

It kind of made his breath catch. "Something like that."

The road was dirt, and bumpy as hell, just like Danny had warned. Worse, the steady incline was muddy with rapidly melting spring run-off. They lurched along, Silas sometimes shifting all the way down to first to get up and over the deep ruts in their path, sometimes pushing the Jeep to thirty, forty miles per hour on the straight stretches, to see just how well she could handle the uneven terrain. More than once Meg, usually much more daring these days, reached up and grabbed the roll bar again for stability. The sight made Silas dislike himself a little: he'd never been the kind of guy who felt the need to impress a girl with machismo. Never *liked* that kind of guy, either.

"We won't get stuck?" she asked him, over the sound of the engine and the wind.

"We're fine," he told her, though in truth he gritted his teeth on every sharp rise, holding his breath as the Jeep's new tires spun for an instant before engaging the muddy road and jerking forward, propelling them up the hills. Behind them, mud churned up in their wake, and before long, the backs of their shirts and jeans were specked with dark stains. As they drove, it grew colder from either the ever-increasing elevation or the waning afternoon light, or both. Silas reached behind him and tossed his sweatshirt to Meg, who pulled it over her head without argument.

"Where does this road go?" she asked almost twenty minutes later. He didn't blame her for wondering. The forest rose up thick on either side of the single-lane dirt drive, which was now swinging in a long arc west to east to west again, snaking back and forth as they wove their way up into the mountains overlooking town.

"I don't know," he answered, but he kept going. For the adventure of it, not because he loved Meg sitting shotgun. Not to keep his mind off Danny stuck at the station, while he, Silas, entertained his girl. But because from just a bit higher, the view would be spectacular.

But Meg frowned, just slightly, for the first time since they'd started off, so he forced himself to add, "Do you want to head back?"

She couldn't hear him over the revving of the engine, so once they had hurdled the next bump in the road, he reached over, his hand touching her leg to get her attention.

She jumped. She recovered quickly—Silas felt the muscle above her knee relax almost as quickly as it had tensed—but her reaction brought his eyes from the road to her face. They stared at each other for no more than a second, but it was long enough to remind Silas of every weighted moment that had ever passed between them, and *definitely* long enough to send them off course. Silas felt the Jeep jerk to the right as the tires caught a particularly deep rut. His eyes flew back to the road, his hands tight on the steering wheel, but it was too late. They lurched forward abruptly before sinking into a ditch at the edge of the road, undercarriage-deep in a puddle of mud, the tires spinning uselessly.

"Silas!"

"Shit!"

He swung his gaze back from the muddy ditch to Meg's face, which didn't exactly look pleased. His face flushed with embarrassment, but something more, too; getting stuck was his fault, for sure, but he'd only taken this road to cheer her up, to try to get her mind off . . . whatever it was.

"Can we get out?" she asked.

Silas pressed down on the accelerator experimentally; if the tires continued to spin in place the Jeep would only sink in deeper. The engine revved . . . and sure enough, down they sank. He eased his foot off the pedal, lowering his forehead to the steering wheel with a groan. Beside him Meg climbed out of the Jeep, clearing the deepest section of the ditch with a cautious side step and hop. Her feet sank in the mud anyway.

"Wait. What're you doing?"

She turned impatiently. "I'm going to find some flat stones we can lay behind the back tires."

He wanted to protest, if only to maintain an illusion of control over this situation, but she was right. If the rear tires gained some traction he might be able to back out of the rut. He jumped out on his side. Lacking Meg's penchant for grace, he stumbled, catching his balance just before tripping headlong into the deepest section of the puddle. "Shit," he repeated, this time in a low hiss just under his breath. This whole mess was starting to feel a lot like karma, for enjoying Meg's company maybe more than he should.

She didn't have to come, he reminded himself. And it wasn't Silas's fault Cairns spent all his time at the station, or that Jessica couldn't pass up a girls' day in town.

Five minutes later they'd laid a decent row of rocks, as well as an eclectic assortment of broken branches, in the Jeep's path and were ready to try again. Meg stood to the side as Silas slid back into the driver's seat. He held his breath and attempted to inch backward. The second he accelerated the tires spun uselessly again.

"Stop, stop!"

He waited while Meg came forward to reset the path of stones. This time she took less care to avoid the mud. By the time she reached the Jeep her shoes were coated in it, her jeans wet to her knees. She shoved the branches back under the tires and retreated again, giving up on her clothes completely; she just sloshed right through.

"Okay," she called when she'd reached the other side of the road.

The second attempt worked better, and the Jeep achieved almost three feet before sinking back into the mire. Silas hopped back out and crouched down by the tires, surveying the extent of the damage. They had only a few feet to go, but now the Jeep was encased even deeper in the mud than before. Shit, shit, shit!

"Maybe if we just try to go forward first? Or if I drive and you push, to get more momentum?" Meg suggested.

They tried both, only succeeding in coating them both in another layer of mud. Silas retreated in defeat, flopping down by the edge of the road in a huff. Meg joined him, knees drawn up to her chest, her arms hugging her muddy legs. She rested her chin against one knee, turning toward Silas with a look of weary resignation.

A fine speckling of mud dotted her face from the side of her nose to her lip, and his hand itched to move upward to wipe it off. But he kept his hands to himself this time, even though it meant curling his fingers around the hem of his shirt to keep them in his own lap.

"You have dirt on your face," he told her.

She shrugged but reached up a moment later to wipe it off. She managed to smudge it across her cheekbone. "Is it gone?"

Silas smiled. "Sure."

"Should we try again?" she asked, nodding back toward the Jeep.

Silas's limbs suddenly felt heavy. They were on the sunny side of the mountain, and the weak rays felt good warming his back. "In just a minute," he told her. To buy himself time. Because he was debating overstepping, and for once in his life he didn't want to push the envelope. "What was it about?" he asked eventually.

Her eyes narrowed. "What was *what* about?"

"C'mon," he chided. "Your fight. With Danny." Who else would get her upset like that?

She bit her lip, but not in a frustrated way. In a nervous way. "A while back, I decided to apply to some of the smaller California state schools. UC Davis, too."

Silas sat up straighter. He'd had his own acceptance letters for weeks now, but unlike Danny, with all his talk of his fire-science plans at the community college, Meg never spoke of any individual goals of her own. It had grated on him all year.

"Meg. That's great," he told her. He meant it. "I can't believe you didn't tell me."

"Yeah, well, I didn't tell Danny, either, figuring I'd deal with that if I got in."

"*Deal* with that?" But even as Silas's hackles rose, the implications of what Meg was telling him sank in. "Wait. *Did* you get in? To Davis?"

Meg offered a shy smile, tentative at the edges.

"Congratulations," Silas breathed. If he spoke any louder, he feared that smile might crack.

"I haven't decided if I'll go."

"Because of Danny?"

"No—well, I don't know." Meg lifted her hands and let them fall limply back to her lap. "He was happy for me and everything . . ." She paused again, and Silas bit his tongue to keep from interrupting. "It's just that Dan doesn't like things sprung on him, you know that. And we've been planning to go to Feather River Community College for, like, forever."

Something about that word, *forever*, made Silas wince. It reminded him of Jessica writing Meg and Danny off as a done deal already. But if he *didn't* want them to be a done deal, what kind of crap friend did that make him?

But he found himself saying, "*Danny* has been planning to go there forever. *He* may be ready to start punching the clock, just like his old man, but *you* can go wherever you want."

Meg glanced away. "Silas. Please. I don't need a lecture."

"No lecture. I'm just—"

She held up a hand again. "Enthusiastic, I know." She tried, but failed, to hide another slight smile. "When aren't you?" She sighed. "Anyway, thanks for listening."

The sun had lowered in the last few minutes, and a slant of light cut across her face through the underbrush. A long strand of hair had come loose from its band to fall across her face, brushing across her jawbone. Silas's line of vision narrowed to that single strand of hair, fluttering . . . teasing . . . And maybe it was the sight of Meg looking so vulnerable, her dreams laid bare for him, or maybe it was his own sense of immobility, stuck here by the side of the road, but for the first time, he let himself admit it:

He didn't care if Meg had a boyfriend, or if that boyfriend was his best friend. He didn't want to be the third wheel, didn't even want, he realized with a fatalistic sort of detachment, to round out the numbers with Jessica, nice as she was. And he was tired of pretending otherwise. He'd known this, deep down, for ages, hadn't he? It was why he'd never tried that hard with Jessica. It was why he tried too hard with Danny. The twinges of guilt. The unexpected longing at the worst times. This was why. This. Meg. It was so obvious, even as the sight of her face, so close, blurred before him, his vision a lens out of focus. He should pull back, he knew this, and he blinked, hoping his retinas would adjust and compensate, but they didn't. She was *right there*, and Silas wanted to touch that jaw, that skin, that hair so badly, a wave of near physical pain sluiced upward from his gut to his chest. He wanted her. And Silas wasn't used to that: wanting but not getting. Not winning. A rising throb of sorrow had him fisting his hands at his side, and he stood up abruptly and waded a few feet away through the mud.

"Silas?" Meg prompted from behind him, and she sounded so confused Silas nearly laughed. How could she *possibly* not understand? He felt so bare and raw and overexposed, the bitterness caught him by the throat and threatened to choke him.

He turned to face her, setting one hand on the fender of the Jeep to steady himself, as she followed in his wake, picking her way through the mud.

"You *should* accept Davis," he managed, and even though the four words fell flat and hollow in the quiet of the forest, getting them out was no small victory. "You'll be sorry if you don't try something new."

She looked at him a bit more closely then, her gaze hot on his skin. "Maybe," she answered, and that familiar dismissal in her tone set Silas's teeth on edge anew. He couldn't understand why she undersold herself; it wounded his own pride on her behalf.

"I'll support whatever you decide," he promised. They were standing face-to-face by the Jeep now. She'd peeled off his sweatshirt at some point during their battle with the mud, and as he said the words he finally touched her, pressing just two fingertips to the hollow of her elbow to gain her full attention, though he knew he already had it. The pads of his fingers burned upon contact with her skin, but if she felt this heat, too, she didn't show it.

Silas's anger quieted to a deep ache. He'd have to break up with Jessica, never mind that nothing could come of him and Meg. It was the right thing to do, but he wouldn't even be able to tell her why. Not really. And of course, he'd never say a word to Danny, though the last thing he wanted was a secret from his best friend. Maybe that hardly mattered; right now, even the thought of conversing with Danny seemed impossible to Silas.

He refocused his attention on the Jeep, making sure the debris they'd placed in front of the tires would provide traction this time. It would work, he decided, but even so, as he climbed back into the driver's seat and hit the gas, fishtailing out of the mud, he felt more stuck than ever.

15

Silas

Matheson search
November 20, 2018
12:20 p.m.
Marble Lake Staging Area

Silas follows the movement of the team of searchers returning from the field from across the circle of vehicles and tents. He feels like a voyeur, but when Meg's in his line of vision, Silas can never manage to look away; yet another thing that hasn't changed. The first thing he notices is the way she holds herself: shoulders tense, thumbs braced around the straps of her pack, redistributing its weight against her back on each stride. The first thing he thinks: *Her shoulders hurt.*

The automatic concern that shoots through Silas for her well-being feels natural, even after so many years, and it's just about the only thing that does. His homecoming to Marble Lake felt more like a hard shake of the shoulders than a warm embrace, and yesterday . . . God. He straightens his shoulders before he can crumble. Racing through the forest? Crying out for his kids? Yesterday was a punch directly to the gut.

So if he finds his eye drawn to Meg's face, softened under the overcast sky, or even to the familiarity of Danny's careful frown, he can forgive himself, if only because he's desperate for any distraction from the misery that's pounding a relentless, staccato beat against the back of his skull.

In all the possible scenarios he has imagined for their inevitable reunion, it's painfully fitting that *this* is how they finally come back together. In the midst of yet more agony. More uncertainty and despair. His thoughts swing from Meg and Danny to Jessica as another wave of remorse dashes upon whatever weak walls he's erected to protect himself in the years since her disappearance. Not that it's worked. That August night in '03 has colored everything in his life since: his choice of career, protecting wilderness even though he can't seem to protect the people in it; trying to form a family with Miranda in an effort to outrun the profound loss he experienced here in Feather River.

Meg catches his eye as she enters the base camp; is she, too, thinking of Jessica right now? She sets a course toward him, Danny pivoting to follow on her heels. This, also, is typical. Everything has changed and yet nothing has changed.

Silas stands just as Meg approaches, and in his haste he catches the heel of his boot on the leg of the metal folding chair behind him, sending him stumbling. He grasps at thin air, and then Meg is right there, her hands steadying him, her arms encircling him, and he nearly loses his balance all over again.

"Hey," she says as he allows himself the count of two, maybe three, to lean into her, his eyes pinched tightly shut against her jacket. "It's okay." And in those simple words are comfort, and camaraderie, and sympathy, and care. The pressure of her hand on his back carries him—just for an instant—away from the deputies and the words they're not saying, and from his children and their cries for help he's not hearing.

Her body radiates warmth from the efforts of her hike, reminding him of his own impotence here in camp, and he pulls away reluctantly to ask, "Any update?"

Danny, standing back, looks immediately guarded, like Silas is breaking protocol again, but Meg's still looking at him with the same open, inviting gaze he remembers. If time or circumstance has jaded her, Silas can't see it. There're a million things he wants to say—to both of them—but his current tragedy trumps everything else.

"Any sign at all?" he presses.

Meg shakes her head. Danny swallows hard and looks away. "It's still early," he says.

"Where did you go? What ground did you cover?"

"We're really not supposed to—" Danny starts, but Meg has already launched into a full report.

"The lodge to the ridgeline, then Lakes Loop trail to Long Lake." Danny frowns at her, and she changes course. "Where else might they have gone, Silas? Can you think of anywhere? I know you must be sick of talking, but try to think."

Where would his boys go, if they're not on the ridge? If they didn't drop down into any of the lakes in the basin?

"Somewhere you explored with them, maybe? Some spot you showed them?"

You know all my favorite spots as well as I do, Silas wants to tell her. Instead, he hears himself say, "I took them to the lookout tower last week." The memory almost allows him to smile, another welcome reprieve from the present. "The one on Marble Peak, where we went that once."

"I remember," Meg says. "That fall. Before the snow hit."

Late autumn of '02. The trail had glistened with early frost, the last of the pale-yellow alpine aster blooms already over for the season, only the dried husks of Wyethia mollis—mule ear—rattling in the wind. The weather was nearly identical the day Silas had introduced his boys to the two-thousand-foot elevation gain culminating in an open-weave metal staircase hugging the granite of the butte at the top of Marble Peak.

"They made it all the way," Silas says proudly. He can't help himself. "They're tough, you know?"

"I'm sure they are," Danny acknowledges tightly.

At the top, Spencer and Cameron stood stock still, not daring to look down at the long drop below their boots. They pressed their backs to the wall of the lookout station as the wind blew, taking a moment to acclimate.

Silas had forgotten how intense this peak was, with its heady combination of staggering height and never-ending view. Past the railing that ran along the deck's edge, the view stretched for miles, and the offering of so much unspoiled wilderness brought moisture to his eyes he couldn't attribute to the wind. From their position against the wall—not even daredevil Spencer seemed eager to step out onto the free space of the deck—Silas pointed out all the familiar landmarks.

"The Marble Lakes Loop is there," he said, one raised finger against the blue sky to indicate the circle of lakes that made up their stomping grounds, shining like tiny green eyes in granite sockets.

"I pointed out the lodge to them from the top," he tells Meg and Danny. "We made a game of them trying to identify each building." A thought occurs to him, and hope takes wing in a sudden flurry. "What if they tried to climb up there? What if they decided they could find the lodge from that vantage point?"

"I don't know . . ." Meg says. She glances at Danny, caution lining her features.

But if she was anticipating an argument, she doesn't get one. "Weren't you just saying not to underestimate them?" he says. Not waiting for an answer, he pulls out his search-grid map, unfolding it so they can all study it anew. He points out the lodge, then runs his finger along the wilderness surrounding it until he reaches the search boundary marked in yellow highlighter. "It's about ten miles," he says.

"To the end of the search radius," Meg interjects, looking over his shoulder. "But that only gets them to the base of Marble Peak, and the lookout-tower trailhead. Assuming they even found that . . ." She studies the mileage key. "They'd have to travel at least another six miles from there." She sighs. "It's not realistic," she admits. Silas looks ready to protest, but she stops him with an upheld hand. "They didn't travel sixteen overland miles in under seventeen hours," she concludes softly. "Not while wandering, lost. Not even your kids."

Silas kicks the dirt at his feet, hard. He takes the map from Danny, not satisfied until he's done the math, too. He doesn't want to admit it, but Meg's right. Even if they thought of the idea, and had the stamina to get there, Spencer and Cameron wouldn't have known which direction to head from the point where they got lost, which was presumably near the ridge. Kids that age, they're big-picture people.

"If I were a bird, I'd fly off of here every day," Cameron said, taking in that epic view from the lookout, and right then and there Silas felt eighteen again instead of thirty-three, standing boldly at the rail instead of the wall.

Don't you just want to launch yourself off? Meg had said, and Silas remembers looking at her in surprise. After all, *he* was the risk-taker. *He* was the extremist. When had Meg joined him at the rail? Now, in the tiny inch of breathing room he's managed to carve out between memory and fear, he lets himself admit a simple truth: he's missed the old trio. Even in the midst of this erected tent city of a staging area, with his life in pieces around him. Even with his kids ripped from him. Why has he allowed pride and pain and, yes, shame to keep him from reaching out to them? Why did he let another tragedy be the thing to bring them back together?

Because I was a coward, he reminds himself, looking between Meg and Danny in their orange uniforms. And he used up any remaining courage returning here to Marble Lake.

"I keep trying to stop thinking about them out there," he admits, "even for just one second at a time."

He braces for disgust—worse, pity—but it doesn't come.

"You must be in hell," Meg says, "keeping up this . . . vigil in your head."

What she doesn't have to say, because it's written all over her face: she knows all too well what that's like. He's comforted by the knowledge that he can still seem to read her. "And yet how can I *not*?"

She shakes her head so resolutely her hair sways back and forth across her shoulders. She still wears it long. "I don't know," she says, and unlike everyone else who's addressed him today, she doesn't retreat. She doesn't pacify or sugarcoat anything.

Danny clears his throat and tucks his search map back into the breast pocket of his jacket. "I'll ask Darcy about the Marble Peak trail, just in case," he says.

Silas is surprised but grateful. Haven't they just decided the lookout is a dead end? "Thank you," he says. "Though like you guys said, even if they had thought of the tower, the boys would have no way of knowing which direction to go."

His mind locks in on the Silva Ranger compass he'd just ordered for Spencer as a Christmas gift, even knowing he is probably still too young to learn how to use it. He thinks of the piles of maps he wants to show them, despite the fact that Cameron has yet to learn to read. Why is he always getting out ahead of himself, flinging himself, like Aunt Mary liked to say, into empty air, no safety net in sight? This time he's brought his little boys along with him. He turns away, choking on the sob that's risen in his throat.

"Knowing they have been introduced to the fire tower might confirm a hunch I had earlier, though," he hears Meg say, and he turns back to look at her.

"What's that?"

"That maybe we should be searching *up*."

"What do you mean, up?"

She explains the basics of search theory, and victims' tendency to travel downhill, and he nods in agreement. "Spencer and Cameron, at least Spencer, anyway, are definitely just as likely to travel uphill as downhill," he says. He doesn't miss the quick look she shoots in Danny's direction, as if to say, *See?* "I always taught them to get their bearings up high. To climb. To reach . . ." His throat tightens again, and he clears it roughly. "You know me. You know how I hike."

Meg smiles. "We do."

Hope swells, finding a foothold in his chest. In all the hours of questioning he endured this morning, no one thought to ask him about the likelihood of the boys traveling uphill instead of down.

"Tanner! Cairns!" Someone in the crowd of searchers waves them toward the com van, and while Meg wavers, Danny pivots on his heel immediately, following orders.

"Ever the Boy Scout, huh?" Silas observes as they watch him stride away.

Meg smiles again, but more guardedly this time. "Ever the Boy Scout." For a second it looks like she might want to say more, but then she shakes her head slightly to clear it. She turns to follow Danny.

"Meg?"

She pivots back around slowly. He touches a hand to her shoulder, feeling the heat of her through her thermal. A modicum of the weight he's been carrying lifts off Silas's shoulders, allowing him to mentally uncurl from around the knot of agony that accompanies him everywhere now. "Thank you," he tells her.

Somehow, she's always exactly what he needs.

16

MEG

At the sound of her name, Meg jerks back from Silas. Sheriff Walters stands right behind her, and she chastises herself for nearly jumping out of her skin; after all, the man has been glued to Silas's side all morning.

"I believe you're needed by the Lemon," he says, jabbing a thumb in the direction of the com van, and though his voice reflects the ease with which they work together, day in and day out, his tone leaves no room for misinterpretation.

She follows orders, turning away from Silas with a million more words caught somewhere in the back of her throat, her thermal shirt still recording his touch where he pressed his fingers into her damp skin. Was Silas really gripping her that firmly? Had she really not noticed?

She fixes her gaze on the com van, where Max and McCrady are clustered by the closed door, waiting for Team Five's debriefing with Darcy. Danny has already joined them, obedient to a fault as always, and McCrady's trying to show him something on his GPS screen. His eyes are boring into Meg, instead, as if he's taken on the collective displeasure of the team for her delay.

"Sorry to keep everyone waiting," she says as McCrady reholsters his unit. By breaking rank to talk to Silas, she's delayed them from their rest and a hot meal.

"No, we get it," McCrady says generously.

"We were just asking Danny how the dad is holding up," Max adds.

"Just needed a comforting shoulder, I think," she says, though it may have been the other way around. She slides out from under the weight of her pack as Darcy approaches to debrief them.

A few other small search teams have returned to base to grab lunch and a rest as well, and now a gathering of twenty-odd searchers circle around the steps of the Lemon so that Darcy can address them all at once. Meg stands between Barb, who runs the local animal shelter, and Steve, who plays in Danny's regular poker game.

"Keep in mind," Darcy says, handing out newly printed search maps with the areas already covered now shaded in gray, "we are still presuming the two boys to be together."

"But lots of people tend to split up," someone objects.

"Not these two," Darcy shoots back. "According to their father, these kids stick together like glue."

"They're really close," Silas announces himself, from somewhere at the periphery of the group. Heads turn to look at him as he adds, "Everyone always says how unusual it is . . ." His voice breaks. "Brothers that age, being just about . . . inseparable."

Faces pinched in sympathy nod at his words, and there's an uncomfortable shuffling of feet and gear as Silas is steered away by Santos. A mercy, Meg thinks. He doesn't need to be here, listening to all this. The mental image his words conjure—two little boys united in their fear—has already sent a quick wave of nausea to rise up in the back of Meg's throat. How much worse must Silas feel? Are his kids hunkered down somewhere, frozen in indecision? Or are they fighting their way through underbrush together, wet and frantic? She remembers what he just said, about trying so hard *not* to think, and the pain laced through his voice echoes in her head long after he's disappeared back into the command-center tent.

Darcy ushers someone else up to the Lemon step to address the group next, and Meg can't decide if she's glad or dismayed to see that Matt Bower from Washoe Medical has arrived in the field, as she thought he might. He tells them a wilderness EMT team has been called in from Reno, adding, "But every one of you need to review your first-aid protocol in the meantime."

Another handout makes the rounds through the group on the heels of the first, with bullet points on treating hypothermia in the field. *Avoid spot treating, warm the core, remove clothing . . .* the list goes on, but Meg retrains her attention on Matt, confident she knows this stuff.

"Darcy says you all have been working under the intel that these boys are likely to be proactive, mobile, and covering lots of ground, but with temps like we've seen last night and today, we need to remember that prolonged exposure to the cold affects the brain as much as it affects the extremities."

"Which means hampered reasoning skills, folks," Darcy interjects.

"And how much reasoning are we expecting from seven- and five-year-olds in the first place?" someone mumbles to Meg's left. She glares at him.

"We need to be prepared for more erratic behavior at this point," Bower says, his voice projecting over the crowd loud enough that Meg worries Silas hears, ensconced in the tent. "If the kids are still on the move, they may be getting clumsy, slower, confused. Injuries could occur, falls, things like that."

"And if they've slowed to the point of immobility, they may be even harder to find, even in one place, if they've taken cover somewhere," Darcy adds.

Meg squeezes her eyes shut tightly, picturing it against her will. Little boys, fighting their way through the brush. Losing the battle. Huddled out of sight of their would-be rescuers. And right on the heels of that image, Jessica, undoubtedly every bit as disoriented. Getting tired. Possibly even hungry. Did *she* trip and hurt herself? How many days did she struggle? How many nights did she spend alone, sheltering as best she could?

It's the never knowing that breaks you. *Please,* she beseeches the majesty of the Sierra, *don't let this be another story with no ending.* Silas doesn't deserve that. She thinks of Teresa Howard wringing her hands in Walters's office and shudders. No parent does.

Santos reemerges from the command tent, Silas, of course, in his shadow. He hands another stack of papers to Darcy, who distributes these, too, through the crowd. Before Meg's fully prepared for it, she's staring into the photocopied faces of Spencer and Cameron. Even in the crude black and white produced by the SAR mobile printer, their childish exuberance nearly jumps from the page, and instantly the theoretical concept of Silas's children is replaced by flesh and bone. These boys are suddenly so real to her, she bites back a sound of distress.

They look so much like Silas, right down to their shaggy mops of straw-colored hair. In their side-by-side portraits their smiles are the same, that enticing blend of mischief and keen interest that draws people like a magnet, and for a long moment Meg can scarcely breathe. Gripping the entire stack of fliers tightly between thumb and forefinger, she tastes the metallic tang of blood from the inside of her lip where she's clamped her jaw too hard.

Eventually she's nudged by someone to her right.

"Can you pass those along?"

"Sorry." She takes one copy for herself and thrusts the pile onward.

Do Spencer and Cameron have their father's charisma, too? Given the search radius, they clearly possess his energy and athleticism. Meg tunes back in as Darcy imparts more facts to the group at large—weight:

fifty-five pounds, shoe size: three . . . *that must be Spencer*—and even though Meg is not a mother and has never met these children, these details of the boys' lives threaten to shatter the last of her resolve. To her dismay, she realizes she's about to cry, right here, surrounded by her team.

The sob builds up hard and fast at the base of her throat, and Meg doesn't wait around for anyone else to notice. She turns abruptly from the circle of people, making her escape in long strides she hopes appear purposeful. She's certain Danny is aware of her departure, but she doesn't turn around, and with each step she takes, she wills him not to follow.

She doesn't stop until she's reached the far edge of the parking lot, where a log barrier marks the start of the forest beyond. Her shin bumps into the rough wood, and in the quick, clean pain of contact, she remembers: This is exactly where they sat, she and Silas and Danny and the Albrights, waiting for help the night Jessica went missing. She pivots immediately, following the boundary of the parking lot around to the dirt road that leads to the lodge, letting instinct guide her toward happier memories.

As she passes the entrance sign, she sees that the white paint has cracked in the deep grooves, and her eyes water again. She has to blink back the swell of tears still threatening before letting her gaze sweep wider, to the main building, which sits perched on its rocky slope tall and square, as though built for the singular purpose of withstanding winters.

She walks toward it without pause. The dirt road curves, and more of the lodge grounds open up before her. She can see the large firepit now, and a few old ping-pong tables, their playing surfaces sagging permanently in the centers from years of rain and snow. The laundry machines still sit encased in a tiny plywood lean-to, and she wonders if the adjacent storage shed is still stuffed to the rafters with linens and towels and the overwhelming smell of detergent and Clorox bleach. How many afternoons did she kill time in there, waiting for the dryer cycle to finish so she could fold sheets for Mary Albright? Silas's crazy stories distracting her from the heat and the heavy, lemony smell?

She stops directly outside the main building, where she takes care not to look up to where she knows she'd see Silas's long-ago upstairs window. Are the maps still on the wall? The constellation posters still on the ceiling? Best to look only forward, where, on the lower level, the huge industrial kitchen and smaller dining room are situated. The same drapes are in the windows as were hung by Mary in '03, and looking up to the second-story balcony, Meg can see the same weathered Adirondack chairs, still set at the perfect angle to catch the sunset.

She's left her jacket with her pack at the staging area, and for the first time since the return hike she feels cold. The wind is picking up, although now that she thinks about it, it's always been more pronounced here, at the crest of this low hill. The windows are already boarded for winter, but the main door is propped ajar, tempting her to seek refuge from the cold. She hesitates—there are still a few deputies about—but no one's paying her any attention. She pushes open the door and blinks into the gloom.

The main room is just as she remembers it, with its giant fireplace on the opposite wall, the historic black-and-white photos depicting mining life, and the rack of brochures pointing guests to areas of local interest propped to the right of the doorway. There's a new rug strewn across the wooden floorboards, however, and the sight of it stops her.

This is Silas's lodge now. All of it . . . not just his teenage bedroom. And she's trespassing without permission. She's no better than the deputies and searchers who are still poking around, opening doors and roping off buildings. She exits immediately, following the wraparound porch to the far side of the building to sit down heavily in a slatted wooden chair.

Marble Peak looms in the distance, off her right shoulder, and she cranes her neck, trying to make out the fire tower at its craggy top. She still maintains that there's an almost zero chance the boys have attempted to reach it; Marble is by no means the only elevation the boys could have climbed. She thinks again of Long Lake, with its slopes they dismissed earlier. She's still holding her newly revised search map, gripped in her hand under the printout of the Matheson boys, and she hastily unfolds it in her lap, rechecking the search margins. Yes, Marble Peak still falls just outside the new search perimeters, but that bowl her team searched just this morning? It begs further investigation, given the Matheson boys' propensity for heights.

With her eyes alternating between her map and the mountain, she doesn't see Sheriff Walters approach until the stiff black tips of his boots catch her eye, and for the second time today she jumps.

Walters reaches out and rests one hand on her shoulder. "Didn't mean to startle you." He looks at her quizzically, then offers a gentle smile. "Again."

"No, no, it's fine." She straightens in her chair, looking up from the map as though she's just been caught with some sort of contraband.

She forces herself to turn and look him in the eye. Under the weight of the search he looks every one of his sixty-two years, but the face that peers back down at her exhibits the same mellow features—thinning gray hair, light-blue eyes—she's observed from her position at her desk in his office for over a decade.

For a brief second the victim-advocacy job he's offered springs to mind. Might as well start advocating right now. She gestures to the map in her lap. "Silas said something a few minutes ago that has me thinking—"

Walters cuts her off. "Cairns already cornered me. You're right: we shouldn't underestimate these kids, so we'll pull teams from the Lakes Loop detail to comb Marble Peak and the lookout."

Meg frowns. Where is Danny's head at today? They've all but eliminated the Marble Peak possibility. "No," she says, "I think you misunderstood." Walters's eyebrows raise, and she's quick to explain. "The boys are familiar with Marble Peak, but we all agreed they couldn't have traveled that much distance. But if they'd be willing and able to climb Marble, they may have done so along the bluffs surrounding Long

Lake." Just because Danny doesn't relish the memories that particular trail holds for them doesn't mean the SAR team should shun it.

But Walters shakes his head. "We go from the inside out, as you know." He places one finger on the dot that represents the lodge, sitting squarely in the center of the search grid. "And Cairns assures us Long has had a once-over already." He looks at her sharply. "By *your* team. Which Susan is still debriefing, by the way. If you had been present, you could have brought up your concerns." Meg flushes at the chastisement before he follows it with: "Are you all right?"

Is she? She replays her conversation with Danny and Silas in her head. She'd been so sure that the consensus was to cross off the Marble lookout. Had she misunderstood? The turmoil of this search, in this location, must be getting to her, because she's doubting herself. "I'm okay," she says slowly. "And you're right. I'll head back." She moves to rise, but Walters's arm comes up impressively quickly for a man his age, clamping firmly on her forearm.

"Take a minute," he suggests, while the pressure on Meg's arm lets her know this isn't a suggestion at all. "I hadn't realized you and Silas Matheson were still so close. You've never mentioned it."

"We weren't," Meg says, and her tongue feels thick in her mouth. "We aren't."

"You aren't?" The sheriff's tone is still mild, but his gaze penetrates. Meg's not sensing hostility, it's nothing like that, but there's a hum of *something* in the air between them. It flusters her; Walters has always trodden gently with her, even back in '03. Certainly more gently than he trod with Silas. And even with Danny.

No matter how she answers, she's acutely aware that her words must maintain equilibrium across the thin wire she finds herself poised upon. "Until today, we hadn't spoken in years."

"Not since the Howard search?"

When Walters's eyes meet hers again, all trace of casual concern is gone. They're sharp in his tired, pale face, and Meg doesn't need reminding that when it comes to an investigation, Walters misses little. *He's always missed little.* Suddenly it's abundantly clear to her why he's chatting with her on a porch while what is possibly the most demanding search of his career is carrying on all around them. She hasn't worked side by side with this man for over a decade without gaining a decent grasp of how his job works. Not to mention her ringside seat for the duration of the Howard search, and the months of inquiries that followed. The *years,* she amends, if she counts her annual petition for an active reworking of the case.

Looking down into her lap, she folds the map and the bulletin of the Matheson boys in half, then into quarters, pressing the creases sharply between her fingers. She folds them again, into eighths, and when she finally feels contained she looks back up. She's glad to hear her voice is steady.

"Is this a conversation, Sheriff, or an interrogation?"

"Does this *feel* like an interrogation?" Walters looks surprised. Or feigns surprise? Meg's not so sure.

"It feels like a lot of questions, that's all," she answers carefully. They're facing away from the center of the property, but she can still hear the occasional calls of the deputies as they walk back and forth across the grounds. She doesn't want to ask, but she has to know. "Are you considering Silas to be a person of interest?"

Walters's look borders on incredulous. He reminds her of Danny in this moment. "Megan. You know perfectly well how these things work. Until a search for a minor ends one way or another and can be definitively ruled just that, the parents are always watched closely. That's all we're doing here. Watching."

And watching other people, too. Like friends.

Walters isn't finished. "I don't have to tell you this is big, Meg. The twenty-four-hour mark is breathing down my neck, we don't have so much as a scrap of a trail, and we're lacking the manpower to cover the amount of ground we need to—hell, you can see the gaps yourself."

He gestures with a stab at Marble Peak on her folded search map, the ink smudged by dirt. "Unofficially? Within the hour I'll be calling in Washoe County for ground reinforcements, maybe even Sacramento." He pauses only long enough to gather breath. "Which is why I'm asking you, as a member of my department, to provide me with any insight you may have."

"Like what?" Her answer's too quick, her voice rising an octave to join the steady wail of the wind leaning into the trunks of the ponderosa.

"Like what the hell we're doing right back where we all started!"

The statement hits Meg like a second blast of the cold air blowing down from the ridge. It's bending the tips of the trees in a low bow as Walters penetrates whatever semblance of self-possession remains to her.

"Like why I'm talking to the same people I questioned at the start of my tenure as sheriff," he continues, "during the only other search of my career that got this big, this fast."

He stands abruptly, the grind of the wooden chair legs into the deck reaching the soles of Meg's feet through her search boots. She's hyperaware of everything now: the pine needles swaying in their struggle against the sky, the damp cold seeping into her fingers, the way her toes press painfully to the front of her boots when she rises hastily alongside him.

"Sheriff—"

He halts her with one hand in the air. "Silas Matheson was at the center of everything then as well," he says. "I can't ignore that, Meg. A case with *another* missing person? Just a kid who—"

"We were *all* kids, then. All of us!" Meg can't believe she's shouting back at Walters, of all people, but she is. She must. She won't apologize.

Walters doesn't seem to be waiting for that. "Yes," he agrees softly, looking back out toward the forest. His inability to meet her gaze suggests victory to Meg, even while it saddens her. "Forgive me," he adds. "It's all just such horrible déjà vu."

"Surely even more so for Silas, with his own flesh and blood out there," she presses, lowering her voice to match his tone. For a moment she wonders if he's heard her.

"Perhaps," he acknowledges. He looks at her long and hard, and she forces herself to hold eye contact. Something about defending Silas has strengthened her.

"And yet," Walters says, "*you're* the one escaping the staging area. Was it something he said?"

Meg brushes a tendril of hair from her face in order to continue looking Walters in the eye. She's not a kid anymore. She won't be running from this, at least any farther than the lodge grounds. "No."

Walters sighs, then nods, taking a step toward the stairs. He looks up briefly at the sky, and Meg follows his gaze to eye the metallic sheet of gray that's settled just above them. "I'm calling in the helo," he says abruptly.

"Today?" It's only midafternoon, but the cloud cover is thick enough for her to already feel the daylight waning. Surely a fog will settle into the lower elevations before nightfall, if not an outright rain- or snowstorm.

"Today," Walters confirms, then pauses. "If you're still looking to get away from it all, I'll recommend you to Santos as spotter."

She stares at the sky for another moment, then back at him. It's a peace offering, but she'd like to reject it. She'd like to prove to him that she's perfectly comfortable with her role as just another ground pounder in this search, and that escape from the slow grind of stress that's eating her alive is the last thing on her mind.

She can't. "You'll consider adding the Lakes Loop to the flight plan?"

Walters grunts an affirmative.

"Then I'll be ready," she tells him, then turns quickly from the lodge.

So much for holding her ground.

17

MEG

Two months prior to Howard search
June 2003
Feather River

Meg, Danny, and Silas all graduated high school on an unseasonably warm afternoon in mid-June. They were back to their old trio, though something felt off, like the three of them were out of stride. Or maybe they were just out of practice, because since Meg and Silas's disastrous Jeep ride, there had been no new adventures. Silas had spent less time in town and more time at the lodge since breaking up with Jessica, leaving Meg as Danny's audience of one as he continuously and incredulously analyzed why. *Why Silas had ended it, or why he was practically ghosting them?* She finally had to beg him to let it go; she was too busy asking herself the same thing.

Jessica took the breakup better than any of them, it seemed, though it was probably just as well the alphabetical seating chart had them all dispersed around the grad platform today. By the time the school band finished playing "Pomp and Circumstance," Meg had already wilted into the framework of her hot metal folding chair, and their assorted parental figures, a rare showing by Silas's mom and dad included, didn't seem to be faring much better up in the football-field bleachers. Sweating through her rented black gown, she wiped the beads of moisture that dripped from under the tight band of her mortarboard.

Silas was voted "most likely to succeed." Not only had he snagged the title as a newcomer to the school; he'd been the sole nominee. True to form, he strode up the main aisle to the podium to give the customary opening welcome to raucous applause.

Meg wondered how it looked to Danny: Silas, top student. Silas, most popular. Silas, who turned everything he touched to gold, and made it look easy. Meg knew what was whispered when Danny wasn't in earshot, and sometimes when he was: that Silas overshadowed Danny, everywhere but at the fire station.

"I'm not jealous," Danny scoffed, when Meg had—just once— brought up Silas's golden-boy status.

"Of course not. You don't need to be." She'd said this too swiftly, and she'd felt her face flush. Yet another example of the awkwardness that had encroached on their dynamic since the Jeep ride.

At the podium, Silas stood before the assembly with careless grace, the sun shining hotly off the crown of his sandy hair peeking in a near-halo around the stiff edges of his mortarboard. His face upturned, his blue eyes shone bright with enthusiasm; somehow he was the only person not melting in the heat. Meg shifted in her seat, peeling the damp fabric of her dress from the backs of her knees, and counted down the minutes until she could finally cross the stage to the podium herself, receive her diploma, and get the hell out of the sun.

They cooled off with half the class at the river afterward, where the Feather widened just outside of town to form a swimming hole surrounded by granite blasted out of the nearby mountainsides, remnants of the area's gold-mining days.

"Which reminds me that we *still* haven't found that old mineshaft up by Long Lake," Silas said as they laid towels out on the smooth rock.

"Enough with the constant challenges," Danny said. "You have nothing more to prove, you know. You've won, like, all the awards. Just chill out and relax for a change." He nudged Silas in the ribs, gesturing across the boulders to where Jessica lay tanning in her bikini. "Or you could fix things between the two of you," he said. "Since you *are* most likely to succeed." He added a good-natured eye roll, but Meg didn't miss the sarcasm it masked.

Silas tensed, too. "Let it rest, man." He flung an arm over his eyes to block the sun, adding into his elbow, "She deserves a way better boyfriend than me."

Danny muttered that he couldn't disagree there, but Meg frowned into the brightness of the afternoon, her thoughts still ensnared on his previous dig. Because it wasn't that Silas tried to prove himself, exactly. It was more that he had to channel himself. Find outlets for his endless energy and curiosity. Take all those maps pinned to the walls in his room, for example, leading him down so many paths. Take his efforts during science class at the creek, or his enthusiasm on the mountain trails, or his stupid prank he'd pulled on the ice.

Her mind shifted back to their Jeep ride and stalled there. Was *she* one of those outlets, too? The energy had been almost electrifying that day, in the mud, as the sun had set behind them, chilling her to the bone. His gaze had drawn her right into his orbit, always set at such a frenetic pace. Ever since, the steady rhythm of Danny's casting and reeling at the river seemed faster. At school, she had worked harder. Silas wanted to see everything, wanted to go everywhere. Could never leave any stone unturned. And it was contagious.

"That boy is a good influence on you," Meg's mother had declared, the day Meg had checked "accept" on her UC Davis offer—at least to hold her spot—a few weeks after their muddy Jeep ride.

But it wasn't just that. Silas's passion—for the mountains, for adventure, for achievement in all its forms—brought out an answering note in Meg. It illuminated something that was, apparently, already inside her. *Like recognizes like,* Les used to say, though he was usually talking about the mating calls of birds.

Her eyes swept over Danny, sunning himself next to Silas. He'd apologized following their fight about college, but much like with their trio, an unfamiliar discomfort lingered between the two of them. Meg wasn't used to swimming against Danny's current. She could always defer enrollment, but if she actually decided to go to Davis, would he applaud her the way she knew her mom and Silas would? Or would he see it as a betrayal? A lack of loyalty? She looked away, already knowing the answer.

She let her gaze sweep downriver, out of the glare of the sun, startling when she accidentally caught Jessica's eye. She lifted her hand in an awkward wave, which Jessica returned shyly, as if embarrassed to have been caught watching the three of them. Jessica was alone, not surrounded by her usual gaggle of friends, and Meg felt a little stab of remorse. She could have made more of an effort with Jessica when she and Silas had been together. Tried to get to know her better. She frowned to herself. *Had* she actually preferred to think of Jessica as a two-dimensional concept, just as Silas had accused her of doing? That remorse deepened into something closer to guilt, bringing her to her feet. She made her way between the rocks toward her.

"Hey," she said, and when nothing more insightful came to mind, she added, "Okay if I . . ." She indicated the space on the rock next to Jessica.

Jessica seemed surprised to see her, but made room for Meg's towel, scooching over while adjusting the spaghetti strap on her shoulder to even out a tan Meg couldn't hope to achieve by August, let alone June. Her jewelry gleamed metallic in the sun: a couple bangles on her wrist and a pendant at her throat. "It's great to be out of school finally, huh?"

Meg nodded. But she was still thinking about how easily she, Danny, and even Silas had erased Jessica from their group, how little an impact she'd made on them when she'd been included in it, for that matter. "Listen, Jessica," she began, not quite sure how she'd end this sentence. *I'm sorry you're not with Silas anymore?* No, she wasn't. *We miss you?* No, they really didn't. God, it was all so messed up. Silas was right: Jessica did deserve better.

She was still reaching for the right words when Jessica came to the rescue of both, interjecting, "So, what's everybody up to?"

"Oh, you know," Meg said. "Glad to have that graduation program finally over." They all had that in common. But Jessica just nodded slightly, waiting for more. "And just hanging out at the lodge, helping with chores, all that." If she underplayed it, maybe Jessica wouldn't feel left out.

"Silas still have that Jeep? I haven't seen it in the school lot."

Meg hadn't anticipated Jessica asking about the Jeep. "Yeah, he still has it," she said slowly. "Though you're right, he hasn't been driving it much." Because it had proven so unreliable in the mud? Or because of her? She changed the subject. "I love your necklace," she said, leaning forward to cast her shadow across them both.

Jessica brightened a bit. "Oh, this?" Her fingers reached up to idly toy with the pendant nestled against her bikini top. Up close, Meg could see it was a flat silver disk, a large letter J etched across the surface in sweeping calligraphy.

"I don't even know who it's from," Jessica said. "It was just on my desk one day, in this cute little box. I asked everyone who sits near me, even everyone on my squad, but no one knows a thing about it. Kind of romantic, right?"

Her eyes flicked over toward Silas, her face unsure. "He felt really bad, he said, when, you know. When he said it wasn't working for him." She fingered the pendant. "But I hope he didn't . . ."

"I'm sure he didn't," Meg cut in, a bit more decisively than she meant to. "I mean, he wouldn't lead you on. He's not like that." She bit her lip. She'd just made it worse, hadn't she?

Jessica looked sad. "No, you're right. He wouldn't."

She'd definitely made it worse. "Maybe it's from Joe Parsons," Meg suggested. The captain of the football team as a potential love interest might cheer Jessica. "Didn't you guys date last year? Or Sam what's-his-name, who you and Silas partnered with in science? He was into you."

Jessica frowned. "Maybe." She glanced again toward Silas, but he'd left his towel, having returned to the swimming hole with a cannonball splash. Something about the lingering hope in her expression had Meg's gut tightening painfully, like she'd taken the old wrench Les used on the Jeep to her insides.

"You could have any guy in our class, you know," she blurted. "Just snap your fingers," she added, trying for a laugh.

But Jessica turned from watching Silas to look Meg in the face. "Those guys are boring, Meg. And when I'm with them, I'm boring, too." She looked even sadder now, her pretty face losing some of its bronze glow in the bright sunlight. "I'm tired of being boring," she added softly.

Her words echoed long after she'd lain back down on her towel with a sigh, as half a dozen responses vied for a place on Meg's tongue. *Me, too,* she could say. Or *Trust me, I understand.*

As they rode back into town three across in the cab of Danny's dad's truck, the June evening had lost its mild-manneredness, and she leaned back, where the vinyl seat still felt a bit warm from the sun. She listened to snippets of the boys' conversation . . . general high school gossip and a joke about how badly the fire trucks would need a washing with Danny at community college in the fall. Meg found it hard to wrap her mind around the fact that this time last year she'd never met Silas. Had never ridden in his Jeep or seen the lodge. *Last* summer, she and Danny had been their well-established duo, fishing the Feather River and hanging out with friends at the swimming hole, and the extent of her plans had been to simply follow his. The topography of that life, that mindset, now felt as far removed as the surface of the moon.

"What's wrong with you these days?" Danny had begun asking, and not just when Meg's college indecision came up. About the little things, too, like the fact that somewhere along the line, Meg's tagging along on the boys' adventures had turned into her leading the charge, at least as often as Silas.

And when she said "Nothing," he pushed back on that, too. "I know you better than anyone," he said, but she wasn't entirely sure that was true. Not anymore.

She heard herself throwing unfair challenges his way: *If I'm not enough for you . . . If there's something else you want . . .*

But Danny was all platitudes and promises, his confusion bouncing back at her. Only in that unguarded moment before sleep overtook her at night could she admit to herself what she'd really meant: *Maybe you're not enough for me,* she whispered into the dark. *Maybe there's something else I want.*

18

MEG

Meg watches, ready and waiting, as Rick Waggins, Feather River County SAR's sole helicopter pilot, cautiously lowers his Robinson R22 to the ground. He hovers briefly over the impromptu landing zone at the edge of the parking lot just as the first media vans roll to a stop directly in front of the roadblock closing off the staging area. Camera operators bail out of the brightly wrapped News 4 and News 6 vehicles from all sides, rolling film, and Meg curses under her breath. How the hell do they always manage to know exactly when the money shots will appear out of thin air?

Susan Darcy emerges from the Lemon seemingly on cue, and the cameras swivel in her direction just in time to catch Silas pushing his way out of the van directly on her heels, the thin metal door crashing closed behind him. He leaps directly to the ground rather than bother with the flimsy steps, and the reporters go wild, deducing his identity immediately.

Shit. They might as well have called a freaking press conference. But Silas doesn't seem to even register their presence. He's staring at the R22 like it's the first good news he's had all day.

It is. The sight of the helo has done more for Meg's morale than any other single moment in this search to date, and she knows how close they came to not having its assistance at all. The sun's all but disappeared, and between the persistent fog and impending storm, today's Helicopter Flight Risk Score—the strict formula pilots adhere to when deciding whether conditions are safe enough for flight—must be questionable at best. The first time Meg stood by, watching Rick tally up the numeric values assigned to visibility, wind factor, weather, and distance needing to be covered, she shifted impatiently from one foot to the other, itching to get up in the air. But one ringside seat as the small R22 attempted liftoff in wind gusts of almost twenty miles per hour—under pressure of a stressed incident commander—quickly changed her way of thinking. A crash, even a minor one, would have taken the focus swiftly off the search at hand, not to mention cost the unit upward of hundreds of thousands of dollars they didn't have to lose.

Bottom line: they're lucky—very lucky—to have eyes in the air today.

The rotors are still revolving at a quick clip as Rick pops open the door, hops down, and trots—hunched nearly double to clear the arcs of the blades—toward the staging area, waving Meg forward. The fact that he has not powered down tells her they'll be loading hot.

"Hey!" Silas shouts. "Meg! Wait!" He waves his arms to get her attention, and the cameras press in closer, too close for comfort really, to the helo.

She knows what Silas wants—to take her place in the cockpit—but he's not the right person for the job. Hasn't she been training for this moment for the last decade and a half?

"I got this," she calls, zipping her topo map into her jacket to keep it secure from the power of the wind generated by the helo. She'd love to put the control Silas craves into his hands, but doing so will not help Spencer and Cameron. There haven't been many times Meg has felt the weight of confidence tip her way while in Silas's presence, but now she knows it's true: she's better at this.

She makes a beeline for the cockpit as Darcy pulls Silas back into the safety zone, and when she turns back—she can't help it—he's standing to the side, obedient but just barely. Meg's chest constricts with a lurch of pity. Silas is only trying to deal with what must be the most impotent moment of his life by doing what he does best: taking action. To be sidelined at this time must be sheer torture.

The reporters show less restraint as they pepper Rick with questions that he ignores, slinging an arm over Meg's shoulder to guide her into a crouch as they give the rotors a respectful berth. Once in the cockpit, she fits the extra helmet over her head and checks the radio frequency. Too much chatter on the same channel clogs the airwaves and makes ground communication difficult. She continues her safety routine by rote, checking her door lock, locating her emergency kit, half her attention still on the thought of Silas, alone on the ground. Cut off at the knees.

Rick glances over, eyes her five-point harness, and makes a quick adjustment; somehow, she forgot the last S-clip. "You okay?" he says, his voice gravelly through his mic.

She gives him a thumbs-up, hoping the low light obscures the heat that she feels in her cheeks. That pull toward Silas feels entirely too familiar, but she can't let it divide her attention now. As a father, he wouldn't thank her for it. "All good."

He nods curtly and fastens his own harness before signaling to the ground-crew chief—in this case, Santos himself—that he's ready for liftoff. They take off into the wind—the steady breeze that seems to be a permanent characteristic of Marble Lake Lodge now a welcome asset—the nose of the helo dipping slightly as they head up and out at an angle of nearly exactly 10 degrees. They follow the ribbon of the dirt road below them for approximately twenty yards before rising significantly.

They clear the tips of the trees and the silver rooftops of the lodge as Meg waits for the buoying rush of adrenaline that accompanies takeoff. Sure enough, it lifts her spirits as her body breaks away from the oppressive pull of gravity, bubbling up through her veins with the heady effect of champagne. Finally . . . she feels useful for the first time in hours.

The R22 careens south, rising several feet a second until it hovers just under the canopy of the gray cloud bank. Within seconds Meg spots the flat blue reflection of Marble Lake. She withdraws her map and finds the path they're navigating upon its surface, her gaze alternating from the paper to the ground as they fly. Rookie spotters make the mistake of focusing all their attention on the terrain, but there's nothing worse than finding a subject—or even a pertinent object—only to have no idea where the find is located in relation to the search grid.

The R22 can fly as high as fourteen thousand feet, but they're nowhere near that elevation. The cloud cover is so low they're just clearing the highest treetops, rising only over ridges as necessary while hugging the underside of the flat expanse of gray sky. It makes seeing long distances impossible, but if Rick flies any higher, they risk losing visibility altogether. They start by heading west toward Marble Peak, and Meg reaches out to tap Rick's shoulder.

"I thought Walters put in an order for the Lakes Loop area," she says into the headset, but Rick waves a hand at the flight sheet in his lap, as if to indicate it should be disregarded.

"Cairns caught me right before I geared up . . . Santos issued a change back to Marble Peak, apparently."

Meg grinds her teeth in frustration. Danny can dig his heels in when he thinks he's right, and hell, he usually is, but this kind of casual disregard for protocol turns small-town search units into jokes. Danny can revisit his and Silas's old teenage pissing matches if he wants, but not on her watch. "Unless it came directly from Walters—"

Rick cuts her off. "We can cover both."

But not thoroughly. Meg wedges herself back into her flight seat, trying in vain to ground herself while they rise upward with the topography. Bureaucracy—and a healthy dose of undermining—may be getting under her skin today, but she still has a job to do. She strains her eyes as they fly toward the peak. Tendrils of precipitation have begun to form; so far, it's only a mist, but it still obscures her vision. With a mutter of frustration, she gets out her binocs and focuses them on the staircase heading up to the tower, then on the tower rail and peak itself. Nothing. Just like they thought.

In the viewfinder of the binocs she works from the top down, following the trail from the tower into the forest below, looking for anything out of place. Any color that does not fold seamlessly into the environment—a tiny trace of red, a swatch of orange or pink through the needles of the trees, even the flash of an aluminum can discarded along the trail—should pop out at her like a firework display.

Whenever she spots for Rick in this particular wilderness grid, she finds herself unconsciously scanning the terrain for two victims . . . whoever is lost at the moment, and Jessica. Always Jessica. She was wearing pink that day in '03, and sometimes, when Meg is especially tired, she can't seem to *un*see the color everywhere. No matter how hard she tries, her eyes play tricks on her, showing her pink Jessica splotches everywhere. And nowhere.

Today, however, she's hyperfocused, even through stinging eyes. Still, nothing. No movement, not even the shadow of the helo upon the earth.

As Rick turns east, she bends nearly perpendicular in her seat to look down at the ground from the rounded side window, the map still spread on her lap. The sound of air-traffic chatter and the engine—distant due to her heavy headphones—resonates in her mind, but it's only background noise, filtered through her helmet as though through a strainer . . . She only retains the small snippets that apply to her.

They finally return to the lower elevation of the lakes basin, where she makes out the low curve of the Lakes Loop trail and the far southern tip of Long Lake. Flying lower, she sets her binocs aside in favor of using the naked eye. This terrain, with this bird's-eye view, is painfully familiar, but memories are easier to stomach from up here, from the sky, where the branches can't ensnare her and the granite embedded in the earth can't trip her up. She studies miles upon miles of green trees and gray granite, randomly interspersed by the dark brown of dense earth.

But just like by Marble Peak, she sees nothing.

The sky is now so flat the entire ground is cast in shadow. Everything is in such low light, Meg is forced to strain her eyes, and even then, anything below the treetops is obscured. The stopwatch on Rick's control panel tells them they've been airborne for forty-five minutes, and Meg knows they'll have to touch down before much longer. While Rick freely donates his time and talents just like the rest of the members of the SAR unit, he cannot afford to extend his volunteerism to include unlimited jet fuel.

Still, neither of them wants to be the first to call it off. They're directly above Long Lake now, reminding her again of Danny's reluctance to extend their search to its far shore. So much memory lies in wait there, she understands this, but then she frowns. What's Long Lake to Danny, especially in the face of two missing kids? She points Rick toward the far shore, determined now to skim the circumference to search the uneven terrain her team wasn't able to cover on foot earlier this morning. It's still nagging at her, all of it: the boys' ability to hike and their penchant to climb, Danny's caution bordering on fear, Meg's tug toward Silas like a gravitational pull. Rick dips lower, hugging the lakeside, and while she can see better here, there's simply nothing *to* see. They fly even lower, so low Meg can make out the individual whitecaps on the lake's surface where the helo rotors are disturbing its smooth, flat plane. Farther on, she can see the ripples of water lapping the pebbled shore, can spot the tangled undergrowth where it hampered their hiking efforts earlier in the day. Even the lowest branches of the ponderosas clinging to the ridge near the access trail are discernible, but there is nothing, absolutely nothing, out of place to her eye. She's looking at acres upon acres of unspoiled wilderness, unmarred by even so much as a discarded candy-bar wrapper.

She spies the thick curtain of rain to the east several minutes before it's upon them. She gestures in its direction, but Rick only nods, apparently having already spotted it. They both ignore the first raindrops to hit the curved glass plane of the cockpit. It's intermittent—a sprinkle, really—one tiny burst hitting the glass of the cockpit, a pause, and then another, each one accentuating its predecessor like a punctuation mark. Rick flies on, and Meg continues to study the ground, but the air is rapidly becoming heavier and hazier. After a few more minutes she's forced to admit her view is as cloaked as if she were peering down through a veil. The branches of the trees are no longer standing out in stark contrast to the sky but rather shimmering in a gossamer film.

When Rick finally radios the ground team to prepare for landing, Meg cannot argue, but even after the skids touch the wet earth, she remains for a moment in her seat, listening to the sound of the rotors powering down. They seem to mimic her disappointment, slowing in time with her heartbeat, which now feels dull in her chest. She lets herself admit now how badly she wanted to be the one to bring Silas good news. He trusted her to take his place in the center of the action, and she's let him down.

She removes her helmet and unbuckles her harness slowly, in no rush to exit and confront the disappointed faces of the searchers, Silas no doubt front and center among them. In no hurry to face Danny, either, with this friction between them. When she eventually deplanes, she jogs straight from the LZ to the com van for her debriefing, hoping fervently that neither is present.

19

SILAS

Matheson search
November 20, 2018
4:45 p.m.
Marble Lake Staging Area

Silas strains to see Meg's expression as she exits the helicopter, hoping to glimpse . . . what? Success? Surely he would have heard already if she spotted Spencer or Cameron from her bird's-eye view. Maybe he's just looking for some standard optimism, then. A dash of hope. A sprinkling of encouragement, like he saw in her expression earlier as she climbed into the R22.

He gets nothing. Meg keeps her eyes trained on the ground as she runs in a crouch away from the helo; by the time she straightens, her back is to him. She meets with Susan Darcy and another officer in a brief team huddle, then makes a beeline for the staging area, shoulders hunched against the wind.

Darcy returns alone, and he knows what she is going to say even before she reaches his side. He decides to beat her to it. "No update? Nothing?"

"I'm sorry," Darcy says, and she does look it, though this is hardly any comfort to Silas. Her face is hardened and lined, more from weather than age from the look of it, and he can tell she's trying to rearrange her features to shift from no-nonsense leadership to something that suggests more sympathy.

He's been told she's good at her job, and he'd rather her get on with it instead of expressing her condolences. "You don't have to babysit me," he tells her. He winces at the harshness of his tone. It's just that everything inside him, right down to his soul, has become as rough and gravelly as this mountain terrain, coarser every minute his boys are missing.

Darcy just pats his back with one gloved hand and, mercifully, leaves him to his agitation and mourning, crossing the staging area to disappear back into her yellow com van. Silas stands there for a minute, feeling utterly lost. Only when the irony of this fact fully sinks in does he manage to drag his feet—like lead—in the same direction. He sees the media van at the last second and pivots on the spot, skirting the crowd of searchers, dogs, and vehicles to duck down the first sign of safety he sees: the forested walkway to the lodge.

Only to be rerouted yet again, because almost immediately he can see that the lodge is still teeming with sheriff personnel. His fingers ball into fists at his thighs, because if this isn't the most colossal waste of time, he doesn't know what is. This sight of so many resources wasted on his property is even worse to endure than the long com-van meetings and the slow-moving bureaucracy. *Search out* there*!* he wants to scream. *In the forest!*

In a blind rage, he nearly trips right over Meg.

She's sitting off to the side of the bustle of the staging area, like she's cast herself into self-exile as well. She certainly looks as lost as he feels. In her hand she clutches her short stack of search papers, including the photocopy of his sons' faces.

"Oh!" she says, half rising before sinking back down just as quickly, as if her legs suddenly decided not to oblige. "Silas. I'm so sorry. About the flight . . . not having the results . . ." She clears her throat roughly. "I was feeling so hopeful, but sometimes, this is just how searches go." She looks up at him. "It's a setback, but it doesn't mean we won't find them."

Silas nods shakily. "I guess we both know a little bit about search setbacks." And search failures.

He leaves this part unsaid, but surely she's remembering? They were just yards away from this spot, in the upstairs landing of the lodge, at 1700 hours on Day 5 of the Howard search as it was officially called off. Silas felt frozen in place, rendered mute by choices both in and out of his control, as the earth continued to rotate on its axis, indifferent to Jessica's plight. Spinning faster and faster, stopping for no one.

Just as it is indifferent now, toward his boys. His young children, innocent of the sins of their father. If this, too, is karma, it is fucking unfair.

He stares at the photocopy at the top of the pile in Meg's hands—Spencer's and Cameron's pictures—until the ink seems to blur on the paper, like those crazy 3D images that take form only with intense and protracted concentration. If he looks at these photos of Spencer and Cameron long enough, will they spring to life?

Meg follows his line of sight to her lap. "I look forward to meeting them," she says pointedly, with an air of confidence—no, of authority—she has mustered from somewhere inside herself in the last five seconds or so. Silas remembers that this is her domain now, more than his: these mountains, yes, but, more so, these search protocols and rules and chains of command. He wills himself to believe that if Meg feels confident that she'll be laying eyes on Spencer and Cameron soon, then so will he.

He sinks down beside her on a nearby log. "I've been wanting to invite you up here to the lodge," he says before thinking better of it. It seems he's been driven primarily by impulse—clamoring, desperate, driving impulse and instinct—since the boys went missing last night. "I mean, before," he adds, "you know . . ."

"Yeah." She looks from the paper in her lap to stare directly forward, where deep shadows are falling over the main lodge building. He's studying her intently enough to see her swallow hard. She doesn't look back at him when she adds, "Why didn't you?"

"I don't know." But he does, doesn't he? He didn't invite her because he has been afraid. Afraid that too much time has passed. That she'll have changed too much. That *he* has changed too much. Or not enough: that Meg will see in Silas the scared boy he was over a decade ago and declare him a coward for leaving the way he did.

He wants to ask Meg if she's sorry to see him, and not just under these circumstances. He's under no illusion: he knew she was still with Danny before he returned, but Silas would be lying if he said he didn't hope that she's missed him at least a little. That his worst fear before losing his kids—that she will have completely wished away their time together—hasn't come to pass. He wants to know: Do they still understand one another like they used to? He wants to say: *Seeing you again has provided the only comfort I've found in the past horrible day and a half.* It has ignited a tiny pilot flame within, glowing weak but sure somewhere deep in the chilled hollow of his core.

But then he thinks of Danny again, and that little ember of warmth is snuffed out as if smothered with a wet blanket. Still, whatever complicated feelings surfaced for Danny upon seeing Silas, he's set them aside to dedicate himself to this search, same as everyone else, and for this Silas is grateful. "I've wanted to invite you *both* up here," he amends. "You *and* Danny." He tries to lighten his tone when he adds, "Though I'm not sure he was too glad to see me this morning."

She inexplicably flushes, and Silas thinks she's about to excuse this with a polite reference to unfortunate circumstances, but she doesn't. "You have to remember," she says so quietly he has to strain to hear her over the steadily blowing wind. "It's not his fault that he doesn't—won't ever—see things the way we do."

She's defending Danny and striking him from the score in the same breath, and Silas has no idea what to make of this. It reminds him, actually, of how he and Miranda view one another these days, as not really part of the other's essential equation. But isn't Danny essential to Meg's?

He wants to know but also knows he has no right. He focuses his gaze on the windows of the main lodge kitchen across the path, which are already darkened by shadow and rain. Jesus, how can it already be getting dark? Again? His mind jerks mercilessly back to Spencer and Cameron, as it does about every ten seconds. They have no light. How will Spencer comfort Cameron, as he knows he will try, afraid as he gets without the glow of his night-light? Are they even together right now? Or is Cameron alone with his fear? Is Spencer?

"What comes next?" he asks Meg roughly, and she looks startled, swallowing again uncomfortably. Silas realizes she might think he means for them . . . what's next for them. "In the search," he clarifies. "What happens after dark?" He tries not to let his voice break. Are there floodlights? High-intensity beams? They won't stop looking, will they? "They'll keep going around the clock?"

"Around the clock," she promises, but then adds, "Although."

"What?"

"The helo will be grounded. Obviously," she adds, almost in apology. "And Darcy will probably call the newbies and novice searchers off until daylight." She explains something about a specialty team of advanced ground pounders. "It doesn't do Spencer and Cameron any good if *more* people get lost. I've seen that happen . . . searchers looking for searchers. It takes people off the original mission."

Silas paces. "What about *other* specialty teams? We should be calling in more resources, shouldn't we? Where are the big-city SAR groups? The experts? The—"

"Silas. Please sit back down."

He obliges, but only because she looks so miserable, and he knows firsthand how shitty it feels to be helpless. They both do. "More teams will come help, just as soon as the jurisdiction is opened up," she promises him. "Walters is already orchestrating cooperation with additional counties, probably dive teams . . ."

She trails off, and he knows why. "Dive teams? You mean, to dredge the lakes?" He remembers all too well how the dredging during Jessica's search took things to a new level of awful, watching the sheriff's-department boats bobbing on the peaceful surface while being forced to wonder what lay beneath.

Meg nods. "But they'll wait until . . ." She hesitates again.

"What? Until when?"

Misery seems to soak into every crevice of Meg's face. She swipes at her eyes, brushing her hair back. "Well, until our team needs longer breaks. After the first few days and nights."

"The first few days *and* nights? Just how long do you all think my kids—my *little* boys—can survive out there?" He flings one arm out toward the mountains, where Marble looms in deep shadow, its evergreen blanket losing definition in the gathering darkness. "God, Meg! Every second is torture, and that's just what *I'm* feeling!" The cry of protest is wrenched from his chest, and he bends double under the weight of it, sobbing into his hands.

"Oh, Silas." Meg chokes back a sob of her own, her professional demeanor broken.

"I'm sorry," he says, through his fingers. He feels her hand on his shoulder, and the touch burns through his flesh same as always, but now, he barely registers the heat. No matter how many pillars of support surround him, he continues to feel so alone in this. He says as much, into his hands.

"What about their mother?" Meg asks softly, her hand still on his back. "Have you connected?"

Silas nods. "She'll be here soon." In his focus on the search, he still hasn't spoken to Miranda directly, but Santos has been keeping him abreast of her travel itinerary, which included a delay in Denver but is now back on track. "But . . ." He wants to say, *It won't help.* Instead, he says, "This is *my* doing, Meg." All his to bear. Seeing Miranda will just mean one more person to pay amends to. He leans back against the trunk of a ponderosa, too tired, too shaky, too depleted to stand back up.

Meg remains right there beside him. After a while, she says softly, "Tell me about them."

He looks at her for a moment.

"Your boys. Tell me. Are they just like you?" She manages a brief tease of a smile. "Wild and unruly and stubborn?" She pauses. "Are they just as smart and strong-willed? I hope so."

"I hope they're far smarter than me," Silas says. "God, I was reckless and stupid and impulsive, wasn't I? And it hurt us all."

"You weren't the only one," Meg says. It makes him feel a little less alone, but it doesn't loosen the grip of dread on his heart. How could it? "I *know* they're smart," he states. "They're also inquisitive as hell, and fast on their feet. At least . . ." He pauses, that dread doubling down, making it hard to speak. "At least Spencer is fast. Cameron . . . Jesus, Meg, what if he can't keep up? I know what I said, about the boys sticking together, but they won't know what to do. What if they got separated somehow? What if they're both all alone?"

She exhales, a long, shuddering sigh, and then her hand is back on Silas's back. "Darcy told us they're the best of friends."

"Ever since Cam was born," Silas says, after he's regained enough composure to speak again. "They had a bit of a rough patch adjusting to the move here, but overall? It's always been the two of them, thick as thieves."

Just last week, when Silas explained that it was time to enroll Spencer in elementary school, didn't he instinctively clutch Cameron's hand in his and squeeze?

"But he'll be lonely," Spencer said, looking to his brother for confirmation that came in the form of an earnest nod. "He won't want to be here all by himself."

"I'll be here," Silas pointed out, but both boys shared another look. Neither of them seemed convinced that this would help much.

"If they're that close," Meg decides, "then they'll be together."

But for how long, in this wilderness so foreign to them? In this cold? "Tell me straight, Meg. How many days will they look?"

She eyes him warily, and he knows why: he knows the answer. They found out together, didn't they, that August fifteen years ago, when they waited and waited as time seemed to stand still until—poof! Time had run out, just like that.

When the Howard search was called off, for the first time in Silas's young life he understood the impulse to turn back the clock. Rewinding his life, and not even that far, either, would have made everything all right, and just the thought of such a simple yet unattainable solution brought the sharp sting of tears to the backs of his eyelids and caused his chest to swell tightly as he swallowed.

Just like now. Silas shuddered, imagining his eighteen-year-old self, privy to the depth of misery that lay in store for him over a decade later. It would have immobilized him. It would have reduced him to rubble. And then time *would* have stood still, and he'd never have grown up and moved away and met Miranda and had his boys.

No, turning back the clock isn't the answer. Waiting around isn't, either. "I'm going to *do* something," he tells Meg, rising to his feet with a sense of purpose that draws a sharp pain of resistance from his quad muscles. "Once and for all."

Meg rises with him, in alarm. "Do what, exactly?"

"I don't know. I don't care. Just *something*."

"You can't just barrel forward, like you always did! Silas! You can't—"

He turns on his heel. "Meg, I *have* to. Can't you see? It can't be like before. It can't end the same way!"

Meg visibly flinches.

"I'm sorry, but you know I'm right. Meg, we have to do differently. We have to—"

"Okay." She turns from him, but not before tears are visible. "I'll find Santos. I'll ask to go along with the night team." The weariness exuding from her reached all the way to her voice.

"No. You sleep. I'll go." He waves away her protests before she can mount them. "They'll let me." Before she can argue, he adds, "I don't plan to give them a choice."

Squaring his shoulders, he makes a beeline for the com van. No more poor decisions. No more waiting for his fate. If high school Silas could see him now, he wouldn't know what hit him.

20

MEG

One month prior to Howard search
July 2003

Feather River hosted its Old-Fashioned Fourth on the first Friday of July. Usually Meg and Danny found a spot on the curb to watch the parade crawl down Main Street, but this year, Silas declared a day of independence to be the perfect moment to finally find the Long Lake mine.

Meg looked at Danny, who shrugged.

"If it will finally get this quest out of your system," he told Silas, "sure. Why not?"

But then he got roped into working the hot-dog booth hosted by the firefighter association at the end of the parade route. No way could Silas's mine trek compete with the chance to hang out with bona fide firefighters all day, even if it did mean he'd be stuck behind a grill in ninety-degree temps.

"You guys should still go," he told her, though not very convincingly.

Meg *did* still want to go. She wanted to test herself on this uncharted terrain Silas had in mind, wanted to see inside this mine. Soon Silas would leave Marble Lake forever, and what if he took Meg's new adventuring spirit with him?

But he might cancel anyway, now that Danny was busy. Meg had noticed he did that lately. Often, actually, since Danny was busy almost all the time now. A new, unwelcome thought occurred to her. Had Danny told Silas he wasn't cool with him spending time with Meg without Jessica in the mix?

"You don't mind?" Meg asked him now. Just to check. With her plans still in the air, things felt perpetually off between them.

But Danny's attention had shifted to ironing a new patch onto his junior-volunteer-fire uniform. "Does this look even to you?" he asked, lifting the patched shirt up to her face.

So she called Silas to make sure they were still on. And she made sure to mention that it would just be her, that Danny had been pressed into service at the booth. And Silas had paused for what had felt like a long time for someone who had been given every out, and then he'd said he'd pick her up at 8:00 a.m. sharp.

"You brought the Jeep," she said with surprise, climbing into the seat the next morning.

"Why wouldn't I?" he said, as if he hadn't stashed it back in the maintenance shed at the lodge for the last three months.

Meg decided to let this go. "At least we'll beat the parade traffic at this hour."

Silas started the engine. "And with the entire Forest Service volunteer corps marching behind the Rotary float, no one will be around to chase us out of the mine."

Was this a serious concern? Meg couldn't tell, without Silas adding his usual swagger to every conversation. She said simply, "If we find it."

Silas scoffed as he turned onto the highway, which was a little more like him. "We'll find it. And besides, it's only Danny who keeps going on about trespassing rules and USFS regulations."

He had a point. She visualized the US Geological Survey map Silas always studied. According to him, multiple caches of abandoned mines—vestiges of the region's gold-mining heyday—dotted the Sierra Nevada landscape. Dense enough in some places to resemble the puckered surface of honeycomb, most had long since been filled in and sealed in the name of public safety by the Forest Service, their locations wiped from the grid forever, but a few remained, tucked into low slopes and rocky outcroppings . . . and plotted by the USGS for anyone to find. On his map, Silas had circled the ridge he sought beyond the far shore of Long Lake.

"I already cross-referenced the topographical coordinates by compass degree," he told her once they'd parked by the lodge. He leaned over her with his Silva Ranger in hand, pointing out the marked mine shafts and deciding where, exactly, along the circumference of the lakeshore they'd need to veer off trail, while Meg fully visualized, for the first time since agreeing to this venture, crawling into some dark, rotting, enclosed space with nothing but a flashlight.

She didn't let it deter her. Twenty minutes later, the sun already felt hot on the backs of their necks as they hiked, the sky a wide-open blue in the stretches of trail between the trees. The trace of tension she'd felt between them in the Jeep faded as they put the miles in, and at the shore of Long Lake, Meg took off her boots and waded into the chilled water until the ripples splashed the hem of her shorts. "Come in!" she called, as Silas eyeballed their destination across the lake. "The water's fine!"

"No, it's snowmelt," Silas countered, mimicking a shiver of cold. "Help me out, will you?"

He instructed her to hold the map flat so he could lay his compass carefully on top of it. He drew his finger across the page to the marked mines, lined the compass dial up with North, and then traced one finger back from the mines to an exact declination mark on the dial.

"Eighty degrees northwest," he said triumphantly. "Remember that, Cass."

And instantly that tension was back, Meg responding to that single syllable like Silas had lit a sparkler under her skin.

Had she always reacted this way? She remembered him teasing her on the hike to Willow Lake, calling her Cass when she tried to break the trail, how it had made her cheeks flush. From exertion, or with pleasure?

And it wasn't just her. Silas was looking at her like he'd just let a curse word slip in the middle of class, not used a silly nickname he'd invented on a whim. He stuffed the map back into his pack and set off briskly in the direction he'd just charted, Meg scrambling to follow him around the lake, fighting the underbrush as the way grew more difficult.

Honestly? She could go for one of Silas's pranks right about now, just to make this all feel more normal. A sudden cry of "Bear!" maybe. Though it wouldn't have worked, she realized. Nothing about Silas scared her. Maybe it was his self-reliance, the way he subscribed so loyally to his faith in himself, that made her feel safe around him. Or maybe it was her own self-confidence she was sensing, rising in tandem with his. Whatever it was, Silas was the kind of person to gravitate *toward* in the event of uncertainty, not flee from. Which made it tricky now, Meg realized, her stride faltering, knowing that the source of her uncertainty was, in fact, him.

As they continued to navigate the lakeshore, Silas settled into a less frenetic pace, though he remained uncharacteristically well behaved. He placed a few strategic stomps in the vicinity of the waterline where the strip of sand they traversed narrowed, splashing Meg with the icy water, but the sun was already high in the sky, and besides, her legs were already wet. She hardly noticed the intermittent sprays of droplets up her calves. They reached the end of the lake more quickly than she had anticipated, and Silas stopped, reaching again for his compass.

"Okay, this is it," he said, lining the needle back up with North and turning the dial to 80 degrees. He must have felt Meg's eyes on him, because he looked up at her. "You know how to do this, right?"

When she shook her head, Silas frowned. "You should know how to read a compass and a map, Meg."

The use of her given name felt pointed, and every bit as charged. It put her on the defensive. She was out here, wasn't she? On his wild-goose chase. *Because you want to be,* she reminded herself.

"You could teach me," she said.

Silas smiled at her tone. "Come here." When he held out the compass, she came to stand in front of him, letting him place her fingers around the edges of the baseplate. He turned her by the shoulders until the red tip of the needle aligned with North, and then guided her hand around the dial until the index pointer at the top of the compass fell even with 80 degrees. "What you want to do," Silas said, looking over Meg's right shoulder in their direction of travel, "is find a point of reference some way off, in line with your course." He pointed to a large spruce in the distance as the proximity of his breath in her ear sent a shiver down her spine, despite the sunshine. "Let's head for that tree, and then recheck our bearings."

She was grateful for the excuse to move. They made their way to the tree, then to a low outcropping of stones, then to a splintered pine lying on its side, and before Meg knew it they had traveled almost a mile at a steady 80 degrees, mostly uphill, and Silas began looking in earnest for any sign of a mine shaft. At his triumphant whoop, she felt the thrill of discovery herself, running to catch up while a hum of anticipation buzzed in her ears. For years after, whenever she bent over tedious map exercises and compass work at monthly search meetings, Meg would wonder whether her love of map reading as a tool for rescue and recovery had been born in this moment.

The mine shaft Silas found had been dug into a low embankment at the end of a small meadow. The entrance looked imposingly narrow, the crossbeams at the entrance bowed and splintered, and when she approached Meg could see they were going to clear her head by only a few inches. Sierra mines traveled laterally rather than vertically, burrowing deep into the sides of mountains instead of straight down, but still, peering in from the outside, Meg could only see the distance of a few feet before the way plunged in darkness. Silas took a step inside, then another, his eyes darting from the rocky ceiling of the tunnel to Meg, standing in the sunlight.

"C'mon," he encouraged, flicking his flashlight on.

When Silas reached a hand out to her she took it, even suspecting that she was going to feel this touch all the way into the marrow of her bones, given how this day was going. She didn't much like the idea of being left out *here*, either, to stand and wait and wonder if he'd been sucked under the surface of a mountain.

She wasn't wrong; his grip on her palm burned in sharp contrast to the sudden, all-encompassing chill of the mine shaft. The cold hit Meg's heated skin and sweat-stained shirt like a leap into the Feather River: goose bumps broke out instantly along her arms and the back of her neck. The relief from the heat distracted her for the first few feet, and then she began to register the low ceiling of the tunnel—already Meg had to duck—and the damp walls on either side of her, slick with condensation and moss. About five feet in, water began to pool in places along the floor of the shaft, and she swatted away the mosquitoes that rose up to swarm around her in the damp darkness.

Still they pressed on, both of them crouched low to avoid hitting their heads on the jagged ceiling of the tunnel. "Good?" Silas asked, turning to check on her. She nodded. Despite his manic energy, when she was in Silas's world, Meg felt strangely calm. Danny called it the eye of the hurricane, but to Meg, the physicality of it all lent a sort of clarity.

After perhaps ten feet, the shaft began to veer to the right, and Meg hesitated, eyeing the gloom in front of them, illuminated only in random spots as Silas's flashlight beam bounced from one side of the tunnel to the other. He was only a few paces ahead of her, and his voice echoed loudly off the walls as he urged her forward. Mine shafts often curved in a haphazard route under the ground, he explained, twisting this way and that as the miners chased the snaking veins of gold at whim.

Meg thought of these long-ago fortune hunters in here for hours at a time, and she shuddered. She was afraid to so much as touch the crumbling walls of this tunnel, let alone actively chip away at them with thousands of pounds of granite directly above her head. When she saw Silas ease down to hands and knees, she hit her limit.

"Can we turn back?" she called.

She expected pushback, but when he craned his head over his shoulder, she caught his sheepish smile in the glow of the flashlight. "I thought you'd never ask."

They allowed their feet to slosh through the muck on their return, and, concentrating as hard as she was on *not* thinking about what might be living in the water, Meg emerged back into the daylight well ahead of Silas. She turned in a circle, momentarily disoriented, but even after she'd gotten her bearings, she had an odd sense she was being watched. She squinted into the sunshine, but her eyes hadn't adjusted yet, and by the time Silas emerged from the shaft, she had chalked the sensation up to the eerie vibe of the mine following her outside.

They climbed the slope to a low ridge, still swatting at mosquitoes. The heat of the sun now welcome, they settled on a long slab of warm granite, peeling off their wet socks while comparing bug bites. And when they'd exhausted that subject, Meg lay back and closed her eyes against the bright-blue sky. She wasn't ready to hike back yet, the heat on the rocks, even the position of the sun, reminding her again of the limited time left to them before summer ended. Left to *all* of them, she amended quickly, with Danny starting fire-science training in September. She shouldn't have left him out.

Silas's voice floated over her. "What are you thinking about?"

She leaned up on one elbow and tried for humor. "I guess I was just thinking it's a lot quieter without the Silas-Danny dynamic today.

You guys would probably be in a rock-throwing contest or something right about now."

Silas offered a smile, but it didn't reach his eyes like it usually did. "Do you want me to find you a rock to throw?"

No, she found she wanted something else. A little clarity. "Why didn't it work out," she heard herself ask, "between you and Jessica?" He'd never really said, and suddenly it felt imperative to know.

Silas looked away from her, studying the minute specks of iron in the granite beneath his hands. "She just wasn't right for me," he said at length.

There was a sadness in his tone that pained Meg in return, an echo, she told herself, of the regret she felt whenever she thought about how quick she'd been to judge Jessica last fall. "I hope it wasn't because of me," she said, "not being super inviting at first." Because she hadn't wanted to hurt anyone, least of all Silas.

He sat up and looked at her, his head blocking out the sun. Finding herself abruptly in shadow, Meg blinked, but she kept on talking, even as a shiver of entrapment ran down her spine. "Because we all got used to her hanging around. It only got weird after you guys broke up."

Something shifted in Silas's eyes, like remembered pain. His shoulders straightened in a familiar posture. Danny called it his Man of Conviction mode, because Silas's air of certainty was unmistakable. "No," he corrected her unequivocally, "it got weird after our Jeep ride in the mud."

He said this slowly, like he wanted it to sink in, and it did, just like the Jeep tires had into the mire. Meg replayed that afternoon in her mind, remembering not only the way Silas had tried to comfort her and support her goals but also the way he had looked at her as he'd done so. Because it was the same way he'd looked at her when he'd called her Cassiopeia for the first time, in the vestibule of the lodge. And again on the shore of Long Lake just today. It was the way he looked at her now.

The charge that had a habit of rising in the air between them surged with an answering spike of her pulse, and Meg knew: She was looking at him in the exact same way.

She scrambled to her feet, nearly sending her pack careening off the rock.

"Meg—"

She didn't wait for him to finish. Just grabbed her shoes and retreated down to a flatter ledge, where she could yank her boots back onto her feet. Silas hopped down lithely, at her side before she could untangle even one lace.

"That day last spring," he said softly, palms outstretched, like when he approached the family of deer that grazed on the lodge lawn. "We talked about plans, and about making choices."

"Silas, don't."

"Just answer me this." He leaned forward. "Do you ever feel boxed in? Pushed down a path you don't want to go?"

"You mean before this afternoon?" she shot back. Silas bit his lip, and this tell of uncharacteristic uncertainty had her yielding. "I'm sorry." And then, more quietly, in the direction of her feet, she added, "You know I do."

"Listen," he said. But then he seemed to struggle for direction, picking his way forward word by word. "You don't have to decide what you want *forever*. Not right now. No one knows what they want forever."

Meg looked at him miserably. "I think Danny does."

Silas's eyes bored straight into hers, reflecting all that misery back to her. His face was only inches from hers, the tanned plane of his jaw in reach, and for an instant she was on a precipice, teetering before the descent, ready to pick up speed. And then she managed to shove herself off the rock, untied shoes be damned, before she could careen down the other side.

He let her go, and Meg scrambled up the embankment and over the crest of another small ridge overlooking the meadow. The slope bore downward at at least a 30-degree angle on the other side, and she skidded gracelessly with each step, her brain screaming *What's wrong with you?* in time with the cascade of shale and rock under her feet. Guilt squeezed tight, souring the scent of Silas's sunbaked skin, the feel of his breath brushing her cheek. Choking out the longing that had tugged like gravity. She needed to put some space between them, just needed to be gone. The low shadow of the ridge crept steadily up her back as she descended, blocking the sun, and for that moment it was a relief to be out of Silas's line of sight.

In her haste to retreat, she almost stumbled directly upon the second mine shaft. At first she mistook the sunken ground for just an odd dip in the steep terrain, but as her weight shifted she heard a creak and a sudden splintering, and then her foot had slid into a lateral tunnel. She flailed a bit for balance, and once she had scrambled away her boots had uncovered enough soil to reveal the thick beam of a side support braced against the mountain.

She must have called out when she slid, because only seconds later she looked up to see Silas's silhouette on the ridge, and then he, too, ran down the hill. "Are you okay?" he called, and she raised one hand up to block the sun, watching him descend.

"Yeah," she called back. "Careful!" He skidded to a stop next to her, and she pointed down at the narrow hole in the slope. "But look what I found."

Silas bent to study the evidence of this other mine shaft and then began brushing away the dirt around the beam. It connected to a vertical support and then to another beam on the other side, and with Meg joining the effort they had the entire frame of the entrance exposed within minutes. This mine shaft looked roughly the same height as the lower one, but this one had been sealed with a thick plank of plywood hammered into the beams.

"Oh, wow," Silas breathed.

He began to feel along the seam of the plank, finally getting his fingers wedged around the back side of the wood so he could pull.

"Wait. If this is a sealed mine, shouldn't we leave it?" Meg asked. "The Forest Service probably closed this one."

Silas halted his efforts long enough to look at her, eyebrows raised.

"Right," she said, and then the thrill of discovery took hold in her, too, and together they wrestled with the makeshift covering. Within three pulls it cracked, and within four the rusted nails slipped out of the beams and she and Silas fell back into the dirt, plank and all.

They peered curiously into the mine shaft. At first it looked just the same as the other. Stagnant water pooled in several places, and while it lacked the hum of insects thanks to its plywood seal, Meg assumed it was only a matter of time until the pests discovered this new paradise as well. Silas took a step inside, then another, and just as Meg was about to urge him back, he bent down and picked something up. "Whoa, check this out," he called back to her.

"Ohhh!" The dirt floor of the tunnel was littered with what looked like shiny black chunks of glass. She picked one up; it was jagged enough to prick her finger, and she shifted it in her palm more carefully. "Obsidian." She smiled.

Silas's eyes shone as he nodded, and Meg registered a jolt of pleasure to have pleased him. "But isn't it unusual here?" he asked. "Obsidian's usually found in volcanic soil."

Meg shrugged, still studying the sleek surface of the stone. "It must have been unearthed in here at some point." She pocketed the rock, then made her way back out into the afternoon light. Silas followed close behind her, and after a somewhat pointless exchange about whether they should try to reseal the entrance—it wasn't as though they'd brought a hammer—they left it wide open and climbed the slope together, dropping back down the other side into the meadow where they'd left their packs. Silas took a minute to fiddle with his compass and his map; lacking a pen, he carefully poked a hole in the thin paper to mark the location of this second, unmarked and now unsealed mine shaft.

And then, the flurry of their find behind them, they looked at one another, neither of them knowing what to say. Meg had just decided it was hopeless, that the Silas she knew so well might as well be a thousand miles away, instead of the space of about a foot, when he said, "You hear that?"

She smiled, grateful to him for closing the distance that had spanned between them with one of his jokes. "Very funny."

"No, I'm serious." And Silas did appear to be, looking now in the direction of the brush behind them. "I thought I heard something."

"Like what, a bat we rudely disrupted from sleep?"

Silas shook his head silently, still looking and listening. After a moment, he said, "Guess it was nothing."

"Yeah, guess I wasn't born yesterday," Meg said, shrugging on her pack.

"I wasn't trying to trick you," Silas protested. "Really."

And then she believed him, which made her feel glad. Because suddenly the thought of him trying to take them back to their old normal held zero appeal.

They both remained quiet on the hike back, Meg fluctuating between wishing she knew what Silas was thinking and gratitude that she didn't. For her own part, she thought about what remained of their summer and the decisions that still awaited her at the end of it. What *did* she want?

Should she stay the course with Danny, or fling herself into the unknown? Silas, of course, had been plenty vocal about what he would pick, and the knowledge made her feel less alone.

When the Jeep came to a stop in front of her house, Meg placed the small chunk of obsidian she'd saved into Silas's hand. "This, at least, will last forever," she said softly. As an answer to his earlier question it was a cop-out, but it was all she could offer just now. A placeholder of sorts, while she gathered up her courage for whatever came next.

He looked from her face to the obsidian almost cautiously, and for a brief second she was gripped by the fear that she was the only one grappling with impossible choices, loyalty and guilt and the possibility of escape vying for dominance in her head. But then his fingers skimmed over hers as he took her offering with a sad smile, and it was all back: the energy, the heat, the weight between them. She climbed down from her seat with a small wave, and then the Jeep roared back to life, Silas popping the clutch and propelling himself away from her.

21
MEG

Meg opens her eyes to the first weak light penetrating the dirty white canvas of a staging-area tent wall. For a moment she has trouble orienting herself. Then the events of the evening before return in a rush: the fruitless helo flight, the disappointment on Silas's face, his insistence that she rest while he continued the search through the night.

Most of the ground pounders retreated to the comfort of the lodge for the night—its fifty-plus beds make for a pretty ideal overnight headquarters—but she crashed here, on one of the cots intended for quick naps and first aid, away from anyone who would want to talk to her, comfort her, help her, or need her. Away from Danny, even, pleading exhaustion to buy herself a few hours alone. It still nags at her, the way he dismissed her opinion about re-searching Long Lake. How he was so quick to go over her head with Santos, pushing the Marble Peak angle. She slept a little, but she still isn't sure she has the energy to spare to confront him.

She last saw Silas around 8:00 p.m., departing with a deputy on a vehicle patrol along the perimeter of the search radius. She wonders: How long did he plead his case before Darcy relented and let him participate? The perseverance necessary sounds like the Silas she knows, and somehow the thought comforts her.

She slept fully clothed, and after rummaging around the sleeping bag and cot for her gloves and beanie, she wrestles her boots back on and steps into the new morning. Outside the tent, base camp is already buzzing with activity. There's no sign of Danny, but the K9 team is in their leads and harnesses, bells jangling, and what looks like at least one fresh team of ground pounders are piling out of a Washoe County Sheriff's van. Reinforcements from Reno.

Silas, looking more ragged than ever, stands in front of the Lemon next to Santos and a woman Meg has never seen before. She first thinks "media liaison" based on the civilian attire and well-groomed appearance, right down to the perfect pixie cut, but as she comes closer, she can make out the tortured expression on the woman's face, and she knows: this is the boys' mother, Miranda Matheson. No, her mind corrects quickly, Miranda Stevens, per Santos's info sheet on the family.

Meg instantly halts, not wanting to encroach but also not wanting to see for herself whether she's been replaced as Silas's primary pillar of comfort, tenuous as their reunion has been. And not liking herself for this reaction one bit. It's *good* the kids' mother is finally here, she reminds herself fiercely. Good for the boys, good for Darcy, trying to keep a rein on Silas. Good for everyone.

As they are both ushered back into the com van, she focuses on Santos instead, glad to see that he's covering all his bases this morning, from fresh boots on the ground to additional tech resources. She migrates to the mess van for a cup of weak coffee and a granola bar as he begins the morning announcements . . . which include more reminders about evidence recording and radio protocol. But then she hears the term "POD," and suddenly, he has her undivided attention.

Gripping her coffee cup, she joins the crowd, finding a place next to Max, who's straining to hear.

"What's he talking about?" Max hisses.

"The POD—probability of detection—determines the probability that a victim will be found—alive." She stumbles over the word. "It's reassessed lots of times during a search. Just like the search radius. It's normal."

Is she trying to convince Max or herself? Because unlike the radius, very little can be done to accommodate a POD or rectify it.

"POD is affected by four elements," Santos reminds the newbies in the crowd. He lifts his fingers one by one, counting off to four. "The searchers, the subject, the weather, and the environment."

"Spencer and Cameron have the first aspect in their favor," Meg tells Max in an undertone. "We're one of the best search units in Northern California." She gestures toward the Washoe team. "And look, we have help now."

"We can do everything right as a team," Santos continues, "but we have to accept that some aspects, like this weather, are out of our control." He pauses, and not for dramatic effect. Because he doesn't want to say what he needs to say next. Meg braces for it. "The Matheson boys' POD is low at this point, people."

Even expecting it, the reality of this situation hits Meg squarely in the gut. She looks around again for Danny, hoping to gain at least a modicum of comfort in his presence, but he's still a no-show.

A mutter blankets the crowd. Somewhere to Meg's right, a searcher calls out, "How much longer until this turns into a recovery effort, Lieutenant?"

The mutters turn into outright protest at the use of the dreaded R-word. Nothing deflates morale faster than a search turning into a recovery. Meg echoes the dissent all around her. It's only been two nights! No way is it time to change this rescue to a recovery. Immediately her training kicks in. It's been *two nights*. In freezing temperatures and rain. The time, whether she likes it or not, is coming. The fact that it's coming for Silas's kids is an extra punch to the gut.

Santos lifts one hand to quiet the crowd. "As of now, we are still operating as a rescue mission, folks! And even if—and it's only an *if* at this point—you're told we're in recovery mode, a quick find is as essential as ever."

Meg squeezes Max's arm in solidarity, because no one knows this better than her. *Fifteen years!* her brain screams. With no answers, no body, no recovery. How does a person just *disappear*?

She refocuses her attention on Santos. If she considers this a lost cause, if she resigns herself to looking for a body instead of a child—instead of two children—she may as well go home right now. Far better to search as if the clock is not ticking. It's the only way to keep putting one foot in front of the other when the hours drag into days.

"Listen," she tells Max, "no one's rolled the evidence tape out yet. So chin up, all right?"

"You mean like the tape at the lodge?"

"That's just protocol," she says swiftly, even as the thought of it makes her granola bar turn to sawdust in her mouth.

"Well, I come out here to search for *people*, not evidence or what-ever," Max grumbles.

"We all do. But while we do our job, we have to help the sheriff's department do theirs." Sometimes searches turned into investigations. And investigations turned into unsolved cases.

Her mind flashes to Teresa Howard, still advocating for her daughter after all these years, and she trashes what's left of her granola bar, her appetite lost. With effort she refocuses her attention on Santos, who has returned to the subject of evidence bags.

"When we find things, we don't touch them, people. We don't move them. We call any object into Command. I don't care if it's a rusted soda can or a cigarette butt or a damned juice box . . . we plot it on GPS. When a representative of the department arrives, they'll bag it."

Santos begins assigning everyone their next tasks, and Max looks relieved to be propelled toward the radio bank to retrieve his walkie, leaving Meg to fight her losing battle against dejection alone. She's just looking around to see if Danny has surfaced when she hears, "Tanner! You're with me again."

She's never been so glad to see Rick Waggins back in the staging area. To burn jet fuel two days running is rare. Despite Santos's less than optimistic "pep talk," Walters is sparing no expense for the Matheson boys. Suddenly she feels buoyant enough to take wing right here and now.

They don't waste any time firing up the Robinson R22, another relief. Waggins must have been up even earlier than her, making all the necessary calculations for the day's flight pattern. Danny finally materializes as she prepares to reboard for their Day 2 sweep of the mountains, offering to get her pack for her as she awaits her turn to climb in.

"Where have you been?" she asks as he hands her her gear.

Danny doesn't answer right away. "Walters had a few questions this morning."

"Of you?"

He clears his throat roughly and doesn't look her in the eye. "Routine, I'm sure. He says he chatted with you, too."

"We ran into one another by the lodge yesterday," she says, "just by happenstance." Though as she says this, she wonders how much of a coincidence that actually was. She looks hard at Danny, who is still stubbornly training his gaze just shy of eye contact. Should they compare notes? Do they need to debrief?

No; she and Danny don't have time for a conversation, anyway. The cloud cover this morning is low and the wind is insistent, but it's not yet raining, and Rick wants to get in the air quickly. She finally feels

Danny's eyes on her as she pulls her SAR hat from her head and stuffs it into his hands before ducking under the rotors to her place in the tiny cockpit beside Rick. The sun won't be an issue today.

"Hold up," Danny objects, his hand on her shoulder. When she turns, he bends toward her, placing a hasty kiss to the exposed skin of the side of her neck. "When you get back," he insists, speaking into the curve of her ear, "please get some proper rest before continuing on."

It's only after she's airborne, Danny an ever-shrinking form standing in the rotors' turbulent wake, the wind causing her cap to dance violently in his fist, that she realizes his words to her were every bit as bleak as Santos's. If he thinks rest is on the agenda, he doesn't expect her to set back down with anything to report other than shadowed ponderosa and craggy granite.

Rick navigates the helo back to the same area they were forced to abandon the night before, starting at Long Lake, at her insistence. As he flies over the flat expanse of the lake, Meg peers down at the endless ripples upon the water. The wind blows just enough to produce tiny whitecaps upon the surface, and the foam, combined with the reflected light of the sun bouncing off the metallic cloud banks, turns the color of the lake to stony gray. Its ominous appearance serves to remind Meg that within a day—maybe even within hours—the county's Emergency Service Aquatic Team, or ESAT, will likely be joining the fray, trolling the bottom in wide sweeps.

She thinks again of Silas back at base having to see these teams preparing, knowing the implications, and her stomach clenches. Then she remembers he has Miranda with him now, just as the helo takes a dip through a particularly nasty air pocket, and she nearly loses her breakfast. She refocuses on what she can control, forcing her eyes open just a bit wider and concentrating even harder on the frustratingly camouflaged terrain below her. She wants to beat ESAT to it. She wants what she knows *they* want . . . for their job to become obsolete.

She spots the first hint of an unnatural object amid the forest approximately thirty seconds after clearing the far side of the lake. The pop of dark blue on the uphill slope isn't anything dramatic. She might have even imagined this slightest shift in the pattern playing out before her eyes, a subtle alteration to the green trees and brown dirt, green trees and gray granite. She doesn't want to get her hopes up but reaches out to tap Rick on the shoulder anyway. Pressing down the talk button of their shared intercom, she asks him to retrace his last sweep, starting back at the eastern edge of the lake.

This time, as he repeats his air pattern, Meg cranes her neck, bending her body nearly horizontal in her attempt to look straight down. The side of one skid blocks her vision, and she leans still further, the chest harness now digging into her clavicle, but this new position has earned her an unrestricted view of the treetops. Rick slows, dropping to the lowest elevation he dares, and from this height, Meg can even see a few patches of bare ground between the tree trunks. She strains her eyes, willing them to once again pick out the tiny scrap of color she's now sure she saw.

At first nothing's out of place: not one branch, not one stone. The forest appears so damn *serene* Meg blinks back the quick sting of frustrated tears. She requests yet another sweep, and this time Rick looks dubious as he yields, signaling to Meg that this'll be the last one.

The last sweep . . . the last sweep . . . She squints, trying desperately to make the most of it, grasping at any chance to return to base with good news for Silas, with a newly written ending to the awful indeterminateness of fifteen years ago. But now the pressure feels too intense, and she's consumed with doubt. Danny was right; she should have slept more. Her eyes are watering . . . she's ill-equipped . . . someone else should have taken her place . . . and still she strains to see, leaning as far as the belt will allow, and then, amazingly—

"*There!*" she yells into the mic, loud enough that she should have made Rick wince. Instead, he shouts in agreement, and she knows he's seen it too. She experiences a heady surge of vindication, the kind that fills the bloodstream like an exoneration, and then they're returning to the site in the tightest circle Rick can manage.

It's a pair of pants. Blue jeans, to be exact. They lie discarded on the ground, their abandoned presence much more ominous than Long Lake's volumes of unsearched terrain directly behind the helo's flight path. Just beyond the pants, Meg can see a very small pond. It sits off trail, which explains how her ground team had missed it, in a tiny clearing like a flat silver dollar. As they hover, the rotors seeming to work double time, she scans it, bracing herself to see what she doesn't want to see: the black speck of a body upon its surface.

The water, however, appears undisturbed, which only builds the suspense in Meg's brain. The pants are here, and while they could be anyone's, they're not—she already knows they're not, in the hollow of her gut—and then, just beyond the jeans, she spots a pair of shoes. From this distance she can't make out the brand—they're looking for Nikes—but they're small, and they're a child's, and even as she alerts Rick, part of her wishes she were anywhere but in this Godforsaken helicopter.

This is why you're here, she reminds herself angrily. This is the break they've all been hoping for, but she's so terrified of the finality of what's in store that Meg can barely stand being in her own skin. She wishes desperately—and so selfishly it hurts—for anyone else's vantage point at this very instant.

They dip still lower, but the trees are dense around the circumference of the pond, and she can't quite make out its banks. They turn south a few degrees, and then north, and Meg is about to pause in her efforts to call in what they've found so far—it's the biggest break all search—when she sees him.

At her cry, Rick whips his head around and sucks in a breath so violently Meg hears the echo reverberate from her headset into her eardrums. The child is lying behind a fallen log, partially obscured by river weed. He's prone, dressed in nothing but a T-shirt and underwear, and he looks so pitifully discarded with his face in the dirt and his wet hair caked in mud, tears instantly obliterate Meg's vision. She strains through the blur, but it's no use. From this height, Meg has no way of knowing if the child is alive or dead.

Rick pauses in flight, and they quiver there in midair like a huge hummingbird while he waits for her to radio in. It's imperative they communicate these coordinates before finding a suitable landing zone, but how can she, when she cannot yet determine status? The image of the child—which one, she's still uncertain—is burning a hole in her brain, and she's not sure she can pick up the mobile radio just yet. Not while Silas is somewhere below, surely standing by.

"Maybe we should land first," she says weakly through their intercom.

"What? No. Call. It. In." Rick's tone leaves no room for argument. "And don't forget to color-code it, Meg."

The instruction hits like a punch to her gut. Eyes smarting, throat constricting, she wraps her palm around the radio, switches to the proper channel—MRA-1—and depresses the talk button.

"Helo One to Base."

"Helo One, this is Base. Go ahead."

"Base, we have a find." She can barely get the words out. Is Silas there? Is Silas listening?

Darcy's voice sounds as clipped as Meg's is cautious. "Status, Helo One?"

A sudden surge of static makes Meg's skin jump. She worries for a second she might retch. "From the air," she transmits slowly, "we see one subject." She pauses again, and then continues in a rush. "Black appears likely."

Even through the squelch of the airwaves, she can hear the thickness to her tone, betraying her attempt to sound neutral. To not further alarm Silas. He won't need a course in radio communication to interpret what she's saying. To know what this might mean.

After she communicates their GPS coordinates, the helo rises below her feet, angling sharply left. Rick cannot land, not right here. It takes him several more sweeps to spot a suitable LZ, and then they lower slowly, putting down in a dry marsh bed. Rick powers down while Meg releases the bulky jump kit of medical supplies from the side of the cockpit. They can't be farther than a quarter mile from the pond, but she charts the coordinates of this new location anyway and relies on the GPS to direct them back to the site. As they take off at a fast jog—following the prompts of the GPS won't allow for an outright sprint—her mind races to recall every bit of first aid she's ever had to learn. Despite her initial assessment, she hopes with everything in her being that her education will be put to use.

They find the boy quickly, still prone, still exactly as they last saw him. Meg sinks to the ground at his side, and after only one glance she determines him to be the older of the two Matheson brothers. *This is Spencer.* The bare skin of his legs is almost as gray as the water. But Meg's seen dead bodies. She knows firsthand the way they elicit an instant, answering response from the living, breathing searcher who finds them, an instinctive recoiling that prickles the skin in a rush of gooseflesh that alerts to the fact that something is off. And she's not feeling it.

This is a case of prolonged and advanced hypothermia. "We need to roll him over," she tells Rick, praying that she's right. She gives a count, and they turn him toward them—he's light, it's easy—and she bends toward the child until she's nearly flat on the ground herself. The marshy earth immediately soaks through her pants at her knees, and the pond water seeps into her boots, but she presses her face directly to Spencer's cold cheek, concentrating solely on the puff of breath she's desperate to feel.

When she detects nothing, she leans in closer. Her hair brushes Spencer's nose, and Meg thinks she feels his breath, just barely. It's nothing more than the slightest stirring of the air—even this kid's chest is unmoving—and as Meg presses two fingers to his carotid artery at the side of his neck to gauge his pulse, she turns back to Rick. "A mirror!" she orders. "In my pack. Side pocket."

He produces it quickly, holding it out just in front of Spencer's mouth. They freeze, and then, unbelievably, they see it. The slightest trace of condensation fogs the surface of the tiny mirror, and for the first time since falling to Spencer's side, both Meg and Rick take a full breath themselves.

Now Meg knows the pulse is there . . . *has to be here* . . . *has to be here* . . . and when she finally detects it, she laughs out loud, even though it's just the faintest thread of a beat against the pad of her fingers. *"Spencer,"* she says, her voice cracking. "We're here, Spencer."

He's breathing, and his heart is beating, and now that they're talking to him, it's clear he's semiconscious. His eyelids flutter, and then close, his lashes shockingly dark against the ashen skin tone of his cheeks, but he's *alive*, and even as Rick digs into the jump kit for an emergency blanket, Meg reaches for her radio. This time, when she connects to Base, she doesn't hesitate.

"Darcy? We're on-site." She doesn't wait to be confirmed. *"We have red."* She's asked to repeat, and she doesn't mind a bit. She hears herself laughing in relief and in elation, but she doesn't attempt to contain it. *"We have red."*

22

SILAS

Silas avoided Meg for two full weeks following their hike to the mines, and he suspected the effort was mutual. Maybe, with some distance between them, the magnetic tug that threatened to pull them both under wouldn't feel so visceral. Maybe betraying his best friend could still be avoided if he and Meg just ran out the clock. He told Danny that Uncle Les had him working morning until night during peak season at the lodge, which wasn't a lie, but only because Silas had willingly volunteered, to which Aunt Mary had reacted by checking his forehead for a fever.

"Let the boy help, if he's got a mind to," Les told her. "He'll be headed to college soon, and then where will we be?"

Where would Meg *be?* When summer was over, would she choose safety or possibility, the expected or the unknown? No matter what else happened, he hoped she'd take a chance at her own path. He remembered how intently she'd bent over the map and compass by Long Lake, eager to learn, ready to explore, and he felt better about those odds, but only just.

And so he cleaned out guest cabins with a zeal that earned him a satisfied nod from Uncle Les, stacked wood for the nightly bonfire in record time, and sorted the linen closet so efficiently Mary couldn't find anything anymore. While, for all he knew, Danny and Meg carried on with their lives down in Feather River, doing whatever they'd always done before Silas had entered their lives.

And this was the tortured thought that broke his resolve. He caved and called Cairns, and that very weekend he and Meg both returned to Marble Lake Lodge to lend a hand with the chores, just like old times. Only it wasn't like old times at all, because that magnetic pull between him and Meg was instantly back, as if it had never been gone at all. Which it hadn't been, of course. Silas noticed how Meg took care to keep some physical space between them, standing apart from the boys at the rail of the upper deck after work, where the breeze tickled the tips of the conifers. The height, combined with the sea of forest below her, reminded Silas of a woman standing vigil at the bow of a ship.

"Let's go to the lake," he said abruptly, because the way she held herself apart—right here but as unreachable as ever—was almost as bad as her not being here at all. He grabbed snacks in the kitchen and led the charge to the Marble Lake boathouse, where he made it a point to rehash Danny's tale of heroism from when they were kids.

Meg shot him a glance—gratitude? Shared guilt?—but Danny seemed unimpressed with Silas's latest rendition, which now had Danny rowing both boats back to safety singlehandedly. Instead of chiming in or rolling his eyes like usual when Silas exaggerated, he mechanically skipped rocks from the lakeshore in moody silence, one after the other.

Had Meg said something to him?

But when he chanced breaking her unwritten arm's-length-apart rule to ask as ambiguously as he could if anything was up, she supplied in a flat whisper, eyes forward on the lake, "He's been in a bad mood ever since I told him I am definitely attending Davis."

Silas felt his face break wide open. "Wait, for real?" he breathed, basking in this slice of sunshine that had just wedged its way through the shadow of their confusion.

She nodded but then frowned. "I just hope I get enough grant money. My mom got the paperwork started late."

But that was okay. Grants could be dealt with. Right? He was still smiling at her stupidly when Danny turned and frowned at them, and the indignation he'd felt when Meg had explained the reason for their argument on the Jeep ride flooded Silas again, popping the bubble of his happiness for Meg. How dared Danny make Meg's college choices all about him? But Meg's face pleaded with him to keep the peace, so the only recourse left to him was a lame "What exactly's up your butt, Danny?" He'd make *him* say it, if Meg wouldn't.

But Danny just tossed one more rock—it skipped an impressive seven times—and then said with a shrug, "Just bored, I guess."

"What he means is, we can't compete with the fire station." Meg forced a laugh. "He's been there pretty much nonstop the last few weeks."

"Oh yeah?" At least that meant Meg hadn't been spending all her free time with him, while Silas had been in self-exile.

"Guess it just felt like it was time to grow up, you know?" Danny looked smugger than Silas thought he had a right to. He was washing fire rigs in the vehicle bay, not pulling babies out of burning buildings.

But Silas could play by his terms. "That mean you don't like gummy worms anymore, big man?" he said, meaner, really, than he'd intended, holding Danny's share of the bag over his head.

Which had Danny lunging for them, knocking into Silas with a force that made him wonder exactly how long he'd been wanting to do that. Silas was in the water now, Danny glowering over him from the boathouse ramp, Meg yelling at them both. When Silas shoved the bag of gummy worms into Danny's chest with a grunted *"Here,"* Danny threw it back at him. They landed in the lake, where they bobbed on the whitecaps erratically until Meg plucked them out.

"Knock it off," she told them, and when Danny turned in protest, she added, "He's only goading you to make me mad."

She clamped her mouth shut immediately, but it was too late. The words hung heavily in the air between the three of them until Danny finally said, "Why would that make you mad?"

Meg opted for offense as the best defense. "Maybe because I don't want to spend my last few weeks of the summer with you at each other's throats!"

As a tension-breaker, it worked, though Danny's mood remained dour. And Meg went right back to careful self-containment. Because she had decided to pretend this thing between them wasn't happening? Or because she wanted to spend these last precious days in Silas's company, however she could? He just didn't know, which was why, when Danny insisted on returning to the swimming hole on the eve of their last Saturday of the summer, Silas didn't argue. He didn't even complain when they couldn't find parking along the BLM road leading to the river, the place was so crowded. It wasn't until they were hiking half a mile along the road that he broke.

"If we're going to trek through the woods anyway, we might as well be up at the mines." He chanced a glance at Meg, but she kept her gaze pointedly on the shoulder of the road.

"We're almost there," Danny said.

"How about tomorrow?" He tried again to catch Meg's eye, just to fail again. "We can see if we can find some new ones. It'll be like a celebration of the end of the summer."

"I work at the station on Saturdays." That *I'm a grown-up and you're a child* look had returned to Danny's face.

"That doesn't mean we should all just sit around. Sorry, but your schedule sucks, man."

They'd arrived at the river, and Danny paused to look for a place to set their stuff. "Yeah," he answered, carelessly enough that it didn't sound careless at all. "Career goals can really get in the way of scavenger hunts or whatever."

Only when they're your *goals,* Silas wanted to shout. Just to get away from him, he leaped into the swimming hole, sandals and T-shirt and all. The shock of the cold didn't manage to shake off his own sour mood, however. Neither did the sight of Jessica Howard standing over him when he broke the surface a few seconds later, dangling his towel out in front of her.

"Come and get it?" She laughed a bit uncertainly.

Silas hefted himself out of the water with a grunt, his shirt clinging to his stomach and dripping water as he climbed back up onto the rocks.

"Keep it," he said.

Color rushed into her face, sending an instant kick of remorse through Silas. "Shit, I'm sorry," he told her, as she just stood there with the towel, clearly trying not to let tears betray her.

"Danny said you'd think it was funny," she managed. "You guys are always goofing off and stuff."

"Yeah, I don't know why I said that," he told her, shooting a look of fury at Cairns.

Something suspiciously like pettiness flashed across Danny's face. "Maybe we can make it up to you," he told Jessica. "What are you doing tomorrow?"

This time Silas pierced him with his best impression of Aunt Mary's ultimate *Now you've crossed a line* face, but clearly Danny didn't give a damn about filthy looks.

"Working. But only until five," Jessica answered, her tone now cautiously optimistic. "Why?"

"We're going hiking out past Marble Lake Lodge in the evening," Danny said. "To find some cool mines. You should come."

"Hold up. We were going to do that during the day. And I thought you had to be at the station on Saturday," Silas interjected.

Danny waved him off. "If we wait until evening it'll be cooler. And then Jessica and I can come." He smiled at her. "It'll be fun," he prompted. "Like old times."

Silas clenched his fists by his sides. How many times had he told Danny to cut that shit out?

"Yeah, sure," Jessica agreed, after a shy glance in Silas's direction. He forced his face to remain neutral. What else could he do, after having acted like such an asshole? "I'd love to join."

Disappointment dropped like a rock to the pit of Silas's stomach. All he wanted was one more day with Meg, however he could get it. He already had to surrender to Danny, with his ever-growing chip on his shoulder. He certainly didn't need to contend with Jessica, too, trying too hard to fit into what was already set in stone. One look at Meg told him he wasn't alone in this, though she replaced her dismay with studied indifference an instant later, disappearing into the frigid water of the swimming hole in a graceful pencil dive.

Just shy of twenty-four hours later, Silas was only a quarter mile down the trail to the mines—his and *Meg's* mines—boxed in between Danny ahead of him and Jessica trailing after, with no room for escape. Meg somehow had taken the lead, a good fifty yards clear of Jessica's now cheerful prattle.

It was already after seven, the sun below Marble Peak, so they took the shortcut up the slope at the far side of the lodge. When they'd connected to the Lakes Loop trail at the top of the ridge, Jessica hadn't let up, Danny peppering her with questions whenever she paused for breath. One more "Then what happened?" or "Well, what did *she* say?" and Silas was going to lose it.

On Danny, to be clear. Not Jessica. None of this was her fault, even if she was giving him a headache, twirling the chain of that J necklace of hers every few steps, the silver pendant catching the light of the sinking sun and flashing like a fish, leaving Silas blinded.

"You can signal for our rescue if we get lost," he said, in as good a humor as he could muster.

"What? Why?" she asked, instantly worried.

"S-O-S," Danny spelled out—literally—from up the trail. "He's joking." But instead of laughing, Jessica fisted her hand around the necklace, stilling it.

"I thought you might like that I wore it," she said.

"Huh? Why?"

She seemed unsure how to answer, but for an instant her eyes flicked past Silas toward Danny. He remembered something Meg had said after graduation, how Jessica had been poking around, trying to figure out who had gifted her with the pendant. And a sinking suspicion dawned. He turned around and forced Jessica to pause on the trail, while Danny hiked on.

"Listen, Jess," he said, "If Danny said anything about your neck-lace . . . like, if he implied it was me who gave it to you or something, I want you to know it wasn't."

Her face fell, and he knew then he'd guessed right. *Goddammed Danny.* It was mean, plain and simple, toying with Jessica like that. Just like when he'd encouraged her to tease Silas with that towel yesterday. And had invited her along today. And why? Just because he'd never been able to get it into his stupid skull that Silas did not want to be with her?

A second possibility made itself known, tingling its way down Silas's spine. Maybe Meg's college plans were not at the source of Danny's recent angst.

Once he allowed himself to go there, Silas's certainty grew. Danny knew something. About him and Meg. And this was his way to throw a wrench in things. But could Danny Boy Scout Cairns be that devious? Silas frowned into the early-evening sunshine.

Jessica misinterpreted the look and gave him a forced smile. "Guess it was from Sam, then," she said with a lightness that didn't ring true. But she tucked the pendant back under the neckline of her tee with two manicured fingers. "Shall we?" she said, gesturing toward the trail. "We're falling behind."

"Yeah," he told her, offering a smile in return. "Want to lead on?"

Jessica waved him forward. "No, no, you're the fearless leader."

He promised himself he'd try to be, to make the best of this shitty night if he could, but as the brush and forest thickened, he grew angrier and angrier at Danny. It wasn't that hard to dredge up more animosity—he was already bitter that Danny was with Meg, already jealous that the two of them were, right this very minute, far ahead on the trail, hiking together and leaving him stuck behind—and now this?

They were waiting for Silas and Jessica at the junction. "Finally," Danny said. "I assumed you'd pulled some dumb prank and we'd be waiting to pick up the pieces."

Silas just glowered at him. "Nothing like that," he said tightly. But when they all resumed, Danny's comment planted a seed of an idea in his head. So, Danny expected a prank, did he? They were on the switchback section of the trail, making their way slowly up the slope toward Long Lake, and if Silas cut a swath directly uphill, through the sagebrush, he could bypass the majority of the zigzagging route, arriving at the ridge well before the others. And if he hurried, he'd have time to hide himself, to wait for Danny to appear first around the bend. And then he would get a taste of how it felt to get messed with.

He stopped again on the trail and made a show of fiddling with his backpack. "Shoot. Something's wrong with my strap."

Jessica leaned in to look, but Silas waved her forward. "You go on," he told her. "It's already getting dark."

She followed his gaze to where the shadows had lengthened over the ridge and nodded solemnly. "What about you?"

"I'll catch up," he promised. When she hesitated, he added a self-deprecating shrug. "So much for my fearless leadership, I guess."

She laughed, and then she was gone, hiking uphill around the bend. Silas wasted no time, legs churning up the slope, sage slapping at his bare arms. Within minutes he had hit the ridge, bent double, panting for breath. He glanced down the trail but couldn't hear anyone coming yet, so he took his time scanning for a suitable hiding place. When he spotted the low-hanging limb of a tall sugar pine leaning heavily over the trail, bent from years of wind and snow, he seized the opportunity, hefting himself into its branches.

And then he waited, breathless, belly to the bark. It wasn't easy; the limb arched steeply and wasn't all that fat, and it took a lot of core work, really, to keep himself steady. He was concealed, he thought, but just barely; any shift of his torso and he'd probably give himself away.

It seemed like forever before he heard voices, and when he did he frowned. Because it sounded like the girls were in front now. A stealthy peek as they approached confirmed that Meg was now in the lead, followed by Jessica, with Danny bringing up the rear. Maybe when Jessica had caught up, she'd explained Silas's predicament, and he'd gone back to check? A prickle of doubt made itself known; it wasn't too late to change his mind. He could just hop down right now, no one the wiser.

But then his boot caught on a branch of pine needles, sending a few fluttering to the ground, and Meg caught the movement. Her sharp eyes traveled from the branch to Silas's face in a heartbeat, and for a brief second he was sure he caught the hint of a smirk on her face.

It was as if a fuse he hadn't known existed had been lit inside him, and he doubled down on his plan, arms encircling the limb tightly. The enthusiasm of his movement unbalanced him, and his body listed right, then left, like a wobbly canoe, but he managed to hold on tight as Meg passed under the tree, feigning ignorance of what loomed above her. He only had to hang on long enough for Jessica to pass, and then Danny would be directly below him and Silas could leap, scaring the living daylights out of him.

And it would have worked beautifully had his hand, gripping the bark, not slipped—sending Silas spiraling downward to fall in a heap not an inch from Jessica's face. He landed with an *"Oof,"* the breath knocked out of his chest, and the only thing he heard for what felt like the span of a full minute was her ongoing, never-ending scream.

When he managed to pull himself to his feet, he was just in time to see the back of Jessica's ponytail disappearing down the trail as she lit out in a full sprint in the direction from which they'd come.

Danny and Meg both yelled in tandem for Jessica to stop. Silas still couldn't draw a full breath. "Oh hell," he muttered, when he could.

Beside him, Danny took on the role of Mr. Responsibility. "*You* get to go chase her down."

"*You* invited her!"

"*You* made this mess!" Danny shot back.

"Enough!" Meg shouted. "We all need to go after her!"

Jessica moved fast for a girl in sandals, Silas could say that much for her. The three of them had run nearly a hundred yards before they caught sight of her again, and even then, it was too dark now to see more than the dull outline of her bright-pink crop top through the trees. Silas knew he should take out his flashlight, but he didn't want to waste the time. His footsteps increased in speed, but Jessica had a heavy dose of adrenaline on her side: she kept the gap between them wide. By the time Silas felt close enough to call out to her, all the air had been sucked from his lungs.

They paused, panting, somewhere midway down the slope.

"We should all split up," Danny suggested, and that was fine by Silas; he was already in motion again, legs churning downhill.

"Head back to the fork in the trail!" Danny shouted after him. "Meg will go up. Who the hell knows where she'd go?"

"Yeah. Okay!" Silas was already several strides down the trail. "You stay here in case she comes back."

He made it to the V in record time, and stopped again, yelling out into the gathering darkness. "Jessica! Jess!"

Nothing.

And so he took off again, heading back uphill this time, because no way was Jessica faster than him, covering this much ground in her sandals. Just above the V, he ran smack into Meg.

"Shit!" she gasped, stumbling backward.

"Sorry!" he shouted.

Her hand clamped down on Silas's arm, presumably to steady him, but it was her expression that stopped him cold. It was that underlying urgency—that lit fuse—that he felt radiating from her nearly all the time these days, staring him right in the face.

"What were you thinking?" she said, kind of shaking him.

"Danny," he gasped, because this was all his mind had room for. "I think he knows."

He didn't have to say what about. That was what Silas snagged on, in that moment, in his mind. Meg didn't ask. She knew.

"But Jessica," she said weakly, and Silas nodded. Jessica would tire herself out eventually; she might have slowed or even stopped already. She was probably just out of sight through the trees, feeling foolish for overreacting. With just one more sprint they could catch her, if Danny didn't beat them to it.

But they didn't try, not even after they'd recovered their breath. Meg just looked at Silas with the same intensity with which he looked at her. It was this one small act of shared rebellion that brought Silas's thoughts full circle to the rapidly waning time they had left together. Tonight had been snatched from them, but they could snatch it back.

Was she thinking the same thing? Did Meg want what he wanted right now?

He wouldn't waste another moment before finding out. One hand on Meg's bicep, he guided her backward a few yards into the trees. The muscle beneath her skin jumped, as it always seemed to do at his touch, but she didn't resist.

"She'll head back down the trail to the lodge," he whispered. It was logical, after all. And even if Jessica *wasn't* logical, and climbed back uphill instead, she'd run headlong into Danny.

Meg nodded, still treading carefully backward with her eyes trained on the ground so as not to snap the scattered twigs underfoot.

She did know, then. What he wanted. And she wanted it, too. Her back hit the rough trunk of a ponderosa, her breath departing her lungs with an *"Oof"* she immediately muffled. They waited, listening, scarcely daring to breathe, their chests rising and falling hard in the quiet.

Neither of them spoke. Silas kept his hand on Meg's arm, and she remained frozen, her back still against the tree. So close. The distance between them finally nonexistent. Down the trail there was only silence; uphill they could no longer hear Danny's shouts, and Silas knew it was a lame cliché, but time seemed to freeze, like the world had paused just for them. But then:

"What was that?" Meg breathed.

The snap of needles and branches. Jessica must have rethought her course and was now heading back toward them. In a minute she'd be upon them. Silas cursed under his breath. Would she never just *go away?*

He didn't know how it occurred to him to do what he did. Ever afterward he'd remain convinced that when motivated, the human mind can conjure up its best and worst brainstorms within a split second's time. In this particular second, his managed to do both.

Just as Jessica came back into view on the trail, still half crying, half whimpering, Silas bent down and snagged the first thing he touched: a handful of small rocks. His gaze met Meg's again in the darkness: she saw the rocks in his hand, could read the desperation on his face. Without a doubt she knew what he was about to do. That he couldn't . . . just *couldn't* . . . let Jessica ruin this last chance between them. Let Danny deal with her. Silas couldn't allow this opportunity to pass.

He let one small rock fly.

Later, he would wonder if it had been that one stone, that single effortless release cast in a perfect arc against an inky sky, that had changed their lives forever. He heard it land on target with a flat thump in the dirt to the right of Jessica's feet and saw her shadowed outline jerk back as if the pebble had come with strings attached.

"Silas? Is that you?" She didn't sound very sure. "If it is, knock it off!"

Silas stared at Meg, who stared back, silent and still, her mouth tightly closed.

"Silas? I mean it!"

There was a slight huff, and then . . . nothing.

They waited, breathing in sync in the dark, listening for any more telltale cracks of twigs or pine needles. Waited for what felt like ages, until the silence blanketed them completely. And then Silas let the remaining pebbles, still clutched in his hand, fall silently to the ground, because finally, *finally,* he and Meg were truly alone. The darkness now complete around them in the canopy of the forest, he stepped close to her. She wasn't crying, but she was close. He could hear the slight shake on each ragged exhale.

"What are we doing?" she gasped.

"You know what we're doing." He reached blindly through the darkness until his hand found the side of her face. He half expected her to freeze, but she yielded, turning hesitantly into his touch as his fingers curved over her jawbone. "You do."

She swallowed, one tiny muscle constricting below the hollow of her ear. Had Silas not been reading her by feel, he would have missed it altogether.

He let his thumb travel across the plane of her lower lip, back and forth, and still she let him, leaning forward just enough that her shorts-clad thighs grazed his in the dark. Her skin was cool. She curled her hand around his wrist to keep her balance.

His mouth hovered inches from hers, and then less, and Meg wavered, and Silas waited for her, his own breath caught tight in his throat. *Cass,* he thought—he was afraid to speak and tip the balance—and then Meg's chin tilted upward, her jaw sliding under his palm, and she was kissing him.

He reacted with an intensity that pressed her back against the tree. She released a single strangled noise, and he slid one hand behind her head, cradling it against the rough bark. Meg *was* crying now—he could feel her tears wetting the cracks between his fingers—but her hands dropped from his arms to his back, pulling him closer as she explored the arched curve of his spine through his shirt. He shifted his weight against her, one leg settling between hers to brace her more securely against the tree, maybe to hear her gasp again, maybe to keep his balance.

They remained that way, bodies pressed hard and close, as time seemed to stretch and fold upon itself. They had months and months to make up for, after all. Silas's hand had just slid under Meg's tee when they heard the single, piercing sound cut through the darkness.

She pulled back. "What was that? That horrible . . . was that *Jessica*?"

It had sounded like a scream, but Silas didn't want to call it that. "Do you think she yelled?" Maybe if he formed it as a question in his head, it wouldn't be true. Because he could see that stone in his mind's eye again, could watch its arc as it had flown. He'd never wanted to hurt anyone. Least of all Jessica.

Meg leaned back against the tree, her hands running a wide swath through her hair. "What-are-we-going-to-do?" she managed in one exhale.

"We'll go find her." It was the right thing to do. It was the only thing to do. "C'mon. It will be all right."

But they didn't know which direction to start in. Turning in circles, they called out to her and then listened, Silas first thinking they should head back uphill, Meg disagreeing, adamant that the cry had echoed from below. Amid the acoustics of the mountains it was impossible to determine where the sound had come from. Jessica could be anywhere within hearing distance. Silas reached out and captured Meg's now-cold hand. Straining to see her expression in the dark, he held it loosely until she shifted her fingers through his.

"We'll find her," he repeated, squeezing her hand. "And then we'll find Danny."

23

Silas

All around Silas, the staging area is in a frenzy of activity. Amid the cacophony of commands and shouts of instruction issuing from the com van, he hears that the subject Meg found is Spencer. He repeats this revelation slowly in his head, relishing it—*Meg found Spencer*—and then again aloud, grasping Miranda in united relief. Her arrival to the scene had brought an atypical tension to their usual dynamic, thanks to Silas's lack of communication, which mercifully dissipates, at least somewhat, in the reprieve this moment has granted them. What he's hoped for most, clutched tight in his fist, has been preserved, at least for one of his children. *Spencer,* he thinks, *Spencer, Spencer,* and while a red status still indicates the subject is in critical condition—he knows this now . . . it's been explained to him—it's *something*. It's something to hold on to when he resigned himself to nothing, and as the ground teams stand by, and Miranda cries softly, and the sheriff's team uses a satellite phone to raise an emergency medic team, which is already en route, Silas paces the narrow confines of the com van. He'll give Darcy only the amount of time it takes to place this call, and then he's headed to the site himself, team or no team.

Of course, in keeping with the horrific pattern of this whole ordeal, his hopes remain cleanly sliced down the middle.

"What about Cameron?" he asks Santos in a tight rush as they wait for Darcy to get off the line with Washoe Medical Center in Reno.

"Yes, where's Cameron?" Miranda echoes. It's not that their younger son's status has only just occurred to them, Silas decides. Just that they've only now gathered the courage to ask.

Santos shakes his head. There's been no mention at all of Cameron via the radio, and Silas's gut tightens anew in a torturous twist. Does he want news? Does he not? He has no idea, his emotions are so thoroughly scrambled. But then Darcy turns toward him, and he has to focus on what they *do* know.

"Thirty minutes," she tells him. In thirty minutes, the medic flight they've had on standby for twenty-four hours will have arrived from Reno, but it will be unable to land in the same narrow meadow the tiny R22 navigated. "It will have to touch down here, in the parking lot, which means Spencer will need to be carried out to it."

Santos pulls the team combing the lodge grounds and reassigns them to Spencer-retrieval duty. "Finding him indicates that Cameron, too, will be better served with all volunteers in the field," he explains, while Silas thinks, *About time.* No more resources will be wasted looking for his kids where he knows without a doubt they are not.

The trail is too rocky and narrow for ATVs, so it's determined that Miranda will wait here at camp for the medic flight, while the field medical team sets out on foot with the additional ground pounders, Silas and Santos among them. They hike at a blistering speed along the Lakes Loop trail over the ridge to Long Lake and then down the other side, cutting off at the shoreline to follow the GPS coordinates

Meg provided. Apparently the pond where Spencer was found is seasonal, swelling after a wet fall, and it takes Silas a moment to orient himself. When he does, he realizes they are uphill from the nearside of the lake . . . confirming his hunch that the boys may have sought higher elevations. How high did they climb? Before Spencer ended up at the pond, was he traveling uphill or downhill? The unanswered questions plague him, needling at him from every angle. His entire body reacts to the sting of it: coming this far, finding Spencer, but with no answers at all. No trace of Cameron.

They're in constant radio contact with Rick and Meg, on scene, as they hike, and then they're *there*, and the sight of Spencer is the greatest jolt to Silas's system he's ever experienced. Because who is this small stranger, ashen to the point of lifelessness? Not Spencer, surely. He's wrapped tightly in a blanket, his head cradled on Meg's lap with his eyes closed, and instead of the critically injured boy in front of him, Silas sees the infant Spencer once was, as though viewing him from the vantage point of a dream. He's a chubby toddler, struggling to walk, and then he's a child with tousled blond hair and bright eyes who trails after Silas every chance he gets, each earnest stride stretched wide to match his father's footfalls. He's starting school, and then he's hiking almost in step, leaning over the rail of the Marble Peak fire tower, narrow shoulders bent in a graceful arc, and *oh!* How can a life—a life sustained and not even his own—be flashing before his eyes?

He makes a sound like a sob and falls at Meg's knee. He reaches out to take Spencer from her arms, but several hands stop him at once. People shout at him. Something about holding C-spine, precautions, preventing shock. He's yanked back, away from his boy, his hands still empty. He has to pacify himself with a featherlight touch to Spencer's forehead, a murmuring of *There now, you're safe now,* and the reward of a fluttered eyelid.

A moment later a team is counting down from five, and then Spencer is lifted, to be carried out of the wilderness on a portable gurney. Silas starts to follow alongside, pressing closely enough for his hip to collide with the edge of the orange plastic backboard, but then what about Cameron? There's a good chance his younger son is nearby, isn't there? He scans the forest, spinning in circles, torn.

"Go with Spencer," Meg urges him, already trotting back toward the helicopter perched on its makeshift landing zone. "We'll keep looking!"

He takes stock of the activity around him and realizes she's right: teams are already being redivided and sent in various directions, and if the helo gets airborne again, the best place for him to be is by a radio. He runs to catch up with Spencer's gurney.

He continues to talk to his son nonstop the entire way back to the staging area, despite still receiving very little in response. He strokes Spencer's head, sweeping the hair away from his closed eyes, and tells him he's loved, and safe, and that soon he'll be warm and fed. He tells him to simply breathe, and once, maybe twice more, Spencer blinks in response, his throat working as though struggling to swallow. Silas shouts for water, but his demands are denied; Spencer's core temperature is too high a risk. Ingesting the cold liquid will only further deplete his son's waning reserve of energy, Santos explains.

Halfway back to the staging area, the sound of the R22's rotors thunders overhead. The promised second sweep. Silas cranes his neck to catch a glimpse of Meg in the spotter position.

"They'll do a focused search of this square mile," Santos tells him.

Others nod in approval as Silas swallows a hard lump that's formed in his throat. It's either hope or dread, or an awful mixture of both. In the hollow space left behind, he finally builds the nerve necessary to ask Spencer the direct question everyone needs to hear. Because what if he knows the answer?

He wills his voice not to break. "Do you know where Cameron is, son?"

Spencer's dry lips close together in a repeat of one syllable—*Cam*— and everyone halts with bated breath. Silas leans nearly prone over the gurney, but Spencer says nothing further. Perhaps his few stirrings of consciousness are simply due to the jostling of the gurney. Perhaps his whisper of his brother's name is nothing more than the slight loll of his small head from one side to the other as they navigate the rough terrain, the board pitching forward or back depending on the grade of the earth beneath their boots or the severity of the incline.

But then: "Cam?" Spencer murmurs again, with confusion, and Silas's heart threatens to beat right out of his ribcage.

"Yes, Cam." He presses in close to Spencer's dry, cracked, cold lips. "Do you remember where he is?"

Spencer's small mouth turns down at the corners, just slightly, like he might begin to cry, if he had the energy. Silas thinks he shakes his head, though the slight movement could be just more jostling.

"We'll find him," Silas promises, heart breaking. "You just rest."

At the staging area, the medic flight helicopter waits with Miranda and Darcy, its blades cutting the cold air and sending it in every direction. A huge part of Silas longs to leap into the bay with Spencer and join him and his mother on his thirty-minute commute to Washoe Medical Center in Reno, but the med flight team assures him Spencer is stable, or will be, at least, once secured in the warm transport cabin, and Silas's brain is still screaming *Cameron,* tearing a jagged line through his conscience, rending him in two. They tell him it's his choice, but when the time comes to step onto the runner to enter the cockpit, he's still immobile.

"Stay," Miranda shouts from the helo, "I got Spence," and he nods gratefully as the rotors send a gust of air in his direction. With their tag-teaming strategy restored, he won't have to leave their younger son in this wilderness alone.

He feels Santos's hand on his shoulder and turns. "The moment he's awake and alert, he's only a thirty-minute flight away."

Silas nods. He knows that right now, Spencer's finally finding some comfort. In the meantime that breath of a word—*Cam*—continues to echo in Silas's mind, fueling him forward.

"They must have been together," he tells Santos. He grips the man's shirt. "We have to continue looking right by that pond."

Santos calmly peels Silas's fingers from his sleeve. "The search area will be narrowed," he agrees, explaining that ground teams have already been dispatched back to the ridgeline and Long Lake as well as the pond. "The best thing you can do right now is trust us."

So when the dust clears from the rotors of the large helo, Silas allows himself to be led back to the com van. Once inside he sits heavily, eyeing the base station radio as if he can will it to crackle to life, bringing him news of Cameron.

What he hears instead is almost as welcome: the now familiar whir of helicopter blades again threading the air. *Helo One is back.*

"Cameron?" he asks immediately, looking swiftly to Susan Darcy, standing near the door, holding her own radio in front of her face. That lump in his throat has returned. It may be irrational to hope for such immediate resolution, but he doesn't care.

She shakes her head. "The pilot needs to refuel," she explains, not unkindly. "The spotter needs to be switched out."

Spotter. Meg. *No,* Silas thinks stubbornly. He doesn't want a new spotter. Meg can pick Cameron straight out of the sky, just as she did Spencer. Not anyone else but Meg.

A minute later, however, the com-van door opens, and he's forced to take this back. Meg stands before him looking exhausted to her core, from the circles under her eyes to her windblown hair, disheveled from the helo. Still, she smiles at him—tentatively at first—and then the jubilation of finding Spencer returns on a tide. Reaching for her hand seems like the most natural thing in the world. He squeezes it in gratitude, and when her grip tightens around his fingers, he's filled with the simple comfort of gaining an ally.

24

Silas

August 28, 2003
8:45 p.m.
Marble Lake Wilderness

The scream had come from somewhere along the ridge. Silas scrambled up the slope, circumventing pine trees and crashing through sagebrush and manzanita. Twice on his ascent the zipper of his hoodie became ensnared on exposed branches, choking him at the neck and upsetting his footing.

"Jessica!" he yelled at intervals. *"Jess?"*

Somewhere above him Danny conducted his own search, and below him Meg traversed cross-country after splitting off from him to follow a natural vein of granite on a diagonal down the mountain.

"Jess!" she, too, shouted. "Jess-*i*-ca!"

For a brief second, Silas's mind snagged on the sound of her voice, and his focus splintered.

"Hey!" she called. "Any sign of her?"

The question drew Silas's attention back to where it belonged. "No sign!" He squared his shoulders and forged onward. He couldn't allow himself to think about him and Meg. Not now. "You?" he called back.

"Nothing!"

By the time Silas reached the trail, any remaining words had been squeezed from his lungs; he bent at the waist, hands on his knees, gasping for breath, fervently hoping he wouldn't be sick. He pictured Jessica, somewhere out here, maybe also panting this hard, maybe still running.

From him.

He scrubbed at his eyes with his fists, wiping away sweat and tears. Why had she worn such flimsy sandals tonight? Why that inadequate crop top? Just so she could show off the necklace she was so proud of? Silas remembered the hurt on her face as she'd worried the pendant between her fingers and had to fight the urge not to sob.

Danny called out to him from above, something about heading downhill, but Silas could only gasp, "*Keep looking*," before taking off anew, following the trail as it made its countless familiar switchbacks toward Marble Lake Lodge. He had to strain to see in the gathering darkness, his feet tripping over rocks and roots. Had Jessica tripped, in those sandals? All he could do was continue to yell, Meg's and Danny's muffled echoes bouncing off the walls of the mountains.

He reached the lodge in record time, but Jessica wasn't waiting. Not by the ring of guest cabins. Not on the lighted porch of the cavernous recreation building. She wasn't at Silas's Jeep, either. He hadn't realized how much he'd hoped to see her there, arms crossed, pissed off beyond belief, until he saw it sitting there, as abandoned as when they'd left it as they'd all set out, just what? Two hours ago? Maybe an hour and a half?

Facing only the ghost of his own reflection in the darkened passenger window sent renewed panic coursing through Silas's veins, and he turned blindly, only to run directly into Meg again. In her own elevated surge of adrenaline and fear, she flailed at him wildly now, hitting him twice across the shoulder and chest before registering who he was.

"Meg!" He reached out to grab her. "It's me!"

But holding her in his arms—again, after what had just happened—only seemed to panic Meg further. "I thought she'd come back here! God, why isn't she here?"

She would have been, had she had any sense.

"Something must have happened to her!" Meg cried. "Up there, where we heard . . . where . . ."

Neither of them could say it.

Meg gripped his arms, her fingers digging into his flesh under his tee. "We need to fix this! God, we need to go back . . ."

He shook his head. "Why? What good would that do?"

She looked incredulous. "Because it's our fault, Silas!"

He took her by the shoulders, willing his hands to remain steady. Because Meg counted on him to be strong. Always. He couldn't let her down now. But could he lie to her? It turned out he could.

"It's not our fault," he told her firmly, kind of shaking her shoulders. She had to believe this.

Meg nodded, hesitantly at first, and then with more vigor. "Right, right." She took her first full breath since coming down from the woods. "And anyway, we don't know where she went. But still, we shouldn't have—"

Danny burst across the parking lot from the trail, completely spent from running, nearly hyperventilating himself.

"Where have *you* been?" Silas shot at him.

Danny waved his arms around in an effort to communicate while drawing in deep breaths. "Up there, where she left us! And then on the trail, now here." He actually looked close to furious, though Silas couldn't make out why. "What are *you* guys doing? Keep looking!"

"Where?" Silas argued. "She isn't down here!"

Danny yelled, "Well, we have to keep at it!"

"What the hell for, man? It's pointless!" It was getting too dark to see, for one.

Meg turned her back on them, arms hugging herself, as they argued. Holding herself tightly against the fray, as if otherwise she might break apart, piece by piece.

Danny had already unraveled completely, but freaking out wouldn't make Jessica magically reappear, shivering in her crop top and jean shorts. Ready to give them all shit. Silas needed to think.

He sent Danny to check the freestanding bathrooms—only for guests, but Jessica knew where they were—and then made for the lodge office, where a light still glowed at Uncle Les's desk. Time to call in reinforcements.

But Meg pulled him back off the porch and into the shadows just as he reached for the service door. "We can't tell him," she hissed, her grip on his arm alarmingly strong.

"Are you crazy? We need help!"

"That's not what I mean." She leaned close. "Us. We can't tell them about us."

Why? Did she want to take it back? Jealousy made itself known, cutting like a whip. "Danny will find out eventually, Meg. Unless you've changed your mind."

But Meg gripped his arm intently, shaking her head hard as tears streamed. "No. We'll tell him, for sure," she said. "After Jessica is found." She took a gulp of a breath, but it did little to keep the hysteria that was right there, on the edge of her voice, at bay. "But you were dating her, Silas. You broke up, sure, but you have history. And then we invited her here. How do you think it will look that you and I were . . ." Eyes wild, she tried to compose herself enough to continue. "That we were together, when she went missing?"

He shook his head. "That's crazy. This was an accident." A nightmare, even, but it wasn't a *crime*. "We haven't done anything wrong," he insisted. But of course he knew that wasn't true.

Despair sank like a rock somewhere in the vicinity of his chest. He willed Meg's logic to sink in along with it, diluting the awful cocktail of panic and pain already taking up residence there. If what she said had merit, if *motive* was really at stake here, their time together in the woods could bounce back on her, too.

No way would Silas let that happen. When Danny returned from the bathrooms, his search fruitless, Silas pushed him toward the lodge door in front of him and Meg. "You do the talking," he told him as he opened the door. Even though this lodge was Silas's home. Even though they were answering to Silas's family. Who better to represent them than the Boy Scout?

But Danny's face registered surprised panic at this request, or maybe it was just the way his skin glowed almost white under the porch light that gave the expression of fear. He nodded once, a sharp, precise jut of his chin. He still looked pissed as well as fearful, no doubt blaming Silas for all of this. Which, of course, he should, even not knowing the half of it. "Yeah, okay," he finally conceded. "Yeah. I can do that."

Could he? Silas looked at him more closely. Or was he going to puke all over the lodge floor? "You got this, Cairns," he said. "Keep it together, all right?"

They'd tell Danny's version of events and leave it at that. Ignoring his own churning stomach, Silas practiced this version in his head as they trotted down the hallway to the office: Jessica got scared. That part was all Silas's fault. But then she ran away, and they couldn't calm her. And now they couldn't find her. All of this was true. The rest didn't matter.

Except it did, so very much, didn't it?

When they all burst through the office door, Uncle Les clambered to his feet in surprise. "We need help, Mr. Albright," Danny blurted. His voice shook with adrenaline, and Uncle Les wasted no time.

"Mary?" he called out. "You'd better get on down here."

She joined them, already in her nightgown, and they gathered in the dimly lit lodge great room. Once there, it was easier than Silas had thought to stick to Meg's plan. To tell only the barest of facts. This was a small blessing, as the rest was lodged in Silas's throat anyway, hard to extract. Telling the full story would have been like picking the meat off a bone, exposing skeletal truths word by word.

"Start at the beginning," Les instructed, after several minutes of words tumbling one over another.

"We were all together," Danny told Uncle Les. "Hiking the Lakes Loop trail."

"And?" Les sounded wary. He liked Danny. Trusted Danny. Always had. "What happened?"

"Well, sir," Danny began. He swallowed. "Silas may have scared Jessica."

"Dammit, Silas," Les said. "How many times have we told you to cool it with the pranks?"

"But people get lost in the woods all the time, right?" Danny interjected. "It happens."

"And they always get found," Meg added. "Right?"

"We tried to call out to her," Silas said.

"But we couldn't catch up to her," Meg supplied.

"We looked and looked," Danny echoed. He took a breath like he was ramping up to say more, and for one long, horrible second, Silas feared he and Meg had miscalculated. Maybe Danny already knew the whole story, and it was about to come pouring out. But Danny only concluded tightly, "There was no trace of her."

Silas exhaled.

Next to him Meg shifted on her seat. Danny looked to her for confirmation, and Silas would have liked to believe he was the only one who could detect the briefest moment of hesitation that followed. It played about Meg's mouth, tugging the corner of her lip downward, just before she nodded. "No trace," she echoed dully.

Her protection of him should have bolstered him, vindicated him, even, but it only brought a sour taste, rising up in Silas's throat.

Uncle Les wanted more details, but Danny, designated spokesman, didn't seem to have many. Guilt bubbled up in Silas, but it didn't spill over. He couldn't let it. He just sat there, censured, because this was the only way to ensure this stayed far away from Meg, too.

"Did Jessica know where you were all headed?" Les wanted to know. "Before you scared her?" He looked Silas's way sternly again. "Did she have a map with her?"

Silas shook his head in the negative. Jessica hadn't had so much as a bottle of water on her when they'd set off, despite Danny's attempt at organizing them all.

Aunt Mary wanted Jessica's parents' names and number. "Did you all think to pack some gear, at least?" she asked. "Did she have a jacket?"

No, and no. Shame heated Silas's cheeks. He knew better than to go into the wilderness unprepared. Even for a last-minute hike he hadn't wanted to take.

"I'm sorry," he found himself saying. He was. He was so, so sorry. But purging himself of the whole story wouldn't help Jessica now. She certainly wasn't where he'd last seen her. And coming clean wouldn't help Meg. It would only ease the pain deep inside him where omission swelled into bloated fabrication.

He needed air.

Back outside, he sat down heavily on the log bench outside the lodge and waited. For what, he wasn't sure. Meg to join him here? To tell him everything would work out? Or to remind him again to keep his mouth shut?

The voices inside continued to roll over one another, but from out here they mingled with the sound of water flowing over the boulders in nearby Marble Creek; Uncle Les's tone stony, Danny's and Meg's grating like rocks in a tumbler. Aunt Mary's voice echoed after. Eventually she joined Silas on the porch, the arm she cast around his shoulder pillowy in her bathrobe.

"Your uncle is making some phone calls," she said.

The others followed shortly, Danny sitting below Meg on the front steps. As Silas watched, he fidgeted with his shoelace, yanking, and yanking, and yanking, his mouth forming a tight, hard line. What was he thinking? Unlike Meg, Danny was impossible for Silas to read.

No one spoke except for Uncle Les, who kept saying, "We'll find her all right, we'll find her," and Danny, who kept answering, "Yeah, I know," between yanks on his shoe, drawing great breaths to—Silas assumed—avoid crying.

He wanted to cry again, too, but he wouldn't.

"The authorities will be here just as soon as they can," Aunt Mary promised. She meant to soothe, but her words, too, felt rough around the edges.

They waited, and waited more, all of them, out in the cool of the summer night. And when the flash of police lights finally rounded the final bend in Marble Lake Road, they all stood of one accord, as though rising to await a sentencing.

25

MEG

Matheson search
November 21, 2018
8:15 a.m.
Marble Lake Staging Area

Inside the com van, Meg enters the coordinates where they found Spencer onto a spreadsheet on Darcy's laptop. She's still waiting on the flight report from Rick, and she swivels her chair closer to the screen, trying to concentrate with the constant chatter on the radio as Santos continues to direct teams through the field.

"Shit, be right back," he says, then excuses himself to deal with some sort of problem with someone's GPS unit. A moment later, Darcy follows, muttering something about doing things yourself if you want them done right.

It's silent for one blissful moment before it dawns on Meg that she and Silas are alone in the van. She looks over at him: so worn down. So tired. "Any update on Spencer?" she asks softly.

Silas exhales slowly. "Stable," he breathes. "But he'll likely be at Washoe Medical for a few days."

She wants to say, *You'll be with him soon. You and Cameron both.* But she can't bear to, because what if it isn't true? She's so weary of lies, even the ones meant to console. He's staring out the window at the lodge grounds in the distance, and after inputting the final coordinate, she gives her eyes a break and follows his gaze.

"It's been over a decade since I've seen this place," she notes. "Your place," she amends. Her voice startles him; he flinches slightly, just like Max when the squawk of the radio seems to come from out of nowhere. It's no wonder he's so jumpy, waiting on any news related to his kids. She can't imagine that sort of agony.

"Over a *decade*," he repeats quietly. "How did that happen?"

She hesitates, unsure what he needs to hear. Not wanting to inflict any unnecessary injury. Silas sits hunched like he's just waiting for the next blow. "One day followed by another, I guess," she says cautiously.

Several more seconds pass in silence. The waste of it weighs on her. There's so much she would like to say to him, but timing has never been their strong suit. The clock on the com-van wall ticks, measuring Cameron's struggle wherever he lies, keeping pace with the footfalls of the searchers out in the wilderness. Measuring Spencer's flight time to Reno. And here she and Silas are, caught inexplicably together. But if experience has taught Meg anything, it's that moments like this one pass in the blink of an eye.

"Listen, Silas—"

But he's already speaking. "If it matters," he tells Meg in a rush, "I'm sorry I left."

It takes her a moment to find the composure to answer. "I'm sorry I stayed," she responds slowly, and the words sink as softly as silt into lake water as she offers him a sad smile. "If it matters."

He looks directly into her eyes. "It matters," he says, and in this single isolated second, hovering and divided from the whole of her life, Meg sees something in his expression that she's done her best *not* to see all these years. The consequences, at least until now, have always felt entirely too high.

The first drop of rain hits the roof of the com van at the very second the door crashes back open. It's Danny, stepping up the metal stairs and into the main compartment, and Meg and Silas both flinch, springing back from one another despite the fact that they were sitting more than five feet apart.

Danny freezes in the doorway, looking quickly between the two of them. Meg surprises herself by looking unflinchingly back. Warranted or not, her and Silas's reaction to his unexpected presence speaks volumes. The truth is too exposed now to hide behind best intentions and penance. The rain begins in earnest, blowing through the open doorway and cascading off Danny's search jacket in big drops, soaking the carpeting. The papers scattered on the counter get wet, but still, no one moves, and no one looks away. Meg is reminded of the GPS units they've been working with all day, triangulating as they search to connect with the satellites far above them.

"I've been looking for you," Danny says finally to Meg. "Guess I should have known you'd be here, right where you always want to be."

"Dan—"

"Don't," he says, holding up one palm. There's something odd in his voice, a strange little catch like Meg's next words could trigger a trap for her to fall through. It silences her as he pivots and retreats back out into the cold.

She stares at that door slammed shut for a long moment, coming to terms with the idea that it just may symbolize far more than this single aborted conversation between her and Danny, and then it bangs open again, Darcy in the threshold, dripping rainwater all over the floor. "A field team has called in near the pond coordinates," she says.

Silas clambers to his feet. "Have they found him?"

"I don't know. Team Eight called in on Santos's handheld but told us to stand by."

"Team Eight?" Meg confirms. "That's a K9 team, isn't it?" Darcy nods, just as Santos joins them in the small space. "One of the dogs has alerted to a scent at the bottom of a ravine," he says breathlessly.

"Bottom of a *ravine*?" Silas interjects, sounding like his heart might have just plummeted into one as well. "What *ravine*?"

"Stay calm," Meg implores even as her own heart starts to hammer loudly, and in the crowded confines of the van Silas curls his hands into fists at his sides. Probably in order to resist the urge to take the lieutenant by the shoulders and shake more information from him.

"Sit back down," Santos commands, and Silas complies, which is good, because otherwise Meg knows he'd be relegated out into the rain to join Danny.

"Is the dog one of ours?" Meg presses. "An air-scent dog?"

The lieutenant darts an anxious glance Silas's way, reluctant to answer, and then concedes. "No," he says, and Meg stifles a moan.

"What?" Silas demands. "What does that mean?"

"It means this dog is trained to search indiscriminately, for any human scent," Santos says. He takes a breath, looking to Silas in apology. "This one is a cadaver dog."

She's glad Santos is the one to say it, especially when Silas sucks in a near-violent gasp of air.

"This could mean nothing," Meg tells him, wanting to soothe even as the tension in the com van ratchets up another notch. Sheriff Walters himself has joined the crew inside the van, and Santos waves him over, pressing through the narrow space to the topo map spread on a table. They both bend over it.

"They called in from here," he announces, his finger marking his place on the map. Meg leans in, craning to see over Santos's right shoulder. He's indicating a steep decline ending in what appears to be a narrow canyon not far off the Lakes Loop trail.

"How far off is that location from where you found Spencer?" Silas asks, muscling his way through, and can Meg blame him? The man is waiting for the radio to crackle to life with news of his son, news that very well could confirm the end of Cameron's life, the end of *his* life as he knows it. Santos consults Meg's coordinates on the spreadsheet, confers with Walters, then frowns as he carefully counts the number of severely arcing contour lines between his finger and the location on the map and then measures the distance. It seems to take him an eternity.

"About a hundred sixty feet, at most?"

He doesn't sound sure. How could he not be sure? Meg grits her teeth; it's hotter than hell in this van, and as Silas jostles against Darcy in his attempt to get even closer to the map, it's also clear that it's way past capacity.

"Well, what does the topography look like?" Silas presses. "Is it even possible for Cam to have walked from one point to the other?"

Santos looks back down at the map. "Um . . ."

"It looks like a very steep slope," Silas interjects again, bouncing forward on the balls of his feet.

"Give him a minute!" Darcy counters. She's shouting, now, too, but Silas isn't listening. Neither is Meg, because the field team is going to call any minute now. Team Eight is going to have a report, and the only thing keeping either of them sane is their focus on this map.

"If I could just see," Silas says. "I'd know if it was possible . . ."

"Sit back down!" Darcy demands just as Meg pivots to allow Silas full access to the map.

"Let him look," she insists simultaneously. She and Darcy are still locked in a standoff when the radio beeps shrilly on the counter.

"Team Eight to Base?"

No one can reach it.

Meg has pushed herself against the wall; Silas is pressed between Darcy and Santos, with Walters on the other side of the table. Whatever scant amount of oxygen remains circulating in the room seems to instantly invert; Meg is standing in a black hole of building turmoil and increasing temperature and—

"Team Eight to Base?" the voice on the radio reissues. *"Come in?"* This time, Santos manages to curl his hand around the mobile unit.

"This is Base. What do you have, Team Eight?"

"A delay, unfortunately. The terrain's inaccessible. We'll need a rappel team."

Silas makes a pained sound, agony with a dash of his typical intolerance for inaction. He moves as if intending to start pacing, but can't, of course. The radio continues to buzz with conversation, requests, plan Bs, but Meg barely hears them, her head already in her hands. They know all they're going to know for now, which is apparently still nothing.

She exits the Lemon to find Danny, surprised that she doesn't have to search far. He's standing just outside the door, the rain pouring off him in thick sheets that pool at his boots. She pulls her SAR baseball cap low over her face.

"What's happening?" he asks immediately.

She shakes her head. "We don't know for sure yet. Team Eight insists a K9 dog is alerting to something, but they're waiting on the specialty team."

"K9? Cadaver or scent?" Danny's voice still sounds odd. Not like himself.

"Cadaver," she's forced to say. She feels something akin to a tide rising, energy pulsing off Danny like the swell of a wave. She glances in the direction of the lodge and the trail. "They're already in the field."

He follows her gaze. "Then they'll know soon."

Something about the fatalistic acceptance in his tone sends a trill of something—warning, maybe?—down Meg's spine. In the com van, she almost welcomed the honesty she sensed between them all, but it's terrifying, too. She and Danny have been pretending for so long. "Listen," she tells him, "there are a lot of emotions at play right now." He says nothing, so she forges ahead. "But I think we should agree to put ancient history aside, at least for today."

"*Ancient history?*" Danny spins away from her with an almost primal moan as that wave she felt between them breaks. "Him back here . . . you two . . . it's like I'm being forced to relive it all over again."

"Relive what?" Meg presses, even as a sense of foreboding floods her, limb by limb. *Say it.* Because it's time.

But he won't give her this. "'Nothing,' I guess!" he says roughly, raking air quotes through the rain. His face is crimson now, spittle flying out of his mouth as he shouts into the storm. "Just like it's been 'nothing' since the start of this god-awful search." He turns to go but then spins back, his fury not yet spent.

"I saw you at the mine, you know! You and him."

"What?" The mine? Meg tries to follow the path of Danny's accusations, but the line of logic runs too jagged.

"That Fourth of July? I blew off the firefighter booth to be a good sport and come join you, and what did I get? I got to overhear a conversation about *you* not wanting to be with me."

What had Silas said? What had she said? God, it was so long ago. But her confusion and dismay only seem to incense Danny further, insult piled upon injury.

"You know exactly what I'm talking about! She saw you, too, you know! She told me, and you know what? I didn't want to believe her, but she was right all along!"

Meg's eardrums ring with a weird, tinny sound. "Who was, Danny?"

"Forget it." His voice has gone flat again as quickly as it rose: a sudden, jarring drop.

Meg's stomach lurches, her gut absorbing something her brain refuses to process. In the rising mist between them, Danny suddenly looks a thousand miles away. The rain is soaking her hair and her face, and she hopes that the sound of it prevents him from hearing the hitch in her voice. "Tell me what you're talking about." Because her gut is insisting. She has to know.

But they're still standing in place, letting the rain run down their search jackets in rivulets when the Lemon door partially opens again and Santos's face appears around the frame. He squints into the gloom, his expression pinched with stress and fatigue. "You two need to come in." When Meg hesitates, still staring at Danny, he adds, "Now."

Inside, Walters has joined Darcy at the radio station. Silas is once again sitting but glances up quickly as they enter. His eyes look almost glassy, like he's been exposed too long to the elements.

"Silas should wait outside, in the command center," she says. He needs shelter from the raw dread of this search.

"I'm not going anywhere," he answers, and she doesn't bother pushing it. Good news or bad, he's right where he always is: in the center of the storm.

"The specialty team is mobile," Walters says. "We're in direct communication with them." He fiddles with the volume on the base radio, and as if on cue, it comes to life. "Sacramento County Team Two to Base," it squawks, pairing a voice to whoever plans to rappel down the ravine. Meg presses back against the wall again, the only space left available.

"Go ahead, Team Two," Santos responds.

The rappeller begins transmitting. "We've reached targeted area," the voice reports, and then gives his coordinates. "The underbrush is thick; we're going to grid search the best we can in this rain."

Grid search? Meg clenches her jaw to keep from protesting. How much longer can they bear to stand by like this, stuck in this endless holding pattern?

They wait as the rain pounds on the metal roof, and Meg forces herself to think of anything but the update that awaits them at the press of a radio button, on the tip of the tongue of some unknown rappelling expert. She watches the clock on the wall and focuses on the accusations Danny has just flung at her, accusations she cannot deny, does not even *want* to deny anymore, as an untried terror churns in her stomach like acid.

"Team Two to Base."

Oh God.

"Go ahead, Team Two."

"Base, we have a subject in sight."

She grips Silas's hand. She can't not.

"Status, Team Two?"

Silas is drawing air into his lungs in deep gulps, like in an instant, he's going to be submerged. Meg squeezes his hand harder. If she doesn't, he's going to sink like a rock to the bottom of this nightmare, and she cannot allow him to drown. *You have Spencer to think of,* she wants to tell him fiercely. *You cannot go under.*

A short pause while the static crackles, and then: "Black."

Beside her, Silas plummets. His knees give way, and then he's collapsing like all the oxygen in the world couldn't save him. Meg tries to brace his fall, but it's Darcy who catches his forearm, guiding him into a chair. Meg knows it hardly matters to Silas where he lands . . . that single word, uttered for the second time in just a few short hours, must be screaming in his ears on repeat.

At the radio, Santos closes his eyes briefly and then reopens them. His voice is laced with genuine sorrow as he transmits back into the receiver. "Can you confirm that the subject is a five-year-old Caucasian male?"

There's another pause. Meg is pretty sure she's not breathing, either, but somehow, she's still here, in this misery. "Negative," the rappeller responds. He sounds shaken. "I'm sorry . . . Sir, I think I jumped the gun."

What? The question is on every face in the room. "Team Two, please repeat. We may have misheard."

"Base, the subject is not Cameron Matheson."

Meg watches Silas spiral downward again, head sinking into his hands, but this time it's with an abject relief that leaves him shaking with sobs. The rappeller is asked to repeat his transmission for a third time, but Meg has stopped listening. It's not Cameron, it's not Cameron, it's not Cameron, and nothing, nothing else matters, until—

"We're looking at skeletal remains," the rappeller explains. "An adult, not a child." His distress transmits over the airwaves like a spiky pulse on an EKG. It's clear that this discovery is more than the man bargained for. "A young adult, we think."

Young adult? Meg feels something vital shift within her . . . her sense of purpose for so many years finally coming to fruition. If this is finally happening, if this is Jessica, Meg's efforts all these years, even her efforts with Danny, all she's given up and all she's settled for, won't have been in vain.

"Do you *think* or do you know?" Sheriff Walters bellows. He picks up the satellite phone, calling in to his department headquarters. "I need our forensic pathologist up here." He pauses for confirmation, then adds, "Yes, in the field. *Now.*"

On the radio, Santos has taken over, and his careful, measured questions are slowly calming the rappeller, drawing out more information. "Partially obscured," Meg hears him say.

"Are there any identifying marks at all?" Santos asks, and on the other end of the radio, the rappeller becomes upset again.

"It's just . . . *bones!*" he insists, appalled. "It must have—*he* must have? *She?*—been here for years, hidden from view in the underbrush."

She must have been here for years. Meg's entire body clenches as certainty cements her in place. She looks sharply to Silas, who's staring back at her with wide, horrified eyes. He's thinking it, too, and across the room, so is Danny, his face ashen. They're triangulating again, as they have for so long. Surely they're not jumping to conclusions, their nerves and their reason shredded to pieces in the course of this entire ordeal.

"Wait," the rappeller says, and Walters frowns.

"No more speculation!"

But Santos has already spoken into the radio. "Go ahead, Team Two."

"There's something here. In the dirt."

In the dirt? By this body?

"It's a necklace," the rappeller reports, and Meg's mind locks with exacting precision on the image of Jessica sunning herself by the river. Of her leaning out into the glare of the sunlight, the flat silver disk glinting as it swung, back and forth, just above the low-slung neckline of her bikini. She draws the memory to the forefront of her consciousness with a swiftness that startles her: through every interrogation following Jessica's disappearance, and then throughout her painstaking attempt at selective memory during all the years since, Meg has never thought of that necklace again. All this time, it has seemed utterly insignificant.

And yet here they are, right back to where they started.

26

MEG

Meg, Danny, and Silas all scrambled to their feet at the sight of the sheriff's-department 4x4's headlight beams bouncing down the drive and flicking off as the vehicle came to a stop in front of the lodge. Another vehicle followed in its wake. Meg coughed on the dust while thinking, *How weird, that you can't see dust when it's dark,* and then the deputy sheriff, or whoever he was, stepped out of his truck. Meg noted his boots first, shiny black in the glow of the vehicle's dome light, and then the crisp cuffs of his trousers. Who would go to the trouble of pressing a uniform to respond to a call at this hour up here in the middle of nowhere?

The man introduced himself first to Mary Albright. "Lieutenant Halloway." He reached for his notepad on the passenger seat of the 4x4. "We have a missing person to report?"

Behind the lieutenant, three—no, four—people stepped out of the second vehicle. They slammed doors as they gathered supplies, then slung packs over their shoulders and pulled headlamps over their heads, the bulbs clicking on one by one. The thin beams of artificial light bounced haphazardly over the drive as the people moved about, and twice, Meg had to squeeze her eyes shut as a rogue glare hit her straight in the face.

"The kids know more about it," Mary answered, and the man's attention fell directly on them. The temptation to lay it all out there, away from where it ate at her insides, appealed in a way that made Meg's stomach ache.

"It's our friend Jessica Howard," Silas said.

The lieutenant readied his notepad, pen poised. "Age? Description?"

Danny jumped in. "She's eighteen. Same as us." He paused, and the lieutenant stared at him, wanting more. He looked sympathetic, but something else, too. Insistent. Danny cast a look, resentful and dark, at Meg and Silas, like, *A little help here?* When no assistance was forthcoming, he blurted, "She and Silas were sort of dating."

This got the lieutenant's attention, and he swiveled to Silas. "You were together?"

"No," Meg interjected. Because that wasn't right. The guy shouldn't write that down.

"We weren't dating," Silas echoed, shooting a look at Danny. "I mean, we used to, last winter, but we weren't anymore."

"Something go wrong between you tonight?" the lieutenant asked.

No, no, no. This was unfolding exactly as Meg had feared. And imagine if she and Silas had already told Danny what had happened between them? He'd sold Silas out fast enough as it was, sending a stab of sorrow through her.

"We were friends," Silas said firmly. "Nothing more."

"Then, what happened? How'd she get separated from you all?"

Silas looked at Les, who nodded once in encouragement. "I scared her," he admitted. He explained it all in one long rush of breath: how he did this all the time, not that he should, how he'd meant to jump out at Danny, but had slipped from the branch.

"Just kids," Uncle Les interjected, "goofing off, you see." But he certainly didn't sound pleased about it.

Halloway didn't comment. He seemed too busy writing all this down. Meg couldn't tell if he'd crossed out *dating*. The silence stretched, save for Halloway's pen still scratching the paper, and Meg felt like she should contribute something, but her arms felt immovable, pressed at her sides. Her jaw clenched. She wanted to help, but she didn't know how to unclench it.

"What was she wearing?" the lieutenant asked next.

At first, Meg's mind went completely blank. "Shorts," Silas supplied. "And a crop top. Pink, I think."

"And her necklace," Danny offered. "The one with the J." His voice cracked oddly on the last syllable.

"Necklace?"

"A graduation present, I think," Silas contributed.

Meg found her voice again. "She told me it was from a secret admirer or something."

The lieutenant paused at this information, his pen hovering over his pad of paper. "Any idea who?"

Silas shook his head.

Halloway looked to Danny for confirmation, who looked pointedly at Meg before saying tightly, "I already have a girlfriend."

Meg felt Silas's eyes on her. Nothing, it would seem, could break the magnetic tug that was always just *there*, drawing them both in. Tangling them up. Even sitting five feet from one another, Meg felt it. She needed to do a better job of fighting it.

And so she looked away again, listening as Danny and Silas recited the order of events from start to finish, just as they had for Les and Mary. Hiking . . . prank . . . running . . . searching. No sign.

"She screamed," Meg said suddenly. How had they forgotten that part? "Right when—right as we were looking for her, we heard her scream."

Silas nodded cautiously, but Danny's eyes flashed with something—surprise? Fear?—at this addition to the story. "What do you mean, screamed? I didn't hear her scream."

Which explained why he'd neglected to mention this detail with Les and Mary. "She definitely screamed," Meg insisted. She had to set that record, at least, straight.

"And where was that?" Halloway asked her. "In which direction?"

Meg began to sweat. "I . . . we ran so much, looking, I got turned around." And yet she could picture that grove, where she'd run right into Silas, so clearly. Could feel the rough bark of the tree where it had collided with her back. She felt a single bead of moisture building at the nape of her neck, poised to drop in one smooth motion down the length of her spine. When it fell, she shivered.

"Aren't they going to go look?" she said, pointing at the searchers waiting in the wings. "Can't you tell them to get started?"

The lieutenant glanced calmly behind him at his team, then back at the three of them. "I need to figure out where to send them first, don't I?"

"Now, John, I think they've told you what they know," Les said.

Halloway didn't appreciate the intervention. He looked like he had swallowed something sour. Meg had seen this look before, on the face of their history teacher when Les had driven all the way down the hill into Feather River to excuse Silas's streak of tardies last spring. His nephew had straight As, so who cared if he preferred to spend fifth period back up at Marble Lake, trekking all over the woods?

The reminder buoyed Meg. Everything always seemed to go Silas's way. This would, too. *Be patient,* she told herself. *Jessica will turn up. Silas will talk to her. We'll tell Danny the truth. No one will be in trouble.*

But in the intermittent flare of the nearby headlamps, Silas's eyes glowed with a pale panic Meg had never seen. Her confidence in his ability to always land on his feet waned, just briefly, like a lantern flickering, low on propane.

The three of them sat vigil all night, isolated by way of a uniformed deputy from the few lodge guests who wandered into the dining room, and by morning they'd danced around the truth—the whole truth, anyway—for so long Meg felt numb. They went over the timeline again with Sheriff Walters, until the individual words began to lose meaning, each one polished as smooth as a stone in a current as it rolled off Meg's tongue. *And then, and then, and then. Trail, trail, trail.* They all just kept talking in circles, the corpse of the truth dashing upon the rocks of this redacted version of events until it became so thin and ragged, she feared it would disappear altogether. What if she forgot what had *really* happened, her brain had been bleached so? The thought both comforted and dismayed.

Every time they reached the end of their story—the part with the lodge and the Jeep and the alerting of the Albrights—they began anew, returning always to the hike and the gathering darkness and the scare. By the time the sun had warmed the eastern window bank, Meg had doubled over in her chair in fatigue, unable to withstand another pass through the gauntlet of the lieutenant's steady line of questioning or the sheriff's stern stare. It was like a furnace in here; she was burning up, slowly, from the inside out.

Guests from the few occupied cabins were questioned next, ushered one by one into the rec room, only to come back out looking as helpless as Meg felt. They took a break midmorning, Aunt Mary plying them all with sandwiches that tasted like lead in her mouth. She sat mutely on the lodge deck, taking in the sight of search teams in orange unloading their dogs and packs. At least half a dozen sheriff's-department vehicles now sat in the lodge parking lot. Even a Reno news van was here, a young woman with a microphone interviewing a smattering of lodge guests.

Silas kept trying to get Meg to talk to him, but she deflected his looks, shook free of his hand when he offered it in support. Because this was precisely what had gotten them here, wasn't it? She wished she could go back to being the Meg she'd been at the start of senior year, before she'd met Silas. *That* Meg had hovered somewhere off-center, unsure and unseen. She hadn't been at the eye of the storm. She didn't know precisely when she'd become illuminated the way the black light at the Cosmos Bowl made her white T-shirt glow when she stood in its beam. But she had glowed last night, in the wilderness by the trail, with the certainty of a woman who finally dared to reach for what she wanted. And now everything had gone horribly wrong. Now the glow was gone.

SILAS

By midday on Day 2, Meg had taken to standing in the doorway of the main lodge instead of sitting in her customary chair next to Silas and Danny. Had she gotten any rest yet? They all still wore the same clothes as the night before, and Meg's pants were smudged with dirt. Her tee had ripped along one sleeve, where a spindly branch of sage had probably cut through to her skin, and dark shadows below her eyes stood out like pillowy bruises on her pale face. *This is all my fault,* he silently promised her, trying to catch her eye across the lodge. *Not yours. His* stupid prank gone wrong. *His* stupid decisions. She might have been the one to suggest they edit their story, but only to help *him*. He couldn't let his choices ruin her by association.

Sheriff Walters set up what he called a command center in the musty lodge dining room, where people fielded phone calls and conducted press conferences via satellite around the clock. Around 7:00 p.m., a surge of radio chatter lifted the reporters' faces from their notes and sent the few searchers grabbing a bite in the lodge kitchen scurrying toward their posts. Silas was still trying to figure out what had happened when Walters strode straight across the room toward them and sat down in Meg's empty chair.

"So," he demanded of the three of them, "which one of you isn't telling me the truth?"

From the periphery of his vision, Silas saw Meg's head snap around, but she stayed in place between the lobby and the porch, her lips a tight line. He didn't dare look at Danny. Instead, he turned his focus back to the sheriff, his pulse accelerating as he took in the sight of his large, calloused hands laying two photographs on the table in front of them. At first glance, they looked like pictures of dirt.

"Our trackers have detected what they call 'sign' in an area within the radius of our search," the sheriff said. "Do you all know what 'sign' is?"

Of course they did. Danny was a freaking Eagle Scout, and Silas . . . well, Silas was instantly transported to the Marble Lake boathouse, stomping around in the mud, trying to throw Uncle Les off his trail.

"Tracks," he said dully.

Danny didn't say anything, which wasn't like him, usually so eager around uniformed types. When he glanced at him, he looked . . . wrong somehow. Amped up and unnerved, his cheeks splotched pink. He couldn't stand it, not being able to help.

"Tracks, yes," Walters was saying. "As well as other detection of recent passage. Here," he explained, pointing at the first photo, "is where someone—two someones, actually—left the Lakes Loop trail, approximately a mile from the Long Lake access trail."

Danny pulled the print closer to look.

"You can see the crushed stems of the sagebrush where it was trampled," Walters pointed out. "And then in this photo"—he drew the other print to the forefront—"a series of footprints are discernible, all within the confines of this grove, approximately ten feet from the trail."

"Where?" Silas asked, staring down at the second photograph. "I don't see footprints." And he really didn't, though that didn't stop the sudden surge of bile that rose at the back of his throat. Because he *did* recognize the area the photo conveyed. He'd remember it forever.

"This is thick forest," Walters said evenly. "The ground here is dense with undergrowth, covered with too many pine needles, twigs, and moss to record exact imprints." His eyes shifted from Silas to Danny and back again. "A shame."

Walters dug into his front pocket and a second later used the tip of a pencil to carefully trace a fine line across the print. He told them it marked a depression, of shoe size approximately ten to twelve, in the earth. Person number one. Silas could only make out the slightest gradient of a shadow, a contrast of depth so subtle he could scarcely believe the trackers caught it at all.

"This is a shoe print of a man," Walters explained. "Or, of course, a teen." He looked at them. "Roughly the size of either of your feet."

Danny stiffened, like he was about to interject, but before Silas could lose his lunch, the sheriff pinpointed another depression slightly overlapping the first. "This one is smaller," he said. "Maybe size seven? Eight?" He tapped the tip of his pencil on the photo, and Silas stared down at it, watching one tiny fleck of lead crumple onto the glossy print. "This one is a woman's."

Danny sat ramrod straight now, the dots of pink on his cheeks crimson. But couldn't Cairns see? The sheriff was trying to turn them against one another. But then the irony of this backfired right in Silas's face. Because they had, of course. At least, Silas had turned on Danny.

For a long second, remorse gripped him. "Mr. Matheson." Walters stared at him. "Do you have something to say?"

Silas shook his head.

Walters shifted in his chair with a little grunt of frustration, then consulted a report, presumably the one they'd made for Halloway.

"You all split up to look for Jessica?"

Silas forced a breath into his lungs. It took a supreme effort, shame encircling to clutch him from all sides. *All my fault.* "Yes," he managed. "But we all started out together." *Tell the truth as far as is possible.* Isn't that what they said, in the movies and stuff? He described running back down the trail to the fork.

Walters set the report down with deliberate care. "Unfortunately, there's a problem with that explanation. My trackers tell me that the evidence within these prints"—he pointed again, two sharp jabs at the photo; Silas wished he'd stop pointing with that stupid pencil—"do not lend themselves to the people in question running and searching. Or even stopping briefly to share information. For that to be the case, you see, the footprints would be more widely spaced. There would be bigger scuffs. These images suggest, instead, that the subjects were standing still. Rather close together, in fact, for rather a long time."

Silas chanced a glance at Meg and immediately regretted it. That guilt was back, pressing in from all sides, but he fought against it. For preservation. For Meg. She was looking back at him like his next words were a carton of eggs she just knew he was about to drop. "We were looking the whole time."

What was one more lie? It escaped from Silas's mouth the same as all the rest. And he was empty now. Hollow-boned as a bird. He'd rise above instead of holding fast.

"Maybe they're the tracks of some searchers," he added.

Walters shook his head. "Today was our team's first pass through these particular coordinates." He frowned as his expression chilled even further. "What we have here should amount to simple mathematics, boys, and yet, it does not."

Danny kind of flinched at this, though he didn't answer.

"Are you nervous, son?" Walters added, not entirely unkindly, which kind of threw Silas off. He had to think Walters did this, tying them all in such knots, on purpose.

But Silas knew Danny. He wasn't nervous as much as quietly fuming. *What are you getting yourself so riled up for?* Uncle Les always said to Cairns with a chuckle, mussing his hair whenever Danny's carefully plotted world went off course, bringing him to the lodge with a scowl. Was Danny just resentful that an authority figure was daring to question his shiny scout's-honor reputation?

Walters continued to stare them down, the room in silent stalemate, and then:

"Maybe it does."

Meg spoke so quietly from her vigil in the doorway that Silas wondered for a moment if he'd imagined it. But both Walters and Danny also stared in her direction, shifting in their chairs to face her.

"The math," she clarified. "Maybe it *does* add up."

Silas's heart began to pound. She looked right at him for the first time in days, which he took for a terrible sign. He closed his eyes, waiting for it. Deserving it. Almost wishing for it.

"Maybe those footprints are someone else's entirely," she said.

Silas's eyes snapped open as Walters leaned forward. "Excuse me?"

Danny chose this moment to jump back into the conversation. "She means maybe somebody else was out there! Some creepo who could have gotten Jessica!" His enthusiasm for this theory carried him to his feet. His metal folding chair clattered to the ground behind him. "Not all hikers are guests at the lodge. Did anyone check the parking lot for other cars?"

For the first time the sheriff looked unsettled, his gaze darting to the door. "Of course we checked."

"Are you sure, because—"

"I said of course we checked."

Walters gathered up his footprint photos and resecured them under the metal clasp of his clipboard with an angry jab. When he spoke again, his voice boomed from one wood-paneled wall to the other. "I did not come out here to share the details of our investigation with you, Mr. Cairns. Not with any of you." A fine spray of spit flew from his mouth as he spoke. "So I'll ask one last time: Does anyone want to change their story?"

Silence prevailed while they all stared at one another. It reminded Silas of a standoff in a movie, when everyone pointed a gun at everyone else, rendering everyone frozen in place. And then Walters rose in frustration, his own chair scraping across the wooden floorboards like nails down a chalkboard.

"In that case," he told them, his expression dark, "I'm afraid we've gotten precisely nowhere."

27

SILAS

The heat in the com van is stifling. The silence deafening as Silas's thoughts ricochet between the past and the present, his mantra now *Jessica. Cameron. Jessica. Spencer.*

Sheriff Walters looks at him, eyes sharp in his face. Nothing gets past him; Silas knows he's remembering Jessica's pendant necklace. Knows he's drawn the same conclusion as the rest of them.

Across the small space, Santos voices what everyone else is thinking. "It's her, isn't it," he breathes. "It must be."

The rain pounds above them, deafening on the metal roof, and the temperature in the com van seems to increase by at least ten more degrees as Silas braces for Walters to confirm this. *Say her name, just say it,* he thinks grimly, even as his own mind is still settled like a rock on *Cameron.*

And then there it is: "Jessica Howard," Walters says, "after all these years."

Against the wall, Meg makes a pained sound in the back of her throat. Her gaze seeks out Silas's, and in it—finally—is the collision of past and present they've both been bracing for. The impact threatens to bring Silas to his knees: he sees her at eighteen, in fear and in guilt, and now, here with him again and yet just as impossible to reach. He sees his sons as he saw them just two days before, young and whole, and then cold and alone, this storm howling at their door. Multifaceted tragedy is refracted like light from a prism off every surface of the van, originating with every terrible decision Silas has ever made. Meg, Jessica, Spencer, Cameron, even Danny . . . what they all have in common is *him*.

"Touch nothing," Walters barks into the radio to his ground crew, and everything picks up speed again. "Mark the area with evidence tape." He lowers the receiver to confer with Santos. "The wilderness EMT with Team Eight is thinking a broken neck, the result of a fall, based on preliminary assessment."

A broken neck. The words come crashing down on Silas like so much rubble, and he suspects that not knowing this missing piece of information may have been the only thing propping up the house of cards that has been his life for the last decade and a half. Hearing the probable cause of death has the finality of a sentencing. But it's his boys who are paying the price. Right this very minute.

"Please," he begs Walters. "Cameron. What about Cameron?"

The sheriff nods. "Team Eight has already been released to resume the search."

It's something, but it's not enough. Silas grabs his jacket and turns for the door. "I'm going to help."

"Wait." It's Meg's voice, and Silas turns back with surprise. He expected further impediment, sure, but not from this corner. He's about to say as much when the look on her face stops him. She's visibly troubled as she works through something in her mind, and though learning

how Jessica died must have gutted her as much as it gutted him, Silas can see it's more than that. Meg has peeled back another layer to all this, and it's a tragic one. His gut tightens anew. *Please, please, not about my boy.*

But it's Danny she addresses. "You know something," she tells him. "What you just said, outside—"

"What I *know* is about you two!" Danny shoots back, flinging an arm wildly between Meg and Silas. He seems to enjoy the startled look on Silas's face as this roller coaster of a conversation takes a new and abrupt turn. "Yeah, that's right. All that summer, you were both plotting together, weren't you? Hooking up behind my back—"

"That's crazy," Silas interjects. Because this cannot be happening. Not right now. "Please," he implores Danny. "Let's not do this." He searches Danny's face, but instead of reason, or even some shred of sympathy, he sees only deep-seated resentment. He looks for the man—the boy—he knows lurks somewhere behind the cold, confident expression. "Dan, please . . . think of my son."

But Danny's too far gone. "They were together that night!" he shouts to the com van at large. He looks away from Silas and Meg, like he can't bear to lay eyes on them. He homes in on Walters instead. "Those footprints you interrogated us about? They were *theirs*! Silas's and Meg's!"

Silas rocks back on his heels with a moan. Is there a statute of limitations on lies of omission?

Walters scrambles to maintain some semblance of authority, turning his attention to Danny. "How do you know this?"

Meg answers for him, her voice ringing in the metallic space. "Because Jessica told you, didn't she, Danny? She found you again, on the ridge, didn't she?"

Danny goes mute.

"The night Jessica died," she says steadily, eyes never leaving Danny's face, "Silas and I were together, yes." There's an audible intake of breath—from Darcy, Silas thinks—but Meg doesn't falter. "Those *were* my footprints, found during the Howard search. Not Jessica's. *Mine*. With Silas's."

Tears flow freely down her cheeks upon this confession, and an answering stab of sorrow slices through Silas. "We wanted to be alone together," she adds, and Silas closes his eyes on the memory. He can still feel the weight of those stones in his palm. "Silas never hurt her, but we knew how it would look, with us—"

"Cheating!" Danny shouts. "You see? It had to have been them!" He sounds more out of control, more immature, than he ever sounded as a teenager. Santos steps in, ready to grab Danny by the shoulders should he advance any farther toward Meg in the tiny space, but Danny doesn't even seem to notice.

Walters remains stoic, poker face in place. "But by your own admission, this happened nowhere near where Jessica has just been found." He consults the topographical map. "The footprints in 2003 were near the trail between the ridge and the lodge," he confirms.

"Even if that's true," Danny insists, pushing forward to grab the map himself, "he had time to get to the cliff and push her off!" His finger beats a staccato drumbeat on the topographical lines indicating the ravine. His nail pulses pink with each jab, he's hitting the desk with such vigor. "He was young"—*jab!*—"and fast"—*jab!*—"and he could easily have been in Meg's pants one minute and shoving Jessica the next!"

A second wave of silence greets this outburst, and in this vacuum of reaction it's entirely possible it is Danny himself who realizes the gravity of his error first. His face goes from red with fury to white with fear in an instant.

Walters breaks the silence first. "No one told you Jessica's body was found in a ravine," he says carefully, his tone so icy Silas shivers. Across from him, Meg just looks numb. "Let alone this exact geographical waypoint." He punctures each point with his own jab at the map. "You were outside, as I recall, when the rappelling team called in." He turns to his colleagues, who nod in agreement, Santos first, then Darcy. "Explain yourself," Walters orders.

Danny takes a quick step backward as if to flee, but there's nowhere to go. "You were cheating on me," he flings again at Meg, who flinches. He swivels around the van, but when no one else reacts on his behalf, he turns to implore Walters again. "Jessica was the only person who understood what I was going through! Why would I hurt her? Why?"

It's like his honor is being questioned, and it's this, even more than Jessica's fate, that seems to completely unravel him. Walters widens his stance, squaring his shoulders in a way only decades of law enforcement can teach. "I'm only going to give you one more chance to tell me how you know the precise location of her death."

Something shifts in Danny as his complete entrapment becomes clear. The rule follower in him causes self-preservation to give way to self-righteous animosity, and he keeps talking long after he should have demanded a lawyer. "She came back up the trail, yeah. But it wasn't to help me find the others. She only came back to tell me she was done."

"Done?" Walters reaches for a pad of paper, but machines whir with life all over the confines of the com van; how many radios, phones, and computers are already catching Danny's words?

"Done trying to get Silas's attention." Danny raises his head, stares Meg in the eye. Meg presses hers softly shut, as if unwilling to view this scene head-on. "She told me I should give it up, too. That it was over for me and Meg." Danny's face reddens again at the memory.

"She saw them, in the woods?" Walters pressed.

"Together," Danny spits out. "And not as *friends*, either." Each word leaves his mouth like shards of glass. "She kept saying it was point-less, that she just wanted to go home, that Silas only noticed Meg and always would. She just kept going on and on and I just . . . I couldn't stand hearing it anymore." He crumples in on himself at this, collapsing against the wall of the com van in racking sobs. "I didn't know there was a cliff, I swear. I didn't know she'd fall in those stupid sandals."

This time the silence in the com van is a roar. It builds on itself as Danny's confession reverberates off the tinny walls. Silas wants to clap both hands over his ears and squeeze. "You?" he says. "You . . ." It takes extreme effort to link the words in the correct order, each stubbornly refusing to fit where he needs it to go. "You . . . killed . . . Jessica? All that time ago? And you never . . . said a word?"

It seems unfathomable: do-gooder Danny, the community-service king. But Silas replays the aftermath of Jessica's disappearance in his mind. The resentment that seemed to radiate from Danny's core. Bubbling underneath it had been the same fury Silas saw today. Aimed at him, he could see now. At Meg. For what they'd done to him. And for the fact that Danny couldn't even confront them on it. Not until today.

Silas feels as though he has been yanked back from a ledge of his own, the role his own actions had in this cutting deep, even knowing how willing Danny would have been to pin the entirety of this on him. Meg still stands frozen, her face reflecting this same conflict. Her eyes are wide on Danny, like she can't believe she was proven right. She's breathing hard, as if midclimb up Marble Peak, and when she does speak, she seems to have the same difficulty stringing together words. "All these years," she gasps. "My God, Danny. All these years?"

It's a complicated thing, to reshuffle years' worth of blame, most of which you've grown accustomed to carrying on your own shoulders. Of course, lessened culpability mattered very little in the face of such tragedy.

"I'm sorry," Danny only says hollowly, hugging his knees to his chest, spine bent like the weight of an entire winter's worth of Sierra snow blankets him.

"Sorry?" Meg has less trouble finding her voice now. "Jessica has been lying there, all this time, and you're *sorry*?"

She lurches toward him, and Silas reaches for her, ensnaring her torso. "Okay, okay now," he says, trying to pull her back. He's furious, too; fifteen years' worth of fury is now battling with all that guilt, vying for dominance as it courses through him in red-hot waves. But if he gives in to it, what good does that do? Danny is a crumpled form on the ground at this point, far from able to withstand the trial of Silas's emotions.

Walters takes the opportunity to regain command of the room. "Get up, man," he says, though his usual authority sounds strained. There can't be any precedent for situations like this, and there's a tremor to his movements as he holds out a pair of cuffs he's unclipped from a holder on his belt. "Stand up and face this."

As he begins to read Danny his rights, Silas feels the fury dilute in his veins as other emotions rush in: despair, regret, sadness . . . for Jessica, but for Danny, too. He pictures the pebble arcing through the air. Can still hear the dull *plunk* it made, landing in the dirt. Hears the startling echo of Jessica's scream off the granite. He and Meg, they went about things all wrong; they caused pain. They told their own half-truths and outright lies so many times, it was easy to forget, until today, that Jessica's story had still not been fully told. All this time, all of them—Walters, Meg, Silas—have been trying to solve the puzzle of her disappearance from the wrong angle.

He thinks of the rides in the Jeep, and the hikes and the dips in the mountain lakes . . . all the minutes that, when combined, led up to this moment. To Danny's anger and jealousy and violence. Eventually, he turns away from watching Danny being led out of the com van, his brain bleached clean with shocking finality.

On his way out, Danny hesitates next to Meg, twisting awkwardly in his cuffs to address her one more time. Her face is now abnormally pale, her hair dark in contrast, the color of rust when wet. "You know me," he says. "You know how I would never have meant for any of this to happen."

"You messed with Rick's flight plans. You told Walters to call off the lake." Her anger is still right on the surface, but somewhere deeper down, she has to be grappling with the knowledge that Danny's not the only one in this stifling van who is capable of sabotaging a search. But then Meg adds, "You could have cost Spencer his *life!*" And Silas no longer has any room in his brain for anything but his boys.

Walters yanks Danny forward, passing him off to an assistant deputy outside. He returns almost immediately, and he looks shaken—Silas imagines they all must—and his face is red with exertion and stress, but he seems just as eager as Silas to refocus their efforts on the Matheson kids. "Listen, folks," he says gruffly. "We'll need to get official statements, but that can wait until forensics confirms cause of death and collects any DNA on the scene." He clears his throat. "Priority number one: we have a search to get back to."

With that, the room slowly resumes a hum of activity. "I'm going to dispatch the forensics team and check in with our ground pounders," Santos says. He speaks into the radio, conversing with Team Eight, who still have nothing to report. Surely, this can't be how it ends, Silas thinks, in this room, in a splintering of memory and pain. He fights back against this possibility. *Some* fragment of redemption must remain to be salvaged today.

Because there's still the key piece to this puzzle, here and now. There's Cameron.

28

MEG

Meg's not sure how she expected to feel after finally purging herself of the secret that's been sitting like a stone in the pit of her stomach for fifteen years, just to have an entirely different truth bomb detonate, but it's not like this. In all the moments she imagined telling Danny what really transpired the night of Jessica's disappearance, it never, in her wildest imagination, included him one-upping her with a confession of this magnitude. It casts every day of their past fifteen years together in shadow, and she bends at the waist, hugging her knees to her chest, willing herself to hold it together.

Next to her pack at her feet, she spies Spencer's jeans, which sit awaiting inventory on Waggins's report, still balled up and wet from when she plucked them from the marsh by the pond. They're filthy, coated in mud and grime, and the denim is so wet the material bends stiffly where she attempted to fold it. Silas wants to believe Spencer shed them after they became soaked: wilderness survival 101. But Meg knows the confused mental state of hypothermia could be just as likely, which calls Cameron's well-being into more question than ever. It's all too much; Meg can practically feel the oppressive dampness, the cold that surely sank all the way to Spencer's bones, the same cold that is undoubtedly still penetrating Cameron's skin, *somewhere out there.*

She bends to grab the jeans, intending to bag them and set them aside. But then her hand freezes midair, her breath caught in her throat. Very slowly, she reaches down and picks up a small object that has rolled out of the front right pocket.

"Silas," she breathes, opening her palm to reveal the impossibly shiny surface of a chunk of jet-black obsidian. Silas stares down at the burnished surface of the stone in Meg's hand as his eyes widen in recognition.

"Oh my God."

Darcy leans in, inspects the stone, then looks between them with a furrowed brow. "What?" she snaps.

Meg can't speak. Her mind is churning too fast, snagging on memory again before being cast back into the present. Obsidian glints in her mind's eye. The sound of splintering wood fills her ears as she remembers the way her foot crashed through the boarded-up, unmarked mine.

"Do you think . . . could he have . . . ?" she says, then stops, still fixated on the rock like it's a sacred object. To her, it is. Dare she hope Silas feels the same?

Darcy's patience breaks. "Will someone *please* tell me the significance of this chunk of rock before my head explodes?"

Meg and Silas look at one another; then both begin to talk.

"There's only one place I've ever seen obsidian up here," she tells her, in a tight rush. "The Long Lake mine shaft."

"My fireplace mantel," Silas counters at the exact same time.

Meg is startled. "Your mantel? You mean this is our—*my*—stone?"

Instantly, she's reliving that day . . . the Jeep and the mine and the summer heat. *You saved it?* she wants to ask. *All this time?*

But Silas rises abruptly, and the moment passes. "It was on my mantel," he says. "Spence must have grabbed it—"

"But if he didn't?" Meg presses. Because doesn't he see what this means? "If this *isn't* that rock, then . . ."

Silas picks up the thread of Meg's logic and takes it swiftly to its conclusion. "Then that means they've been there. In the mine." His face falters. "But I've never told them about it."

"That doesn't mean they didn't stumble upon it."

Silas weighs this possibility, a thin thread of hope that's beautiful to see teasing the corners of his mouth. "Do you really think he could have wandered that far? To our—the—*mine shaft?*"

She envisions it . . . the hike around Long Lake. The climb up the slope. What has she thought more than once in the past twenty-four hours? That any kid of Silas's would push boundaries. Test limits. Go the distance. "I do."

Silas nods. "Which means we're close, but we're searching in the wrong place!"

Their eyes lock on one another, the tight confines of the com van narrowing to include only her and him and the few short feet between them. When Darcy's voice cuts back across the small space, they both startle.

"What mine shaft? Start at the beginning. Because if our people are wasting their time on the wrong grid, I need to know."

"I have a rock just like this," Silas explains. They all study it. Is it the same one Meg gave him all those years ago? "This may be it . . . I don't . . ." He looks closer, the pad of his thumb tracing the smooth planes. "I don't know. But if it's not . . ."

"We know where Spencer got this one," Meg finishes for him.

Darcy picks up her radio to contact a deputy standing by at the lodge. "On the mantel in the dining room?" she confirms before transmitting, and Silas nods mutely. She relays the location into her handheld, and they wait while the deputy goes in search of it. A minute goes by before her radio squawks back to life.

"Base?" the deputy prompts.

"Go ahead."

"The item in question is here. Chunk of obsidian about two inches in diameter."

At first the words are devoid of meaning. Could this all be falling into place? If they're just grasping at straws, why is Silas already pushing past her to the topographical map on Darcy's desk, his finger tracing a path from Long Lake due east, toward the mines? Why is Santos already on the radio, confirming the current location of each field team in an attempt to gauge which one is closest to their new target area? Darcy is standing by, ready to relay the coordinates once they have them at their fingertips, and Meg cautiously allows herself to believe: it's not just her, clinging to nothing but thin air. This really is their big break.

"I can't remember the bearing," Silas says in frustration, bent over the map.

Meg joins him, running a finger over the thin, curving lines that lap across the topo map's surface. She pictures his map from so long ago, probably long lost, with the unmarked mine punctured so perfectly with his pencil tip. She closes her eyes, recalling that hike through the woods to the mine in the heat of the sun. It's Fourth of July and they're standing at the edge of the lake and he's turning her by the shoulders, pointing her in the direction they need to go. The compass needle is quivering, hovering between the tiny white numbers spanning the dial, and she can feel the rough edge of the baseplate in the crook of her fingers. She recalls Silas's breath on the back of her neck as he bent forward, his hands braced on her shoulders, and she remembers the needle swinging and vacillating and, finally, resting.

"Eighty degrees!" she blurts, and Silas looks back at her. "At the edge of the lake, that's the bearing."

Silas reroutes his finger on the map, following her direction. "Yes, this is it!"

The contour marks become dense and rounded, indicating a steep ridge, and just around the opposite side, where their direction shifts like the flow of an eddy, is the location of the mine that still exists in the eyes of the Forest Service. If that one—the one they crawled into, dark, dank, the buzz of mosquitoes echoing off the walls into her ears—is there, the *other* one, the one they stumbled upon accidentally, the one covered in a carpet of obsidian, is right . . .

"Here!" Silas says sharply, tapping his finger forcefully against the thin paper. Meg reaches around him, her arm snaking to mark the place he's pinpointing with a single pencil dot. She grabs a ruler, tracing the point of her pencil lightly along its edge from the marked spot to the grid of coordinates framing the map. She relays the GPS coordinates to Darcy.

They're not exact. There's no way to be. But she knows that's close enough to give the searchers a place to begin looking for Cameron.

"Do you really think he's there, in that mine shaft?" Silas asks, and she nods.

"I think Spencer was, at least," she clarifies after a moment. "I've been all over this area for the last decade and a half," she says softly, "and I've never seen obsidian anywhere else."

"Then we've got to go. Now." He barely looks to Darcy and Santos as he decides this, already at the door of the Lemon, urgency practically humming off of him.

Meg couldn't agree more. She grabs her pack from the floor and crosses the room to join him.

"Meg!" Sheriff Walters barks, and she halts, the rush of her pulse beating in double time to the seconds ticking on the clock on the wall. "Take a radio," he commands, and she closes her eyes in relief before moving again, strapping the receiver to her chest and following Silas out the door.

The rain is still a driving force before them; it's hitting their faces at a punishing angle, and Meg pulls her hood over her head, ducking her face to shield it as best she can from the deluge. Her hair refuses to stay in place, plastering to her forehead and neck in wet tendrils when not whipping about in the wind, and she swipes at it impatiently, trying to clear her vision.

Silas sets a pounding pace, and for a while it's all she can do to keep up. She doesn't have the luxury of thinking too hard about Jessica, of the horror of her body—*her remains*—cradled all this time at the foot of a cliff, nor the horror of Danny's confession, and for that, Meg is grateful. She concentrates on the pull of her muscles in her calves as they navigate the first uphill slope and then on the rhythm of her breathing as they hit the trail at as fast a clip as they can manage given the muddy, slick conditions.

In her haste to find Cameron, it occurs to Meg too late that their route to the mine will take them directly past the spot where they lost Jessica. Maybe it's the rain obscuring her view, or the overtaxed state of her mind, but when they finally come face-to-face with the exact bend in the trail where Silas had leaped and Jessica had cried out and she and Silas had set everything after in motion, the significance hits her like a slap.

Their location is not lost on Silas, either. She knows by the way his shoulders tense. He continues on, slightly hunched, ducking a little too sharply from the force of the rain. Is he experiencing the same impulse to silence his footfalls and creep past this stretch of trail instead of jog?

She's acutely aware of how Silas took the heat in the com van and can't shake the feeling that she, too, owes Jessica so much more. *It was me,* she said, *the footprints were mine,* and even though the statement resounded with a satisfying ring of finality—silencing Danny, gratifying Silas—it only makes Meg a woman half-absolved. She's straddling redemption and damnation, and if it weren't for Cameron and his gift of possible atonement, she's not sure she'd be able to find her way today.

But she *does* have Cameron to think about, and when they reach the outlook over Long Lake, it's still raining too hard, the wind blowing too forcefully for anything more than a few clipped words. She's grateful. The radio strapped to her chest is issuing a steady stream of jumbled conversations as Team Eight attempts to meet them from the field in their search for the mine, and they descend to the lakeshore at a half trot. They're searching in the thinnest of light; the cloud cover blanketing the sky casts an oppressive shadow over the treetops, and Meg stumbles more than once, sending streams of pebbles to cascade down toward Silas, several feet below her on the trail. He turns back, and when he reaches out to steady her, his fingers on her skin are stiff with cold. The shock of it sends an answering chill straight down her spine. His bare hands have been exposed to the elements only minutes, not hours—and certainly not closing in on forty-eight hours—and she hopes he's not thinking what she's thinking, assessing his discomfort and multiplying it by two full nights and a day.

As they fight their way through the dense underbrush at the shore of the lake, it's hard for Meg to believe that she was here only yesterday, *this close*, calling for the boys while Max flipped rowboats and Danny checked the locks on the storage shed. Everything's coming around full circle, spinning madly, faster and faster, and this time she doesn't even notice the sage slapping her thighs or the branches of low-slung pine scratching her face as they push their way onward.

When they finally reach the far shore, Silas tries to take the GPS unit from Meg's hands—she graduated from a standard compass years ago—but she's already pulling off her gloves, and his dexterity is too compromised for him to argue when she takes it back.

"I've got this," she shouts over the wind, and she *does*.

She inputs their bearing of 80 degrees, and they begin walking directly into the wilderness, following the direction of the digital arrow on her screen. Humidity clouds the plastic face of the unit, and the overcast sky filters the light to such a degree that Meg has to stop every few feet to keep to the course. She retrieves her headlamp from her pack, and this helps a bit, but the going is still so slow that Silas keeps striding too far ahead, rattling her, and she keeps shouting at him to wait.

They reach a clearing, and Meg stops, turning in a circle. Nothing is at all familiar in this sideways-spitting rain, and her self-assurance slips. Silas stops beside her, awaiting direction for once, and she spirals in a crisis of confidence. Did they turn off the trail too soon? Have they walked far enough? Fifteen years ago they were talking as they hiked. She wasn't paying as much attention as she should have been. They had the benefit of the full light of day.

She calls in her coordinates to Base, but she knows it's just protocol. The assembly in the Lemon does not have another bearing for her. Only she and Silas have ever been where they're going, and right now, in the rain, they're staring down a debilitating, terrifying loss. This is their chance at redemption, she thinks desperately. They have to get this right.

"How far have we come?" Silas shouts, and she fumbles with the GPS, her bare fingers cramping painfully as she scrolls through the menu to find what she's looking for.

"Four hundred ninety feet?" He frowns, and he's right: it makes no sense. She peers closer. "No, wait. Forty-nine *hundred* feet."

He says something about miles, or milestones, but she can't hear him. "What?" His words are lost on the wind the instant they leave his mouth. Panic closes in. They're wasting time. "Silas! *What?*"

Grasping both her shoulders, he pulls her to him to speak directly into her ear. "We're close!" he says. "Last time we went almost a mile in from the trail."

She nods mutely. She thinks that's right. It has to be right.

"We traveled uphill, and then we came upon the marked mine first," Silas reasons. "From there, the other one, with the obsidian, is just over the ridge."

She knows . . . she remembers . . . and they begin to run. They reach the meadow, and yes, this looks right. Even in the rain, Meg has regained her bearings. They're at the marked mine. The dark chasm of the entrance to the open tunnel is right there, gaping in what was then a patch of sunlight where they tossed their packs before eating lunch and what is now a deepening puddle of runoff. This is not the shaft where they'll find Cameron, she feels sure of it, but even so, as they look in to make certain, her gut tightens in anxious anticipation. When the beam of her headlamp bounces off nothing but slick bare rock, she doesn't know whether to be disappointed or relieved.

"It's empty!" she calls to Silas, who is already pivoting, anxious to search the unmarked, obsidian-carpeted mine. She calls in these new coordinates; she wants everyone possible on hand.

The team member who responds is from Team Eight, and he tells her they're close by. With the coordinates she's given, they can be there within minutes, and Meg allows herself a fleeting instant of relief. She knows she's unprepared for the multitude of contingencies revolving in a slow circle in her brain. Cameron will be hypothermic, he could be hurt; the list goes on and on. And that's if they're lucky enough to find him here at all. When the others arrive, maybe a fraction of the weight of responsibility will be lifted from her shoulders.

Silas runs up the steep slope ahead of her between the two shafts, and she follows after him, her boots slipping in the mud as she struggles to find purchase on the incline. He crests the ridge and drops down the other side to where the mine lies in wait, and suddenly Meg knows she can't let him do this alone. She has to be the first to cross that threshold and see what there is to see, because what are the odds this will end the way they all hope? If there's any justice at all in this world, they're slim to none, aren't they? Certainly for her and Silas.

She calls out to him, but of course he cannot hear her, and still she climbs up the slope . . . slipping, falling . . . her fingers sinking into the loosened soil. She reaches the top and practically slides down the other side just in time to see him bend, and duck, and then enter the mine they opened all those years ago. He calls for Cameron, and then he's calling for *her*, and she realizes belatedly that he doesn't have a light. He must be blindly feeling his way along the blackness of the tunnel as he yells. The muscles of her thighs burn as she propels herself downward, willing her legs to go faster.

He's still calling— *"Cameron! Meg! Cameron! Meg!"*—as she reaches the halfway point on the downhill slide, but then, with a shift to his tone like the flipping of a switch, he's screaming. It's a wail that slices straight to the core, shaking Meg in a way that would have made her legs give out altogether had she not already been there, *just now*, at the entrance to the mine shaft. Her light catches first the glint of blackness in the tunnel—obsidian? Simply the void of daylight?—and then it shines upon the image of Silas, bent forward on his knees, his hands groping wildly as he reaches for the pale shape of his son.

She falls to her knees beside him, offering her light, but Silas is frantic, skimming his hands along the planes of Cameron's face, his fingers trailing over his nose and then his mouth in the most desperate of tactile sweeps. To Meg, it looks as though he's trying to absorb two days' worth of pain and suffering from the parting of Cameron's lips and the bell of his ear to the awkward clasp of his hands pressed between his chest and the stone floor of the mine. Her light is on them now, and it's clear that Cameron is completely unresponsive—not a twitch, not a blink—his skin a reflection of the sky in the coldest, stoniest gray. What Silas is really doing is refusing to see.

She wants to do the same, but instead she angles the headlamp more carefully, holding it aloft. Silas begins to moan in a strange cadence that unnerves Meg more than his screams did, echoing unbearably through the tunnel. When he leans forward to sink his face into the curve of Cameron's small shoulder, she shouts at him, trying to pull him back even as she sobs that she's sorry.

"Let me see him!" she yells, because maybe, just maybe, the light is playing tricks on them, desaturating the hue of Cameron's complexion to this particular shade of unnatural white. She's seen hypothermia before—she saw it on his brother only this morning—and if she can just hold the light higher . . . if she can just press her cheek to Cameron's chest and feel for the sigh of a breath, she'll know for certain that—unlike fifteen years ago—she's done everything she can.

That this time, she hasn't hidden, hasn't withheld, and hasn't run away.

29
MEG

The Howard search officially ended at 6:00 p.m. on Day 5. What Sheriff Walters, and Halloway, and Les, and Meg's mother said this meant: there was nothing more the kids could do. They were free to go.

After five days of constant vigil, interrupted by only a few hours of rest in Feather River in between, it felt so wrong to be home. *Home.* For good. In her room with her posters on the wall and her graduation tassel hanging from her bedpost, while Jessica was . . . Jessica was who knew where? As much as Meg had hated the hours spent sitting in the cloying heat of the lodge, at least she had been doing something, if only standing vigil. She imagined Jessica, isolated against miles of empty forest and craggy granite, scared and alone. She imagined her as she'd been before, happy and tan, chatting with Silas on the trail.

Silas.

A strangely euphoric feeling rose through Meg, only to turn to nausea when it hit the guilt churning in her gut. Like thinking of something very pleasant, then remembering it was a dream. Not real. Couldn't be real.

She couldn't stop seeing the look on his face when she'd stopped him outside the lodge, urging him not to tell the authorities everything. Once she'd gotten through to him, she'd seen her own fear reflected back at her. Her own doubt, too.

Just days ago she'd dared to hope things could be so different. As they'd set out on that hike, she had been ready to leap toward a new future, at the college of her choice. And in the shelter of those trees with Silas she'd discovered the awakening of an enticing possibility. Jessica, lost, still missing, changed everything.

Meg wanted a do-over. She'd never wished for anything so hard. Turning the clock back could fix what she had broken by wanting too much. Reaching too far. Altering just one day could make everything all right again. Could return her to the status quo.

But what good was wishful thinking? In the quiet of her bedroom, the rush of the interrogation, with all its frightening intensity, fell away until only one truth remained. Jessica was still *out there*, all alone, and no one knew where to look for her.

The wave of loneliness this thought sent through Meg propelled her out of her bed. She pulled on a pair of jeans blindly, then reached for her shirt, sweeping a pile of papers off her desk in the process. On the top of the stack: the welcome letter to UC Davis. She stared at it for a moment before crumpling it and tossing it in the direction of her trash bin.

Crossing the empty living room, she slipped out her front door in silence. Wanting a change of trajectory had led to all this horribleness. She should have just stayed steady. Maybe she couldn't have a do-over, but she could at least pivot, turn back, and reset her course.

She made her way down the street at a speed walk. It was late; everyone was either in their beds, like her mother, or on the red-eye Union Pacific run toward Reno, like Danny's father.

Later, she'd try to convince herself that what she was about to do was premeditated, but halfway to Danny's house, she realized she'd forgotten her sweatshirt, the cotton shirt she'd tossed on about as useful as tissue paper against the night air. Her shoes weren't doing much for her, either, left back on her front stoop. So much for preparation.

She jogged around the back, careful to avoid tripping over stray logs from the woodpile, and tapped on his bedroom window. Waiting for him to respond, she stared down the darkened glass. *Open up, open up, open up.*

His face registered surprise as he slid his window wide to help her inside. "What's wrong?" he whispered. He looked leery and aged beyond his years, like what he really meant was *What's gone wrong now?*

She squinted into the gloom of his bedroom. "I don't want to be alone."

Maybe she could still be redeemed. It was irrational, but what choice did Meg have? Burning bridges was all she had left, if she wanted back on the straight and narrow.

Danny made room for her on the bed, and she sank down onto the mattress while he stood awkwardly over her. He looked out the window again, as though half expecting Silas, too, out of habit, before shutting it.

"It's just me." She tried not to hear the hollow sadness of this. She slid under the bedcovers, still warm from Danny's body.

"Are you . . . do you want to stay?"

"Yes. I'm sure." There was a first time for everything, wasn't there? She just hoped he wouldn't question this tonight. *Just this once,* she thought fervently, *don't be a Boy Scout.*

He stretched out beside her, still hesitant, not touching her. "Listen. I need to talk about—"

She cut him off, redirecting his hand to her chest. "Not now, Danny. Please."

Danny sucked in a quick breath, and she dipped her head to kiss the side of his neck, her mouth on his throat as she threaded one long leg between his. She wouldn't think about the search. She wouldn't think about Jessica or . . . Silas. She felt Danny respond, but a moment later, he'd untangled himself from her.

"What's wrong?"

He looked wretched, really, now that she looked closer. Haunted but also hardened, somehow. Not the Danny she'd known for so many years. She swallowed a new swell of guilt. This had to have been so hard on him, Danny the public servant in the making. Had she, so caught up in her own tangled story, just not noticed what this search was doing to him?

He regarded her at arm's length. "Are you sure you want this? Do you really want to be with me?"

He looked almost . . . distrusting, and she felt herself flush. "Why wouldn't I want to be?"

His jaw clenched, and when he offered an apologetic smile it didn't reach his eyes. They remained trained on Meg in the dark. She reached for him, but he deflected the caress.

"It's just . . . this isn't how I wanted this to happen."

"What?"

He pinched his eyes closed with his fingers. "Any of this." But his body, still pressed against hers, said otherwise.

"There's no point in waiting forever," she told him. The commitment her mother warned her against had never looked so good. "I think we need this right now." Something about this argument, weak as it was, spoke to something within him. He cupped her face in his hands and nodded, at first hesitantly and then with more conviction.

"Yes, it's you and me, right? Just you and me. *We* are who we need right now."

She didn't answer him. Just resumed where she had left off, her leg wrapped around his hip once more, her face back in the hollow of his throat. She pushed up Danny's shirt, kissing his chest, all the while willing her own tears not to fall. She couldn't let them wet his skin and expose her.

He rolled her from her side to her back, his hands fumbling with the button of her pants, and she let him, willing herself to believe that as restitution went, this just might work.

30

SILAS

All Silas wants to do is curl into the prone form of his son and lose himself. Seeing Cameron in the light of the headlamp feels different from seeing Spencer carried out from the pond. Everything about Spencer's condition felt reversible, the whole universe on fast-forward, trying to beat the clock. Everything in this mine shaft feels carved in cold, hard stone, from the unnatural bend in Cameron's knees to the rigidity of his skin. He presses Cameron's body directly to his torso, rocking him up and down as the cold from his son's body seeps in, clinging to him. If Silas can just hide here for a moment, burying his face into the wet cotton of Cameron's sweatshirt, he'll be ready when time sweeps forward again, carrying him with it.

From far away, Meg pleads with him. "Silas! Lay him down."

She falls to her knees beside him, trying to wedge herself between him and Cameron. Her fingers curl around Silas's bicep.

"Silas! Please!"

He looks down at her fingers gripping his jacket, ghostly white in the beam of the headlamp. They're just as far away as her voice, as if he's looking through the wrong end of a telescope.

"No! Just let me be with him!" He doesn't mean to yell. He just . . . has to.

She sobs with frustration and something else, something Silas wants to soothe, but cannot. He's glad she's here, just her, no one else but her and him and Cameron. Even as he thinks it, other voices call through the dark behind them, and people who are not Meg appear in the rectangular frame of the tunnel entrance. A searcher crashes forward through the crowd of packs and dogs, and someone shouts, "He's a medic!" and someone else says, "Let him through!" and then this EMT is helping Meg pry Cameron from Silas's grasp.

Silas is thrown off-balance, his back hitting the rock wall of the tunnel. The accompanying stab of pain shocks him into the present in a way that Cameron's prone body did not. The EMT lays Cameron flat and stretches out on the ground beside him, belly to stone, listening for him to draw a breath. Everyone else holds theirs. He presses two fingers to Cameron's neck hard enough that Silas yells out in protest. Everyone else yells for quiet. He bites his tongue, hard, watching the medic feel for a pulse as the rain drips in a steady *plunk, plunk, plunk* from the tunnel roof. When he looks up and shakes his head, Silas wails.

The sound echoes off the stone, setting the search dogs pacing restlessly outside the tunnel to bark and howl. Somewhere to Silas's right, someone reaches for a radio, and he braces for the word *black* to cut yet again across the airwaves, but it doesn't come. Instead, the EMT clamps a hand down over the intercom, halting the searcher midmessage.

"Call in red," he orders. "We don't know anything for sure until he's rewarmed." He bends back over Cameron.

"He's not dead until he's warm and dead," someone else intones, and Meg hisses, "Shut *up*, McCrady!"

Silas's mind lurches like a pendulum swinging. Dead? Not dead? Around him, a flurry of questions and commands bounce against the slick walls of the tunnel: "Is he too fragile to actively rewarm?" "Someone hand me an emergency blanket!" "Can we maintain the heat here in the field?" Words like *protocol* and *circumstances* follow fragments of *how do we?* and *where should we?*

After interminable debate, the medic begins removing Cameron's clothing carefully. It seems awful, stripping what little protection a cold child clings to, but someone is still holding Silas back, and someone else is saying, "It's okay, it's okay," over and over again. It takes Silas far too long to realize this voice is Meg's.

As the soaked layers are stripped away from Cameron's body, Silas notices for the first time that he's wearing not only his Dinosaur Days sweatshirt he begged for at the science museum last spring but Spencer's Riverside Elementary one as well. An unexpected surge of pride in his older son swells within him. Once Cameron lies completely bare on the rock surface of the tunnel, heating pads line his groin, armpits, and neck. Meg wraps the space blanket someone produced loosely around him, then pleads to Silas, "Don't watch."

He doesn't have time to ask what she means before the EMT begins CPR. The heels of the man's palms come down hard on the barrel of Cameron's little chest, and his son's entire body bucks. Silas screams, but the medic does it again. And again. Cameron scoots half a foot across the floor of the tunnel like a limp rag doll; the effort loosens one of his hands from the folds of the space blanket. It hits the ground with a soft plop, seemingly lifeless and blue against the silver of the blanket.

"His hand!" Silas cries. "It will be cold!"

He rocks forward on his knees, reaching to tuck Cameron's fingers back under the blanket, his own fingers clumsy with cold. It makes no difference; Cameron's hand flops away again on his next compression. Meg is still there, and Silas whirls back on her for help, but instead she takes her own firm hold of Silas's arm to help halt his reach.

"Don't," she says, and for the first time since they entered the mine, she doesn't sound in control. "It doesn't help!" Someone nearby says something about warming the core before the periphery, and Meg explains, "We can't rewarm his hands yet. Not here."

She leans in to Silas, watching Cameron, and eventually he lets himself collapse back against her. Multiple flashlight beams dance over the walls of the tunnel, adding visual confusion to the cacophony of shouts and instruction, and Silas trains his gaze only on Cameron, rigid and gray, and the medic, compressing and compressing in his horrible, jerky rhythm. The denim of Silas's pants clings to his cold skin, wet with rain, and his fingers remain too stiff to bend. It's only the hum of body heat radiating from Meg as they sit, hunched together, that's keeping him from splitting apart.

He's just allowed his face to drop into his hands when the EMT straightens and lets out a triumphant yell. It rings like the crack of a whip in the hollowed-out space of the tunnel, and Silas's head snaps up. Beside him, Meg springs to her knees.

"I have a breath!" the medic calls, and then, one carefully timed minute later, the pads of his fingers still pressed to Cameron's carotid artery: "Three beats per minute!"

Three. Isn't it supposed to be thirty? One hundred and thirty? Silas doesn't know, but . . . *three?*

The pendulum that's rocked him since setting out for this mine swings again. He falls forward over Cameron and weeps into the folds of the space blanket until they pull him away again. He doesn't fight them: his son's heart was still and is now pumping. He won't ask why or how. Beside him, Meg watches Cameron with a look of awe in the flicker of the lights, and Silas knows that redeemed or not, fair or not, what they have just witnessed is nothing short of a resurrection. He'll take it, deserved or no: in his experience, very few people truly get what they have coming.

31

SILAS

Silas couldn't sleep. It had been awful, staying every night at the lodge with all the search crews and media, but it was even worse now that it was quiet again, just him and Uncle Les and Aunt Mary. Just before 2:00 a.m., he rolled out of bed, retrieved his key ring from the peg above the check-in counter, and slipped out the side kitchen door. He climbed into the Jeep and then sat for a long moment in the parking lot, bracing for the turn of the ignition to prompt the quick illumination of lights in the living quarters upstairs. When he finally worked up the nerve to twist the key, the lodge remained dark, and he rolled down the access road to descend the highway toward Feather River at a reckless clip.

Meg had been avoiding him, not even answering her phone in her room when he rang her at night, but it was time to talk things through. They had been cast into a surreal, awful landscape, but finding one's way out was simple navigation . . . they just needed to study the lay of the land, find their bearings, and set a new course. Silas could plot his way out of any terrain.

Even after what happened to Jessica? Even after this week?

The memory of Meg's touch returned to him, her lips on his, her breath, like little gasps, that kept time with the heavy beat of her pulse in her wrist. Yes. They could find their way back to one another. Silas knew they could.

He parked at the end of Meg's drive, shutting off the lights a full block in advance, but the minute he reached her bedroom window and glanced inside, he knew she wasn't there. He stood at her sill, peering through the dark to make out her still-made bed; the shirt she had worn at the lodge two days ago lay on the floor, her shoes tossed in the direction of the closet. Her mom's car sat parked in the drive, all the lights in the house were out, and, all at once, he *knew* where she must be spending her nights.

Why hadn't he seen it coming? *We need to fix this,* she had said, in that first terrible hour of searching for Jessica. *We need to go back.*

She hadn't meant back up to the trail. She'd meant back-back . . . to when it had been Meg and Danny, not Meg and Silas. Back to when her life had been predictable and manageable and safe.

He shouldn't have been shocked by how badly it hurt, and yet the pain cut him down so swiftly he practically staggered back to the Jeep. Ironically, the first stab wasn't betrayal, although he imagined that would come. It was loneliness. In all the time he'd known Meg and Danny, he'd never truly felt like the odd man out until tonight.

He had shared five stolen minutes with Meg, whereas Danny had spent years. Had Silas really thought he could compete with that?

Yes. Of course he had.

He sat in the Jeep until the sun rose over the mountains to the east, not knowing whether Meg would sneak back home before full daybreak or risk staying at Danny's all day. It didn't matter, because he didn't plan to confront her. He wouldn't do that to her. But he did need to be sure.

He drove around the corner from Danny's house and waited, watching for her while hidden from view and detesting himself for it.

Was it really necessary to go to such lengths to garner proof of how thoroughly his life had fallen apart?

Again, yes.

When he finally saw Meg heading back home sometime just past six, she walked with focus, her eyes trained on the dark asphalt. Her hair fell forward across her face, and she marched with shoulders squared. She wore Danny's navy-and-red fire-station sweatshirt, and it didn't fit, of course. It hung down well past her hips to brush the backs of her pajama-clad thighs, and she wrapped her arms around her torso, drawing the material tightly to her throat. Watching her clench the material to her body, Silas had to concede: if she needed to try this hard to make her relationship with Danny fit, there was nothing Silas could do. She walked steadily on, the sweatshirt billowing behind her like a cloak in subtle resistance to the early-morning breeze, and if this warmed her, if this layer was the protection Meg needed, Silas would never deny her it.

The rest of that morning he packed haphazardly, throwing books and clothing into the boxes already awaiting departure to college. He overstuffed each cardboard box, not caring what went where, despite Aunt Mary's attempts at interjecting organization. Silas only wanted to rid his room of everything. One by one, he hauled the boxes out to the Jeep in the driveway, then climbed the narrow staircase one last time to survey his room swept clean. The bed sat bare and boxy in the center of the floor, the spread peeled away and packed. The star maps were gone from the walls, the topography scrolls no longer cluttering the oak desk by the window. Standing in the doorway, he stared down the empty walls and wished himself already gone. All the lies and even the truths he had told over the past week crowded his brain, churning in a violent way that made him want to punch the wood paneling and cry at the same time.

Convincing his parents by phone to allow him to drive himself to college—*right now, today*—wasn't easy, but it was the only thing left for him to do. He couldn't stay here and receive Uncle Les's and Aunt Mary's condolences and support. He couldn't even deal with reinserting himself into his parents' whirlwind life, distracting as that would be. And he definitely couldn't remain in Feather River. Maybe if he fled— no, maybe if he took himself out of the equation completely—in his absence, everything for Meg would make sense to her again.

He hadn't even hit the highway before he wanted to pull over, find a phone, and call her. The only thing stopping him was what to say: *Sorry to take off on you? What did you want from me? Why didn't you give us a chance?*

Maybe she'd say she'd given him the only chances she could while they sat in the lodge, looking anywhere but at each other throughout the vigil of Jessica's search. But he hadn't been able to move from his chair then, much less cross the room to sit beside her, for fear of upsetting the delicate balance that was their version of the truth.

He felt afraid now, too. In lieu of calling her, he settled for imagining their final conversation as he rounded each bend along the Feather River. She'd ask him where he was, and then why. He'd tell her he knew about her choosing Danny.

"Do you hate me?" she'd ask, and he'd say no. It was true, but what good did truth do him? She'd heard Silas tell so many lies. He'd want to say something about martyrdom and false bravado and giving up before good things could begin. He wouldn't know whether he meant her or him.

She'd say, "You're leaving me with all this?"

And he'd say, "No. I'm taking it with me."

He grimaced at the grind of the Jeep's gears as he took the hairpins along the river. If she were here right now, she'd tell him to slow down. He eased up on the pedal but still took the corners too tightly, barely in control, outracing the storm.

32

SILAS

One day post–Matheson search
November 22, 2018
Reno, Nevada

Under the bright light of the ICU unit, Silas learns that Cameron's rebirth is due to a physiological phenomenon known as a metabolic icebox. He leans against the pale-green hospital wall with Miranda, and they listen as their son's doctor tells them about unresponsive hypothermia victims essentially stopping time in their own bodies, reducing their need for energy to nearly nothing. Silas imagines Cameron in the tunnel of the mine, his small body hibernating, waiting to be awoken.

Cameron sustains no neurological damage. When Silas hears the words *full neurological recovery*, the promise of them, uncoiling from the fear at the pit of his stomach, lifts him like a balloon on a string. It enables him to finally have the conversation he owes Miranda.

"I'm sorry," he tells her simply, standing outside Spencer's room, where she's been keeping their older son company. The two words carry the heft of bricks as he finally lays them down. He's still ashamed for tasking Santos with delivering the initial news that should have come from him. "I'm so sorry for letting this happen on my watch," he continues. "For thinking I could do this, give them this life here." What he doesn't add, because he's never fully opened up to her regarding Marble Lake and can't possibly start from the beginning now: *I felt like I cursed our children, bringing them back here.*

Her eyes have been down on the linoleum squares at their feet, but now she lifts her head. "You *can* do this," she says. "You *are* giving them this life." She cocks her head slightly to peer at him steadily, a sad smile touching her lips. "But one day you're going to realize, Silas, that not everything is up to you and you alone." She lifts one eyebrow. "You don't get to take responsibility for *everything*."

He tries to smile back. "The boys get some credit, too?"

"Don't push it. You *are* the one who convinced them they could scale mountains."

She lays a hand on his shoulder, giving it a soft pat that feels like forgiveness and farewell all in one touch. The boys' discharge imminent, she says her goodbyes to them as well, promising to see them again soon, and the trust conveyed in her departure makes Silas feel pounds lighter as he returns to Cameron's side. He listens as every shrill *beep* of the monitor punctuates another step along a path to revival, feeling his confidence return by slow degrees with each flash on the screen. In the end, Cameron loses only one pinky finger to the effects of frostbite. Lying beside him on the extra bed that's been wheeled into the room, in between visits from various members of the sheriff's department and the media—Walters needs his statement to close out the Howard case; News 4 wants a sound bite about Cameron—Silas stares at his younger son's bandaged hand. This penance is small, but Miranda's forgiveness notwithstanding, it strikes him squarely in the chest, dagger-sharp. He won't get used to this: the thankfulness and the fear, the agony mixed with the relief. He takes comfort in Spencer sitting beside him, released back into his care just today, the warmth of his body sinking into Silas's shirt where he curls in to his side.

"When do we get to go home?" Spencer mumbles, twisting deeper into the blanket the hospital has brought him. His breath, too, is warm against Silas's ribcage.

A new, second agony arises in him. Does Spencer mean home to Portland? Did he ask Miranda about this, even though Silas knows she explained that she can't whisk him away? Because why *wouldn't* Spencer want to get as far away from this place as possible, after what happened? It was, after all, exactly what Silas had done. But even as he thinks this, he knows that this time he wants to stand his ground. Wants a second chance, with his kids.

This desire feels horribly selfish until Spencer adds, "'Cause I want to put those star posters in my and Cam's room. You know . . . the ones you said you had hung up when the upstairs was yours?"

Silas exhales. "Yeah. Okay. We'll do that as soon as we can."

Spencer snuggles deeper. "Which stars did I see last night, do you think? And the night before that?"

That damned agony gives another lurch in Silas's belly before rising like bile. "I'm not sure," he chokes. But he knows how bright the night sky is here in the Sierra. He knows how the entire Milky Way can glow. "Did they help you see at all?"

Spencer lifts his head and thinks about this. "The first night they were like a night-light, they were so bright." He pauses, and his face clouds. "Last night was darker."

"It got cloudy," Silas confirms. "Getting ready to rain."

"And Cam wasn't talking anymore."

Silas stifles a low sob. He hasn't pressed Spencer yet for detailed information, and he isn't sure he's ready to learn more now, either. But Spencer isn't done sharing. "Before that we pretended we were playing *Green Laser*," he tells Silas, "in the tunnel." He's talking about their favorite game app on Silas's phone, and he immediately pictures the black lines of the maze the boys love to navigate their little green avatars through.

"You explored the mine, huh?" he manages.

"We just pretended that, too. Sitting against the rock wall. Cam was too tired." He adjusts under the blanket, pulling his knees up tighter to his small chest. "And after a while," he adds, "Cam didn't even wanna pretend anymore."

"Is that when you left the mine? To go get help?" Silas works hard not to picture Spencer, facedown in the marsh of the pond, where Meg found him.

Spencer nods. "With Cam so quiet, it felt like game over in *Green Laser*, but with no restart button." He kind of laughs at himself. "That's silly, but I decided it was time to stop pretending."

"That was right," Silas manages tightly. "That was the right thing to do." He draws him in closer, squeezing him to his side almost roughly, trying to let the solid warmth of him be enough. To let his son's well-being—his *two* sons' well-being—make up for all the wrongs Silas has done. It doesn't, it can't, but that's not on Spencer. Spencer is breaking the cycle. "You did so good, son," he tells him. "You saved him, you know that, right? You saved your brother's life."

MEG

Meg wakes at home to the sound of the automatic coffee maker percolating. She was dreaming of rain, and for a moment she's disoriented by the sight of the sun filtering through her blinds. Storms in the Sierra are like that; they commence and then they break with identical flair, their weakness for high drama unmatched.

She's told that Danny is still at the station awaiting bail; there's time to see him, should she have anything to say. Questions arise in a flood: How could he have lived, all this time, with what he did? How could he have borne witness to Jessica's mother's grief and not shared what he knew about her daughter's final resting place? How could Meg have? And how could they all have justified their roles in the destructive triangle they had all become entangled in?

But when she gets to the dark little trailer in the parking lot of the sheriff station for what they call a reception visit, she finds herself overwhelmed by the sheer magnitude of fifteen years' worth of secrets and lies. She starts with what feels like the smallest piece of the puzzle, intending to work her way outward.

"Why did you stay with me all these years?" she asks him. Did Danny ever really love her at all? She wants him to connect the dots for her, orienting her like Silas used to, so long ago, with the constellation book in his bedroom at the lodge. Help her see where their stars all crossed paths. *Please,* Meg implores silently, *explain to me how a man I've known almost all my life, a good man, a community servant, could have gotten from this particular point A to point B.*

Danny doesn't meet her gaze, his eyes trained on the countertop he's resting his cuffed hands upon. "Jessica could never seem to keep Silas's attention," he tells the countertop. "In life, I mean. No matter how much I wished she could." He finds the courage to look up, and she can see that a deep bitterness still shines in his eyes. It makes them look foreign to her. "But in the end, it was her death that managed to destroy you two. I couldn't let that be in vain, could I?"

Meg stares at him, horror-struck. He almost looks . . . vindicated. In light of what he did to Jessica, she can see more plainly now what he did to *her,* too . . . what, essentially, she allowed him to do: dismissing her ideas about going to college, telling her that victim advocacy wasn't for her, casting Silas as the villain for the past fifteen years. She felt it for so long, like an ache under the skin. That viselike grip of manipulation. How had Silas described it, that day at the mine? Being boxed in.

She decides she won't allow him to manipulate her or her reality for a single second more. She walks away without another word, taking the long way home along the river, past the trestle Silas once dared her to climb, past the forest road where the Jeep got stuck in the springtime mud. She doesn't know how it will end for Danny, whether he will serve time after what promises to be an extensive and grueling trial. But she knows his departure from her life will leave a void, because she already feels a vast and satisfying sense of space.

After so many years of denying herself room to move on, she feels lighter than air.

She realizes she's gripping the steering wheel too tightly as she watches the cloud banks shift, finding new sky to darken. Despite the patches of blue, serious weather is still on the horizon, and this doesn't feel over. She wants to call Silas. She wants to be wherever he is now, in Reno at Washoe Medical, facing whatever it is he's facing with his kids. When she gets home, she calls the hospital instead, where identifying herself as the SAR member who found the Matheson boys earns her a basic report on Cameron and Spencer. She tells herself that's enough.

It's been fifteen years. She can wait a bit longer.

She's called in to the sheriff's department the next day for questioning. Sheriff Walters has scheduled this appointment one hour prior to the official Matheson search debriefing, and already members of her team mill around, buzzing about the search while they get the coffee on. She hears the name *Cairns* whispered from several corners of the room, but her fellow volunteers have the grace to pinch their lips closed as she passes by. A few offer sympathetic smiles. Others look at their shoes. McCrady takes the initiative to clap his hand on her shoulder. "Chin up, kiddo."

She walks directly into Walters's office and stops. What she thought would be a simple interview includes the county prosecutor, her paralegal team, several deputies, plus Walters, Lieutenant Santos, and a tech aid she doesn't know setting up a voice recorder on the foldout table in front of her. She sits, equal parts nervous and sad. Walters turns on the recorder. He tells her to start from the beginning.

She fiddles with her hands as she talks: flat down on the tabletop, then palms up, then folded together before she finally settles on crossing her arms over her chest. She looks at Walters as steadily as she can, and once she gets used to the whir of the recorder, it feels good to pry this final wedge of truth from the dark place it's inhabited until now. She extracts each answer from her mind one by one, admiring the shiny legitimacy of them from every side. *It was Danny who invited Jessica on the hike. He pushed it on me and Silas. Yeah, Danny had an agenda, but Silas was the one who scared her. It was kind of his thing.*

"And after she ran away, then what?" Walters's follow-up questions are harder to answer, each one a pill Meg's so painstakingly swallowed. Danny may have committed the unthinkable up on that cliffside, but Meg is not without culpability.

"We all split up to find her."

Santos sits quietly beside him, taking notes.

"But at some point, you and Silas crossed paths again?"

Meg looks down at her crossed arms. "And when we did, we hid ourselves out of view," she says softly. "We wanted to be alone." She looks up, looks Walters in the eye. "When we scared her off, that was the last time Silas and I ever saw her," she says tightly, regret thick enough to coat her throat.

"But you heard her scream?" Santos prompts.

Meg nods, then remembers to add the audible "Yes."

"How long after you scared her was that?"

Meg thinks. Remembers Silas's arms around her. Remembers the feel of his mouth on hers. She hopes her face hasn't heated. "Five minutes? No more than ten. And we went in search of her, but we couldn't tell where the noise had come from. It was dark, and by then . . ." By then it had all unraveled. "We knew we needed help, and we called you guys."

Outside the room, she can hear the search teams getting restless, waiting for the debriefing to start. Before the interview can end, she asks, "Was any DNA evidence recovered?"

The prosecutor shakes her head in the negative. "No soft tissue remains intact, and while we can positively identify Ms. Howard based on her skeletal matter and dental records, any incriminating evidence, like fingerprints, blood, or bruising is of course long lost."

"We wished so badly that we'd known where she was," Meg says.

Walters studies her. "We?"

"Silas and me," she clarifies.

"Silas and you . . ." he repeats, and Meg waits, but that's it. That's his point. "You sure it was always 'we'? Not 'he'?"

She's not sure what he means.

"Silas was with you the whole time? Never left? Never acted on his own, or with Danny?"

She returns the sheriff's gaze and finally sets her hands, folded calmly, in her lap. This question is easy. *"Yes,"* she tells him. She's sure it was always *we.*

33

MEG

Three days post–Matheson search
November 24, 2018
4:30 p.m.
Feather River

Jessica's cause of death is officially ruled first-degree manslaughter. Danny is also charged with intent to impede a search-and-rescue operation and the endangerment of minors. It's the leading story in the local paper, and the reporter has done a very thorough job of linking the longtime mystery and horror of the Howard search to the fervor of excitement and celebration currently attached to the Matheson search. Even though Meg now knows how the story ends—and, more importantly, how it began—it's startling to see it laid bare in black-and-white print across her kitchen table after so many years.

Through a series of circumstances both coincidental and calculated, the article states, *the search efforts for Cameron Matheson essentially led authorities to the location of the remains of Jessica Howard, who had been missing since 2003.* The story quotes Sheriff Walters, who expresses gratitude for the Matheson boys' safe return before adding, "All of us at

Feather River Sheriff's Department are saddened and dismayed at the evidence that has come to light in the Jessica Howard missing-persons case, which is now an official criminal investigation. Our thoughts and sympathies go out to the Howard family, and they can be assured this department will prosecute the accused to the full extent of the law."

It's something, Meg supposes. It's a small shred of the atonement she's so long sought, arising from the boys' ordeal. But it's not enough. The article focuses on the sensational, detailing how Jessica Howard died of a fracture of her C2 vertebra as the result of a fall, only to remain hidden by the dense underbrush for fifteen years. It's not until Meg reaches the end of the story and sets the paper down that she realizes what's missing: the short window of time from when Jessica first fled to the time of her death. The reporter doesn't speculate on what led Jessica away from the trail to the cliff by the mines; Walters didn't see fit to make this detail from the official report fodder for the media, his act of kindness to Meg and Silas.

Teresa Howard, too, has shown kindness beyond what they deserve, requesting that only Danny be listed as a defendant in her daughter's criminal and civil cases.

"Why?" Meg felt compelled to ask her, standing under the fluorescent lighting of the sheriff's-department hallway.

Teresa Howard gripped Meg's hand in both of her own. "I need justice for Jessica," she told her candidly, watery brown eyes holding Meg's with earnest appeal. "But enough lives have been all twisted up by her death already, haven't they?" She assessed Meg a moment longer. "And, my girl? You've done so much, for so long. Forgive me if I'm wrong, but I imagine you've done your time."

Meg is grateful to be omitted from the article and from Teresa's process of closure, but she still finds herself half wishing the reporter could have pinpointed what still eludes her—where her guilt leaves off and Danny's responsibility for Jessica's death begins. She closes her eyes, sinking inward on the downfall—*her back is hitting the rough bark of the*

tree, the stone is arcing through the air—and rising on its redemption—
Cameron is drawing breath, Spencer is smiling. Down. Up. Fall. Rise. Will
she ever feel balanced, or will she live in this lurch for the rest of her life?

She knows one thing for certain: she has outgrown the careful
monotony of her existence here in Feather River. She can't go back to
sitting at her same desk job next week, and the week after that, and with
sudden certainty, she knows she wants the victim-advocacy job Walters
has put her forth for, if it's still on offer. Her unique perspective on the
Matheson search, privy as she is to Silas's struggle, gives her confidence
she'd be good at it, but there's also something about facing her past that
lends a sense of propulsion, ironic as it may be.

Silas is still a moving target, even in her memory. In her mind's eye
she sees him standing before her for the first time, carrying her through
a conversation so effortlessly it leaves her breathless. He's lying beside
her on the bed in his room, his arm outstretched, tutoring her on the
cosmos, narrowing their scope to include only her. He's pointing out
Cassiopeia, giving Meg a tour of the nuances of her own psyche. He's
looking at her in a way she knows—she's always known—he's never
looked at anyone else . . . across a pond, in the woods amid darkness,
under the rotors of the helo, braced against the wind. He's kissing her
in a way that makes her wish for so much more. In a way that makes
her not care, and do the wrong thing, and then he's gone, and she's left
to remember.

Danny once told her that bracing for a punch to the gut made
it hurt worse: this is true. She replays the shock of hearing of Silas's
departure secondhand, so many years ago, then the startle of his return.
She sees his earnest frown as he imparts his apology in the silence of
the com van.

If it matters, I'm sorry I left.

She believes him, she does, but people make the same mistakes over
again all the time. Hasn't she made fifteen years' worth with Danny?
She knows Cameron was released from the hospital only this morning.

They'll be back at the lodge by now, letting both boys recuperate, but what if their recovery is the only thing holding Silas to Marble Lake? They've all had Jessica's whereabouts hanging over them all for so long. What if finally laying her to rest closes a chapter in Silas's book?

The possibility is unacceptable. Meg rises from her chair fast enough to send a swell of vertigo to her head. She can't do anything more for Jessica, but she can still fix her own life.

The break in the weather lasted longer than anyone anticipated, but now the low clouds are back, waffling between frozen rain and tiny, icy flakes. It's getting dark, and it's starting to snow, but she's out the door, turning over the engine of her truck. As she eases out onto the slick road, she decides she's channeling neither Silas's impulsivity nor Danny's reason but following, rather, some unique impulse of her own making.

She makes good time along the highway, but just as she makes the turn onto Marble Lake Road, fat flakes begin to fall from the sky. Within minutes, they're so thick Meg's windshield wipers can't keep up. She clicks her headlights down to low to avoid being blinded by the ever-spiraling expanse of pure white against the blackening night and bends forward over the steering wheel.

She's driven in whiteout conditions before, and this can't even be considered one, because Meg can still make out the occasional flash of a snow-marker reflector along the shoulder of the road. Still, she can feel the tires crunching the powder as her truck lurches within a single set of deep ruts, already iced over; only one other vehicle has paved the way before her. Silas, just hours before, bringing his boys home?

She passes the midway point to the lodge, where a permanent sign marks the end of the plow route. From here on out, the snow will accumulate unchecked. Even if she can make it up the hill, she won't be coming back down anytime soon. The warning only makes her press her foot down more firmly on the gas. This is exactly what she needs. No way out. A one-way path.

SILAS

The lodge living quarters feel empty with the boys both asleep, Spencer in his own bed, Cameron on the daybed in Silas's room despite his preference to be with his brother, just in case of lingering complications. The wind wails as the storm does its best, and he ought to feel at peace now, with all of them together under one roof. With all of them back home.

Instead, he paces in front of the fireplace. The past days of doctors and reporters and follow-up questions with Walters have left him little time to process the discovery of Jessica's body and Danny's blurted confession. He knows he will need to come to terms with this soon, but not this week. Not tonight. So many people have come and gone: medics and specialists, Santos, Miranda. For Silas, the search had acted as a sieve, shaking and sorting his priorities.

When he hears the knock at the heavy front door, he first thinks it's icicles breaking from the eaves. The sound persists, a steady drumming, muffled but distinct, and he opens the door to swirling snow and a cold gust of air. In the way that's become a hazard to his health, the blood begins to pound in his temples as he makes out the shape of the woman waiting on the deck.

"Meg." Snow covers her pants up to her knees, and fat flakes cling to her hair. He looks past her to where her vehicle must sit, already accumulating snow. He flips on the outside light.

She blinks as though he's surprised her and not the other way around. Steam rises from her mouth to dissolve into the night when she speaks. "I thought maybe you had left and gone back to Portland."

The sentence ends on a slight uplift that's not quite a question, and not quite fear. "I thought about it," he admits. Hasn't the lodge just been feeling too empty? Too large for his little family of three?

Meg's gaze searches his face, her eyes almost green in the light, but she doesn't ask why he didn't retreat again. He's glad, because he doesn't want to admit he didn't know why until now.

She's still standing on the lodge steps. "Meg, come inside."

She remains in place. "How are the boys?"

He tells her, and she smiles at the news before sobering again. She shifts on her feet, her face cast in shadow as she steps sideways out of the weak ring of porch light. "I saw Danny," she tells him, but then goes quiet again, only shaking her head. "I still can't believe, all this time, he kept such a tragedy from me."

"Working at the station, volunteering in SAR . . . I think he may have kept it at arm's length from himself, too," Silas says. Maybe he has been giving this enigma more attention than he realized, on some level. "Or at least kept the full truth at bay."

Meg nods. "He deluded himself somewhere along the way." She changes the subject, for which Silas is grateful. "There was an article in the paper today about Jessica. And the boys. Did you see it?"

He didn't. Is this why she is here? "No," he says. "Should I?"

A few wisps of wet hair cling to the side of Meg's face, and she peels them back. "There's nothing in it we don't already know."

Snow falls on her cheeks and nose, each flake landing with a delicate precision only to instantly melt, and he stares at her before saying again, "Please. *Come in.*"

"Silas?" she says instead.

He steps toward her, straddling the entry and the snow.

"Do you think it would have made a difference—back then—had we told them everything we knew?"

Her fingers twist nervously in the cuff of her coat, but her eyes are on his with an intensity he's seen before. The need reflected in them would unnerve him were he not certain of his answer. "I don't."

She studies him, waiting.

"That doesn't mean we made the right decision, staying silent. It just means we could have relieved our guilt, but it wouldn't have helped Jessica. Our confession would have been an admission, but not a solution."

She nods, her chin ducking into the folds of her coat. "Not an answer."

"We weren't the one privy to the answers, Cass."

Her eyes snap back up to his. "I know." She swallows, and then takes a step toward him. "But the choices we made . . ."

"We make choices every day," he points out, reminded of Miranda's words to him in the hospital hallway. "Everyone does." He waves his arm back into the lodge. "Spencer and Cameron did, and we lived the consequences for over two full nights of terror."

She offers him a sad smile. "They're just kids, Silas."

"*We* were just kids," he answers softly. "Some of our choices were very wrong, and some . . ." He takes a chance, reaching for one of her hands. It's red with cold. "Some were right, if only for a moment." She looks down but makes no protest when he threads his fingers through hers. He can feel the pulse point of her wrist through his thumb.

"We're not kids now," she answers finally, like it's her last card in a hand she's determined to play. Her fingers curl around his.

"No," he agrees, "we're not." And unlike so many years before, when he stood in the darkness of the woods and gave her every way out, this time he simplifies the equation. With a firm tug on her hand, he pulls her through the doorway. She brings with her tracks of snow that pool on the floor, and when he kisses her, the chill of her mouth sends a tremor down his spine. Her cheeks and nose and eyelids are wet with beaded water, her hair stiff with ice when he combs his fingers through it.

Her hands rise to the back of his neck, her cold fingertips digging in to the cotton of his shirt, and Silas closes the door behind her with a hefty kick, still kissing her. The warmth of the room melts the snow clinging to Meg's coat and pants and the tips of her hair, and in the span of a minute Silas's shirt is equally wet. When he releases her, her smile is everything he remembers it to be: the startle of happy surprise laid bare and breathless. He peels away her coat, letting it fall in a puddle on the rug, and resumes kissing her until the vibration of her laugh tickles his lips.

They talk into the night, and as their touches become softer, the questions become harder. He tells her about his years away, they compare their long-overdue interviews with Walters, and she recounts the past decade-plus in Feather River and search and rescue. They indulge in hindsight: how Danny's reluctance to participate in Meg's determination to reopen Jessica's case now adds up, how Silas's return to the lodge may have been a subconscious attempt at finally making things right. As they talk, Silas studies the pale hue of Meg's complexion in the firelight and wonders that she doesn't bruise more easily. The search for his sons will haunt him forever, and Jessica Howard will haunt him forever; perhaps being with this woman will feel akin to living with a ghost.

Tonight, however, she's flesh and blood, capable, as always, of both redemption and transgression. She smiles at him again, and this time it's somehow Meg at eighteen *and* Meg at thirty-three. Now that they've filled in a few lines of their story, Silas can see the depth fifteen years of shading will bring. For the first time he doesn't feel the need to scale mountains, and outrun the competition, and beat the odds. There's no single pin to place to mark where they went wrong or where they're going, so he stops looking.

The snow falls outside the window until dawn, and when he wakes to fresh powder reaching the sill, Silas knows what he told Meg is true. Their lives didn't irrevocably change after one impulsive choice that August night, even if Jessica's had. One decision—to go, to stay, to run, to tell—built upon the next, until minutes became hours, and hours became days, falling like snow to cover the earth, burying the good and the bad.

ACKNOWLEDGMENTS

Writing a novel is an intensely solitary endeavor right up until it's not. This book would not be in existence without my team. I want to extend my thanks to my agent, Abby Saul of the Lark Group, for being the first champion of my work in the professional world. I am profoundly grateful for your belief in me as a writer from that very first manuscript to land in your inbox. And to my team at Lake Union: my acquiring editor, Erin Adair-Hodges, who took a debut author under her wing; my developmental editor, Tiffany Yates Martin, who guided me in polishing each word to a shine; my production manager, Kyra Wojdyla; and the entire Lake Union editorial team, who collaborated to make this story what it is.

I am also thankful to my past colleagues and fellow volunteers at Jackson County Search and Rescue and the Lost But Found educational program in Southern Oregon. My time hiking and teaching alongside you all allowed me to step into Meg's world and Spencer and Cameron's mindset, though I am glad none of our searches proved quite so exciting.

To my earliest readers of my roughest drafts: your belief in me as a writer when the publishing path felt so distant and daunting kept me going. You know who you are. And to my amazing critique group: Kathleen Basi, Brian Katcher, Heidi Stallman, Ida Fogle, Joseph

Marshall, and Kelsey Simon, this book would not have become all it could be without you. I am grateful for every Zoom meeting.

On the home front, a heartfelt thank-you to my personal cheering squad: my parents, Julie and Jerry Hagstrom, and my three wild and wonderful sons, Nate, Calvin, and Tobias Whitley. Thank you for never getting lost during all our treks into the wilderness together. And last but far from least, thank you to my partner in all my own adventures, my wife, Erika Balbier, for standing by me through marathon writing days, editing days, and every day in between. I wouldn't be the woman I am without you.